SHADOW SUN
PROGRESSION

BOOK FOUR OF THE
SHADOW SUN SERIES

By
Dave Willmarth

The story so far...

A race of ancient aliens has seized earth, using the power of the sun to transport the entire planet closer to the center of the galaxy, and making it a part of the Universal Collective of Planets.

Earth now has two suns, one dark, and one light. The planet is ruled by a game-like System that has determined the human race is a contaminant that must be wiped from the planet. The survivors find they are now able to cast magic spells, control their attributes, and level up as they get stronger.

The initial one-year Stabilization period is over, and aliens have begun to colonize earth. Allistor has earned the title of Planetary Prince on Earth, and after several hard-won battles with a goblin clan, become Emperor of a planet he has renamed Orion.

He's established his Princedom and its Capital City, both called Invictus, by claiming the lower half of Manhattan island in what used to be New York City. While he works to secure his new city, Allistor tries to recruit more humans to become citizens of Invictus under his protection. At the same time, he's learning that not all non-humans are evil, or even bad.

After a year of dating in the midst of the apocalypse, he's finally asked Amanda to marry him and become his princess/empress. Preparations for the wedding have begun, bringing a whole new set of challenges in the form of interactions with the various alien factions that will want to attend.

Allistor must find a way to help his fellow humans to survive, and thrive, before their planet is irrevocably overrun by colonists. At the same time, he must figure out how to navigate interplanetary and interspecies politics, without offending any factions powerful enough to wipe him and the human race completely from the face of Earth.

Chapter 1

Baldur moved with purpose through the mists in Odin's hall, his progress pushing the mists before him, transmitting his movement and his mood ahead of him to his father's throne.

"You are troubled, my son." The Allfather motioned with one tentacled arm for Baldur to approach and sit, another tentacle's motion causing a chair to appear near his throne. Baldur took the offered seat, but did not speak, choosing to consider his words carefully. Odin gave him a place to begin. "You wish to tell me your brother and niece have interfered with the human planet."

Baldur's agitation grew, the mists swirling about his head becoming more active. "I know it to be true, but I have insufficient hard evidence to put before you."

Odin chuckled, the sound emanating from deep within his rubbery chest and transmitting through the mist to fill the room. "In the myths of the human world, I am known as all-seeing. You and I know this is not true. Yet I, like you, do know that Loki and Hel have violated the sanctity of Stabilization. They cover their guilt well, with the deaths of those who might bear witness against them, with subterfuge, intimidation, and bribery. Loki breaks our laws out of contempt for me, and out of pride. He believes himself to be the master of deception. To be smarter than the rest of us. Hel, on the other hand, acts out of boredom, and an overarching desire to end her father's mortal existence."

"And will you accommodate her desire? Will you punish Loki?"

"Ah, my son. You ask the wrong question. Of course I will punish Loki. And his wayward daughter. Both have earned death sentences many times over. The proper question is *when* I will punish them." Odin watched as Baldur considered his words. Baldur was the best of them. Honest and loyal, beloved by all. He shared Odin's fondness of the humans, having joined him on visits to the planet every few millennia to observe their evolution. Both beings had been sickened by the System's determination that the human race was a contaminant. Odin himself had wept over the loss of billions during Stabilization. But there were immutable laws that pre-dated even his ancient race. The creators of the System that nurtured his own people, as well as the thousands of younger races within the Collective, followed some arcane plan that no one but them fully understood. And the System punished those who dared interfere. All he had to do was call the details of their elusive machinations to the System's attention, and challenge them to deny his charges. The System would know if they lied.

Baldur finally spoke. "You delay because they serve some purpose of yours with their actions..." Two of his tentacles waved in front of him in a thoughtful manner. "The Prince. On that first day, I showed an interest in him. Their attempts to annoy me by destroying him have failed. They have instead made him stronger. And he in turn has

6

strengthened those around him. He stands on the precipice of a path that could make him a force within the Collective."

Odin's tentacles moved in an affirmative sign. "A force for good, I hope."

"But he hates us, father. He is driven by his vow to destroy us in retribution for taking his world and destroying his people."

"You speak true, son. Yet he is not the first to swear such an oath. And he is many years, many challenges away from being able to threaten us. Much like the others, I expect he will gain the wisdom in that time to know that we are not directly responsible for the genocide. We could not prevent the System from carrying out its imperatives once the determination had been made. And I hope that he will have the compassion to forgive us."

Baldur again took a long moment to reply. "And if he refuses to forgive, Loki and Hel would make excellent scapegoats. After all, it *was* Loki who initiated the relocation of Earth, and the subsequent induction into the Collective. But what if ending their lives does not satisfy?"

Odin exhaled deeply, a wave of sorrow washing through the hall. "We failed them, my son. They should have had another thousand years or more before induction. It was our responsibility to protect them from Loki, Hel, and those who would take advantage. If they demand our lives in retribution, so be it. I tire of this physical existence, and would not mourn its loss."

*****

Planetary Emperor/Prince Allistor sat in his smithy on the roof of the Invictus tower, staring into the furnace, but not really seeing it. The drink in his hand went unnoticed, as were the grunts of William, his ten year old squire, who was standing behind him and doing his best to crush Allistor's noggin with a staff. Allistor had a lot on his mind, between his upcoming wedding, the development and expansion of his nation, taking care of his people, and the galactic political arena he found himself thrust into. Which is why he didn't notice when his *Barrier* spell collapsed under William's onslaught.

His only warning was a sudden intake of breath, and a wicked little chuckle from William as he swung his staff with extra enthusiasm, aware that he was going to get a rare chance to actually hit his target.

With a wry smile, Allistor re-cast the spell. The barrier popped into existence behind him a fraction of a second before William's weapon struck. The young squire cursed loudly, the unexpected impact vibration of the staff stinging his hands.

"Shit, that hurt! I almost had you that time."

"Close only counts in horseshoes and hand grenades. And AoE spells." Allistor turned to face the boy. "And don't let any of the ladies hear you cuss like that."

William looked grumpy, shaking his hands to get rid of the sting. "I know. Just around us guys." He blew

8

on his hands, as if that would make them feel better. "Why does it hurt more when I hit the shield than when I hit you?"

Allistor cast a small heal on the boy, raising one eyebrow as he did it, to remind William that he could have healed himself. The boy had learned the same basic skills every citizen of Invictus had been given. "It has to do with physics. First, my head is softer than the shield. So when you hit me, there's a little bit of give. But also, you loosened your grip. That allows the vibration of the impact to sting your hands more."

He took hold of the stick and demonstrated a tight two-handed grip. He was about to instruct his squire to hold the staff like he would a baseball bat. Instead, his lips pressed together as he realized that William had only been eight or nine when their old world ended, and may never have had the chance to play baseball. Or many of the other games kids of Earth normally played.

"With practice, you'll learn to adjust your grip for the circumstance. In the meantime, you have to remember that you can heal yourself during combat."

William shook his head. "Lady Amanda said I shouldn't heal little things like stinging hands. Says if I tough it out, it'll raise my stats, and make me mentally tougher."

Allistor suppressed a grin. "Well, as my squire, the most important thing I can teach you is to never argue with Lady Amanda." He patted William on the shoulder. "The second most important thing is to never stick around when she wants to test a new spell."

Williams eyes widened and he nodded his head solemnly. "Yeah. The other day she said I could earn a lollypop if I helped her test something. She said it would just sting a little…" The boy shook his head, remembering.

Allistor winced, then chuckled. "Yep. That's how she gets you. Next time, just run. Tell her I need you to do important squire stuff." He held out a fist, which William bumped with a conspiratorial smile.

Noticing that the metal he'd set in the furnace was getting overheated, he got to his feet. "That's enough for today. You've put in a good workout. The rest of the day is yours. I think Sam and his crew might be clearing another building this afternoon, if you want to tag along."

"Yes!" William carefully set his staff against a wall. "My *Stamina* went up another point about an hour ago. And my *Strength* is at three already." He waved at Allistor as he turned to head toward the elevator.

"That's great, buddy! But remember, the next few times you level up, I want you to put points into *Intelligence* and *Will Power*! It'll be a few more years till you're big enough to be a melee fighter. Until then, I want you to level up your casting skills!"

William didn't even slow down, just waved over his shoulder to acknowledge that he'd heard.

Allistor grabbed his tongs and used them to pull the heated metal bar from the furnace. Not really in the mood to craft anymore, he simply set it on the anvil to cool. Taking his drink in hand again, he moved over to the lounge area to sit and think.

He'd finally summoned the courage to ask Amanda to marry him! It had been two days since she agreed to become his queen, and that was all any of his friends and family talked about since. All of Invictus seemed to be scurrying around making preparations for the wedding. He'd wanted it to be a small affair, but was quickly shouted down by every single person he knew. They unanimously agreed that the wedding of a Planetary Prince, who was also a Planetary Emperor, was an affair of state, and had to be celebrated as such!

At the same time, Gralen and Harmon had been working to colonize his new planet, Orion, which he'd taken from the goblins. Gralen's initial estimate of twenty thousand beastkin wishing to become citizens of Invictus had turned out to be conservative. The number was closer to thirty thousand. Allistor and his advisors were scrambling to arrange housing for all of them as quickly as possible. In addition to filling the three main Strongholds on the planet's surface, and Harmon housing nearly three thousand of the beastkin on his orbital trade station, there was a small army of orcanin and beastkin technicians and engineers working to bring the two dilapidated habitats that orbited Orion back online. Between them, they could house another twelve thousand, as well as create more jobs for the immigrants. And as Allistor had hoped, nearly five thousand of the beastkin, including most of the original mercenary crew and their families, were willing to live among the humans on Earth.

Allistor had put the word out that he wanted a few human volunteers to join the beastkin on Orion, in the interest of further improving human/alien relations. After the funeral for those who'd died taking the new planet, he'd made a short speech asking his people to accept the beastkin, orcanin, elves, dwarves, and other races that were not responsible for Earth's apocalypse. Though some were less accepting than others, there had been no violent objections. And with the ability to travel between the planets using the teleport system, the fifty or so humans that volunteered would never be more than a few minutes from home.

"Pardon the interruption, Sire. Analyst L'olwyn has requested a word." Nigel's voice rang out from thin air. *"Analyst Selby has made a similar request as well."*

"Send them on up, Nigel. Thank you."

Allistor got to his feet and walked behind the rooftop bar to refresh his drink while he waited for two of his four alien analysts to arrive. L'olwyn was an unhoused elf with noble blood and a reserved bearing, while Selby was a feisty little gnome who had, in the short time she'd been on Earth, developed a bit of a crush on Logan.

The elevator door opened and the two analysts stepped out. As they approached across the rooftop, Allistor called out. "Can I fix either of you a drink? Got some really good Jamaican rum here." He held up his glass and shook it, making the ice clink.

Selby began to nod her head yes, opening her mouth to accept, but stopping when she heard L'olwyn reply. "Thank you, sire, but I must decline. It is improper to imbibe while performing one's duties."

Selby sadly changed her nod to a shake. "No thank you, Sire."

Allistor coughed, covering his mouth to suppress a grin as he walked around from behind the bar. Taking a seat in one of the lounge chairs, he motioned for the others to sit as well. "Listen guys, I don't want to have to keep saying this. When it's just us chickens, I want you to call me Allistor. And it's okay to let your hair down a bit and share a drink with me when I offer. They tell me I'm the boss around here, so I think I get to decide what's proper, or not, yes?"

"Chickens, Si… Allistor?" L'olwyn frowned at him while Selby hopped back out of her chair and headed for the bar.

"It's a silly Earth expression. Don't even remember what it's from. Forget it. Just… if we're not in a formal setting, let's lay off the titles, alright?"

"Of course, Allistor. I will endeavor to… how did Lady Meg put it? Loosen my jockeys?"

Allistor snorted, nearly spitting out the sip of rum he'd just taken. "Yes, thank you L'olwyn." He wiped his mouth just to make sure none had escaped and was running down his chin. "Now, what did you wish to speak to me about?"

"I have been in contact with the Or'Dralon elves of Vermont. Specifically, Commander Enalion, with whom you've had some previous discussion?"

"Ha! You mean when I talked him out of blasting us into oblivion on our very first day in space?"

"Indeed. You also extended an invitation for him to join you for a meal."

"Indeed I did!" Allistor was having a hard time resisting a few pokes at the tightly wound elf. If Nigel could loosen up and even make jokes, Allistor had hopes that L'olwyn would do the same. Eventually.

"Yes, well, the commander has heard of your upcoming nuptials, and reached out to me this morning to enquire as to why he had not received an invitation."

Allistor's amusement fell away, and a cold sense of dread began to creep up his spine. The Or'Dralon faction was capable of swatting him, his people, and all of Earth if he offended them a second time. L'olwyn's own faction had been wiped out in a similar way.

"Shit. It never even occurred to me that they'd want to attend." Allistor set his drink down and leaned forward, placing his elbows on his knees and running both hands through his hair. Selby emerged from behind the bar with a glass of rum in hand, hopping back up into a human-sized chair without spilling a drop.

"Oh, the Commander is quite interested in attending, Allistor. He seems especially intent on introducing you to his daughter."

14

Allistor's head jerked up, and his eyes focused on L'olwyn in time to catch what he suspected was a suppressed smile. Maybe the elf had a sense of humor after all, if a little twisted.

"Ohhh, no. No daughters. Harmon told me if I married Amanda, I could hold off any attempted arranged marriages for like a year!" His eyes got wide and he slapped a hand over his mouth as he realized what he'd just said. After a few seconds, he lowered it enough to whisper, "Not that that's the reason I'm marrying her. Let's just keep that whole topic between us, shall we?"

Selby raised her glass and gave him a knowing wink as L'olwyn replied, "Of course."

His gut beginning to roil and his forehead beading with sweat, Allistor asked, "So what did you tell Commander Enalion?"

"Fortunately, I was able to tell him the truth. That he would of course be welcome to attend. And that Lady Amanda had yet to choose the method and style of formal invitations. I assured him that as soon as her selection was complete, Or'dralon would receive said invitation along with everyone else."

Finding himself both relieved and further alarmed by the elf's response, Allistor asked, "Everyone else?"

Selby broke in at that moment. "That's actually why I'm here. There have been several requests for invitations from various factions. I have compiled a list of those, as well as others we feel should be included. Based on our combined analysis of your current supporters, potential future supporters, and-"

She paused when Allistor raised a hand. "Thank you, Selby. I don't need to hear the gory details just now. I trust that your list, and the reasons behind your selections, are entirely correct. I'm still recovering from the fear that I'd accidentally offended Enalion again." He used a cocktail napkin to wipe the sweat from his brow. "How... many are we talking about?"

Selby tilted her head to one side as she looked at him. Gralen had told him before her interview that Selby was nearly a hundred years old. But the little gnome looked, and often acted, like a twenty-something human would. Allistor found her care-free attitude refreshing.

"How many... factions? Or people?"

"Let's start with factions. I'm guessing each faction will send more than one representative."

"You guess correctly. The current list includes nineteen factions. That is not counting Harmon, or Gralen, who will represent their peoples."

Allistor began considering a leap off the edge of the tower's roof.

"As I'm new to this whole *Prince* thing..."

"Emperor thing." Selby corrected him.

Exasperated, Allistor leaned back. "Okay yeah let's settle this once and for all. I'm both an emperor, and a prince. The title Emperor Prince sounds silly to me. Like I can't make up my mind. What do I call myself?"

L'olwyn actually smiled at him. "It is not common for one being to have held the same combination of titles for two different worlds in the past. We actually did a little checking. It seems that while on Earth, it is most proper to address you as Prince. And while on Orion, Emperor is proper. Anywhere else, including aboard ship in open space, the higher title of Emperor is appropriate."

Selby added, "You may also refer to yourself as Imperial Prince. Though that is somewhat misleading, as it implies that you're the son or heir of an Emperor."

Allistor continued to sweat. Visions of formal occasions from old books and movies flashed through his mind. Hours of rehearsed speeches and studied customs to be observed while wearing uncomfortable clothes. With the threat of oblivion, should he make a mistake, hanging over his head.

"I'm not ready for this." He mumbled.

Both the elf and the gnome, having excellent hearing, gave him sympathetic looks. Selby was first to speak. "Take a deep breath, Allistor. L'olwyn here is a noble, trained from birth in proper etiquette. He can help you and Lady Amanda learn what you need to know."

"Though, it may take some time." L'olwyn's dry tone made Allistor snort.

"Can't be easy to teach the hairless apes how to behave properly." Allistor quipped.

"Exactly so, Allistor." This time the slight grin on the elf's face was clearly visible. "I suggest setting the wedding date at least three months hence, to both relieve some of the pressure you feel, and to allow for sufficient preparation."

Allistor nodded. "I'll speak to Amanda about it. I know she's excited about the wedding, but making a mistake because we move too quickly might cause a disaster." He took a deep breath and let it out slowly. He thought Amanda would understand, but he wasn't absolutely sure. "Was there anything else you wanted to discuss?"

Selby nodded her head at the same time L'olwyn shook his. When Allistor motioned for her to proceed, she reached into her storage ring and pulled out a pad. "It has come to my attention that you, and your humans, have not been training as you leveled up."

"Training? I mean, most of us have leveled up our spells and melee abilities at least a little bit. I've been raising my *Barrier* skill by having William try to kill me nearly every day this week."

Selby giggled. "Yes, he has told me. He's quite determined to, as he puts it, give you a beat-down." She watched Allistor roll his eyes. "But I was speaking about class training. For example: You selected the Battlemage class. At that time, you learned the basic starting class abilities, is that correct?"

"Yeah…" Allistor saw where she was going, and was feeling foolish. His eyes unfocused as he pulled up his

Battlemage tab. "You're going to say I should have been getting more spells or abilities as I leveled. But I don't see them here on my interface."

Selby shook her head. "The initial abilities are awarded by the System when you choose your class. Those abilities can be leveled up as you use them, modified as you achieve higher levels, combined with other abilities, and so forth. You can, as you know, learn spells from scrolls you purchase or loot. But any additional class spells or abilities must be obtained from a Battlemage of a higher level."

Allistor nodded, not all that surprised. "So class trainers are a real thing. Gotcha. But how do I go about finding one? Or finding trainers for the rest of my people, for that matter. Is there a class quest or something?"

"You are in somewhat of an unusual situation here, Allistor. Normally when a new world is colonized, only a small portion of the indigenous population have reached a level where they can choose a class. And indeed, even here on Earth, the average level today is likely to be between ten and twenty. You and your people are an exception to the rule, as I'm sure you've been told." She paused until he nodded his understanding.

"Normally, the factions that colonize a planet will import a cadre of class trainers shortly after they settle. They either bring their own, or contract with outside trainers. There is even a guild of class trainers. New planets like Earth, where the system determines the locals need culling – no offense - offer rare opportunities for leveling in the early days after stabilization. There are abundant menagerie spawns to hunt, and experience to be gained. Especially when the creatures have killed so many of the local population, and achieved higher levels themselves. The trainers teach those factions' members who take advantage of the windfall. As the locals, in this case, humans, reach the proper levels, the factions can sell them training at exorbitant prices."

Seeing that Allistor's face was darkening, she quickly continued. "You and your people, with your access to the Library, and your willingness to copy and share the spells from any looted scrolls, have fared much better than a local population in Stabilization normally would. You have been able to remain alive, advance to higher levels, and capture vast territory. Other humans here on Earth will have been much less successful, and will need to pay dearly for training when they eventually reach the required levels."

Allistor's fear from a few moments before was turning to anger. Anger at the reminder of the genocide forced upon his world. Anger at the way the System encouraged other races to take advantage of his people. "That's not happening here." He clenched his jaw as he spoke, his voice quiet and flat. "Nigel, do you have a list of everyone's chosen class? And how many people do we have that haven't chosen yet?"

"I do have a list, Sire. And there are four hundred thirty citizens, mostly children or elder citizens, who have reached level ten, but not selected a class as of now. There are thirty one, all small children, who have not yet reached level ten."

"Alright… let's fix this right now. Nigel, loudspeaker please, everywhere."

"*Go ahead, sire.*"

"Good morning, everyone. Allistor here. It has just come to my attention that all of us who have chosen classes need a class trainer in order to receive additional spells and abilities above the ones we were given at level ten. I will be recruiting class trainers from off-world immediately. Any of you who are level ten or higher, who have not yet chosen a class, I need you to do so by the end of the week, so I know which trainers to hire. If you have questions, let Nigel know, and someone will get with you to provide answers. Don't choose without thinking it over. Once you choose a class, you're stuck with it. And I want each of you to have a class that feels right to you. I'll update you all as to timing as soon as possible. Thank you, and have a great day."

Looking both his advisors in the eye one at a time, he gave orders. "I want you to contact this trainer's guild, or whomever else you need to, and hire us some trainers. One for every class chosen by Invictus citizens, including yourselves, if that's possible. Get back to me with costs and timing. I authorize you to offer citizenship and land in lieu of gold where you think it's appropriate. Land can be here on Earth, or on Orion."

Both advisors nodded their heads. "Anything else we need to discuss?" Both shook their heads no. "Great! Now I feel the need to let off some steam. I think I'll see if anyone's headed out on a raid. Thank you both. And please, don't hesitate to come to me anytime something like this pops up."

Elf and gnome got to their feet and bowed their heads before leaving. Allistor sat for a while, feeling foolish. He thought he'd learned his lesson about learning the System's details when he discovered he could give quests. In the year since he'd reached level ten and chosen his class, it hadn't once occurred to him that he should be learning new class spells or abilities as he leveled. Worse, he knew that was how it was in nearly every VR game he'd ever played. But he wasn't the only gamer still living, and none of the others had brought it up, either. At least, not to him. That in itself seemed... suspiciously odd. Had the system been manipulating their minds somehow? He closed his eyes and opened up his character sheet, taking a few minutes to look at it. He had reached level forty nine after clearing and claiming Orion, but hadn't taken the time to assign his attribute points. Rather than do it right then, he decided to wait until he hit level fifty, and had spoken to a Battlemage trainer. For all he knew, he was mismanaging his stats up to this point. Level 50 was typically a significant level as far as character development. So he'd just wait and see.

Designation: Emperor Allistor, Giant Killer	Level: 49	Experience: 18,215,000/25,000,000
Planet of Origin: UCP 382, Orion	Health: 48,000/48,000	Class: Battlemage
Attribute Pts Available: 4	Mana: 15,000/15,000	
Intelligence: 24 (28)	Strength: 10 (18)	Charisma: 10 (14)
Adaptability: 8 (10)	Stamina: 12 (19)	Luck: 6 (12)
Constitution: 19 (24)	Agility: 11 (17)	Health Regen: 1,400/m
Will Power: 24 (32)	Dexterity: 7 (11)	Mana Regen: 1,100/m

Chapter 2

Allistor found Fuzzy in the sculpture garden located between the Invictus tower and Harmon's building. He was playing with several young children, serving as a dungeon boss for them to battle. The bear cub that had been so small and cute just a year ago now stood almost four feet tall at the shoulders, and weighed at least four hundred pounds. As a yearling, he still had the 'cute teddy bear' face with the rounded ears and fuzzy fur. Normally at his age he'd be about half this size. But in this new world, each time he leveled up he seemed to get a bit larger. Having been by Allistor's side for most of his battles, the cute bear cub had leveled up to forty five.

Now Allistor watched as the ferocious beast romped around with children one tenth his size, taking a fake 'fatal' blow from a stick held by Cody, and promptly falling onto his side, playing dead with his tongue hanging out one side of his massive jaws. The children squealed and shouted with glee, grabbing handfuls of fur and climbing atop the oversized beast for a victory pose.

Allistor smiled as he watched, his earlier itch to go kill something fading away. A little girl roughly Chloe's age, whose name he didn't know, spotted him standing there, and shouted, "Prince Allistor! We killed Fuzzymonster! But I didn't level up." She stuck out her lower lip and crossed her arms, pouting.

"Oh, well let's see what we can do about that!" He called back, grinning widely. Everybody but Fuzzy, come over here. I have a super-secret quest for you."

The kids leapt fearlessly off the bear's corpse, shouting enthusiastically as they ran toward Allistor. By this time, several parents and passersby had taken interest, and they too gathered 'round, leaning over top of the children and Allistor as he squatted down to whisper to them.

"Okay, are you ready? Here's the quest. You have to defeat Fuzzymonster by getting him on his back, then tickling him until he farts!" He awarded them all an actual quest called "Take Down Fuzzymonster" with enough xp to give most of them a level.

He smiled like a twelve-year old planning some shenanigans as the kids responded with "Eww!" and "Yess!" and various other exclamations before turning and racing back toward a suddenly suspicious Fuzzy.

"Good luck, buddy!" Allistor waved to his bear companion as the adults around him laughed. They all watched as the bear was mobbed by seven tiny warriors. He put up a mock resistance, growling at the children and swatting them gently with paws larger than their heads. One mother gasped in panic as Fuzzy latched onto her child's head with his jaws and gently lifted him off the ground. A moment later he dropped the boy, who fell on his butt and began wiping slobber from his face.

"Ugh! That's nasty, Fuzzy!" the kid used the front of his shirt to clean himself off, then stuck his tongue out and shuddered. Then he was back on his feet and tackling the grizzly's flank, trying to push him over. Fuzzy obliged, falling onto his side after checking to make sure he wouldn't squish anyone. When the children continued to push, he rolled over onto his back and languidly swatted at them as they climbed onto his belly.

Fuzzy was just laying his head back on the ground and preparing to play dead when the children began to jump up and down on his belly, shouting, "Fart! Fart! Fart!" Not one to worry about social convention or etiquette, Fuzzy let loose.

Approximately two seconds later, the children were covering their noses and falling off the bear's belly, scrambling to put distance between themselves and the chemical attack even as a golden glow surrounded them. The completed quest had leveled each and every child.

The parents and bystanders applauded as Allistor called out his congratulations to the tiny raiders, who were throwing him looks filled with betrayal and disgust. He pulled a big chunk of dragon jerky from his ring and tossed it to Fuzzy. "Thanks for your help, Fuzzymonster!" Fuzzy's little nub of a tail wagged as he gnawed on the jerky held between his paws.

Taking his leave, Allistor continued across the street to the building Harmon had claimed for his shop. Stepping through the door, he was immediately greeted by an imp that bowed low, waving one hand in a flourish. The grey-skinned creature was maybe two feet tall, with painfully thin arms and legs, a pear-shaped body, and a large round head. "Welcome, mighty human Prince. How may we serve you today?" It spoke in a smooth, cultured voice.

"I was… hoping to speak with Harmon, if he's available? I'm sorry, I don't know your name."

"This one is called Scrit, great Prince. And master Harmon left instructions that he is always available for you. Please, be comfortable, and this one will let the master know you have arrived." The imp led him through the shop and motioned toward the seating area outside Harmon's office. As Allistor took a seat, the imp sprinted toward Harmon's door. Allistor jumped slightly when the imp pounded on the door hard enough to make it shake, and shouted "Hey boss! The human boss wants ta see ya!" sounding more like a Jersey dock worker than the butler persona he'd had a moment earlier.

Harmon emerged from his office and strode toward Allistor, who was back on his feet and staring at the imp. Catching the direction of his gaze, the orcanin merchant chuckled. "Yes, Scrit is quite the character. I never know who he's going to be from one minute to the next. He's completely insane, but generally harmless."

Behind him the imp gave a friendly wave, then stuck out his tongue and made a hand gesture that was pretty universally rude, before dashing off across the shop.

Harmon motioned toward his office door. "Please, come in. Always a pleasure to see you, my friend." Allistor preceded the orcanin into the office, taking a seat in one of the chairs. Rather than move behind his desk,

Harmon chose to take the other chair next to Allistor's. "What can I do for you?"

"Well, first… I just this morning found out about class trainers. I've instructed the analysts to recruit a small army of them for my people right away. So if you have any recommendations, please let me know."

Harmon nodded, looking thoughtful. "That's odd. It never occurred to me that you weren't aware of class trainers. Even though I clearly haven't seen any here on Earth since I arrived. Or heard you discuss them."

Allistor decided to change the subject. He wasn't ready to consider the possibility that the System was messing with all of their minds. Especially regarding something so vitally important. So he asked the other question he'd been meaning to bring up with Harmon.

"My smithing is still improving, but I'm a long way from being able to make a blade worthy of a prince. So I was thinking of purchasing or commissioning a weapon. I have some materials that might interest a master craftsman, and I can certainly pay them well for their time. I was hoping you might recommend someone?"

"What kind of materials do you have?" Harmon began tapping on his wrist, calling up a holo-display.

"Well, off the top of my head, there's the purple Ancient Shellback Heart. A couple of drake hearts, claws, and fangs as well. I have a forearm blade and heart from a giant mantis, and an Occulant Sentry Elite power core. There may be more that have slipped my mind."

Harmon had stopped typing almost as soon as Allistor mentioned the shellback heart. "What is your chosen class?"

"I chose Battlemage. I like the idea of being able to deal ranged damage as well as get in close for melee attacks. And the *Barrier* spell has come in handy more times than I can count."

Harmon dropped both hands to his lap, his wrist holo winking out. "Do you remember the day we met, I showed you this?" He pulled the master-crafted wooden blade from his boot sheath and held it up for Allistor.

"Sure. Made by the elf who took you in. I remember. I don't expect a weapon nearly that valuable or pedigreed. Just something I wouldn't be embarrassed to wear at my wedding, for example. Which apparently about twenty different factions will be attending."

Harmon didn't seem to hear that last bit. He was tapping one of his tusks with a fingernail, lost in thought. Allistor took a moment to admire the dagger again, until Harmon spoke. "Master Daigath is the elf that created this blade. I make no promises, but I will reach out to him on your behalf. You will have to be willing to surrender the shellback heart."

Allistor's heartrate increased, and his mouth hung partway open for a moment. "I... of course. But why would such a legendary being come here, even for a purple crafting ingredient?"

"Not just for the crafting, Allistor. Master Daigath is, or was, a Battlemage. Easily the most formidable I've ever heard of. Imagine having thousands of years to learn and perfect your skills and abilities." Harmon chuckled to himself. "Daigath is so old, he may have *invented* the Battlemage class!"

"And you think you could convince him to come here?" Allistor was already picturing himself wielding a purple glowing wooden sword.

"I will attempt to make contact, and ask him. It is likely that if he takes the trouble to travel here, he will want to stay a while. I know you have many parks under your control. It may be that he'll want to inhabit one of them, if he finds a forest he likes. Like the one where we first met. Your... Wilderness Stronghold?"

Allistor nodded. "He can have his pick of any forest I control. Or any that I can claim, buy, or steal for him."

"Then I will make the request on your behalf. I'll let you know as soon as I hear from him. It may be several days, as Master Daigath is not easily reached."

"Thank you Harmon. Oh! My analysts have recommended we delay the wedding for three months. To give us time to prepare, both logistically and personally. It seems there's much we have to learn in terms of etiquette."

"Ha!" Harmon thumped the arm of his chair. "Wise decision, my young friend. And it brings the added advantage of three more months during which you will have good reason to decline or delay other offers without offending anyone."

Shaking his head, Allistor got to his feet. "Yeah, that doesn't hurt. Now I have to go explain the situation to Amanda. The part about delaying. Not that bit about fending off alien brides."

Harmon just chuckled as he watched Allistor walk toward the door. "Good luck, my friend. Maybe wait until she's not in her infirmary full of sharp implements."

*****

Allistor was just entering his tower again, headed to find Amanda, when Nigel sidetracked him.

"Sire, you have several human visitors awaiting an audience. I have asked them to wait in the street outside the lobby. They are not citizens."

Allistor looked across the lobby through the tall windows to where three of the Juggernauts were still parked. There were two men and two women standing around, one of them pacing nervously. All of them looked like they hadn't had a decent meal in a while. "Thank you Nigel. I'll take care of it." He noted that his mini-map displayed four red dots at their location as he walked across the lobby. Exiting the doors, he waved with one hand. "Hello there. I'm Allistor. I understand you want to speak with me?"

One of the women stepped forward. "I'm Leila. Been waiting to hear from you, but got tired of waiting, so I've come to talk."

Allistor was confused. "Uhh... okay. Come on in. Let's sit and talk." He held the glass door open and motioned toward his usual sitting area in the lobby. Several of his people, upon seeing him coming, vacated the area to give him some privacy.

When they were all seated, he held up a finger, asking them to wait a moment. "Nigel, would you ask whoever's in the kitchen to bring a cart with some sandwiches and drinks? Thanks." Turning back to Leila, he smiled. "Welcome to Invictus. I'm afraid I don't know what it is you want to talk about, or why you've been waiting on me?"

One of the two men, a tall and scruffy-looking specimen, snorted. "You have a lot of nerve. Welcoming us to our own home." he growled, clenching his fists. Leila put a hand on his knee and gave him a look that calmed him down some.

"Your home?" A light was starting to dawn in Allistor's brain. "You live in one of the Strongholds here in the city. One of the ones that are now inside my walls?"

Leila pursed her lips and nodded. "We do. Got the notification when you claimed this part of the city, and saw the walls go up. We expected someone would come and try to oust us."

"Shit, I'm sorry guys. I have you on my list, I mean, not by name or anything, just like… visit the other three Strongholds. But things have been pretty hectic. I don't know if you heard, but I met with Jesse, and invited him and his roughly four thousand people to join us that first day. He and some of his friends tried to kill me. It wasn't the best start. I hope things between us can be friendlier."

Allistor paused when Meg approached, pushing a wheeled cart full of food. "Meg, thank you. This looks wonderful. This is Leila, and… I'm afraid I don't know the rest of your names?"

Leila patted the knee of the grumpy scruffy guy. "This is Josh. Over there are Stacey and Ben."

"Nice t'meet ya" Meg favored them with a smile as she pushed the cart closer, then proceeded to unload the food and drink onto a coffee table between them. "Help yourselves, there's plenty more where this came from." She looked at Allistor and added, "You should try some too. The girls have been practicing their singing, and the buffs are getting pretty substantial."

Allistor looked over the spread. There were sandwiches of thinly sliced red meat that was probably canid steak. Several types of pastries, some grapes, and tiny carrots. He waited for the others to dish up plates before grabbing one of the sandwiches and a cup of liquid that turned out to be apple juice. Setting the plate on his lap, he said, "Please, eat while I talk. I'll give you some background, and maybe answer some of your questions before you even have to ask them."

Leila nodded, then took a big bite of her sandwich. She chewed slowly, then began to talk with her mouth full. "Meg, this is delicious."

Meg winked at her. "This is just thrown-together leftovers. Hang around for dinner and we'll get you a proper meal!" She turned and headed back to the kitchen, leaving them to eat and talk.

Allistor had taken a quick bite of his own sandwich, and noted the buffs. He was seeing +4 Stamina, +4 Strength, and +10% health regen, which were very nice. Then he noticed the duration and nearly choked. "Meg! Eight hours? Holy shit!" he shouted after the retreating woman, who didn't even turn around.

"Sorry guys. That was rude." He apologized to the startled visitors. While they resumed their meals, he gave them his standard speech about his background, their battles over the past year, and how Invictus City came to be. When he was done, he took a moment to drink some juice before continuing.

"And that brings us to today. I truly meant to stop by the other Strongholds that wound up inside the walls. To bring you the same offer I've made to the others. You have several options. Ideally, I'd like you and your people to become citizens of Invictus. You can continue to live in your Stronghold and run it your way, if you choose. Or you could choose to live here, or at any one of our properties across the country." Allistor watched all of their faces as he spoke, trying to gauge their level of interest.

"Option two is that you elect not to become citizens, but we remain friendly. You agree not to attack me or my people, and I agree to the same. We can trade, and you remain in your Stronghold, which will eventually become a much safer place as we clear the monsters from the city. Option three, you tell me to screw off, and I invite you to relocate somewhere outside my walls. I give you food and other supplies to last you a week, and an escort to your destination. I'll even have my battle droids clear a building or two for you, and give you and your folks all the xp for the kills."

He stopped talking and took another bite of the tasty sandwich. It was up to Leila and company now, and he felt unusually calm as he awaited a response.

Leila took the time to chew and swallow the last bite of her sandwich, then take a long drink of water. When she was through, she looked up at Allistor. "I can't decide if you're completely full of shit, or just an inconsiderate ass who's in over his head."

Allistor had expected questions, not hostility. "I've told you the truth. So I guess it's the second one. The inconsiderate ass one." He didn't smile as he answered.

Leila used a napkin to wipe her mouth, then threw it down on the ground. "I've lost eleven of my people since your walls went up. Two of them children. Why didn't you come to us sooner? You have this big building full of food and weapons and... and robots. This whole time we've been fighting monsters and half-starving to death." Her voice hitched, and she took a moment. When she spoke again, her voice was barely more than a whisper. "Damn you."

Allistor set his plate on the table and clasped his hands in his lap. Leila was right. He was an ass. He had shuffled the notification about the other strongholds into a folder and marked it as a priority, then forgotten all about it. People had died while he was on the roof crafting, or taking the fight to the goblins. He didn't even know how to begin to answer her.

"I'm... you're right to be angry. I'm sorry. I should have gone to find you in those first few days. I don't have an excuse. I was wrong." He paused to take a deep breath, his hands shaking. "I can't bring your people back. But I can do my best to make sure that you don't lose any more. Please, don't let my failure keep you from accepting my help." He wanted to reach out to touch Leila, but didn't dare.

The woman stood and began to pace. Her companions remained were they were, clearly used to her movements. Allistor looked to each one of them, hoping for some hint of what they were thinking. He got nothing.

Leila sat back down, her left knee bouncing as she tapped her foot. "If we join you, I can keep my Stronghold?"

Allistor nodded. "Absolutely."

"And my people?"

"Free to stay with you, or move to any of our locations. They can even claim their ten acres of land, and we'll help them with resources to build Strongholds or Outposts of their own."

Stacey spoke up next. "How do we know all of this is for real?"

Allistor looked her in the eye, which was more difficult than he expected. Her eyes held the haunted look that so many of his people had in the early days after the apocalypse, when survival was in doubt. "Take some time, explore this place. Speak to anyone you like. They'll answer all your questions. Or you can teleport to any of our other locations and look around, speak to the folks there. I have nothing to hide."

That seemed to satisfy the woman, and beside her Ben was nodding his head. When Leila didn't speak for a full minute, Allistor asked, "How many of you are there?"

Grumpy Josh spat on the floor before saying, "Eleven less than there should be."

Leila looked up from staring at her hands. "Josh, enough." Turning to look at Allistor, she replied, "We have just over three hundred people."

"Hungry people." Josh added. Allistor was trying his best not to dislike the man, but he wasn't making it easy.

"Well, I can fix that, at least. Your people are invited here for dinner, and to spend the night. I'll send a company of battle droids back with you, and they can escort you safely here. If you have folks that can't walk, I'll send vehicles. We have enough empty rooms here in the tower to put you up for the night. Tomorrow you'll be rested and well fed, and can all explore and ask questions, then let me know what you decide."

"How do we know your robots won't just murder us all when we get to our home?" Josh again.

Allistor sighed. "How bout I go with you? I'll bring a few healers along in case you have wounded that need attention. If the droids get hostile, you can shoot me first. They won't enter your gates, just wait outside to escort you back here."

Leila nodded her head. "Fine. Let's do it. How long do you need to get your people together?"

"Nigel, please inform Prime I need a hundred battle droids for an escort. Also ask Amanda and Helen to grab five or six more healers and join me in the lobby. And let Meg know we're expecting more than three hundred hungry visitors for dinner. Tell her to pull some staff from other Strongholds for a few days if she needs them. And make sure we have rooms for the same number of people ready by this evening."

"Of course, sire. The rooms are ready and waiting. Would you like Lady Kira to prepare the ship?"

Allistor snapped his fingers. "I hadn't thought of that, Nigel. One second." He turned to Leila. "Is there a large open space near your Stronghold? Like, a park, or a big parking lot, big enough to park a battleship-sized spaceship?"

"What?" Ben asked. "I mean, there is…"

"Okay well, that gives us the option of saving everybody the walk. And some time. We have a spaceship large enough to transport everyone. That will also reduce the number of droids we need for protection, if that'll make you more comfortable."

Surprisingly, that got a positive response from Josh. "I'm up for a ride in a spaceship."

Leila nodded her head in agreement, not saying anything.

"Yes, Nigel, please ask Kira to fire up the *Phoenix.*"

"*She is already aboard sire, and will be ready to go when you arrive.*"

Amanda, Helen, William, and a half dozen others approached as Allistor got to his feet. He introduced everyone, then quickly explained to his people what they were up to.

"I'm coming with you." William informed him. Allistor considered for a moment, then decided there was no serious risk.

"Good idea, William. There may be some frightened children who could use a brave squire to reassure them." He put a hand on the boy's shoulder. "But you don't leave the ship, no matter what. On your honor, as a squire."

This was exactly the right button to push. William's face took on a solemn look, his chest swelled, and he placed his fist over his heart. "On my honor, as a squire."

With that issue resolved, Allistor and Fuzzy led the group down the four blocks to the parking structure and the *Phoenix*. He had Prime bring along one of the industrial hoverpads, pulled by battle droids. Once everyone was aboard, Kira lifted off and hovered. Allistor took Leila to the bridge so she could direct Kira on where to land. It turned out Leila's Stronghold was a single city block located on the northwest corner of 10th Ave and W. 21st Street. From above, Allistor could see that there was a red brick church building and attached school, with a square courtyard in the center, as well as a couple small commercial buildings that filled out the block. On the back side, there was a raised platform that looked like an abandoned railway track.

There was a small wooded area across the street that was large enough to land the ship, but Leila directed them a couple blocks north. The wide open intersection of 10th and W. 23rd – both roads having six lanes – allowed Kira to squeeze the ship between the buildings and land on the street.

As Leila walked Allistor and the others south along 10th Ave, she pointed to the park. "That's Clements Park. We've been using it as a community garden, even though it's outside the walls. I haven't had the resources to expand them, or I would have. That's where we've lost the most people lately. Trying to harvest food." Allistor saw there was a low iron fence around the park, and several rows of corn inside, as well as other plants mixed in among the trees.

To the right, directly across the street from the park, was Leila's stronghold. It had thirty-foot walls, and a gate that faced east toward the park. Allistor didn't see any weapons atop the wall, though he did see a few sentries with rifles. With a whistle from Josh, the gates opened slightly. Inside, Allistor could see the front of the church, with a stone cross above the door and a faded banner that said *Guardian Angel Church.*

Noticing the direction of his gaze, Leila said, "Yeah, that's where we started. When the apocalypse happened, and monsters began spawning, myself and a bunch of neighborhood folks filled the church, and prayed. I think we were hoping that somehow holy ground would save us. You know, like in the vampire movies?" She looked down at her feet, shaking her head. "But it didn't. Monsters spawned in the cellar on the fourth day. Killed dozens of my neighbors before we managed to put them down. We got organized, and raided a few of the hotels and restaurants close by for food and bedding and such. Folks just sort of drafted me as leader because I was a Marine. Eventually the System said we had enough resources to form a Stronghold, so I did."

Amanda took charge. "We'll wait out here. I expect you'll need a little while to gather your people and speak to them. When you're ready, bring out your injured and infirm, and we'll begin doing what we can for them.

Those that can't walk, we can transport on the pad there, or a droid can carry them to the ship."

Josh looked suspicious. "How do we know you won't just attack with these battle droids while we're inside?"

Allistor stepped close to the man, their faces less than two feet apart, and leaned in, growling, "I'm getting a little tired of your attitude, Josh. I'm here to help. If I wanted to kill you and take your stuff, you being out here wouldn't stop me. I could have done it already."

Stepping back and turning to face Leila, he added, "You've seen our tower. I have plenty of space, weapons, and food. The only resource inside these walls that means anything to me is you and your people. Human beings are the most valuable resource on Earth right now, and I want to preserve as many of us as I can. I'm sorry for failing you before, I truly am. But I'm here now."

Leila nodded, throwing Josh a look that caused him to lower his eyes. "I'm convinced, Allistor. I apologize for Josh, he lost family last week, and is understandably angry. I'll bring my people out as quick as I can."

As Leila and her people entered the gates, the battle droids spread out to form a perimeter. Fuzzy wandered over to the iron gate leading into the park and pawed at it until Allistor opened it for him. He then wandered inside to sniff around the trees, and do what bears do in the woods. While they waited, Allistor took a seat on the hoverpad and opened up his file on the other Strongholds. There were two more within his Capital City's walls, and Leila had given him a harsh reminder that he needed to reach out to them as soon as possible.

It took nearly forty five minutes before Leila's people began to emerge from the front door of the church and exit the gate. The seniors came first, some using canes or walkers, others being helped or carried by their younger neighbors. Amanda had them lifted onto the hoverpad as she began using *Internal Analysis* on each of them. Once she'd scanned them, she would inform one of the healers of their issues, and move on to the next patient. In total about thirty elder citizens and badly wounded were triaged and given at least preliminary attention.

As the healers did their thing, Leila brought the rest of her people out. Most of them carried bundles of supplies and belongings on their backs, or in shopping carts. As she approached Allistor, he said, "I'm guessing you've decided to come stay with us? That's great! If you like, the droids can carry some of those loads for you."

Leila let out a long breath. "They're tired of being hungry. And a safe place to sleep is hard to pass up. Not all of us wanted to relocate. But for the sake of the kids and the weaker folks, we agreed to go. And yes, please ask your droids to help."

As Allistor gave instructions to Prime, Leila called out for her people to hand their packs to the nearest droid. In short order they were all moving at a good pace up 10th Ave. Survivors pushed carts, carried or led children by the hand, as the healers walked alongside the platform, still working as two droids pushed it north toward the *Phoenix*.

The droids kept at least one gun hand unburdened, and maintained a loose perimeter around the now much larger group of humans.

In less than ten minutes the entire procession had boarded the ship via the cargo ramp. There were many exclamations and expressions of wonder from the survivors as they took in the sights. William began introducing himself to the children, passing out lollypops that Amanda had thoughtfully provided for the occasion. Allistor reported to Kira that they were all aboard, and she closed the door before lifting off.

When they landed, they found the three *Juggernauts* awaiting them. Bundles were piled atop the vehicles, and children were loaded inside. As the vehicles drove down the ramps, the rest of the survivors rode the elevators down and met them at the street. Again, the procession only took a few minutes to cover the four blocks to the tower, and Allistor's people began the process of getting Leila's settled in.

Chapter 3

The following morning Meg and Sam, with the help of Sydney and Addy, and an expanded kitchen staff from other properties, served everyone a meal featuring delicious breakfast burritos. Scrambled eggs, sausage, and peppers wrapped in a soft tortilla, that gave the same improved eight-hour buffs as the sandwiches from the day before. As they ate, Allistor stood on a chair and made a quick speech.

"Good morning, everyone. I hope you slept well. I'd first like to say a big thank you to our chefs and kitchen staff for this amazing meal." He paused while the combined crowd of Invictus citizens and Leila's people clapped and cheered in appreciation. "Now, for all of our newcomers. I've held off on having you swear the oath that will allow you to become Invictus citizens. I promised Leila that you'd all have the opportunity to explore, to check out this place and our other properties, and to ask questions. So today is for you to do just that. My people will answer questions for you about this place, our other properties here on the continent and the Caribbean. And..." he paused, a wicked grin on his face. "You can even travel through the teleport to *another planet!*"

There was a full minute of murmuring before he held up his hands for quiet. "Take a look around, and decide what you'd like to do. I have assured Leila that she will retain ownership of her Stronghold at the church. And we'll focus several raid groups on clearing the neighborhood around it, to make it safer for you if you choose to remain there. We'll beef up the defenses, expand the walls to include the park, whatever is needed. Or you're welcome to claim your ten acres of land pretty much anywhere outside Invictus City, including on the planet Orion if you like."

Again he gave them a little time to absorb that info. "At the end of the day, I want you all back here. Let's say by 5pm local time. At that point, I will expect each of you to take the oath, or leave. You can remain at your stronghold even if you choose not to become one of us. But you won't share in the same benefits our citizens enjoy. Leila can explain that to all of you. So, enjoy your breakfast, and have a good time exploring today. I'll see you all this evening."

Hopping down, he took a seat and quickly ate his own breakfast. He planned to visit the other two Strongholds within the city, and his conscience itched for him to get moving. During the previous evening's meal, he had asked Juanita, Rhonda, and Leila whether any of them knew the locations of the other Strongholds. He'd hoped Nigel could just pinpoint the non-citizen humans on the map for him, but apparently it wasn't that easy. Nigel's sensors didn't work throughout the entire lower half of Manhattan yet. Only in the vicinity of the walls, and any buildings that Allistor and his people had cleared and claimed. Juanita said she knew the general direction of one Stronghold, having run across fellow human scavengers moving in that direction several months back. All three ladies had promised to ask their people to see if anyone had better information.

46

His meal finished, Allistor moved to his usual spot in the lobby lounge area and waited for the ladies to report in. He'd also arranged for Amanda, the teen sisters, Prime and a company of droids, as well as Bjurstrom and his raid team to join him. Just in case the occupants of the Strongholds were hostile. The *Juggernauts* outside were fully fueled and loaded with supplies, and Allistor had loaded his ring with enough jerky, fruit, and apple juice for a hundred people. He hoped that the other survivors would be in better shape than Leila's, but planned for the worst.

Rhonda was the first to approach him. She had a man with her, whom she quickly introduced. "Allistor, this is Chuck. One of my best scavengers. He says there was a stronghold near the Empire State building a couple months after the apocalypse. But when the building fell, it buried the place. He doesn't know if there were survivors or where they moved to, but our guess is they wouldn't have gone far."

"When the building fell? What happened?"

Chuck answered first. "In those early days, it happened pretty regular. Most buildings were damaged in the battles between the military and the monsters in the first weeks. Add in fire damage, wind, weather… lots of the taller buildings collapsed. The ones further north seemed to suffer worse. Possibly because of all the bombs and tank shells from the heavy fighting, combined with that nuke in the Bronx."

"But you saw this Stronghold?"

"Not exactly. We ran into a couple of their guys as we were out scouting. Turns out we were all eyeing the same grocery store. We agreed to work together to clear the building and share whatever we found inside. I had a chance to talk to one of the guys for a while as we waited for the sun to come up. He told me they'd chosen a building just south of the Empire State, that had a bank in it. There were secure cages, and a vault, to hide in at night in the early days before they made it a Stronghold. There was a drug store full of medicine, and a sandwich shop with a full commercial kitchen. I was a little bit jealous." Chuck paused, scratching his head, and Allistor joined him in remembering the first few days when there was no such thing as a safe place to sleep.

"Anyway, a few months ago we were ranging further away from our base, looking for food, and we heard a building fall during the night. When daylight came, we saw the Empire State was gone. Remembering what that guy had said, we went to investigate. There wasn't much left of the tower, or the entire block. It fell toward the south, wiping out a few blocks, including the one where he'd told me the Stronghold had been. We saw some blood, and called out for survivors, but nobody answered. By the time we reached the place it was late afternoon, so we didn't hang around long." He looked a little bit guilty. "Bodies, even buried bodies, tend to attract the monsters. Especially after dark."

Allistor reached up and patted Chuck on the shoulder. "I totally understand. My parents were killed when a void titan destroyed our house. My mom died in

48

our front yard, my pop was crushed when the whole front brick wall of the house fell on him. I had to run, and couldn't come back for a few days. By then, the canids had taken my mom's body. I didn't uncover my father, figuring he was better off buried the way he was. Even days later, the canids were still hanging around, and nearly killed me."

By this time, Amanda, Juanita, and Leila had joined them. Amanda, hearing the last half of Chuck's report, offered, "At least we have a general area to start from. I agree, if there were survivors they probably wouldn't have moved far. Especially if they had wounded. It was nighttime, and they would have wanted safe shelter as quickly as possible."

"It's as good a place to start as any." Allistor agreed. "And I'm hoping that since the System is telling me there are still occupied Strongholds, some of those folks did survive and recover."

Juanita raised her hand, then grinned sheepishly. "Uh, one of my guys said he ran into some folks over on the lower east side. When they saw our people, they retreated. Headed toward the area of the housing authority high rises over near the FDR. Not too many other places they could go in that direction. Beyond that is the river, and the army blew up the Williamsburg Bridge, so there's no crossing. I guess they could have used the FDR to go north or south…"

"Great, thank you Juanita. Not being from here, I have no idea where that is. But Kira has a good map on the

Phoenix, and we can search from the air. Strongholds should stand out pretty clearly."

Chuck stepped forward. "Hey, if you don't mind, I'd like to tag along? I spent a lot of time poking around out there, and I know the area around the Empire State a little. I might be useful."

Juanita added, "I'd like to join you, too."

"Absolutely! Grab your gear and meet back here in ten?" Chuck nodded and dashed off toward the elevators. Though all of Allistor's original survivors had storage rings, many of the newcomers from the City hadn't acquired them yet. There was a limited supply available on the open market, and there were four thousand new people. Allistor made a mental note to speak to Harmon and make sure they all got one. Allistor had gifted Juanita a ring the same day he'd given her Jesse's properties.

"Nigel can you patch me through to Kira, please?" Allistor had spoken to her the evening before about using the *Phoenix* to search for more survivors.

After just a few seconds, the AI replied, "*Go ahead, Sire.*"

"Good morning, Kira. You all set for a little search and rescue?"

"You know it, boss. Ready when you are."

"Okay, we'll see you in about fifteen minutes. First target is the Empire State building. Or.. what's left of it."

"Roger that. See you in a few."

50

William showed up while they were waiting for Chuck to return, trying to slip unnoticed behind Amanda and Juanita. When Allistor cleared his throat to get Amanda's attention and pointed behind her, both women turned and exposed the lurking squire. Allistor frowned down at the boy, crossing his arms.

"What? There might be kids there. You need me, just like yesterday!" William crossed his own arms in imitation of Allistor, and set his jaw.

Allistor had actually expected the boy to want to come, and didn't mind. But one should never pass up an opportunity to give one's squire a hard time. "Fine, but same deal as yesterday. You do not leave the ship for any reason." Juanita held up a hand, and William had to jump to claim his high-five.

Chuck returned, and they headed out. Since they were taking the *Juggernauts* anyway, everyone piled in, and they proceeded toward the parking garage. Prime and the droids ran along on either side of the vehicles, easily keeping pace. Once they were all loaded aboard, Allistor escorted William up to the bridge where Kira could keep an eye on him.

Upon entering the bridge, he was surprised to see Kira's two young daughters sitting at two of the command stations. "Hello there, Brooke. Hillary. What a surprise!" Allistor smiled at them, taking each of their hands and kissing them, making the girls giggle. He gave Kira a questioning look. "New crew trainees? Recruiting a little young, aren't we?"

Kira rolled her eyes at him. "Gene's gone out to Vegas this morning, and I figured it wouldn't hurt to bring them along. If we get in any fights, this is a safe place for them to earn some xp." She glanced at William, then raised her eyebrows at Allistor.

He got the point. "Well, this ship has never had a lovelier bridge crew! You think you ladies can do me a favor and make sure William doesn't get into too much trouble?"

Both girls nodded their heads, and Hillary shot William, who was close to her own age, a look that said he'd better behave, or else. William just sighed, and took a seat at the weapons station. Having flashbacks to their first day in space, Allistor picked him up out of the chair immediately. "Ohhhh no you don't. Let's put you on the sensors station. You can help us look for the survivors." Having been given a legitimate job to do, William didn't complain. He immediately began to pull up the station's displays and try to learn how to operate the sensors.

Kira lifted off, saying, "The building is still inside the City walls, so it will only take a minute or so to get there. I noticed it when I was flying to the park to pick up Mira and the others. It's a big pile of rubble now."

"So I hear. Hey, you said Gene was in Vegas? What's going on there?"

Kira snorted. "Well, you know he flew the raid group out there that first day. And he went to Hoover Dam with them, mainly because he's a huge engineering nerd and wanted to see the machines inside. Now he's claimed

52

his ten acres right next to the dam, and built a small airstrip. And he thinks he can use the alien tech you've given him to improve the power generation at the dam. I'll let him tell you about it."

Allistor grinned. That sounded like Gene. "Did you ladies claim land next to his."

"Nope! We claimed the pirate island!" Brooke bragged.

Allistor looked to Kira, who explained. "Well, after they claimed the dam and set up the Stronghold, the raid crew went back to Vegas. They started claiming sections of the strip, and the hotels. Gene thought it would be a good idea to claim one for us, too. He has a plan to get the hotels and casinos up and running again. Sort of a… retirement income. Anyway, Brooke really liked the pirate ship out front, so we chose Treasure Island. Turns out with the main hotel, parking garages, and everything, it's right about thirty acres. So the girls and I claimed it."

"We're gonna be pirates!" Brooke thrust a fist in the air.

"Shiver me timbers!" Allistor looked at her with one eye closed, pirate style. "I hope you'll let me come visit the pirate ship when you get it in tip-top shape?" Brooke nodded her head vigorously, smiling at him.

"Okay, we're here." Kira reported, maneuvering the Phoenix to hover over the fallen monument to early twentieth century engineering. The displays across the front of the bridge switched to the view directly below them. Allistor saw that Chuck had been correct. The tower had leaned toward the south as it fell, smashing into and crushing several smaller buildings on the adjoining city blocks.

"Damn." Allistor was in awe of the destruction below them. It looked like a giant hand had reached down and crushed a section of his city. After staring for a moment, he headed for the door. "I'm going to join the others in the cargo bay. We'll open the door and look around, while you watch the monitors up here. We're looking for a Stronghold, so walls, etc. When I give the word, start circling in an outward spiral."

"Gotcha, boss. Good luck."

Allistor rode the elevator back down to the cargo level, then jogged the short distance to join the others in the main cargo bay. He asked Nigel to open the door, and explained what they were going to do. After making sure everyone was secured, he spoke through Nigel. "Alright Kira, let's go."

She had set the ship to hover at about two thousand feet, high enough to clear any of the nearby skyscrapers. Turning the ship toward the west, she said, "If it was me, and that building had just fallen on me, I'd go east, or south. There's too much rubble to the north and west." The ship began to move slowly eastward as everyone gazed down at the ground, searching for signs of life. Kira passed over Madison Ave and continued west as far as Park Ave. From there she turned south for a couple of blocks, then circled back toward the west.

It wasn't long before Chuck shouted, "There!" Pointing down toward a small building at the intersection of 5th Ave and E. 32nd Street. "That has to be it. Man, they really didn't go far at all. I wonder why they didn't answer when we called out?"

The building he pointed to was close enough to the disaster zone that there was still some rubble on 5th Ave not far north of it. It was brick, just four stories tall, and there was a wall that sprang up in the middle of the wide street, thirty feet or so from the front of the building."

"Kira, we think we've found them. Hover here for a minute, please. And start looking for a good place to land. Nigel, can I have loudspeaker at full volume, please? Just here on the ship. I want the people below to hear me."

"*Go ahead, Sire. I will route your voice through the external transmitters.*"

"Hello down there in the building! Anybody home? This is Allistor." His voice echoed off the street and buildings below.

They waited and watched, but nobody emerged from the building. There was a garden of sorts growing on the roof, but that was the only sign of life.

"Hello? We're friendly. We're here to help. We have food, and healers." Allistor tried again.

Kira's voice came to him. "I think I can squeeze the landing in here on the street, but it'll be close. Might snap off a few light poles. Easier to land on Park Ave to the east, it's a couple lanes wider."

Allistor thought about it, looking down at the street, then spoke again to the people he hoped were below. "Listen, we're going to land this ship a few blocks away, and come back. I promise, we're not here to hurt you. My name is Allistor. You might have seen a couple notifications about me? I'm human like you. We're here to help! So... yeah. We'll be back shortly."

Kira took the hint and drifted the ship along above E. 32nd Street to Park Ave, just two blocks east. She turned the Phoenix so that it oriented roughly north-south to match the eight-lane wide street, and set her down gently.

"Prime, I want you and your troops to hang back a full block from the Stronghold . I'll shout if we need you. I don't want to scare these people. Fuzzy, Amanda, Juanita, Chuck, Bjurstrom, you and your people come with me. Addy and Sydney, you can come too, but stay behind us. Call out if you see anything or anyone." Allistor quickly created a raid party, inviting everyone including Kira and the children on the bridge.

Allistor and company descended the ramp and began to walk the two long blocks to their destination. The droids followed behind and on either side, scanning the buildings and alleys for any threat. When they reached Madison Ave, Allistor motioned for Prime to hold. "If I call for you, come as fast as you can."

Prime saluted without a word, and the droids began to move into the nearby buildings and alleys, out of sight in case anyone in the Stronghold stepped out to look. Allistor and the humans, and one bear cub, continued on. When they were within fifty yards or so of the wall where it jutted out into the street, Allistor paused and called out again.

"Hey in there! It's Allistor again. I'd like to talk to you!" He put his hands in the air and continued to move forward toward the corner, around which they'd find the gate. The others raised their hands as well, and followed. Every eye was glued to the top of the wall as they went, watching for any kind of movement. Just to be safe, Allistor cast *Barrier* on Sydney, who was walking between Addy and the wall. Sydney saw the glimmer, and nodded her understanding. She lowered one hand long enough to move Addy slightly closer behind her.

Allistor turned the corner, keeping his distance from the wall. As he moved in front of the gate, and his party swung out into the middle of 5th Ave where there was no cover close by, a dozen people with guns rose up atop the wall, pointing their weapons.

"Hold it right there!" A man called down in a clear New York accent. "Keep your hands where we can see 'em!".

Fuzzy growled low in his throat, and Allistor whispered, "Easy, buddy. Let's not scare the nice people with guns pointed at us."

"Whatever you's want, we ain't interested!" The man shouted again. Allistor was able to identify him this time. He was taller than the others, with wide shoulders and a white streak in his otherwise jet black hair.

"I'm Allistor. Ruler of Invictus City, which your Stronghold now sits within. I've just come to talk, and hopefully, help."

The man spit over the wall, but said nothing. The guns remained leveled at Allistor and his party. Allistor decided to try again. "Look, are you the folks who had the Stronghold closer to the Empire State building before it fell?"

"Yeah, so what?"

"So I heard you might have suffered casualties. And maybe lost a lot of your resources. I'm here to see if we can be friends. Offer you a chance to join us. We have plenty to go around."

"Why would you wanna do that?"

Allistor sighed. This wasn't going as well as he'd hoped. "Because we humans need to stick together! We need to help each other survive, and get stronger. There are so few of us left, I'd like to think we could find common ground."

"This is *our* ground! And *you're* trespassing. We don't need nuttin' you's are offering."

Allistor was about to try again when Juanita lost her patience.

"Hey, moron! Yeah, you, goombah." she shouted. "This man's trying to be nice, here. He owns half the damn continent, has something like twenty strongholds, all bigger than yours. Hell, he owns his own damn *planet*. You pull that trigger, and he'll scrape you and your people off the face of the earth like gum off his shoe. Get your head outta your ass and get down here! It won't hurt ya to listen."

As the rest of the party looked at Juanita with surprised faces, laughter could be heard from atop the wall. "Ha hahaha! You, I like. Hold on, I'll be right down."

Juanita looked at Allistor and shrugged. "New Yorkers. Sometimes you gotta get in our face and prove yourself."

It wasn't long before the gate opened, and the man with the streak in his hair walked out. His gun was lowered, held in his left hand. He approached the group, and reached his right hand out to Juanita. "Francis DiMarco. Most folks just call me Big Frankie."

"Of course they do." Juanita looked him up and down as she took his hand and shook it. "Juanita. Most people call me Juanita." Frankie chuckled at that, then turned to Allistor. "So you're the Prince. Yeah, we been seein the notifications about you. What gives you the right to come here n claim our territory? You ain't from the city."

"No, I'm from out west. Way out west. From a town that would barely cover four or five of your city blocks. As for what gives me the right... well that's a long story. You want to stand out here while I tell it? Or invite us inside?"

"I ain't ready to let you in just yet." Big Frankie looked over the rest of group, smiling brightly at Amanda.

When he reached out to shake her hand, she stepped closer to Allistor and put an arm around him.

Doing her best impersonation of his accent, she said "I ain't ready to shake yer hand just yet."

"Ha!" Big Frankie barked a laugh, continuing to smile. "I'll give ya this much, mister fancy prince, you gots good taste in women."

"That's Prince Fancypants." Amanda corrected him, pinching Allistor's butt as she spoke. Allistor did his best not to squirm, but it hurt. Despite himself, he reached around and rubbed the injured spot.

This time Big Frankie was surprised. Fuzzy gave Allistor's hand an experimental sniff, and the two teenage sisters, who'd also seen Amanda's pinch attack, tried to stifle their laughter. To Big Frankie, who was directly in front of Allistor, it all looked quite odd.

Allistor quickly changed the topic. "Listen, we have food, we have healers if any of your people are wounded, or sick. We really are just here to help. And there's no need for the titles. I'm just Allistor. Nice to meet you." He held out his hand.

For a moment, he thought Big Frankie would refuse. But the man cracked a smile and shook his hand. "And you as well. I suppose you can come inside. Not for nuthin, but a good meal would hit the spot."

"How many of you are there?" Allistor began to worry he hadn't brought enough.

Big Frankie looked down at his feet. "Eighty five of us, now. There were over four hundred… before." He looked up the street toward the pile of rubble. "This place was just an Outpost. Most of us still living were already here when the building fell. Only a dozen made it out of the rubble."

"I'm so sorry." Allistor's voice was quiet.

"Thanks. Anyway, we been getting by okay since then. But this place don't hold a candle to what we had."

Allistor pulled some dragon jerky from his ring and handed a piece to the man. "I've got enough of this for everyone, plus some fresh fruit. If you'll gather everyone together, I'll tell you about us, and what we can do for you."

Big Frankie took a bite, chewing thoughtfully. His eyes widened a bit when the buff notification appeared. "This is good. The name, though. This is really dragon meat?"

"Yep. Well, drake meat, technically. We've had to tangle with a few of them now."

"Right. Well, that's worth hearin' about. Come on in. Leave your robots where they are." He nodded down the block.

"No problem. I'll even send them back to the ship if it'll make you feel more comfortable." Allistor offered, not surprised Prime and his droids had been spotted.

"Nah. There's all kinds of nasty things walkin around out there. Better they're close by." Big Frankie led them in through the gate. Already his people were emerging from the building, and all but a few of those on the wall were climbing down. Half a dozen remained as lookouts. Most were wary of Fuzzy as the group walked closer, but Allistor reassured them by patting the bear's head, and giving him a piece of jerky.

"Fuzzy won't hurt you." He gave them his best smile. A few of them ventured close enough for the bear cub to sniff at extended hands, then give them a friendly lick. The group was led inside the building's ground floor, into what looked like it had been an Asian restaurant of some kind. There were dozens of tables surrounded by black-lacquered wood chairs with bright red satin seats.

Allistor emptied the food and drink from his ring onto a large table near the center of the room. "Please, help yourselves." He said to the gathering crowd. Amanda stepped forward and added some bread and pastries he hadn't known she had. She just smiled at him.

Big Frankie motioned to another round table near the window, and they took seats, watching as the food was quickly distributed, and the residents took seats of their own, most of them murmuring thanks of some kind. Two of the children were sent outside to deliver food to the guards on the wall.

Big Frankie stood and said, "This is Prince Allistor and his people. You've all heard o' him. He's here to make us some kind of offer. I'd told him we'd listen, but that's all." He sat down with an air of finality.

Allistor got to his feet, once again wishing he'd put more points into *Charisma*.

Good morning, everyone. I'll get right to the point. Big Frankie here asked me to explain how I came to claim this part of Manhattan as my Capital City, which is called Invictus, by the way..."

He spent about fifteen minutes relaying the highlights of his story to the gathered audience. He spoke about fighting void titans and drakes, seizing the gold depositories, and taming the murder chicken matron. He talked a bit about the friends and family they'd lost, but mainly focused on all the ways he'd helped his people get stronger, and all they'd accomplished. Then he spoke about Leila's stronghold, and his regrets for not helping them sooner. When he was done, he added, "And that is why we've come here this morning. Any questions?"

A woman sitting two tables away leaned back in her chair and crossed her arms. "It sounds like bullshit to me. No way you did all that."

Juanita started to get up, but Allistor shook his head. "Which part don't you believe, miss...?"

"I ain't no miss. You can call me Deborah. I don't buy most all of it. Friggin leprechauns. Pull my other leg!" Several in the crowd nodded their heads and spoke quietly to each other.

Allistor thought for a moment. "Okay, well…
you've just eaten dragon jerky, so will you accept that at
least the part about killing drakes was true?"

Deborah looked around at the others for a moment,
then nodded her head. "I guess so."

"Good! That's a start. Now, let's see. He opened
his inventory, looking for a specific item. He'd ignored it
when he first looted it, being busy with other things. But it
would come in handy right that moment. When he found
it, he pulled it out from his ring and stepped toward the
woman. "Do you know how to use the *Examine* spell?"

"'Course I do." She glared at him like he was
stupid.

Allistor simply handed her the item. "I looted this
when we cleared the depository. Could you *Examine* it
please, and read what it says to everyone?" Deborah took
the item and stared at it, her eyes crossing a bit as she read
the description.

> *Leprechaun Clan Mother's Wand*
> *Item Quality: Very Rare*
> *Enchantment: Greater Illusion*
> *This wand was crafted for the matron of a*
> *leprechaun clan.*
> *It can cast a powerful illusion of her choosing that*
> *will last up to one hour.*

The room was silent as she finished reading and
quickly set the wand on the table. A few seconds later, a
man cackled loudly, making everyone jump. In a strong

Irish accent, he called out, "Ha! Leprechauns be real! I knew it!"

This got everyone chuckling, and broke the serious mood in the room. Allistor just looked at Deborah with one eyebrow raised as he held out his hand for the wand. She grabbed it like she didn't really want to touch it, and thrust it back into his hand. "Fine! The leprechaun bit is true." She grumped.

Next Allistor pulled the staff he'd looted from Goblin Chief Borzgl. He handed it to a random man seated nearby. Without needing a prompt, the man read the description, then handed it back.

"Fine. I agree, you're not totally full of shit." Deborah pronounced, earning more laughter. Allistor noticed she was struggling not to smile herself. "So what do you want from us?"

Allistor turned a full circle, meeting the eyes of as many of the survivors as he could. "Well, what I'm hoping for is that you'll all choose to come join us as citizens of Invictus. You can live in the tower here in the city, or one of the other buildings we're clearing. Or you can live at any one of my Strongholds, including one of those on Orion, the former goblin planet where I got this staff."

Not ready to give up quite yet, Deborah followed up. "And if we don't wanna join you?"

"Then I hope we can be allies. You can stay here, live your life. We'll trade with you, and you'll be mostly protected inside the City walls. Though it'll be some time before we've cleared all the monsters from all the buildings, tunnels, and so on. You won't get the same benefits of a citizen, but we'll leave you in peace."

"What kinda benefits?"

"Well, that would take quite a while to explain. Let me tell you this, instead. I mentioned Leila's people earlier. Right now, they're poking around my various properties, asking questions and deciding whether they want to join. I invite all of you to do the same. My ship is just a short walk down the street, and I can have you all back there in just a few minutes. Then you can ask any random person you see, whatever question you like, since you seem to have a bit of trouble believing me." Allistor smiled, reaching down to take Deborah's hand, then kissing the back of it while waving his free hand with a flourish. She snatched it back, blushing slightly.

Standing straight again, he spoke more loudly. "That invitation is for all of you. We'll go wait outside while you discuss it. If you want to come investigate, grab whatever gear you want to bring with you. We've got enough rooms for you to spend the night. You can all eat a good lunch, then explore until dinner." After a pause, he added, "And while you talk, I'll give you all a small gift. I'm about to send each of you an invitation. Please accept it."

A minute later he motioned for his people to follow him, gave Big Frankie a nod, smiled at Deborah, and exited the Stronghold. Knowing it would take them a while to talk, he walked back to where Prime and the droids were waiting. Prime stepped out and saluted. "I am glad to see you safe, Sire."

"Thank you Prime. We have a little time while the folks inside make up their minds. Would you please have your droids clear these buildings as quickly as possible? I'm looking for as many kills as you can rack up in… the next hour?"

"It shall be done, Sire." Prime saluted again, and disappeared into the nearest building.

Allistor led his group back to the Stronghold gate area, where they took seats on some of the larger chunks of concrete that littered the street. It wasn't long before the sounds of battle echoed down the block toward them. Allistor grinned to himself, and settled down to wait.

Fifteen minutes later, Big Frankie walked out to join them. With a big grin on his face, he said, "You oughta see them in there. They were talkin' all serious-like about whether to join you, then they started poppin off, one after the other. Started with the kiddos, leveling up again and again. Then some of the ones who ain't been out huntin' much. Pretty much everyone's leveled up at least once since you walked out. Lemme guess, the droids, right? I gotta hand it to ya, that was clever."

Allistor returned the grin. "Just one of the benefits of being a citizen of Invictus. We send our low level people in behind the battle droids to clear buildings. They get experience and loot, with minimal risk. And there's always a healer with them, just in case."

"Yeah, yeah. I'm guessin' I don't need to tell ya that we're joining yous for lunch. They're grabbing their gear and will be out in a few."

"Great! There's room for everybody on the ship. I don't know how much of a wilderness guy you are, but I recommend taking the portal to Orion and having a quick peek around. There's a whole planet that is basically empty." Allistor held out a hand, and Big Frankie shook it.

"Thanks, but I'm a city boy. Eighth generation of DiMarco's born here in this city. This fancy-schmancy high rise you talked about sounds like my kinda spot. Think I'll settle in there and see if I can't start the ninth generation." He gave Allistor an exaggerated wink.

It wasn't long before the survivors began to emerge from the Stronghold with packs on their backs. Even the kids had makeshift bundles made from sheets slung over their shoulders. When they'd done a head count and confirmed everyone was out, Big Frankie first locked the building entry, then closed the Stronghold gate behind him.

Even as they walked down East 32nd Street toward the *Phoenix*, members of the crowd continued to level up. Most often it was the children, but several of the adults were surrounded in the golden glow before Allistor called out for Prime to form up and escort them the last block back to the ship.

Because he had the other Stronghold on his mind, Allistor asked loudly if anyone knew anything about another group of survivors south of Central Park as soon as he had everyone in the cargo bay. No one spoke up, and a moment later they were all distracted as the ship lifted off.

It took another twenty minutes to offload everyone, get them back to the tower, and situated in the dining area. Allistor checked in on Leila's group, several of which he spotted milling around.

"Nigel, have Leila's people begun exploring?"

"Yes, Sire. I have transported two hundred and thirty seven of them to other locations, many of them to multiple locations. I am tracking their whereabouts, and answering questions for several of them. Would you like an individual list?"

"No, thank you Nigel. That won't be necessary. But I would like to know if any of them traveled to Orion."

"Seventeen of the newcomers have transported there so far. Along with eight citizens who agreed to escort them."

"Thank you Nigel. This new group has been given the same offer. Please allow them to teleport around and explore. And please give everyone a reminder at 4:00pm local time that they need to return here by 5:00pm."

"Certainly, Sire."

Allistor raided Meg's kitchen storage, stocking up on more food and drink, this time for two hundred people. Finding Amanda and the others waiting for him in the lobby, Allistor headed back to *Phoenix* to start their search for the next Stronghold.

Chapter 4

Kira took the Phoenix up, and Juanita directed her roughly northeast from the parking garage. As they moved above the city, they could see that both the Brooklyn Bridge and the Manhattan Bridge had been destroyed, large sections right in the middle having been blown apart. There were cars on both bridges, but many were crushed and shoved to either side of the bridge, as if tanks had pushed through them.

It was the same when they reached the Williamsburg Bridge a moment later. This time the bridge had been blown apart closer to the Manhattan side. Kira hovered for a moment over the base of the bridge, and pointed downward. "I think that right there's your Stronghold. But they're in trouble!"

Allistor was noticing the same thing on the bridge monitors even as Kira pointed it out. The view beneath the ship was of several oddly shaped high-rises just west of the FDR freeway. The two buildings nearest the freeway and bridge intersection were enclosed in a standard thirty-foot high Stronghold wall. It encompassed both buildings, a couple parking lots, and a few acres of green space that looked like it had been partially cultivated. A double-wide gate was situated in the eastern wall, facing across the freeway toward the river flowing just a hundred yards or so away.

Outside the gate, the road was clogged with abandoned cars, several of which were on fire. Swarming between the cars and massing near the gate were hundreds of goblins. Smoke poured from one end of the building closest to the gate. Even as Kira spoke, balls of flame were rising up from the goblin horde, arcing over top of the walls, and impacting the building. The goblins outside were using bows and slings to shoot upward, while a group of them were pushing a truck to ram into the gates. Allistor could see humans running around inside the wall, and defenders shooting down at the goblins from the ramparts.

"Kira! Get on the weapons station and start firing! Nigel, take over control of the ship and keep us hovering just out of range of their weapons! Bjurstrom, get your people ready, we're gonna be landing soon, and there's a goblin horde below us. Open the cargo door and do whatever damage you can do from up here until then." Allistor started running off the bridge toward the elevator. "Nigel! Get me Gralen, now! Prime, send a droid from the tower to get Harmon, tell him we're fighting a goblin horde, and it's lunchtime!"

"*I have Gralen, Sire.*"

"Gralen! We've run across a goblin horde, attacking a human stronghold. I can't tell how many there are, but it's a lot."

"*There are one thousand one hundred and eight hostile entities below us, Sire.*" Nigel flashed up a display over top of Allistor's map showing masses of red dots.

"You hear that? Gather up as many people as you can fit in your ship and get over here!"

"Right away, Allistor!" Gralen's voice came back. "I'm getting the feed from Nigel here on *Opportunity*. We'll be there in twenty minutes." Gralen and his crew were currently with their ship, which was parked in Denver after returning from Orion.

"Shit, twenty minutes might be too long. Just come as fast as you can." Allistor replied.

"*Sire, Prime is relaying a message from Harmon.*" Nigel made a hologram of the giant orcanin's face appear in the air in front of him as he ran into the cargo bay.

"Harmon! I've got a horde of tasty treats down here for you. Over a thousand of them. Think you could grab some of your orcanin and my people, and get over here in your ship?"

"We're already on our way, Allistor. A hundred or so of your people are joining my troops. It'll take us about five minutes to load everyone, and another couple to get there."

"Great! We'll keep them busy. I'm sending you a raid invite, designating you as a Commander. Please include everyone on your ship. See you when you get here."

Allistor was approaching the open cargo bay door, where the others were looking down at the horde. The two sisters were singing a battle song, stomping their feet to create a beat as they enhanced the damage of the spells their raiders were hurling downward. The ship's guns were firing plasma bolts and repulsor charges into the horde.

Each strike took down several of the little monsters, but they were hardly making a dent.

Bjurstrom looked up as Allistor approached. "Really wish we had one of those bombs on board about now."

Allistor grimaced. "We used all we had on Orion. Gene's guys might be making more, but it's only been a few days." Grabbing hold of one side of the cargo door's frame, he leaned out. He saw one of the raiders toss two of Meg's napalm grenades out, and watched them fall for several seconds before they exploded near the rear of the goblin horde that was still trying to bash open the gates. There was some confusion among the goblins, but when nothing happened other than a foul-smelling soaking, they shook it off. One of the shamans began casting another spell.

That was a mistake.

The moment the goblin began to summon the fireball between his hands, he caught fire. Followed quickly by dozens of goblins around him who'd either been splashed with the liquid from the grenades, or were standing in small puddles of it. In seconds, an area thirty feet wide became an inferno of screaming goblins. Allistor took a moment to *Identify* the shaman.

Goblin Shaman
Level 35
Health 6,270/9,500

"Nigel! I need you to take us down. Bjurstrom, I need three drivers for the *Juggernauts*. We're gonna break up that group by the gates."

The ship descended, moving a short distance east away from the horde. Allistor looked down and saw they were about to land on a wide patch of artificial surface that encompassed a dozen tennis courts in three rows. Plenty of room for the *Phoenix*.

The moment they touched down, Bjurstrom and two other raiders drove the vehicles down the ramp. Kira continued to fire ship's weapons at the horde across the freeway, the plasma bolts screaming through the air above the *Juggernauts*.

A moment later, the lead vehicle smashed through the four-foot iron fence between them and the FDR, and sped onto the road. Allistor immediately saw a problem. He hadn't taken into account the concrete K-rails that separated the northbound and southbound lanes. The vehicles had stopped, and Allistor could just hear Bjurstrom thinking about trying to ram his way through. He quickly scanned north and south as he jumped off the ship. There wasn't a break in the wall that he could see. He picked a spot to one side of the *Juggernauts*, and cast *Dimensional Step*.

As soon as he was in range, he cast *Levitate* on the section nearest the lead *Juggernaut*. Immediately, he felt his gut twist and the blood burn in his veins as he tried to use his magic to lift the multi-ton section of concrete. "Bjurstrom, push it!" He screamed as he tried to hold the spell. The concrete hadn't risen into the air at all, but when Bjurstrom advanced and slammed into the K-rail it slid along in front of him as if it weighed almost nothing. The moment there was space for the vehicles to get through, Allistor cancelled the *Levitate* spell and gasped for air.

When he cast *Restore* on himself, hoping to ease the burning in his veins, the pain only got worse. So he pulled a healing potion from his inventory and drank that, instead. The pain lessened as he watched his three demolition drivers start to plow through the rear of the horde. Goblin bodies were flung aside, or were crushed under the oversized wheels. Others turned their attention away from the Stronghold and began to bash at the vehicles with clubs and spears. Shamans began throwing fireballs at the moving targets as they completed their first pass through the horde and were turning for another.

Allistor was debating whether to try and cast another spell, when he saw the defenders atop the wall dump buckets of what looked like oil onto the truck the goblins were using as a ram. A moment later a flare dropped from the wall, there was a deep *whump!* sound, and thick black smoke began to rise as the vehicle and monsters caught fire. The thick black smoke rose into the air, pushed by the breeze off the river to join the much larger column of smoke billowing out of the high rise. From where he was standing, Allistor could see the upper floors at the near end of the building engulfed in flames. The defenders atop the wall above the gates had to retreat before they were overwhelmed by the smoke.

Bjurstrom and his drivers were plowing through the back lines of the horde for the second time, but without the element of surprise. All three vehicles looked like moving piles of goblins as they pushed through, the little monsters covering every inch and pounding at the exteriors. The upside of this was that there were no more fireballs. The shamans had either stopped targeting the *Juggernauts* to avoid killing their own, or they'd all been run down.

On the other hand, goblins along the walls on either side of the gate had begun scaling dozens of ladders, and were reaching the top of the wall. Human defenders were hacking at them with machetes and what looked like kitchen knives, while others were firing guns at the climbing monsters, or trying to push the ladder tops away from the wall. But already there were goblins atop the wall in half a dozen places.

Bracing himself, Allistor ran closer to the wall, and the horde. When he was within one hundred feet, he chose a spot of relatively clear wall, and cast *Dimensional Step*. The moment he appeared atop the wall, his body screaming in pain again, he lost his balance. Only his recently improved *Agility* stat let him fall inward to land atop the walkway, rather than outward and down into the screaming horde.

Gritting his teeth, he got to his feet and started shouting. "Here! I've got weapons!" He began pulling plasma rifles from his ring, handing out his entire supply of six of them to nearby humans. "Just point and shoot!" They all seemed to get the hang of the weapons quickly enough, and began blasting goblins off of ladders as they spread out down the walkway.

He found a couple of Meg's grenades in his inventory, and grabbed them as well. He chucked the first one sideways along the outside of the wall so that it smashed into several goblins at the base of a ladder near the burning vehicle. Instantly the napalm lit, and those goblins, along with the ladder itself, began to burn. Allistor repeated the process with another nearby ladder, using the flames from the first one to light the next two on fire.

Grabbing a man who was standing a few feet away stabbing a goblin in the face with a Bowie knife, he drew his sword and handed it to the man. "Hey! Use this. Keep them off me for like a minute, okay?"

The man nodded and began to hack wildly, knocking the top goblin off the ladder without a big chunk of its head. Allistor grabbed the wall with both hands to steady himself, and targeted the lead Juggernaut, which was still buried in goblins. He began to cast *Storm*, the burning in his veins not quite as bad as before. But as he channeled the spell, and the clouds gathered above the horde, the searing pain increased. He gritted his teeth and held the cast, watching bolts begin to blast the little green monsters off of his vehicles as they moved slowly through the AoE storm. As the strikes increased in frequency, Allistor let loose a scream of pain. Five seconds later he could no longer concentrate enough to hold the spell, and he let it go. Feeling dizzy, he stepped back from the edge of the wall and stumbled. The only thing that kept him from falling off the rampart was the man to whom he'd handed the sword.

As the man helped him lower himself to sit with his back against the wall, Harmon's ship came screaming over top of them from the southwest. Speakers blared something in a harsh orcanin voice as weapons fire rained down upon the horde. Allistor couldn't see what happened next, as he didn't have the ability to stand back up and look. He produced both a health and mana potion, downing one right after the other, then held his head in his hands as he hoped for the pain to recede. The man with the sword returned to hacking at the goblins on the nearest ladder, splashing Allistor liberally in monster blood.

Less than a minute passed before the sounds of the battle changed. Allistor could hear the screams of terrified goblins and the roars of hungry orcanin, and assumed Harmon's troops were making a charge. He looked up at his sword-wielding companion, and saw the man's eyes widen. It occurred to him that the defenders probably thought their situation just got worse, that the orcanin were attacking them.

Slapping the man's leg, he shouted "The big ones are friendly! Pass the word! They're on our side!"

The man stared for a moment, then nodded and began to shout. Echoing shouts began to run up and down the wall. The man looked back down at Allistor, and offered him a hand up. Allistor gripped the man's hand as tight as he could, and pulled. Now on his feet, he once again held onto the wall for support.

"I'm Angel." The man shouted above the screaming. "Thanks for the help." He held up the sword, then pointed over the wall. "That was some badass magic."

"Allistor. And you're welcome. Those big guys that look like orcs are called Orcanin. Allies of mine. They eat goblins." Allistor gave a half-hearted grin as the man looked over the wall again and shook his head.

"They can have them." He spat over the wall. The ladder in front of them had apparently cleared. Angel used the sword to push it away from the wall. He quickly scanned in either direction to confirm there were no more goblins coming over, then turned with a worried look toward the burning building.

Allistor shook his head. "You can't help them right now. Focus on this fight."

Angel nodded, his face grim, and began to stalk down the wall, looking for something to kill. Allistor let him go, leaning over to look down. The ladders within twenty feet of him in either direction were all down or burning. The juggernauts had freed themselves and were turning back toward the gates for another run. All of them appeared to be intact, though they were covered in goblin blood.

Harmon's hundred or so orcanin troops had the remaining several hundred goblins trapped between themselves and the wall, and were happily scything them down with long swords and hammers. Allistor's people were firing spells nonstop into the goblins closer to the wall, and the few who were still on ladders.

A small number of remaining goblin shamans cast fireballs from near the center of the horde. Some screamed into the orcanin line, knocking the burly fighters off their feet when they struck, singeing but not killing the tough orcanin. Other fireballs flew up and over the highway to splatter against the shield surrounding the *Phoenix*. A single fireball flew upward toward the wall's defenders, targeting one of the humans firing a plasma rifle. It struck the wall just below the man, flames splashing upward to engulf his face and arms. Screaming, he fell back, dropping the weapon as he instinctively tried to cover his burning face with burning hands.

Allistor traced the path of the fireball back to the shaman, who was doing his best to blend into the horde. But his staff gave him away.

Not wanting to risk the pain of using more magic, Allistor pulled the Barrett .50 from his ring and set it upon the wall. He didn't need the scope to zero in on a target just a few dozen yards away. Using the gun's sights, he took a few seconds to breathe, then squeezed the trigger. The shaman's head exploded even as the round continued through the bodies of three more goblins in a line behind him before burrowing into the concrete.

Allistor heard Angel whistle from beside him before murmuring, "I gotta get me one of those."

The sounds of screeching metal distracted Allistor before he could respond. The goblins had organized, working together to flip one of the *Juggernauts* onto its side. The vehicle continued to roll until it sat wheels-up on its roof, rocking back and forth, and spinning slightly as the horde pounded and shoved.

Harmon's orcanin had decimated the goblins facing them, chanting and stepping forward in rhythm as they sliced and smashed the much smaller and weaker monsters. Nearly half of the horde was dead or dying now, and many of the remaining goblins were frantically trying to break through to escape.

Behind Harmon's ever-tightening line, Allistor saw the rest of his raiders had formed up and were casting both dps and healing magic into the fray. Addy and Sydney were still singing, though Allistor couldn't hear the tune above the din of battle. Looking down the wall, he could see several of the wounded defenders were receiving heals, but he couldn't tell whether they were coming from his people, or the locals.

Taking aim at another shaman, Allistor saw three of them grouped together, each of them chanting and moving their arms, each waving a glowing staff. A chill crept up Allistor's spine as he thought he recognized the spell. A moment later, something close to four hundred goblin fighters began to grow larger, and stronger, as their eyes began to glow a crimson shade of pure hatred.

Allistor squeezed his trigger again, causing one of the three shamans to burst like an overripe watermelon. Even as he targeted the next, he began to scream. "Get back! Get down! They're going to explode!"

Angel immediately picked up the cry, shouting both directions down the wall, repeating himself to make sure the message was understood. Word began to pass down the wall, but it wasn't moving quickly enough.

Bjurstrom and the other raiders recognized the spell, and began to retreat. As did Harmon's troops. The only ones who didn't move away were Allistor's people that were trapped in the overturned Juggernaut. Which was still encircled by enlarged and enraged goblins. And even as the orcanin stepped back in a rapid and orderly fashion, the goblins charged forward, diving into the line, sacrificing their bodies without care, wrapping themselves around their foes' arms and legs.

Allistor managed to put a round into another of the two remaining shamans, but the third caster finished his chant at nearly the same time.

The entire area in front of the gates erupted as if Allistor had dropped one of his bombs. Hundreds of tightly crowded goblin bodies exploded, showering the orcanin, raiders, and defenders in bits of flesh, organs, and bone. The orcanin line was blasted apart, several of the warriors torn to shreds by the berserker goblins who'd latched onto them. Others were sprayed with shrapnel, the force of the explosions knocking them down. When Allistor's ears stopped ringing from the blast, he could hear roars of pain and anger from the orcanin, nearly drowning out the screams and sobs of humans who hadn't gotten word quickly enough, and had still been looking down from the wall at the battle.

The gates themselves, now peppered with bone fragments and flesh, had buckled inward when the burning truck the goblins had tried to use as a ram was lifted by the force of the explosion and slammed into them.

Allistor saw two of his raiders' icons go grey. His gaze immediately went to the line of raiders that had formed behind the orcanin, looking for bodies. It took him several seconds, as he watched all his people get to their feet, to realize what had happened.

There had been two people trapped in the overturned *Juggernaut*. Chuck, the new recruit who'd volunteered to lead them to the other Stronghold, and one of Bjurstrom's regular raid team, a man named Frank that Allistor had met once or twice.

Shifting his gaze to its location, he saw the sturdy vehicle now sat on its side, the windows all shattered and the body of the vehicle badly dented, with several areas showing multiple holes grouped as if they'd suffered shotgun blasts. Red human blood mixed with the goblin blood splattered everywhere.

Not a single living goblin remained, including the final shaman that had completed the suicidal casting. The human defenders realized this at roughly the same time as Allistor. A ragged cheer went up from the people atop the wall, even as most of them immediately turned to rush toward the burning building. Others crouched down over wounded comrades to try and help. Allistor saw more than a few of those shake their heads in resignation, finding their friends had died, then move on with faces grim.

Without thinking, Allistor cast Restore on the nearest wounded defender, a woman who'd fought the climbing goblins and taken a nasty stab wound just below her collarbone. The spell worked, but the pain within him dissuaded Allistor from casting more. He needed to find out how badly he'd damaged himself, and whether there was a remedy.

Grabbing the nearest of the able-bodied defenders, he handed them a bag he pulled from his ring, followed by a score of health potions. "Use these on the worst cases. Keep them alive long enough to receive full healing. I have healers outside, if you'll open the gates and let them in?"

"Who are you?" the woman asked. "I saw what you did for us. The magic, and the weapons. But you're not one of us." She looked up at him, her five-foot-nothing frame shaking from the adrenaline of the battle.

"My name's Allistor. This is my city, now. You might have seen some system messages…" He stopped when she nodded her head.

"We were wondering when you'd come to kick us out. Figures it would be now. We've fought the goblins for months to keep this place, and we'll sure as hell fight you, too. Even if you wipe us out with your ships and your magic!" she growled at him, setting the bag of potions down and balling her fists, looking as if she were about to swing at him.

Allistor raised both hands in surrender, taking a step back. "Easy, there. I'm not here to kick anybody out. You're welcome to stay here if you like. Or join me, and live at any one of my properties. All of you. But we can discuss that later. Right now, my people and I are just here to help. Including the orcanin. The big guys. They're friendly." He motioned toward the bag of potions. "Might want to hurry."

The woman looked down, her fists unclenching as she bent to retrieve the potions. She had the grace to look slightly embarrassed when she met his eyes again. "In that case, thank you for your assistance. I've got to get these to the folks who need them. Someone will come find you to talk. When they can." She looked toward the smoking high rise briefly before she stepped past him, shouting down to the gate. "Open up! Got healers outside that can help!"

A man's voice echoed up from below. "No can do, Maria! The doors are all bent and busted! They won't budge."

"Shit." The woman, whose name Allistor now knew was Maria, turned back to him. "Any way you can help with that?"

Allistor turned to lean over the front of the wall, shouting, "Harmon! Need to open the gates! They're jammed. Got any ideas?"

Harmon, who had been supervising the orcanin tending to their wounded, simply nodded his head. He barked a few quick orders in his own language, words that almost made sense to Allistor. A dozen of his troops trotted over to the gates, first lifting and tossing aside the mangled truck that was partially embedded in the doors. Next they produced massive prybars, each at least six feet of thick metal, and jammed them into gaps along the seam between the warped and dented doors. With a low chant, they levered the bars in unison, the screech of straining metal drowning out their guttural voices.

When there was sufficient space, half of them dropped their bars and inserted tri-pointed grappling hooks attached to cables. The others then let go of their prybars and took hold of the cables, two orcanin for each. Now able to use the strength of their legs and backs, instead of just their arms, they resumed their chant, leaning back and hauling the cables in bursts every fourth beat. More sounds of straining metal echoed across the courtyard as one of the doors finally gave way, moving outward far enough for even a wide-shouldered orcanin to pass through.

"Thanks, guys!" Allistor shouted down from the wall as the warriors removed the hooks and gathered up the cable and prybars. "Bon appetite!" he added, waving to the small sea of goblin parts at their feet. He heard a few deep-throated chuckles as the orcanin waved their acknowledgement, moving off to loot and butcher the few intact goblin corpses.

Allistor spotted Bjurstrom and the rest of his people moving toward the blood-splattered Juggernaut. He called out, "They're gone. Healers, come inside and help whomever you can! We'll deal with the bodies later."

Bjurstrom shook his head. "I'm sorry, boss. There isn't enough left of them to bury." He hung his head, wiping his eyes with the back of one hand. A few of the nearby raiders stepped aside and vomited at the sight.

"Alright, I need ten of you guarding the Phoenix, in case more goblins show up. The rest of you, get in here and see what you can do to help. There's still a fire burning in the high rise, and dozens of wounded that I can see."

Allistor stood where he was, as Maria had instructed, watching his people move through the gate and spread out. He noticed the sisters singing a light, upbeat tune that sounded vaguely Celtic, and felt his pain ease a bit. Checking his UI, he confirmed that his health, stamina, and mana regeneration rates had each increased. Smiling down at the teenagers, he gave them a double thumbs-up, which they returned without pausing their song.

More and more of the defenders were getting to their feet after Allistor's people cast heals and applied potions as quickly as possible. There were many handshakes and pats on the back as introductions were made, and thanks offered. In less than five minutes, the only humans still laying on the ground or atop the walls were the dead. Allistor estimated there were about fifty bodies. "If we'd gotten here just an hour earlier, most of them might be alive." He mumbled to himself, shaking his head.

"And if you'd arrived even ten minutes later, we might all be dead." A man's voice answered from behind him. Allistor turned to find an elderly black man with snow white hair and beard, and a friendly smile that created deep wrinkles along his jaw and next to his eyes. He held out a hand. "I'm told you're Prince Allistor. I'm Remington, but most folks just call me Remy." The man's voice was deep, with a cultured accent that reminded Allistor of one of his college history professors.

Allistor took the offered hand. "Good to meet you, Remy. What can we do to help? Have you got more folks inside that need heals?"

The man shook his head, his smile fading quickly. "We have our own healers inside, helping those we still can. We had some folks trapped in the fire, lost at least a dozen."

"I'm sorry for your losses, Remy. Truly. Every human life is precious these days." Allistor spoke softly.

Remy's head jerked upward, and he looked directly into Allistor's eyes. "Each human life has always been precious, Allistor." His eyes blazed with challenge.

Allistor's eyes widened at the seeming hostility the man suddenly displayed. "Of... of course, Remy. I didn't mean to suggest otherwise. It's just that there are so few of us left, now. I've been doing my best to protect as many as I can, but still it seems we lose too many, too often."

Remy's gaze softened, and he nodded slightly. "I'm sorry. I know you didn't mean anything by that. It has been a rough day, and I'm afraid emotions are a little raw just now." His gaze moved along the wall and across the courtyard, taking in the bodies that would never rise. "We lost a lot of good people to those little bastards. Too many, I'm afraid. My... youngest son was among the first to fall." His voice faded to a whisper, and he looked down toward the gate. "He was outside when they attacked, escorting a foraging party that was gathering fruit in the orchard across the road. He made sure everyone else got through the gate first, took a spear in the back just as the gates closed behind him."

Allistor placed a hand on the old man's shoulder. "It sounds like he was a true hero. A son to be proud of."

Remy wiped a tear from his cheek. "I'd rather have a live coward than a dead hero." He kicked at the wall half-heartedly. "So would his wife and kids."

"I know what you mean." Allistor commiserated. "I'd give almost anything to get back the family I lost right after the world ended. Or any of the adopted family I've lost in the last year." He paused until Remy eventually met his gaze. Pointing over the wall at the blood-spattered *Juggernaut*, he added, "I lost two of them just now. Maybe we can work together to make it so that neither of us lose any more?"

Remy shook his head, stepping back out of Allistor's reach. "You can't promise that. Being a prince doesn't make you god."

"No, it doesn't. And you're right, I can't promise nobody else will die. But I *can* greatly increase our people's chances of survival. Help them get stronger, more prepared for what comes. Provide safe places to sleep, food, training, and weapons. That's why I came here, in fact. To introduce myself, and ask all of you to join me as citizens of Invictus."

Remy stared into his eyes for a long moment before speaking. "Angel told me how you helped in the fight out here. And Maria said you weren't here to evict us like we've been expecting." He waved a hand to encompass the area inside the walls. "And your people saved a lot of mine here today."

"It was the least we could do. I'm sorry I didn't stop by sooner to speak with you. It was a gross oversight on my part. I hope that once we've gotten you back on your feet here today, we can talk?"

Remy nodded his head. "The fire's out, and cleanup has already started. We've had lots of practice since that horde showed up a few months back." He spat as if to rid himself of a bad taste. "We need to bury our dead. Outside the walls. Think you and your people could watch our backs while we say goodbye?"

"Absolutely. It would be an honor. There's another ship arriving soon with a hundred or so more of my people. We'll make sure you aren't disturbed."

"Thank you, Allistor. We'll hold the burial in the park, just across the road." Remy shook his hand again before taking his leave to go organize his people.

Allistor likewise joined his own people, thanking them for their help, and listening to their reports of leveling up from killing nearly a thousand goblins, all above level thirty. Even sharing the experience with all of the humans inside the walls, there was plenty to go around. All but the most experience Invictus raiders leveled up more than once. Allistor himself reached just past the halfway mark toward level fifty. As soon as he could, he pulled Amanda aside and told her about how he'd strained his magic somehow.

Chapter 5

Allistor and the raiders, including those from the *Opportunity* that Gralen had brought, along with the remaining orcanin, formed a perimeter a respectful distance from the funeral service in the park. After some discussion, Remy had elected to burn the bodies, as digging so many graves would have taken a great deal of time, and space. Between the casualties along the wall, and those from the fire, the settlement had lost sixty four people, including seven children.

Remy spoke first during the service, naming each of the dead and sharing some small fact or short anecdote about each of them. Allistor felt slightly ashamed, listening to this man who knew each of his people so well, when he himself barely knew the two men he'd lost in the battle. A few of the settlement's citizens took the podium to speak about lost family or friends, but the entire funeral service was completed in less than two hours. One of their casters cast flames upon the covered bodies, and a short time later everyone began to file back into the Stronghold.

Remy had used his Stronghold's interface to begin repairs on the gates and the fire-damaged building immediately after the battle, so by the time the service was over, the gates were back in serviceable condition. Once everyone, including Allistor and Harmon's people, were inside and the gates secured, Remy called them together on the grassy area between the two buildings. There were nearly one thousand of Remy's people there, with another hundred or so still keeping watch on the walls.

"It has been a rough day for us." Remy called out, the crowd instantly going silent. "Roughest we've had maybe, since those first days." There were murmurs of agreement, along with sobs and ragged tears from a few. A mother who'd lost two children in the fire had to be supported when she nearly collapsed from grief.

"I want to thank Prince Allistor, and all of his people, for coming to our aid, fighting alongside us when we were very nearly beaten. And for their generous aid in healing our wounded. Without them, we'd have lost many who are standing here with us now." He paused for some applause and quiet cheering from the crowd.

"Allistor came here today to speak with us about joining him and his people. You all saw the messages when he claimed this part of the city. And the ones that came before. It's clear from the ships he brought, the high-level fighters who fought alongside us, and the… orcanin allies that terrified the goblins, that Allistor has accomplished much in the last year. But before I give him the chance to speak here today, I ask all of you whether you even want to hear what he has to say. If you're willing to listen, raise your hand."

Remy raised his own hand as he finished speaking, then waited patiently for about fifteen seconds as people talked amongst themselves, hands going up, then back down again. Allistor tried his best to keep his face neutral but friendly as he observed. Finally, Remy nodded his head. "It's not a big majority, but it looks like more than half of you want to hear what the man has to say. Allistor, if you would?"

Allistor nodded and smiled at Remy, stepping closer and shaking the man's hand before turning toward the crowd.

"Thank you, for your willingness to hear me out. And my sincere sympathies for your losses today. We've all felt that ache in our hearts since the apocalypse. More than any of us should have to. Our world of relative safety became a hostile environment created by aliens who decided from day one to try and kill us all. Or so many of us that it makes no difference." He paused to take a calming breath, as his own anger was turning his voice into more of a growl.

"I'm here to make you all an offer. To help make you stronger, better equipped, better trained, and above all, safer. I'm not saying I can keep you one hundred percent safe. That I can not promise, and I won't lie to you about it. But I *will* promise to do all that I can to make you better prepared to live in this new world. We have more secure Strongholds here in the city, and other properties across this continent…" He spent the next five minutes giving what was becoming his standard recruitment speech. He watched as some heads nodded, others shook in denial. He saw hopeful looks, and angry faces, some of which even turned from him and walked away.

In hopes of catching those people before they were too far gone, he quickly finished up.

"I'm not asking you to decide here and now. Instead, I extend to all of you an invitation to join us for dinner at Invictus headquarters tonight. You can enjoy a good meal and a safe place to sleep for the night. Explore the property, use the teleports to check out other Strongholds. Talk to my people, and the people from other Strongholds we recently adopted, ask them whatever questions you like. Then tomorrow, you can decide what you'd like to do."

More heads were nodding now, and Allistor decided to quit while he was ahead. "Any of you who'd like to join us for the evening, there is room on the three ships to transport all of us. Don't worry about your property here. I'll assign some battle droids to guard the place. They can alert us of any trouble, and we can have a whole army here in minutes. Your homes will be safe for the night."

He let the crowd talk for half a minute or so, then raised his hands to get their attention again. "Before we get set to depart, I'm sure you have questions?"

About a hundred hands went up, and Allistor looked to Remy for assistance. Remy pointed to someone near the front. "Gerald?"

The man spoke loud enough for all to hear. "You have this title of 'Prince'… if we join you, does that make us all your subjects? Do we give up our rights?" About half the hands went down when he asked this question.

Allistor nodded, then shook his head, causing a few in the crowd to chuckle. "Yes, I have earned the title of Prince, and in fact I'm also Emperor of the planet we now call Orion. And I suppose technically if you join us and take the oath, the system will consider you my subjects. However, I consider all my people to be citizens. With essentially the same basic rights we all shared more than a year ago. A few things will be different. You can't vote to elect a replacement prince..." He paused for a moment, looking thoughtful before adding, "If you don't like how we're living, I suppose you just kill me and take my place." He smiled as he said it, giving a little shrug. "Way faster than all the campaigning and vote counting hassles."

Directly behind him, Harmon loudly cleared his throat, then quietly mumbled the word, "Oaths." It took Allistor a moment to realize what his friend was saying, and when he did, he rolled his eyes.

"Uh, actually, Harmon just reminded me of something." He paused again, realizing he hadn't introduced the orcanin yet. "Everybody, this is Harmon. Merchant extraordinaire, and leader of the orcanin who joined the fight today." There was applause, some head-bobs, and a few waves. "Anyway, Harmon just reminded me that if you decide to kill me and take over, you probably need to formally challenge me according to the rules of the System. Otherwise, if you were to try and poison me or something, the System would punish you for oath-breaking." He lowered his head and shuffled his feet a bit, his cheeks turning slightly pink with embarrassment.

"Sorry guys, I'm new to this whole Prince thing, and I'm just learning as I go, the same as all of you. I didn't ask to be a leader. It just sort of happened. But I accepted the job, and I'm doing the best I can. For all of my people, and hopefully for all of you."

He took a deep breath, looking toward Gerald. "And I just got sidetracked before I really answered your question. The rules will be basically the same. Don't kill people. Don't steal. Everyone contributes to the community in whatever way they can. Everyone works to get stronger, develop a skill or two, or three. I'm not a tyrant. I won't be looking to steal your daughters for a harem." He motioned for Amanda to step close, and he put his arm around her. "This is Amanda, my future queen. You're all invited to the wedding celebration in a few months, by the way." This time there were some smiles, and the cheering was a little more enthusiastic.

Hating to break the mood, but needing to be clear, he added more solemn thoughts. "I have been forced to kill other humans in the last year. Some attacked me or my people. Others were murderers, slavers, rapists, and the like. People who thought the end of the world meant the end of the rules, the end of common decency. I don't want to have to do that ever again. But I will, if I have to. Without hesitation." He looked at Gerald again. "Does that answer your question?"

The man nodded, again speaking loudly enough for all to hear. "It does. And thank you for your honesty."

Remy chose a woman next. "Leandra?"

A tall woman with dreadlocks stepped forward. "Will we get paid for our work?"

Allistor smiled as the people behind her made noises of agreement. "Well, some of you will. Those who work on behalf of the community will be paid to do so. The ones who take support jobs like teaching, building, cleaning, cooking, etc. will receive salaries. Those who take up crafting, for example, will initially be provided materials for free. You'll have the opportunity to sell your finished product to me for a fair price, sell to fellow citizens at a fair price, or sell them on the open market using the kiosks. In which case you can gouge your customers for as much as you can get away with!" Leandra smiled at this, and a few behind her nodded their heads. "Also, any loot you get from raids is yours to keep, or sell, as you like. We only ask that any spell or skill scrolls be turned over to our Sage, so that he can copy them to be shared with others. A copy will be returned to you so that you don't miss out. And we have the entire southern half of Manhattan to clear of monsters over the coming months. So you'll have plenty of opportunity to fight and grow stronger."

He turned and indicated Harmon. "Harmon's troops looted all the goblins on the field today. They'll be depositing all of that loot here, or somewhere back at my place, for you all to divide up amongst yourselves. In addition, if you decide to become citizens and swear the oath, you'll each be provided with a few spell scrolls. A light spell so you're never lost in the dark. A healing spell, for obvious reasons, and at least one combat spell to help you defend yourselves. Those who choose to fight, and have the ability to learn more complex spells, will be given some of those, as well."

The question and answer session went on for nearly another hour. Allistor paused to ask Prime to relay a message to the kitchen at the tower, warning them of another thousand mouths to feed. He also confirmed that Prime had a hundred troops on the march toward their location to act as guards. They would arrive in twenty minutes. Then Allistor stood there and answered the questions from the crowd honestly and frankly, until no more hands were raised. Finally he looked to Remy. "How about you, sir?"

Remy, who had been staring off into space thinking about his son, blinked a few times and focused on Allistor, who could see tears forming in his eyes. "Son, I decided to join you five minutes after I first shook your hand. You jumped into a shitstorm to save total strangers. That says something. The patience and understanding you've shown my people just now only reinforced that decision." He patted Allistor on the back, then turned to the crowd. "I'm going to join Allistor at his place for a free meal! Anyone who wants to come along, you've got fifteen minutes to change your clothes, grab your toothbrushes, whatever you need for an overnight stay. Then meet at the gates, and we'll get loaded up and go."

In the end, about nine hundred of Remy's people decided to make the trip. Some stayed because they were afraid to leave their home unguarded. Others didn't trust Allistor or his offer. Whatever their reasons, neither Allistor nor Remy pressed them on the issue. Allistor simply made it clear they could change their minds after getting reports from their friends in the morning.

It only took a few minutes to load everyone into the ships and fly them back to the parking garage. Allistor and his people chatted with the newcomers as they walked the four blocks to the tower. He stopped in the street just outside the lobby and held up his hands again. When the crowd didn't immediately quiet, Remy gave a loud whistle that silenced them.

"Welcome to Invictus! Please feel free to look around and talk to anyone you like. All I ask is that you remain on the ground level for now. We'll be serving dinner soon, and making arrangements for all of you to have a comfortable place to sleep tonight. Between dinner and bedtime, you're welcome to travel through the teleport system to wherever you like. Or we'll give you some more time for that in the morning, after breakfast. By lunch tomorrow, I'll expect you all to decide whether you want to join us, or not."

He stepped back and pulled open one of the lobby doors, and a few of his people did the same with the others as the newcomers streamed into the lobby and began to spread out. When they were all inside, Allistor went to sit in his usual spot in the lobby. Amanda moved to sit in his lap, planting a kiss on his cheek as she leaned her head on his shoulder. "I already notified Nigel to assign sleeping quarters for everyone. There's enough room here in the tower, still. Some of our people from other Strongholds will arrive shortly with more pillows and blankets. And a couple of companies of droids are scouring nearby buildings for more beds and chairs. We should have enough for everyone by the time they retire to their rooms."

"Thank you, my queen." He squeezed her briefly, kissing her forehead.

"Yeah, about that. I don't think queen is correct. Depending on what you decide to call yourself, I should be either a princess, or an empress. I vote for empress." She smiled up at him, not moving her head from his shoulder.

He poked her gently in the belly, causing her to tense slightly, fearful of a tickle attack. "I think it all depends on where we are in any given moment, proper title-wise. The advisors tried to explain it to me, but my brain sort of fuzzed out. How bout I just introduce you to everyone as 'my main squeeze'?"

She frowned at him. "Is it too late to trade you in for a new model?"

"Yep! Much too late. I'm crazy about you, now. You wouldn't want to break your prince's heart by rejecting him, would you?"

Amanda sighed, feigning resignation. "No, I suppose not. And you are sort of handy to have around. Like when I need heavy things lifted." Her eyes widened as she remembered about Allistor's issue after trying to *Levitate* the k-rail. She immediately sat upright, activated her *Internal Analysis* and stared at him with glowing eyes. "Try casting a heal. Tell me if it still hurts."

He did as he was told, casting *Restore* on a random person walking across the lobby, causing them to spin around, looking for the source of the spell. He suppressed a grin as he ignored the pain and acted casual, turning back to Amanda. "It still burns a bit. Not as bad as before."

Amanda stared a bit longer. "I... can't see any difference. Or, if I'm seeing one it isn't registering. Try to levitate something, and hold the spell so I have more time to scan you."

With a sigh, Allistor embraced the coming pain and cast *Levitate* on a nearby empty chair. His blood burned slightly as he held the chair a foot off the ground and moved it back and forth. "The pain is less than when I was on the wall, but definitely still there."

Just then Allistor spotted Rhonda moving in his direction. He dropped the chair as his concentration was shattered by the realization that Chuck, who had died in the *Juggernaut*, was one of her people. And he hadn't sought her out to let her know.

Amanda, having felt him tense up and seen him lose the spell as the chair crashed to the floor, turned to follow his gaze. "Ah, shit." She mumbled before getting up.

Allistor got to his feet as well, unsure whether to move forward or just wait for Rhonda to join them. He raised an awkward hand in greeting, deciding to wait for the woman. "Hey, Rhonda. I'm so sorry. We lost Chuck in the battle. He was in one of the Juggernauts, and..." His voice trailed off as Rhonda pulled him into a brief hug, then stepped back slightly.

"I know. Kira called in and let us know right after the battle. Chuck was a good man."

"He was. If it's okay with you, we'll hold a service for both Chuck and Frank after dinner? I'm afraid we don't have bodies to bury."

Rhonda lowered her eyes. "Bjurstrom just told me. It sounds like they went quickly, at least. That's something. After dinner is fine. We could maybe just do it in the dining hall where there's room for everyone."

Allistor just nodded as Amanda took the opportunity to give Rhonda a hug and whisper something into her ear. The woman nodded, then departed. Turning back to Allistor, Amanda updated him. "So, there's something… wonky about the way the little nano-thingies are moving through you when you cast."

Allistor sat back down. "Right. So I'm suffering from a mild case of wonky. Thanks, doc." He gave her a small smile. "I'm guessing that since it hurts less now, I'm getting better? Like, maybe tomorrow I'll be fine? I've played lots of games where if you drain all of your mana or stamina, you suffer a nasty, but temporary, penalty."

She didn't look convinced. "I have no idea, babe. This is all new to me. Looks like you get to be my guinea pig again. Let's just say don't cast any spells the rest of the night, and we'll test again in the morning."

*****

The dining area was considerably more crowded during dinner. In addition to nine hundred of Remy's people, and the Invictus citizens, there were roughly four

104

hundred of Leila's and Big Frankie's people who'd all returned for the evening meal as agreed.

All the groups mixed together, asking questions, sharing information and war stories, and getting to know each other. Sam, Meg, and the kitchen staff went above and beyond. They brought out a thick stew made from fresh vegetables from Nancy's gardens, and real beef from the herds around Cheyenne. There were loaves of freshly baked bread, still warm inside, and bowls of fruit on each table. Meg had recruited the sisters to assist during the final stages of prep, and their singing increased the buffs from the meal. By the time they were done eating, everyone in the room was feeling the rush of +6 to *Stamina* and *Strength*, and +5 to health and mana regeneration for six hours.

Allistor smiled to see that William had claimed a table in one corner, and was surrounded by wide-eyed children who clapped and cheered as he waved his arms wildly, telling the tale of some adventure.

As folks finished their meals and began to focus more on conversation, or get up in preparation of doing some exploring, Allistor stood on his chair to get everyone's attention.

"For all of Remy's people, you are welcome to resume your explorations for the next few hours. We ask that you report back here by 9:00pm so that we can get you all settled for the night. If you wish to use the teleporters, just tell Nigel where you want to go. He'll remind you

105

when it's time to head back." He took a deep breath, then continued.

"Our visitors from Big Frankie's and Leila's groups, I'd like you to remain here so we can discuss your decisions. Also, it is my sad duty to announce that we lost two of our own in today's battle. We'll be holding a memorial for Chuck and Frank here in just a few minutes for any of you who want to pay your respects."

With that, he stepped down to wait for everyone to arrange themselves according to their own plans. To his surprise, nobody left the room. After a couple of minutes, he took the hint and moved to the front of the room. There was a lump in his throat that he had to try twice to clear before he could speak.

"Thank you all for being here. It warms my heart to see all of you remain to say goodbye to men that many of you never even met."

Remy stood up and spoke quietly but clearly. "They gave their lives defending us, even though as you say, they'd never met us. Of course we want to pay our respects to them and their loved ones. We only wish we could have thanked them in person." Across the room his people murmured their agreement. Following his lead, they all stood and bowed their heads. The rest of the crowd quickly followed suit.

"Thank you, all of you. I'm proud to be among you this evening as we pay tribute to Frank and Chuck, who volunteered without hesitation to charge into battle this afternoon. They sold their lives dearly, taking out dozens of the enemy before being overwhelmed. They will be remembered as heroes."

The crowd applauded as Allistor motioned for Rhonda to come forward and say a few words. She was followed by Bjurstrom, who spoke about Frank, offering up a funny story about the man. A few others spoke about each of them, and the ceremony came to an end, everyone taking their seats.

Allistor was about to step forward again when Big Frankie and Leila beat him to it. They exchanged a look, and Leila cleared her throat.

"First, I'd like to say thank you, Allistor. For being open and honest with us, even when we were a bit hostile toward you. For allowing us to explore, to ask questions, and to choose for ourselves." She looked up at Big Frankie, who took over.

"We're pleased to say that all of our people, Leila's and my own, have chosen to become citizens of Invictus. What you've accomplished in the last year is nothing short of amazing. We want to be a part of what you're building here. So we're ready to swear the oath."

The citizens in the room cheered and applauded the news, shaking hands and patting the backs of the newcomers near them. Allistor joined the two leaders, giving each of them a quick hug. Turning to the crowd, he shouted, "Welcome! If you'll please stand and approach, Helen will get the oath out of the way."

Five minutes later there were roughly four hundred new citizens of Invictus. Nearly all of Remy's people had remained to witness the oath, and several seemed surprised by the simplicity of it. They had been expecting a more detailed, uncomfortably binding oath to be required.

Sam and Logan emerged from a side door, each carrying two steel kegs on their shoulders. They plopped them down and tapped them, filling cups and passing them out as quickly as possible. Less physically developed kitchen staff rolled several more kegs out behind them, or carried tall stacks of red plastic party cups.

Allistor watched as some of Remy's people joined the wake, while others filtered out of the dining area to go exploring. A few hesitantly asked if they could just retire, and were quickly directed to the elevators where Nigel took over and guided them to rooms.

Harmon caught Allistor's eye from the back of the room, then exited to the lobby. Allistor and Amanda followed the orcanin to their usual spot, where they all took seats. Allistor quickly said, "I'm sorry about the warriors you lost today."

"Don't be sorry, Allistor. They died well, doing what orcanin love more than almost anything, slaughtering goblins!" Harmon grinned at him, showing more of his sharp lower tusks than usual. "Which is why I am here. We are holding our own celebration next door. While I know you don't wish to partake in goblin meat, I thought you might want to make an appearance."

"Of course!" Allistor was immediately on his feet. "Should I bring something?"

Harmon chuckled. "That is not necessary. I have supplied large quantities of spirits for my warriors, much as you have here. And there is no shortage of food after the battle. As leader of the battle, you need only speak a few words, and raise a glass."

"I can absolutely do that." Allistor took Amanda's hand, the two of them following Harmon out of the lobby's back doors, across the courtyard, and into his building. They stepped into a nearby elevator, which took them up to the tenth floor, where they could hear the celebration long before the doors opened.

Harmon led them from the lift into a large open space where a hundred or so orcanin were partying alongside all of the aliens of various races that Allistor had seen working in the store below. Allistor and Amanda followed Harmon to a long table at the far end of the room, where he motioned for them to sit. Large crystal mugs were placed in front of them, then quickly filled with a clear liquid. Harmon thumped the table a few times, then roared so loudly that the spirits in Allistor's mug trembled.

Instantly, the room went silent. All eyes turned toward Harmon, who stood and raised his drink. "A good fight! And a good death!" he shouted. His words were echoed back at him a hundredfold, and Allistor thought he felt the building itself shake slightly.

After draining and refilling his mug, Harmon motioned for Allistor to rise. Once again the room grew silent, and Allistor felt a bead of sweat run down his spine as all eyes focused on him. Doing his best to look composed and princely, he raised his own mug.

With the most commanding voice he could muster, he shouted, "To the warriors! Both the fallen, and the victorious! May the hearts of your enemies give you strength!" He lowered the drink to his lips and tilted his head back. The answering roar made him choke slightly, sputtering the clear liquid on his face and down his front. Which only made the warriors roar again in appreciation. Allistor took another gulp, the spirits burning through him much like the pain he'd felt when casting magic earlier.

He felt a little better when he noticed Amanda's eyes bugged out and her forehead sweating after taking a significant gulp of her own drink. Harmon shouted something the human's didn't understand, but it was clear they should drink again, so they did. The trend continued until both of them had emptied their mugs, and neither of them could stand. Amanda barely managed to cast *Restore* on each of them, clearing their minds enough to bid Harmon a good evening and wobble their way through the enthusiastic throng to the elevator. Before the lift reached the ground floor, she hit them both with another *Restore*, then a third. "I don't know what that stuff was, but I think we should keep it away from Bjurstrom and Goodrich." She mumbled as they exited the building and walked unsteadily back across the courtyard.

"Agreed. No more murdershicken shen...shenanigansh!" Allistor's voice was still a little thick, his speech slurred as Nigel obligingly opened the lobby doors for them.

As they boarded their own elevator for the ride to their penthouse suite, Allistor grinned mischievously. A moment later, just as the doors were closing, Amanda screamed in response to a stealth tickle attack. She quickly turned to fight off the lout who'd launched such a dastardly attack, causing both of them to lose their balance and tumble to the floor. Where they remained, laughing and pointing accusatory fingers at each other, until the car came to a halt.

When the doors opened, neither tried to regain their feet. They simply crawled into their sitting room before collapsing onto a soft carpet, both of them rolling onto their backs.

"That was fun!" Allistor observed, staring up at the ceiling, which was slowly spinning.

"Yeah, it was." Amanda answered, her voice sounding sleepy. "Let's not do it again."

A minute later, Nigel dimmed the lights as the prince and princess of Invictus began to snore. A curious Fuzzy, who had retired to his corner after failing to mooch treats from the teenage sisters, sniffed at his humans. The sharp smell of orcanin spirits assaulted his sensitive nose, and he snorted several times to clear it. Plopping down on the floor between them, he rested his enormous snout on Allistor's chest and closed his eyes.

Down in the lobby, Chuck and Frank's names appeared on the wall below the names of the other lost citizens.

Chapter 6

Morning found Allistor, Amanda, and Fuzzy still snoring on the floor as the sun broached the horizon, blasting cruel sunlight through the floor-to-ceiling windows of their sitting room. Amanda simply grunted, rolling onto her side to face away from the light. Allistor, with the weight of his massive bear cub's head on his chest, didn't have that option.

He covered his eyes with one arm, successfully blocking the sun. With a sigh of relief, he attempted to drift back into dreamland. But the uncharacteristically loud sound of teenage laughter and voices pounded through his ears to his defenseless brain.

"Why are they on the floor?" Addy pondered aloud.

"I think they're drunk!" Sydney's declaration was much louder, and Allistor could hear the smirk on her face. "You know, like uncle Rick used to be. We should wake them up!"

"No… you should not." Amanda's strained voice replied. "You should tiptoe away and not make any more noise. At all." Allistor removed his arm from across his eyes and opened one of them to gaze in the general direction of Amanda's voice. The evil sunlight pierced straight through the exposed eyeball into his soul, where it went to work with an ice pick.

"Gah! Bright light!" he complained, closing both eyes tightly. "Nigel, please close the blinds."

"Of course, Allistor. The blinds are closing. Also, you should know that I've requested breakfast for you and the others, which will arrive in approximately five minutes. It might be prudent for yourself and Lady Amanda to arise from the floor and make yourselves presentable before then."

"Nigel, don't make me cut you." Amanda's voice was now muffled as she'd used both arms to try and cover her face and ears.

Allistor snorted, taking a moment to cast Restore on himself. When the magic healing made him feel slightly more like himself, he did the same for Amanda. He heard her sigh in relief as the magic took hold. He also noted that the pain of casting was greatly diminished, though still present. Pushing Fuzzy's oversized head off his chest, he said "Yep. Time to get up. Stuff to do today." before rolling to one side and using a sofa arm to pull himself up.

"I might not be able to actually cut Nigel, since he's an invisible voice from space or some shit, but you *know* I will cut *you*."

The girls giggled as Allistor opened his eyes, which began to blink rapidly of their own accord and tear up as he tried to focus. At least the blinds had muted the ungodly brightness from outside.

Fuzzy, who was now wide awake after his chin hit the floor, gave Allistor a dirty look. He rolled onto his back, swatting Allistor's leg and demanding belly rubs. The girls quickly dropped to sit on the floor on either side of the bear to oblige. Fuzzy rumbled his pleasure deep in his chest.

"Easy for you to say, buddy. You didn't drink that orcanin death-juice last night." Allistor rubbed his face with both hands, still trying to focus. He noted the time on his interface clock. "More than ten hours since we left that party, and I still feel drunk."

Fuzzy just snorted, completely ignoring Allistor.

"Amanda, sweetheart. Love of my life. My future empress. Time to get up. Can't have the folks downstairs gossiping about finding you passed out on the floor."

Amanda grunted as she rolled over, mumbling something distinctly unladylike that made both girls gasp, then giggle. Fuzzy actually opened one eye and looked at her with a hint of respect. Taking a seat on the sofa next to Allistor, she ran her fingers through her hair and used one sleeve to wipe away the dried drool that was crusted to her left cheek. Then she leaned her head back and closed her eyes again. "There better be coffee with breakfast."

Allistor agreed wholeheartedly, though he didn't bother to speak the words. Instead he just watched his bear soak up the belly scratchings the girls were providing. A minute or two later, the elevator ding made both adults wince. The doors opened and Meg appeared, pushing a cart. Instantly recognizing the condition of the royal couple, she grinned.

"Up and at 'em!" She called loudly. "It's a beautiful day! The sun is shining, the birds are singing…"

"Meg, I love you. I truly do. But if you speak again, I have to kill you." Amanda opened one eye and rotated it toward Meg without moving her head. The older woman just snorted, giving the cart full of platters, silverware, and cups an extra rattle as she wheeled it over.

"Here, drink some coffee. It'll help. And I have eggs, and sausage, and toast." She quickly dished up plates for all four of the humans as she spoke. Then she reached underneath and pulled out a large bowl of cooked meat and fish, which she set on the floor for Fuzzy. "Come on, eat up. The food will do you good."

Allistor and Amanda both leaned forward and addressed the plates on the coffee table in front of them. They lifted forks and mechanically shoveled a few bites of food into their mouths as Meg watched, shaking her head.

"Tsk tsk!" Meg called out. "You can't even see what you're eating." She moved toward the blinds, and Amanda dropped her fork.

"Meg, don't you dare – aaaack!" she covered her face with both hands, mimicking every movie vampire that had ever been surprised with sunlight.

Meg chortled, patting Amanda on the head as she moved back toward the elevator. "I'll leave you to it. Girls, I could use your help down in the kitchen. Sam's group and a couple others are going out to clear buildings this morning, and could use the extended food buffs."

The girls hopped to their feet, leaving behind a disappointed Fuzzy as they followed Meg into the elevator.

Addy called out, much more loudly than necessary, "Have a great day!" as the doors closed.

Amanda slowly uncovered her eyes, blinking rapidly against the sunlight as she muttered, "I'm gonna put that girl over my knee, later."

Allistor was content to eat in silence, pushing the delicious food into his maw and barely chewing it before swallowing. The less motion his head was involved in, the better. After a few minutes, the food in his belly and the caffeine flowing through his system from the coffee actually did make him feel better. And his eyes had adjusted to the sunlight.

Speaking quietly, he extended a hand toward Amanda, his pinky finger sticking out. "Pact? We never let each other drink that stuff again?"

Amanda extended her own hand, latching onto his finger with hers. "Pinky swear." Despite her pounding head, Allistor saw a faint smile on her lips. "But maybe we should serve that at our wedding reception? Might be fun to see L'olwyn and the other elves get all funky."

The mention of the wedding reminded him he still needed to speak to her about the scheduling.

"Hey, about that. How do you feel about delaying the wedding a bit? Say, three months-ish?"

Amanda set down her coffee cup and turned toward him. Her face was completely devoid of expression. Allistor couldn't tell if it was from the hangover, or because he'd just stepped in a steaming pile of relationship poo.

"For what reason?" Her voice was just as neutral as her face.

Allistor took a deep breath. He was knee-deep in it now, and he might as well go all in. "I was talking with Selby and L'olwyn yesterday before all the excitement. The Or'Dralon elves reached out, and were wondering why they didn't get an invite. That got us into a conversation about what factions should be invited, how many people would be involved, and the formalities of a state function. There are a lot of things we need to learn, etiquette-wise, to be sure we don't offend anyone and, you know, start a war."

He watched her face turn thoughtful as he spoke. It didn't take long for her to give a brief nod, which then caused her to grimace slightly. "That makes sense. And more time to prepare is probably a good thing. I'll let the ladies know, so everyone's not so frantic, trying to get ready."

Allistor let out a breath he didn't know he'd been holding. Scooching closer to her on the sofa, he took both her hands in his. "I'm glad you're not upset. This whole nobility business is crazy. There's so much involved in every little thing. And so much we don't even know yet." He paused, his mouth beginning to dry out as he psyched himself up for the next bit.

"I also learned something from Harmon that I need to share with you. But I don't want you to get mad at me."

He gave her his best puppy dog eyes, squeezing her hands gently.

"Uh oh. This must be serious. Okay, hit me." She looked suspicious.

"Well, Harmon says that some of the other factions are likely going to try to ally themselves with me, with Invictus, through… arranged marriages." Allistor froze, watching as the meaning of his words sunk in, and Amanda's eyes widened, then narrowed.

"Then maybe we shouldn't wait three months to get married. Once you're spoken for, it won't be an issue." Her voice was sharp, her words clipped.

Allistor sucked air through his teeth, not wanting to contradict her, but having no choice.

"That's exactly what I said." He gave her a weak smile, then began to jabber, the words just fumbling out of his mouth. "But Harmon says that marrying you will only hold them off for maybe a year. That nobility within the Collective often have multiple wives, and that it's almost unheard of for a prince or an emperor to have only one. Arranged marriages are accepted political maneuvers, and rejection of offered brides can have dangerous consequences." He watched her face as the words piled out, wanting to stop himself but unable to. When he was done, he had to resist the urge to retreat and let her mull things over.

"So… you're telling me you want to build yourself a harem?" Her eyes flashed dangerously.

"No! Not at all. What I want is to marry you, only you, and live happily ever after. And I'm hoping between you and I, with the help of our advisors, we can find a way to avoid more wives without causing issues. But the problem is looming out there, and I didn't want to keep it from you." He exhaled, having said all of that in one breath, then took in a lungful of air. "I love you, Amanda."

He sat there, holding her hands and waiting for her reaction. He could see her thinking, and wished he had something like her *Internal Analysis* spell so he could tell what was going on in there. He caught movement out of the corner of his eye, and saw Fuzzy sitting nearby, his head tilted in a curious manner, as if he too were awaiting the response. Not for the first time, Allistor wondered just how intelligent Fuzzy had become. Amanda withdrew her hands, and leaned back against the sofa. "This has been bothering you, hasn't it?"

Allistor nodded. "Worrying about how to get out of it, *and* how to tell you about it."

She nodded, still looking thoughtful. "It's not like you created the problem. As you said, we're just learning a lot of what's involved in the political arena we've been sucked into." She paused and caught his gaze with her own. "Don't get me wrong. I really want to be mad at you about this!" Her eyes flashed for a moment before her face softened. "But I can't find a good reason to blame you. And it's sort of sweet of you to have worried so much."

"So... you're not mad at me?"

"Oh, I am *so* mad at you! I just don't have a good, rational reason. But I love you, and I'll figure out how to get over it." She flashed a wicked smile at him. "I can't say the same for Meg and the other ladies when I tell them. My guess is they won't be so understanding."

Allistor groaned. "Oh, come ON!" He was opening his mouth to try and negotiate secrecy when Fuzzy chuffed, his own form of laughter, from the other side of the coffee table. Turning toward his bear, he grumped. "This is funny to you, fuzzball?"

Fuzzy nodded his head, his tongue lolling out one side of his massive jaws. Despite himself, Allistor smiled at the bear cub, and Amanda outright laughed. The tension of the past several moments gone, Allistor looked back to Amanda. "Thank you, for understanding." He took her hands again and pulled her toward him for a hug. She squeezed him tightly, then gave him a slow, soft kiss.

As she pulled away, she said "That was just a reminder, in case you're tempted by pretty young elf girls or… gnomes, or something."

"I dunno, Harmon tells me that orcanin females are pretty sexy…"

She slapped him lightly, a hint of smile in her eyes. "I might let you have one, just to see if she rips you in half!"

*****

By the time Allistor made it downstairs, most of the people within the tower had finished breakfast and moved on with their day. His citizens had disbursed to begin their crafting, or teaching, whatever their daily routines involved. A few of Remy's people were hanging around, talking amongst themselves or asking questions of citizens.

"Nigel, have the visitors been checking out the other properties?"

"Indeed, Sire. Eight hundred and sixty two of the most recent visitors have made use of the teleport system. Seventy three of them have visited the planet Orion so far."

"Heh. Way to anticipate my next question, Nigel. I take it we were able to provide proper shelter for everyone last night?"

"We were, Sire. Many of the visitors have commented that they had not slept so well in quite some time. They were also quite pleased with this morning's meal."

"Thank you Nigel. Please remind them all at about 11:30 that they must return here by noon to meet with me."

"Of course, sire."

"Anything else I should know about?"

"The battle droids assigned to mister Remington's Stronghold reported some light scouting activity during the night. Goblin scouts observing from a distance. No significant forces detected."

"So the horde wasn't wiped out yesterday. Which means we'll have to track down their nest and finish them off."

"General Prime made a similar assumption, and has assigned a few scouts of his own to follow the goblin scouts. No significant results have been reported as yet."

Allistor was impressed by the initiative taken by his lead battle droid. "Thank you, Nigel. Please ask Prime to join me in the lobby. Also, is Ramon here in the city?"

"General Prime is already on his way to this location. He will arrive momentarily. Baron Ramon is at his Citadel on the island. Shall I summon him for you?"

"No, thank you Nigel. Please just connect me so I can speak to him."

There was a slight pause, then Ramon's voice seemed to echo up from the floor. "Morning, boss. How's the head? I hear you overindulged a bit last night?"

"Oh, man. If Harmon or any of the orcanin offer you that clear stuff that smells like licorice, don't drink it. I might still be a little drunk right now." Allistor grinned at nothing in particular. "Listen, clearly you're up on the latest gossip, but I wanted to be sure you're aware that we picked up about four hundred new citizens yesterday, and may bring in as many as a thousand more today and tomorrow. Not to mention the thirty thousand or so beastkin that will be joining us soon. I wanted to talk to you about beefing up your capabilities when it comes to scrolls and such."

Ramon coughed once before answering. "I'm glad to hear you weren't expecting me to just pull thousands of scrolls out of my ass. And yes, let's talk about increasing our capabilities. Want me to come over there? Or would you like to stop by my workshop here?"

Seeing Prime crossing the lobby toward him, Allistor replied, "Prime and I will come there. Anything you'd like me to bring with me?"

"Scroll parchment. We're working on a way to craft our own from wood pulp, but for now we still need to buy it. Luckily it's cheap and available in large quantities. Load me up with a few thousand sheets?"

"You got it, man. I'll be there in a few. Just need to poke around and take care of a couple things here, first. Oh! And it seems we didn't kill all the goblins yesterday. So if you and Nancy want in on hunting the rest, we'll need to handle that very soon."

"You know it. Always up for some sweet xp. See you in a few."

Prime stopped in front of Allistor and saluted with a fist to his chest. "Good morning, Sire."

"Good morning, Prime. I wanted to commend you on your decision to send droids to follow the goblin scouts. Thank you for taking the initiative."

"You are most welcome, sire. I endeavor to anticipate and provide for your needs."

"And you're doing a fine job. I wanted to ask, when you upgrade your troops, I know there is a tank variant with heavier armor, and a flight-capable variant. Is there a scout or stealth configuration?"

"There is, yes. Currently I have thirty battle droids modified for scouting. Their armor now features a light-bending tech that renders them nearly invisible to biological entities. It also masks their already reduced internal heat signature to avoid heat-sensing abilities both biological and technological."

"That's awesome! I don't suppose that material is available for armor my people could use?"

"I believe there is a mercenary guild that makes regular use of such armor for its fighters. However it is not as effective as the natural stealth abilities many biologicals are able to employ."

"Right. That makes sense. I'll ask Michael to look into it. Maybe he can learn to craft something similar, but better. In the meantime, how are you doing as far as troop strength? Do you have enough to cover our rapidly expanding territories?"

"I have sufficient forces for your current holdings. However, if you continue your current rate of expansion, I will need to increase our capabilities, or reduce deployment levels to free up units for new duties."

"Then let's get you some more troops. I don't have plans right this minute to expand further, but stuff happens.

And I want to be prepared. How about another five thousand battle droids?"

"That would allow for significant additional expansion, sire."

"Nigel, I'm authorizing Prime to order an additional five thousand troops, modified as he sees fit. And an appropriate number of charging stations. Please let Chris know, as well?"

"*Certainly, sire.*" Nigel replied. "*Also, Master Longbeard wishes to speak with you.*"

Have him join me here, please. In fact, ask all four of the analysts to join me. I want to discuss a few things."

There was a delay of approximately fifteen seconds before Nigel reported. "*Your analysts have been notified of your desire to meet, and will arrive in two to three minutes.*"

"Thanks Nigel. Prime, I'm heading to Ramon's Citadel for the next hour or so, if you need me." The general saluted again and departed, heading toward the teleporter. While he waited for the advisors, he spotted William headed his way, staff in hand.

"Allistor! I got six levels during that fight yesterday! I'm almost level nineteen!" the boy was practically jumping up and down with excitement.

"That's great, William! Did you do as I instructed and put points into *Intelligence* and *Will Power*?"

The young squire nodded his head. "Some of them. I got twelve points, so I put four each into those, then I put two into *Constitution*, one into *Stamina*, and one into *Adaptability*."

Allistor put a hand on the boy's shoulder. "That was good thinking, buddy. Never hurts to have a little extra health and energy. And I'm pretty sure *Adaptability* is what kept me alive in those early days. I'm proud of you."

William beamed up at him, then a look of consternation crossed his face. "I want to pick Knight as my class, but the system won't let me."

Allistor crouched down so that he was face to face with the boy. "That might be because of your age. Or the fact that you've just become a squire. I'm not really sure. But we'll check into it. There's no rush. You just keep training, learning, and getting stronger."

"But your announcement said everybody who could pick a class needed to hurry up!" William's eyes looked worried.

"That was just so I know what kind of trainers to hire, buddy. And I already know what you want, even if you can't pick your class yet. So I've got you covered, okay? Don't worry."

Looking relieved, William just nodded his head. Allistor stood and waved at the approaching advisors. "I won't be doing any crafting today, so you've got the day to yourself. Though if you want to come with me to visit

Ramon, Nancy, and Chloe, you can tag along. Maybe do some fishing, or play with Max?"

"Yesss!" William nodded. "I bet I'm a higher level than Chloe now!"

Grinning, Allistor greeted the analysts. In addition to Master Longbeard the dwarf, there was L'olwyn, Selby, and Droban the minotaur, who he hadn't seen much of since the massive creature had accepted the analyst position. Droban's specialty was research, and he tended to stay locked away much of the time, buried deep in his various information sources.

"Thank you all for coming. If you wouldn't mind accompanying me, I'm headed to see Ramon at his Citadel. There are some things we need to discuss that I think you all should be up to date on."

Each of them nodded in respect as they fell into step with Allistor and William, all of them moving toward the kiosk, where Allistor quickly purchased ten thousand sheets of scroll parchment. After inserting the material into his ring, he led them to the teleport pad and through to the Citadel on what was formerly Governor's Island. Chloe greeted them at the pad, immediately dashing forward and throwing herself into Allistor's arms.

"Allistor! I missed you. Welcome to our castle!" She wrapped her tiny arms around his neck and squeezed, and gave him a peck on the cheek. Then, realizing there were other guests, she squirmed to be let down. As soon as she was on the ground, she gave a slight bow to the advisors. "Welcome, honored guests. Please allow me to escort you to…" She paused and whispered to William, "Where do they want to go?"

When the boy just shrugged, Allistor helped her out by whispering, "Ramon's new workshop."

"Allow me to escort you to the workshop!" The little girl smiled brightly at Allistor before taking William by the hand and leading them all toward the old fort building that Ramon had recently modified. As they walked, Allistor heard her quietly tell William, "Momma is teaching me stuff like the proper way to greet guests. You should learn it too." William looked thoughtful, then nodded. He took his duties as a squire quite seriously.

It only took a few minutes for them to reach Ramon and his new workshop. Which was basically a giant open room with bookshelves covering every wall from floor to ceiling, except where they were interrupted by doors or windows. Crafting tables and reading tables littered the open space in the middle, and at least a dozen citizens were hard at work. Some were inscribing scrolls, others mixing ingredients to create different colored inks.

"Allistor! You brought a whole posse with you. What's up?" Ramon nodded a greeting at each of the advisors, then gave William a wink and a fist-bump.

"Well, you know I wanted to talk about scrolls for the new recruits. And we have a few other things to cover. Is there someplace private we can sit and talk? Also, the new place is awesome!" he scanned the room again, smiling.

Ramon quickly led them through a side door into a dining room with a long table. Everyone except William and Chloe, who disappeared to go find Max and do kid-and-dog stuff. When everyone had taken seats, Ramon got things started. "Okay, about scrolls for the new people. We're cranking them out as fast as we can, but it'll take us months to produce more than thirty thousand of each of just the basic three healing, light, and fire scrolls. Let alone the more advanced spells."

Allistor sighed. "I figured as much. We could recruit more helpers for you, prioritize scrolls for those who are going to be fighting. New raiders, people who join the crews clearing buildings. And if we have to choose one spell to focus on, I say make it the heals."

Ramon raised a hand to stop Allistor. "We were thinking along the same lines at first. But I think we have a better alternative. You know that Nancy has mastered her growth spell, and has been able to teach it directly to others without using a scroll. If we can do those basic spells that way, with several of us having mastered those spells and being able to teach them directly, it would save a lot of time, and materials. And it would free up my people to focus on the more advanced items, which we'll need fewer of."

Allistor grinned at his friend. "And do we have people who have mastered all the spells?"

Ramon shook his head. "No one person that I'm aware of has mastered them all. It takes a lot of practice casting each one before you reach the level where you can teach. Nancy was fast-growing veggies and fruit trees for the better part of a year before she reached it. But there are a dozen or so healers that have cast the basic *Restore* spell enough to teach it. And two of the raiders I've spoken to can teach the *Light* spell, having used it in many raids. There might be more. Four of them have mastered the basic *Flame Shot* spell. I think with a little time, several more could reach mastery of those two."

Allistor quickly checked his own skill sheet, and was surprised to find that the only spells he'd mastered were *Restore* and *Barrier*. The others were advancing, but he hadn't used them often enough, apparently. "I can teach *Restore*, and *Barrier*. But I don't know if *Barrier* requires a specific class?" He looked toward the advisors.

Droban's deep voice was the first to answer. "There are indeed a few spells that are restricted to specific classes. Though they are mostly higher order spells that require certain other class skills be learned as a prerequisite. Most spells can be learned by anyone with sufficient personal level, *Intelligence* and *Will Power*. Some spells that are more physical in nature, like *Berserker Fury* or *Levitate* have additional *Strength* or *Stamina* requirements."

Allistor's pulse quickened when the minotaur mentioned *Levitate* in relation to requirements, and he made note to clarify that. "Right! Some of the scrolls we found, like *Dimensional Step*, had minimum requirements. Which is why I was the one to use it."

"Exactly so, Allistor." The minotaur nodded.

131

"Thank you, Droban. Since we're on the topic, I want to quickly ask you more about *Levitate*, specifically. I tried to use it to lift something very heavy yesterday, and I seem to have injured myself. It burned my insides until I let the spell drop, and then each time I tried to cast after that, I felt significant pain."

Selby spoke before Droban could, standing up in her chair and leaning across the table toward Allistor. "Did you pass out? How bad did it hurt? Does it still hurt now?" she rapid-fired questions at him, a concerned look on her face. The other advisors shared similar looks.

"Uhhh… on a scale of one to ten, the pain was a solid nine when it first happened. No, I didn't pass out, but I did scream like a little girl. It hurt less toward the end of the day, yesterday. And I actually only cast restore a couple times this morning. The pain was much less." He grinned at them before adding, "Amanda grounded me from casting last night."

Selby snorted, hopping from the chair up onto the table and walking across until she was face to face with Allistor. She reached out a tiny hand and pried open one of his eyes, looking deep inside. He saw her own eyes begin to glow with magic much like when Amanda cast her *Internal Analysis*. After a few seconds, the glow faded and she turned to walk back to her seat. "You'll be okay. But you got very lucky. I think you just damaged a few pathways instead of burning yourself out altogether."

Both Ramon and Allistor spoke the same word at the same time. "Pathways?"

Selby looked at them both like foolish children for a moment, then sighed. "I keep forgetting that you've not had trainers here before now. Or anyone to explain the basics of your abilities." She looked left and right at the elf, dwarf, and minotaur, but none of them volunteered.

"Okay so you know that your bodies contain a finite supply of mana, the extent of which is indicated by the blue bar, and the numeric designation in your personal interface." She waited as both men nodded. Ramon held up a hand for her to wait, then stuck his head out the door, shouting instructions. Returning to his seat, he asked, "Can you hold on for about two minutes? I want Nancy and the others in the building to hear this. Then we can pass the information on to everyone else."

Allistor took it a step further. "Actually, do you mind if we just transmit this to everyone? I'm sure we all need to know what you're about to reveal."

"I don't mind at all." The little gnomess smiled. "This isn't top secret or anything. In normal circumstances you would learn this in your first lesson from a trainer."

"Nigel, can you record and transmit a hologram of this in each location?"

"*Certainly, sire. It would take a few minutes for your people to gather in significant numbers.*"

"Please give me loudspeaker, everywhere. Can you project the images in... the courtyards of each Stronghold? Or the dining areas?"

"*Either, as you prefer. Whenever you are ready.*"

"Hey everybody, Allistor here. We're about to transmit a hologram of Advisor Selby laying down some vital information about how magic works here on Earth. I need as many of you as possible to stop what you're doing and move to either your Stronghold's dining area, or the courtyard, so that you can see and hear. We'll start in five minutes. If you're in the middle of something you can't put down, don't sweat it. You'll be able to get the info later." Allistor made a cutting motion across his neck, letting Nigel know to turn off loudspeaker, and start the timer. Nancy walked into the room and sat down next to Ramon, giving him a quick peck on the cheek.

"Okay, while we wait for everyone to gather, a few quick things. First, I spoke to Amanda, and she has agreed that we should delay the wedding for three months. I also told her about the likelihood that other factions would try to marry their daughters to me. She wasn't so agreeable on that point." He paused as Nancy snorted, giving her a dirty look that made both her and Ramon laugh.

"Anyway... I need all of you advisors to help us figure out how we decline any additional brides for me, without offending the other factions. This is important. We've got three months at least to come up with a strategy. And longer if we can convince everyone that my 'first wife' wants me to herself for a while." The advisors all nodded their heads, none of them feeling a need to speak. When Nancy chuckled softly, Allistor added, "Maybe I can pass potential brides off to my ministers and vassals, like Baron Ramon?" Nancy glared at him, sticking her tongue out as Ramon coughed in surprise.

"Next, L'olwyn we'll need some of your time to train us on proper behavior, manners, which fork to use, whether to stick a pinky out when sipping tea, whatever. Assume we're barely more than trained apes with no social graces whatsoever, and start there." He grinned at the elf.

"Of course, Allistor. I would be happy to help."

Allistor looked at Ramon and Nancy. "Now that I think about it, it wouldn't hurt for all of my ministers and advisors to attend the lessons. Since you'll be attending formal functions alongside us."

Nancy nodded her head, smiling even as Ramon rolled his eyes and asked, "Is it too late to resign?"

Nigel interrupted before Allistor could poke at his friend. *"Sire, approximately ninety two percent of your citizens have gathered in appropriate places."*

"Thank you, Nigel. Please begin the projection. First myself, then Selby. And anyone else in the room who offers up additional information."

"Go ahead, sire."

"Hello again, folks. I hope all of you can see me clearly, or at least hear my voice. A few minutes ago I asked our advisors about a situation during the battle yesterday." He paused and sighed. "For those of you who haven't heard yet, we found approximately a thousand other survivors in a stronghold here in Invictus City. They were under attack by a goblin horde. There was a fight, and about a thousand goblins died. We lost Frank and Chuck, two of our own, and the Stronghold lost about sixty of their people. During the fight, I tried to *Levitate* a K-rail, and hurt myself. Apparently I overdid it, which is dangerous. Selby is about to explain to all of us what I did, and why none of you should ever, ever do what I did. Selby, if you please."

The little gnome chuckled, then repeated her initial statement.

"All of you should know that your bodies contain a finite supply of mana, the extent of which is indicated by the blue bar, and the numeric designation in your personal interface. What we call *mana* is the energy that is the driving force behind the spells that you cast. What you humans know as magic. In truth it is an energy that permeates everything around us, affecting all matter. Within us all are tiny nano-molecules that allow us to manipulate and control that energy." Selby paused for a few breaths to let that information soak in.

"When you learn a spell, even a basic spell like *Light*, what you're learning is how to convert the mana within you to a specific energy with a specific task. The mana is channeled through certain pathways within your body and mind as its converted to external energy. Think of these pathways like your veins and arteries, which deliver oxygenized blood from your lungs through your heart to be distributed into your arms, legs, and brain." Again she paused, waiting for Allistor, Nancy, and Ramon to nod their understanding.

"Now is where things get a little complicated. No two beings are exactly alike when it comes to mana conversion. Some develop a single pathway from their source, through their body and mind, and out into the universe. Others develop a new pathway for each spell that they learn. For example, some of you might just think the word *Light* and the thought becomes reality. Others may need to focus their vision on a certain spot or object, or hold out a hand to channel the spell through. There is no single correct way to channel mana for most spells. Though there are a few that have to be channeled through an enhancement item. We don't need to cover that just now. The important information here is that we all channel our mana through pathways."

"What Prince Allistor did yesterday was terribly dangerous. He attempted to *Levitate* an object that was many times his own body mass. When casting a physical spell such as that one, more than just your spell skill level and mana supply come into play. His *Strength, Stamina, Will Power, Constitution*, and *Luck* all factor in as well. I won't go into the complicated formulas involved. For now, what you need to know is that Prince Allistor very nearly killed himself by far overreaching his ability. The resistance, both physical and magical, of the object he attempted to move caused a backlash through the pathway the mana traversed through his body and mind. Think of suddenly tripling the blood pressure in your arteries, only applying the pressure in the *opposite* direction of your normal blood flow."

Allistor felt slightly sick as Ramon mumbled "Holy shit."

Selby smiled at the man. "Indeed. Allistor's attributes, especially his *Strength*, *Constitution*, and *Luck*, negated much of the backlash that should have killed him. As it was, it damaged his pathways such that even casting other spells like healing caused great pain. Humans with lesser attributes who attempted similarly foolish castings would almost certainly end their mortal existence." She nodded at Allistor, indicating that she was through.

"Uhm. So you all heard the lady. I nearly destroyed myself by overdoing it. For you gamers out there, it's like when you completely drain your mana in a fight. Only instead of simply being useless and maybe feeling slightly sick for a while… your head might explode. So for everybody casting spells of any kind, take it easy. Build up your skill with each spell slowly, and be careful not to overdo things. And don't ever drain your mana completely." He looked at the others at the table, and none appeared to have anything more to add.

"Right! Good talk! I hope you all take this warning to heart, and use the valuable information that Selby has provided to help develop yourselves safely. I think we may do more of these little online classes in the future. Hope you all have a great day!" He made a motion for Nigel to cut the feed, and leaned back in his chair.

"Well, shit."

Chapter 7

Allistor and William spent a little more time on the island after the meeting, enjoying a bit of sunshine and romping around with Chloe and Max. They visited the chicken coops, and the gardens, Chloe proudly showing off the work they'd done since moving in.

"We even have bees! But I'm not allowed to get close to them, yet." The little girl pouted slightly.

Allistor tried to lift her spirits. "I bet when you have honey, Fuzzy will abandon me and just move over here with you!" he gave her a wink. "That bear would sell his soul for belly scratches and honey."

"I'll be sure and save him some!" Chloe beamed at him, her sorrows forgotten.

Noon approached, and Allistor said goodbye before returning to his tower. Remy's group were due to gather and let their decisions be known. Allistor was concerned that so many of them having stayed behind at their Stronghold might cause the others to feel that they needed to decline his offer and go back.

When he and William stepped off the teleport pad, he found Amanda waiting nearby. Next to her stood Remy, his face neutral. Stepping forward, he gathered Amanda into a hug, then shook Remy's hand.

"Remy, this is William, my squire and constant companion." He motioned toward the boy, who gamely stuck out a hand for Remy to shake.

"Nice to meet you, squire William." Remy smiled down at him. "What exactly does a squire *do* in this day and age?"

William grinned up at him. "Well, mostly I try my best to bonk Allistor on his noggin with a big stick!"

Remy's eye's widened for a moment, then he chuckled, thinking that the boy was kidding, or at least exaggerating. Allistor explained, "It's true. I'm leveling up my *Barrier* spell and my *Weaponsmithing* at the same time. My faithful squire stands behind me and swings a staff at my shield until it breaks. Then it's a race to see whether I can recast it before he cracks me on the head. It's a good motivator, let me tell you. And he is leveling his *Strength*, *Stamina*, and weapons skills as he does his best to brain me."

Remy chuckled, shaking his head. "Sounds very… efficient."

"I also help out as bridge crew on the *Phoenix*! The battle at your place yesterday got me six levels!" William puffed out his chest, proud of the accomplishment.

Seeing the look on Remy's face transform from amusement to sadness, Amanda quickly corralled the boy and made mumbled excuses before escorting him away. Once they were a safe distance, she quietly explained to the squire that Remy had lost his son in the battle, and that maybe it was too soon to talk about gaining experience from it. Allistor caught tears in the little guy's eyes as he looked back.

"I'm sorry about that, Remy. He's very taken with the idea of becoming a knight, and enthusiastic about anything he sees as getting him closer to that goal."

Remy waved a dismissive hand, taking a deep breath and attempting a smile. "No need to apologize. I raised children, I know what they're like at that age. I take it he's an orphan?"

Allistor nodded. "Found him and a few others at the Santa Monica airport. They were vulnerable and half-starved after an earthquake wiped out most of their group."

"And you've taken him under your wing."

"Ha! More like the other way around. I invented the squire position when I first met him, to sort of break him out of his shell. He promptly demanded a salary of one hundred dollars, and has been pretty much running things between us ever since."

"Is that why he was on your ship during the battle yesterday?"

Allistor paused, sensing that the question was more important than it sounded. Since he was hoping to recruit this man and his followers, he spoke carefully.

"Well, to be fair, we weren't expecting a battle. Our plan was to visit and talk with you. But in this new world of ours, every minute of every day presents the possibility and danger of battle. For that reason, we've done what we can to level up even our little ones, doing so as safely as possible. That ship and its shield could withstand pretty much any attack short of a nuclear strike. He was kept on the bridge with our pilot and her two girls. Had things not gone our way, she would have lifted off and brought them back here. And because he's been involved in a few fights, he's now almost level nineteen."

Remy didn't respond immediately, his gaze measuring and thoughtful.

"Two years ago, you might have been jailed for child abuse, knowingly putting children in harm's way." he mused. "But you're right, this new world of ours doesn't care about the niceties of civilized society. It'll eat our children and spit them out without hesitation or mercy. We have all had to make certain adjustments to survive the last year, and I suppose this is just one more." Remy nodded and turned toward the dining area. "I think it's about time we headed in."

The two men walked the short distance in silence. They found the dining area packed with Invictus citizens and visitors, mingled together amongst the tables and in the chow line. Allistor and Remy joined the back of the line, both men observing their people as they waited to dish up their lunches. Remy touched Allistor's shoulder, and with a smile, pointed toward a table where once again William was surrounded by children. They mostly ignored their food as they listened to a description of the formidable murder chickens, and the pending glory of the murder chicken cavalry.

Chuckling, Allistor shook his head. "I've had to practically tie him down to keep him from trying to ride one of the little ones. Had to promise that one of our cowboys would give him horseback riding lessons. And even then, I had to sell it as a preliminary skill he needed to learn before murder chicken riding."

"Murder chickens?"

"They're actual name is Kyllings. One of the menagerie creatures the aliens seeded, I think. Possibly just a mutation of earth animals. Imagine a chicken mated with a velociraptor, and its offspring grew to be seven or eight feet tall. Then give it a bad temper, and a taste for fresh meat."

"Damn. And you're raising a flock of these things?"

"We stumbled across them out in the wilderness, and killed all but the boss lady. We captured her and snagged a bunch of eggs. And yes, we did it because my inner twelve-year old thought it would be cool to have them as mounts." He grinned unabashedly. "And if we can't properly tame them, well each one provides several hundred pounds of meat when full grown."

They reached the front of the line, and Allistor spotted Sam behind the counter. "Hey, Sam. We got any murder chicken meat left?"

The older man shook his head. "With all the extra mouths to feed all of a sudden, we've burned through it all. Sorry, Allistor. We've sent hunting parties out to the

143

Wilderness Stronghold, though. Might be they'll run across some more."

"No worries. Thanks Sam. You and Meg have done a great job here." Allistor dished up a plate of what looked like chipped beef, pouring a ladle of the stuff over top of a couple biscuits. He also grabbed an apple from a large bowl of fruit, and a glass of ice cold water, before leading Remy to a table.

They ate their lunches as they chatted with the folks seated around them. Two people across the table, a young couple from Remy's group, were describing the massive towers that the beastkin were already working to renovate near the main Stronghold on Orion.

"I still can't believe it. You step on the teleport pad one second, and a blink later you're standing on a planet that's like a bazillion miles away. The light is a little different, and the air smells so fresh!" the young woman added. "If we moved there, would we still be called Earthlings? Or would we be Invictus…ians? Orionians?" Several people around the table chuckled.

Allistor replied, "I think just humans would work fine in most instances. As far as I know, we're the only ones around."

"But are there other kingdoms, or princedoms, or empires or whatever? Here on earth, I mean?" the woman persisted.

"I haven't seen any notifications of anyone else reaching Planetary Prince status here on earth." Allistor mused. "But I was off of earth for a few days when we were taking Orion. Did any of you see any notifications that I might have missed?"

Everyone at the table shook their heads. "Yours is the only one we've seen." Remy replied. "And while we're on that topic, now is as good a time as any to discuss becoming citizens of Invictus." He looked around at his people sitting close enough to hear. Each of them nodded their head yes. "I plan to join you. As do most of my people. There are a few who aren't ready yet, mostly because they have people who remained behind at the Stronghold, and don't want to commit before speaking with them."

Allistor nodded his understanding. "I'm happy to hear that, Remy. And I hope the others will come around soon. But if they don't, I hope we'll find a way to live together peacefully inside the city walls."

"About that." Remy cleared his throat. "What if some, or all, of my people want to continue to live at our Stronghold? After swearing the oath, I mean."

"I said yesterday that citizens of Invictus are free to live at whichever of my properties they like. If you want to continue to own your Stronghold as a citizen, that's fine with me. Most of my advisors have Strongholds of their own. Ramon just became a Baron when he and Nancy built their own Citadel." Allistor looked around the table. "Look guys, I'm not trying to run your day to day lives. You take the oath, you work to support each other, contribute in a useful way, and we're good. Your lives

145

don't have to substantially change, except that you'll be better prepared, and hopefully get stronger."

"What about the goblins?" A man further down the table spoke up. Several others added their voices. "We didn't kill them all. They'll be back to try again."

Allistor's lips pursed and he drummed his fingers on the table. He had some suspicions about the goblins, and he needed to speak to Harmon about them. But regardless of whether or not he was correct, they needed to be dealt with.

"We've got scouts tracking the goblins now. Hopefully we'll find their home base soon, and we can go finish them off. We killed more than a thousand of them in that last fight, so I don't imagine there are very many left. Or so I hope."

The man who'd asked the question nodded his head. "That's good enough for me. I want to go with you when you find them. I owe them."

"That's okay by me, so long as you follow orders. If I have my way, we won't be doing any face-to-face fighting. Ideally, we'll drop a bomb or two on them, wipe them out completely, loot whatever's left, and head back home. Everybody gets some good xp, and none of our people get hurt."

The man nodded his agreement, as did most of the others around the table, both Remy's and Allistor's people.

Remy stood up, raising his hands and calling for silence. "People, please… if I might speak for a moment?"

It took about half a minute for conversation to die down and all eyes in the dining area to be turned in his direction. "For those who haven't met me, my name is Remington. Leader of the Stronghold that Allistor and some of you here helped us defend yesterday. Thank you for that, from the bottom of our hearts." He gave a small clap, which was picked up by his nine hundred or so people, who also let loose a few cheers. "We were strangers when you came to our aid. Now, we've fought together, eaten together, shared some of our stories, and I'd like to think we've begun to become friends. Toward that end, I have decided to swear the oath and become a citizen of Invictus. And if there are any of my people here now who feel the same, I invite you to stand and join me." He moved to the clear space at the back of the room as one by one his people stood and followed.

When all of those who were joining had grouped together, Allistor noted his people staring at a dozen or so of Remy's people still sitting. He was considering whether to ask them if they still had questions, or a specific issue, when Remy called out to them.

"Juan, Tara, the rest of you who are still sitting… I know each of you has family that chose to remain behind. I suspect you're waiting until you can speak with them." He watched as several heads nodded. "Are any of you actually opposed to joining with Allistor? Or do you have a concern you want to address? If so, raise your hand. Now's the time to speak up."

Now most of them were shaking their heads in the negative. Just one man raised his hand, then stood. Remy pointed to him. "You don't wish to join, Juan?"

"I don't know, yet. My wife and son are back at the Stronghold, and I do need to speak with her before we decide. But I'm not even sure I want to join myself."

Remy looked to Allistor, one eyebrow raised.

Allistor asked, "Juan, have you seen or heard something that concerns you? Is there a question I can answer?"

Juan looked down at his feet for a moment, gathering his thoughts and taking a deep breath. He clasped his hands in front of him, then met Allistor's gaze. "This is all happening so fast. Everything, since the first day the monsters came. We've been running, and fighting, and reacting to all the ways the world has tried to kill us, every day for over a year. We've dealt with more pain, more losses in that time than most of us would normally experience in a lifetime. And now you're asking us to do it again. To react, to make a big, life-changing decision right after a battle that nearly wiped us all out. That claimed friends and loved ones." He held his hands up in a placating gesture toward Allistor.

"Don't get me wrong, I'm very grateful for you and your people, for all you've done. I bear you no ill will at all." He paused to lower his hands and take another deep breath. "I just... I feel like I need some more time right now, to think things over. I'm sorry."

Amanda appeared next to Allistor, taking his hand. She quietly whispered, "He lost somebody in that fight."

Allistor hadn't needed her to point that out. It was clearly written on the man's face as he spoke. He squeezed her hand in thanks.

"Juan, there's no need for you to apologize. What you say makes sense. In fact, I think I should be the one to offer an apology. You lost someone in the last battle. In fact, Remy, I'm guessing all of your folks lost friends, if not family. I should not have pressed you to decide so quickly." Remy nodded, though it really hadn't been a question.

"Alright. Those of you who *know for sure* you want to take the oath, Helen here will administer it. The rest of you, take some more time. If you have family who remained behind, go talk to them. Try to bring them here so they can see and investigate for themselves. I'll give you the rest of today and tomorrow to look around and ask questions. Beyond that point, if you still aren't ready, I'll ask that you return to your home. I'm sorry I can't give you more time than that, but recent events have made it clear that I can't have unsworn people wandering around unwatched. That mistake cost several innocent lives. And I can't spare more of my own people's time guarding those who are unwilling to join us."

Remy gave a slight bow. "That is more than fair, Allistor. As I said, I have made my decision, and will swear the oath now." He smiled at Helen, who moved to stand in front of him. Even as she crossed the room, four of the visitors who'd stood with Remy now crossed back to sit with Juan and the others, apologetic looks on their faces. Helen just smiled at them as they passed.

Allistor gave them another chance. "Really, guys, I understand. We understand. None of us has made it through this year without losing someone. And we've all felt the constant fear. If you need the extra day or so to think, then take it." He watched the people still standing behind Remy for half a minute, but no more of them left the group.

Smiling, he said, "Helen, if you would?"

And a few minutes later there were roughly nine hundred new green dots clustered in the dining area on his interface's map.

"Welcome, new citizens of Invictus! Those of you who wish to return to your Stronghold can do so now. Kira and Gralen will fire up two of our ships, and taxi you back in... 20 minutes. They'll remain there for two hours, so that any of you who wish to come back and relocate to another property can do so. And for those of you who want to bring back the hundred or so of your family or friends who stayed behind and show them around." He waved at the crowd, and they began to disperse. With a nod toward Remy, he stepped back into the lobby and led the man back to his informal meeting spot. The two men took seats.

"I take it you wish to remain at your Stronghold?"

Remy nodded. "Maybe not long term. I like this place better, to tell you the truth." He spread his hands to indicate the tower around them. "But I think a lot of my people will want to stay. Juan was the only one to speak up, but many of them are going to need some time to adjust. And if we're going to take out the rest of the goblin horde, I don't see any harm in giving them that time."

"I agree. And since the Stronghold is inside my city, I can do this…" His gaze unfocused as he moved through the tabs on his interface. A moment later, Remy's eyes widened when he received several notifications. Allistor laughed. "As Prince, I can promote favored citizens who advise me or serve as leaders for segments of my people. Let me be the first to congratulate you, Baron Remington." He held out a hand, which Remy shook.

Remy shook his head. "Shit. If there's one thing I learned in the army, it's to never accept promotions that put you in charge of more people!" He grinned at Allistor. "But since I was already sort of serving as step-daddy to everyone at my place, I accept."

"The position allows you to take certain actions as my vassal. That includes claiming more property outside the city in my name, disciplining those who reside on your property, arranging the resources of your Stronghold as you see fit. Though I would strongly recommend you add some defensive turrets and such. I'll allocate some city resources if you don't have sufficient points of your own."

Remy shook his head. "I think I'm good. I just got some System Points and experience for becoming a noble." He chuckled. "If my mama could see me now."

Allistor let him enjoy the moment for a bit, then changed the subject. "We need to talk about what happens if some of your people choose not to join us. Not right this minute, unless you feel the need. It may be that, given another day to think, they'll all join, and we won't need to talk about it.

"Just one question." Remy held up a single finger. "Should any of them refuse to join, will they be banished? Because if that's the case, they need to know that before they decide."

Allistor sighed, leaning back in his chair. He took a long time to think it over before answering. Remy, realizing the importance of the answer, waited patiently.

"This is a new situation, sort of." Allistor began. "I've made the offer to Stronghold leaders before to let them remain in the city as allies. To trade with them, if possible. But I made it clear that I wouldn't assist them beyond that, and the tacit protection they receive from being inside the city walls." He tapped his fingers on the arm of the chair. "But that offer was made for the entire group. Everyone inside the Stronghold, from the leader on down, as a single unit. I'm not sure how to deal with a situation where there are a few holdouts within a group."

"Might I offer a suggestion?" Remy leaned forward and put his elbows on his knees. His face hardened. When Allistor nodded, he continued. "As a leader who's responsible for the people under me, I don't like the idea of having people around who are unwilling to swear a simple oath not to hurt or betray their neighbors. If you were asking more of us, I might feel differently. But basically, those who refuse to swear are saying they want to keep open the option to steal from, or in some way hurt their own people. My people. As cold as it may seem, I say put them out. We live in a practical world where, as Juan pointed out, we have to fight to stay alive. There's no room anymore for sentimentality and one-sided loyalty that might endanger us. Even if we're getting stronger, and the world is getting safer, I see no reason to invite trouble."

Remy paused for a moment, forcing himself to relax. "That said, I don't wish them dead. Maybe we could arrange for them to have a safe place somewhere else? Give them some supplies and weapons, or something?"

Allistor didn't hesitate. "I would have done that, regardless. Every human life is precious, and I will do what I can to help preserve them, as long as they don't act against me or mine." He watched Remy's face as he spoke. "Let the holdouts know that if they decline to join us, we'll clear and secure a place for them to create their own Stronghold. But it'll be outside the walls here in New York, or outside any of my other properties. And Orion isn't an option. As humans, they have certain rights to claim land here on earth. That doesn't apply on other planets. I'll supply them with plasma rifles, and enough food for a week. After that, they can trade for more if they have something of value."

Remy nodded. "That'll do. Enough of a stick to encourage them to join us, but leaving them a viable option. Thank you, Allistor. I'll join my people heading home, and do my best to bring all the rest into the fold." Remy stood and offered a hand, which Allistor shook.

"Good luck, Baron Remington." He reached into his inventory and pulled out one each of the standard three scrolls. "We have a limited supply of these right now, but we're working on a solution that'll allow everyone to learn at least these three as soon as possible. How high are your *Intelligence* and *Will Power* attributes?"

When Remy told him, he smiled wide. "Then you can learn a few more. Here you go." He handed the man scrolls for *Mend*, *Vortex*, *Mind Spike*, and *Fade*. "When you come back, I'd like you to set aside some time to sit with me, and a few of the others. We've got a lot of information regarding how the world works now, and I want to bring you up to speed, so that you can do the same for your group."

"Thank you, Allistor. These are… quite a gift. I'll put them to good use."

*****

It didn't take long to get all of Remy's people back to their home. As instructed, Gralen and Kira parked their two ships in the same spot near the river and waited for those who wanted to make the return trip.

Allistor found he was nervous about the potential for holdouts, and soon found himself pacing back and forth across the lobby. He decided to try and channel that energy

154

into something useful. "Nigel, has prime finished adding and upgrading his troops?"

"*He has, Sire. Would you like to inspect them?*"

"No, thank you. Please ask him for an update from his scouts. I want to know if they've found the goblin horde's base, yet."

There was a short delay before Prime's voice replaced Nigel's. "*My scouts have continued to follow a dozen different goblins. So far the individual targets have moved about in a seemingly random pattern, hunting and gathering food, but not returning to a base of any kind. Groups of two or three have come together to share shelter and sleep in rotation, then separated again afterward.*"

"Do you think they've spotted your scouts? Are they putting on some kind of show?"

"*I do not believe so. It is not uncommon for goblin scouts to remain away from camp for long periods, filling their bellies and searching for valuable items, before returning. It may be another day or two before we can track one of them back to their horde.*"

"Alright, thank you, Prime. Please report immediately if your scouts discover anything important."

"*Of course, Sire.*"

Allistor, still feeling fidgety, was considering heading up to the roof to pound on some metal. He actually took a few steps across the lobby toward the elevators before he spotted Harmon approaching across the courtyard, holding up one massive hand to wave at him. Stopping where he was, he waited for his large friend to step inside.

"What the hell did you give us to drink last night?" Allistor scowled at the merchant. "I thought my head was just going to fall off when I woke up this morning. And I only had *one* mug of the stuff."

Harmon chuckled, patting Allistor on the shoulder. "It is called Tiq. Distilled from the juice of a cactus that grows in abundance on my homeworld, along with a few secret ingredients. Our people drink it like water, my diminutive friend. You will eventually develop a tolerance for it."

"The hell I will. Never touching that stuff again. Next time I celebrate with your warriors, I'm bringing milk, or something." Allistor grumbled, making Harmon laugh even louder.

"I came to tell you that I have spoken with Master Daigath. He has agreed to come and meet with you, and will arrive first thing in the morning. Assuming you allow him access to your portal hub."

Allistor's spine shivered for just a moment as visions of an elven army bursting through into his headquarters flashed through his mind. He shoved those thoughts aside, trusting in Harmon, who so far had not led him astray. "That's wonderful news, my friend. Thank you."

"It's the least I could do after you invited us to that battle with the goblin horde. Have you found their nest, by the way?" Harmon did his best to look uninterested. Allistor wasn't buying it.

"Ha! Your warriors want a shot at more snacks. Well, you are welcome to them as soon as we locate their… nest, did you call it? Prime's scouts are tracking them, but no luck yet."

Harmon nodded is massive olive green head. "If I were you, I would arrange for a nice box in which to present that Ancient Shellback heart to Master Daigath. He has not decided to work with you, as yet. Only to meet with you. It would be a good idea for you to impress him. He likes fresh fruit and vegetables. And brandy. That stuff you seized from the goblin ship would do nicely. I've not tasted human brandy, but if you have some handy I would happily taste test it for you."

Grinning along with the merchant, Allistor said, "I'm sure we can find some local versions. I'm not sure I've ever tasted brandy myself. I guess I'll have to learn. We can experiment together this evening."

"Good! A fine meal prepared by lady Meg, followed by brandy tasting? Excellent! I'll see you this evening." Harmon began to walk back toward his building. Before he exited the lobby, he turned and added, "Oh, and for Master Daigath, and elves in general, first thing in the morning means an hour or so before sunrise."

Allistor rolled his eyes as the orcanin exited the building, chortling happily to himself. Fuzzy took advantage of the open door and entered the lobby from out in the courtyard, where he had once again been romping about with Invictus' smaller citizens.

"Hey, buddy. Let's go see Meg. I need to speak to her about a couple menu items, and I bet you could convince her to fork over some tasty hunks of meat. I'm guessing you worked up an appetite out there, rolling around like a puppy." Fuzzy just grinned and fell into step beside him.

Chapter 8

Not having time to have a proper box crafted for presenting the Ancient Shellback Heart to Master Daigath, Allistor took a little time to shop the open market via the kiosk. He did a search for gift boxes, and was bombarded with nearly a thousand options. Narrowing his search, he tried wooden gift boxes, and added some dimensions. This reduced his choices considerably, and it didn't take him long to find an attractive wooden box that looked as if it were made of mahogany. It had silver hinges and an ornate silver clasp that was stylized to look like an eagle's claw. Allistor quickly purchased it for five thousand klax, and retrieved it from the kiosk window.

Pulling the rare crafting item from his inventory, he placed it into the box, which turned out to have been lined with a soft, silvery fabric that reflected the glow from the heart. Closing the box, he put it back into his inventory ring as he headed toward the dining area.

Remy had sent over every single one of the people who'd stayed behind at the Stronghold after the battle. Along with about two hundred of his group who had opted not to stay at his Stronghold. Most of those had already filtered away through the teleport system to other locations. Some had stayed at Invictus tower to escort the newcomers around or introduce them to new friends.

Allistor was gratified to hear that about two dozen of Remy's people had elected to try living on Orion. He wanted as many humans as possible to begin mixing with the beastkin, and vice versa. In fact he was considering offering some kind of incentive to his humans to try out the new planet. He'd already effectively bribed some of the beastkin with land on Earth if they'd be willing to stay there.

Prime's voice interrupted Allistor's musings. "Sire, I am pleased to inform you that my scouts have located the goblin horde's nest. We were able to follow a small group of them who returned to deliver food and loot. The nest is less than a mile from Baron Remington's Stronghold, almost due north. They appear to be inhabiting a large, primitive power generation facility."

"Great! Have your scouts been able to tell how many of the goblins remain?"

"Unfortunately not, sire. The goblins appear to have settled in subterranean levels, and my scouts are unable to follow without alerting sentries. We have been able to locate three separate entrances to the lower levels, but all three are well guarded."

"Alright, thank you. Please have your scouts form a rough perimeter, and locate any other possible exits. Keep a sharp eye on those. When we attack the nest, I'll want at least a hundred of your battle droids at each exit, and several thousand others surrounding the place. I don't want a single enemy to escape."

"It shall be as you say." Prime saluted, remaining nearby in case Allistor had other orders.

"Nigel, please put me in touch with Remy." Allistor waited a moment until Remy's voice greeted him. "Hey Remy, the battle droid scouts found the goblin nest. I don't know the city at all, and my map's not fully filled in. Prime says they're in a large power plant due north of you, less than a mile. Ring any bells?"

"Oh, shit. That's the Con Ed plant. Straight up the FDR, not very far at all. The place is huge, and sits behind high brick walls and fences with razor wire."

"So… just dropping a bomb…?"

"Would do no good. You'd need like, twenty big bombs. Or one really, really big one. And that brings up another question. It's the main power plant for the area. If we're going to rebuild this part of the city, aren't we going to need that?"

Allistor shook his head for a moment before realizing Remy couldn't see him. "I don't think so. I mean, all of our facilities come with this sort of automatic electricity and water that are, as far as I can tell, some kind of magic or extremely advanced System tech. And we can always use the hydrogen engines to create power on a large scale if we need to. We could probably replace that great big power plant with something that takes up less than an acre?"

Allistor looked at Prime as he spoke, and the general nodded his head.

"Yep, Prime is nodding his head at me. So we could bomb that place into oblivion… if we had that many

161

bombs. Which we don't. I think Gene and his guys might have one or two ready by now. We'll have to try a strategy that worked pretty well before with the goblins. Piss them off, draw them out, kill as many as we can with a bomb, then get down and dirty inside the nest to kill whatever's left."

Remy sighed through the audio link. "I defer to your expertise. But even after the last battle, I'm not sure that many of my people are prepared for that kind of fighting."

"If this horde is anything like the previous ones we've fought, the highest level and toughest goblins will be the ones we have to go in after. My raiders can handle it." Allistor wasn't as confident as he sounded.

"When do you want to hit them?"

"Let's say noon tomorrow. Maybe a little later. I have a VIP coming to visit first thing in the morning. And I want to see if we can have a few bombs made before we go. Any of your people that want to join us should start preparing."

"Roger that. See you tomorrow." Remy signed off.

"Nigel, can you put me through to Gene, please?"

"What's up, Allistor?" Gene's voice came through a moment later.

"Hey, buddy! So… we have this goblin nest to wipe out…"

162

"And you want bombs." Gene finished for him. "We're working on it. I made them a priority as soon as I heard about the battle the other day. We've got two bombs just about done. Working on two more."

"Just about done? Like, how many can you have for me if the fight happens at noon tomorrow?"

"Two for sure. Probably three." Gene's voice was thoughtful. "If we work all night, definitely three."

"I'm sorry to ask this, but please work all night. The nest is in a giant power plant complex. I'd like to be able to turn the whole place into a crater, and not risk any lives."

"Well, that changes things. We designed the previous bombs for pressure waves. More damage to soft bodies, less damage to buildings and such. If you just want to level the place, we might be able to use some conventional bombs. I think there are even a few bunker busters stored at Andrea's place. I'll reach out to her."

"Great, thank you Gene. Let's still bring along two of your bombs, just in case. If we can lure most of them out and pulp them into jelly first, then Harmon and his guys can grocery shop before we destroy the rest of it."

"That's just gross." Gene replied before signing off.

*****

Dinner was a relatively quiet affair. A bunch of Remy's holdouts sat interspersed with citizens, talking

163

quietly about what they'd seen at the various properties, or asking questions. Some shed tears as they remembered lost family and friends.

Allistor's table was filled with his advisors and analysts. He'd called a few of them together to update them on the visit from Master Daigath, the location of the goblin horde nest, and the plan for the next day. It was a casual conversation, and they mostly talked in between mouthfuls of deliciously seasoned steak, seared and served in sizzling butter with grilled vegetables and freshly baked rolls.

Droban the minotaur, who was actually sitting on the floor so that the table was at a workable height for him, was making deep-toned nom-nom noises as he ate. As the steaks were from the Cheyenne cattle herd, some mischievous part of Allistor couldn't resist. "How's the steak, Droban?"

"It is quite tasty, Allistor." The deep voice rumbled back after Droban swallowed the mouthful he'd been chewing. "I especially like the white, crusty spice that lady Meg has applied to the meat."

Allistor was confused for a moment, staring at his own steak until Amanda helped him out. "You mean, the salt?"

"I believe that is it, yes." Droban nodded again.

Allistor's jaw dropped. "You haven't tasted salt before?"

Droban shook his head this time. "Not before arriving on Earth. But I have grown quite fond of it."

"Well, don't eat too much of it." Amanda warned. "It is bad for your blood pressure."

Allistor was barely listening. The fact that the minotaur hadn't tasted salt before had knocked him ass over teakettle. It was so common on Earth that it never occurred to him that alien planets were not the same. Could it be that simple sodium chloride could be a marketable, even valuable commodity on the open market?

Down the table, Bjurstrom snorted. "Droban, I'm calling you Kaz from now on, big fella. FOR THE SALT!" He pumped a fist in the air, and the confused minotaur copied him after a moment's hesitation.

Amanda gave the man a scowl, making it clear he should quit teasing the minotaur. Bjurstrom coughed and lowered his eyes, quickly cutting himself a piece of steak and shoving it into his mouth.

When the meal was over, Allistor did some quick traveling. He stopped at Luther's Landing to visit with George and ask for a few bottles of the brandy the old man had salvaged from the wrecked military train. "Hey old man, I've missed your ugly mug! How're things going here?" Allistor made a bit of small talk before getting right to the point. "I'm expecting a visit from an even older man in the morning. Master Daigath is a battlemage trainer and master crafter. I'm trying to convince him to come stay here for a while, and he's a big fan of good brandy, according to Harmon. Can you spare a couple bottles?"

George snorted at his prince. "What? You think I'm that easy? You don't come visit for months, then all of a sudden you come here tellin' me how pretty I am cuz you want my prized happy juice?"

Allistor pretended to think it over. "Yep. You got it exactly right."

Half laughing, half grumbling, George pulled three bottles from his inventory. The label read "Hennessy Cognac XO" and the liquid inside had a deep amber hue. Allistor picked up one of the bottles, the textured glass feeling good in his hand. It felt like quality to him, but he knew nothing at all about brandy, except that you sipped it from those funny shaped glasses, and it warmed your belly on cold days. "Is this good brandy?"

"Well, yes. It ain't the fanciest in the world, but that's a solid brand from France. They quit making it a few decades back, so it has become rare. I'm guessing some officer or smuggler was transporting their entire stash on that train. It's a miracle they weren't all smashed." George started to reach for the bottles as if to take them back, then pulled his hand into his lap. "They're pretty rare, now."

"I appreciate your sacrifice, my friend. I'll pass on your compliments to Master Daigath. Maybe he'll reward you with a crafted weapon or something."

The old man didn't look impressed. Allistor shook the man's hand and took his leave, stopping at the Citadel to find Michael. The man was in the smithy, working with some of the crystals that Nancy had grown using her magic.

Allistor waited outside the private room Michael worked in until his friend sat up and took a deep breath.

"I was worried you were about to make something explode. Again." Allistor teased.

"So was I." Michael looked around, making sure nobody else had heard. "I'm working on figuring out the limits of how much enchantment magic a crystal will hold. I've pushed it too far a couple times, so far. FYI, don't overfill a crystal. I'm still picking slivers out of my skin. Anyhow, what's up, boss?"

"A lil birdy told me that you and Ramon figured out how to make apple brandy. Master Daigath apparently likes brandy. I thought I'd offer him a bottle or two of our home-grown stuff..."

"Ha! Only if you let me be there to see him taste it. I'd love to hear the opinion of a multi-thousand year old elf." Michael pulled a couple sealed mason jars from his inventory. Looking at them as Allistor took them in hand, he spoke in a sheepish tone. "I'm afraid we don't have any fancy bottles or even labels, yet. We're basically still at the experimental moonshine stage of development." His face brightened a bit. "Maybe Daigath would give us some suggestions?"

Allistor put the bottles into his ring. "Let's convince him to stay, first. Maybe let him settle in a bit before you involve him in your shenanigans?" He patted Michael on the shoulder. "You coming with us tomorrow afternoon to take out the rest of the goblin horde?"

"Hell yes! Not all of us got a dozen or more levels just for inheriting a bunch of land. Some of us have to *work* for it!" Michael thumped his prince on the back. "I'll be there with bells on."

Taking his leave, Allistor went back outside. "Nigel, where are you storing the brandy from the goblin ship cargo?"

"Those crates were confiscated by Sam, sire. He claimed them for medicinal purposes. He is currently storing the remaining supply in the kitchen pantry at the Invictus tower."

Crossing to the teleport pad, Allistor rolled his eyes. "Medicinal, my butt. Nigel, please ask Harmon to meet me in the tower's top conference room in ten minutes. I'm going to go liberate some of Sam's *medicine* and meet him there."

"Of course, sire."

Stepping off the pad at headquarters, Allistor went directly to the kitchen. It was mostly empty, the staff having just finished cleaning up after dinner. He found Meg there mixing some kind of dough. "Hiya, Meg. Is Sam around? And whatcha making, there?"

"Sam's in the back, taking inventory. This is bread dough for tomorrow's breakfast. If I mix it now and let it set overnight, I don't have to get up quite so early."

Allistor stepped close, leaned in, and gave the woman a quick peck on the cheek. Then he hurriedly jumped back, in case she felt inclined to bust his nose again. "Don't get hostile! I just wanted to thank you for all your hard work."

Meg pretended to wipe her cheek with her shoulder. "So you slobber on my face? You wanna properly thank me, give me a reward! Like... Yellowstone! I always wanted my own supervolcano." She eyed him sideways as she continued to knead the dough.

"Ha! You want Yellowstone, it's all yours, lady." He realized that he really hadn't done much to thank his core group for all they'd done over the past year. He'd given Ramon and Nancy their own Citadel on Governor's island. And it occurred to him that this might have made a few of the others jealous, or made them feel unappreciated.

"Hey, Meg... you know I owe you and Sam everything, right? You've saved my life several times, fed our people every day, even when I surprised you with hundreds or thousands of new mouths to feed. You are the backbone of Invictus, and my family. Anything you guys want, I'm happy to give you. Just ask."

Meg stopped what she was doing, wiping her hands on her apron as she turned toward him. "We've been happy to pitch in, boy. We opened the diner because both of us loved to cook, and to socialize with our neighbors. Sam and me, we both love you like a son. When the time comes, we might ask for our own place off in the woods somewhere." She paused, a grin forming. "A really big, fancy place. With a whole staff to take care of us."

"Ha! You got it. Just say the word. In fact, I could make that happen here in the city right now. Pick a building, or a penthouse, or whatever, and it's yours. I'll find somebody to clean and cook for you…" Allistor stopped when Meg's smile turned to a frown and she reached for a nearby rolling pin. "Or just clean for you. My bad!" He started backing up, hands in front of him. Then he turned and dashed for the back. "Hey, Sam! You back here somewhere?"

He didn't hear Meg mumble, "Silly brat." or see her angry frown turn back to a gentle smile. Or notice the tear that ran down one cheek, which turned into a glob of flour when she wiped at it with the back of her hand before returning to her work.

Sam called out from behind some shelves in a huge walk-in pantry. Allistor hadn't been in this room since claiming the tower. It was huge. At least thirty feet square with floor to ceiling shelves along the outside walls, and more in rows that ran front to back. "In here, boy. Got the munchies?"

Allistor located the man in a back corner, writing on a clipboard. "Nope. I'm here to reclaim some of that medicinal goblin brandy you confiscated, old man."

Sam looked over one shoulder, his eyes narrowing. "If you're lookin' to get drunk, that ain't what you need, boy. That brandy's for sippin', not gulpin'." Allistor noticed the man took a couple steps to the side as he spoke, positioning himself between Allistor and a small stack of crates against the back wall.

"Ha! I don't intend to do more than sip, you old hoarder. Harmon says Master Daigath likes brandy. I'm rounding up as many different samples as I can. If you want to join us upstairs, Harmon and I were going to do a little tasting to decide which one to offer as a welcome gift."

Sam immediately relaxed. "Why didn't you just say so!" He turned his back to Allistor, reached into the top crate, and removed two bottles. "What else are we tasting?"

The two of them headed up to the conference room, where Harmon joined them almost immediately. He held two bottles in each hand, the different shades of liquid making it clear there were at least two different brands. "I brought along a few suggestions from my own private stock." He set the four bottles on the table.

Sam set his two bottles next to them, while Allistor pulled his collection from his ring. As soon as he set the two mason jars down, Harmon scooped one up, sniffing at it. "What is this?"

"Homemade apple brandy. Michael and Ramon figured out how to distill it from apples that Nancy grew at the Warren." He watched as the orcanin unsealed the lid and sniffed at it again. "I haven't tasted it myself, and I have no idea whether it's any good."

Harmon produced a box from his inventory and set it next to the bottles. When he opened it, Allistor and Sam saw that it was filled with small shot-sized glasses with rounded bottoms and wide mouths. "We shall soon see." Harmon commented as he took three of the glasses and poured small quantities of the homemade concoction into them. Passing them to Sam and Allistor, he added, "It has a pleasant odor. Lighter color, and clearer than one might expect."

All three took an initial sip. Allistor definitely tasted the apple, along with a few other elements he couldn't quite place. He'd never understood people who could sip a glass of wine and call out things like "Oaky, with a hint of citrus, toffee, and cinnamon." But he liked the pleasant, warm, gentle burning in his belly after he swallowed.

"Damn, it's better than I expected." Sam commented before taking a second sip.

"Indeed. This is quite promising, for an experiment." Harmon agreed. "And I rather suspect that Master Daigath will appreciate its home-grown origins." Finishing the sample, Harmon resealed the jar before pulling out three fresh glasses. "Let us try one of Earth's more established offerings." He reached for the nearest bottle of Hennessy and opened it, smiling as the scent of the amber liquid reached him. "Ahhh, yes." He poured samples into the three clean glasses and passed them out.

Again, Allistor's first sip made him believe he was born with defective taste buds. While he enjoyed the taste, he couldn't pick out any specific flavors. And again, the best part was the warmth in his belly.

"That's what I'm talkin' bout!" Sam thumped one hand on the table. "Good ol' Hennesy. Can't go wrong with this."

"Yes, this is quite agreeable." Harmon took a second sip, finishing the sample. "I'd like to purchase a few of these for my own cellar, if that's possible."

Allistor nodded. "I'll let George know. He's got a small supply that he scavenged. But he guards them like each bottle is one of his grandchildren. I practically had to mug him for these two. So be prepared to pay dearly!"

Both Harmon and Sam chuckled as the merchant produced three more glasses, and began to pour the goblin brandy. "For such offensive little beings, the goblins make more than passable brandy." He handed glasses to both humans before sipping from his own.

Aware that his opinion here meant nothing, Allistor simply enjoyed the flavor and the burn, which he was feeling less and less with each sip. The goblin brandy had a little more of what he would call *bite* to it, a slightly harsher flavor than the others he'd tried.

Sam seemed to agree. "Got a lil kick when it first touches yer tongue. But I like it!"

Harmon grinned, revealing the full length of his tusks and lower teeth. "It's made from a fruit similar to Earth's pears, distilled using a digestive enzyme from a large insect that is also a delicacy among the goblins."

Allistor felt slightly green, though he could not see his own face. Sam gulped once, looking uncertain for a moment, then grinned. "Hell, I've eaten my share of bugs when I had to. This stuff's still tasty!"

Allistor didn't finish off that sample. He slid it aside next to his empty glasses as Harmon poured the next. "This is my second favorite. It is called "Firebelly", and if you cannot guess from the name, is a dwarven contribution." He passed them out. "I must warn you, this one has a significantly sharper flavor, and a longer burn, as its name implies." He raised his glass in a salute before taking in the entire sample."

Allistor took his first sip, and immediately his mouth lit up. For the first time he thought he tasted cinnamon, some kind of pepper, and maybe honey?. But that was all he got before his tongue began to tingle, and his eyes started watering. He swallowed the small quantity of liquid, which did indeed burn quite enthusiastically all the way down his gullet.

"Really good." He rasped, thumping his chest.

"Hell yeah!" Sam had downed the entire sample, not wanting to be outdone by the large orcanin. He was thumping his own chest, then wheezed slightly. "I need to get me some of this. Maybe a bottle for Meg's birthday. She'd love this."

Harmon chuckled, producing a few items from his inventory. "For this next one, I wish your palettes to be fully cleansed. I would not contaminate your first experience with my favorite brandy, with aftertaste from lesser vintages." The orcanin produced a knife and a wedge of something that looked and smelled like cheese. Taking three thin slices, he placed them onto thin wafers, and motioned for the humans to take one. Allistor slipped his into his mouth, and closed his eyes as a smoky flavor made even his defective taste buds take notice. The cheese was soft, yet firm, a counter-texture to the crispy and tasteless cracker-like thing.

Harmon poured them each a glass of water from the pitcher in the middle of the table. Once all three had washed down the food, he began to pour the final brandy. "This is made from a rare fruit, cultivated by druids on the planet Octia." He handed Sam and Allistor their glasses, but didn't lift his own. His attention was laser focused on Allistor's face.

Allistor raised his glass, and immediately noticed a spicy, flowery scent before taking a sip. Colors burst across his tongue! That was the only way he could describe it. This was what he'd imagined LSD would be like. He could actually *taste* colors. The flowery scent disappeared, and the spice was enhanced by a sweetness that reminded him of strawberry and possibly honeydew. When he reluctantly swallowed, there was minimal burn in his throat. The liquid went down smoothly, and the warmth spread beyond his belly all the way to his fingers and toes."

"Wow." was all he said before taking a second sip. After a moment, he added, "This is the best thing I've ever put in my mouth!"

Sam was quiet, his eyes closed and a smile on his lips as he licked them clean. After a moment, he opened his eyes. "I didn't know this was even possible. These druids, are they elves? Cuz this tastes like magic potion made by elves in all the old stories."

Harmon shook his head. "Not elves, arachnoids."

Sam's eyes went wide. He gulped once before asking, "Arachnoids? Like, arachnids? As in eight legged spider people?" Allistor sat down, not liking where the conversation was going.

"Indeed. Planet Octia is inhabited by a race of what you would call spiders. Though octians are not typical arachnoids. The race is generally aggressive, much like goblins. Though with higher intellects, a stronger prey instinct, and a hive mind social structure. They also have an affinity for technological trades. Except for the octian druids, who long ago isolated themselves from their brethren and strove to return to their roots by rejecting technology and embracing nature."

"Do I even want to know how they make this stuff?" Allistor asked. He was pretty sure the answer would ruin the experience for him. "Tell me this isn't made from giant spider pee."

Sam leaned forward, setting his elbows on the table. "I gotta hear this. So I can tell Meg. She hates spiders." He grinned happily.

Harmon chuckled. "The octian druids make their homes among the fruit trees, living in web hammocks strung between branches. When the fruit ripens, they pluck it free and masticate it, squeezing the juices into containers fashioned from the wood of that same tree. The juice is left to ferment for some time before being taken and distilled into the liquid you've just tasted."

Sam laughed loudly as Allistor's thoughts whirled. He suspected this was in part due to the multiple samples of brandy he'd imbibed. On the one hand, he was relieved he hadn't just tasted spider pee. On the other... pre-chewed fruit from a giant spider's mouth did not sound the least bit attractive.

"Can I have a small refill?" Sam asked. "I want to take this down to Meg, let her taste it. Then tell her the story." He grinned at Allistor. "I might need to sleep in a spare room tonight, but it'll be totally worth it!"

Harmon obligingly refilled Sam's sample glass, then offered a refill to Allistor, who held up a hand to decline. He had moved on from the slight revulsion toward the drink's origin, and was now experiencing a different conflict.

"This spider brandy is clearly the most delicious of all of these. But if I gift this to Master Daigath, do I risk offending or alienating him when he learns its source?"

Harmon shook his head. "Master Daigath is familiar with both of the samples I brought with me this evening, and indeed, enjoys both. It is a wide universe, Allistor, and most other races would not blink at this brandy's origin. Consuming the flesh of other species is commonplace. Orcanin are not the only ones, for example, to consider properly roasted goblin flesh to be a delicacy."

"Then I should gift him a bottle of this." Allistor nodded, feeling relieved, and slightly tipsy.

"Not necessarily. This is a safe choice, one that he certainly would not reject. But as I said, he might appreciate the novelty of a local product. At his age, anything new is a welcome change. I believe either of your Earth samples would please him."

Sam, on his feet and headed for the door with his surprise for Meg, paused to offer his input. "I'd go with the Hennessy to start with. Just for the fancy presentation. Then, when he knows us a little better, offer him some of our moonshine." He looked at the sample in his hand, then at the bottle on the table in front of Harmon. "Hey uhh... how much for the rest of that open bottle?"

Harmon resealed the bottle and held it up. "Since we are among friends, how about you and Lady Meg cook one of your special meals for my people?"

"Deal! Whatever you like!" He paused in the middle of reaching for the bottle. "Uhh... except there's no way I can talk Meg into cooking goblins."

Laughing, Harmon handed over the bottle. "Some of your earth beef, or... what did you call it? Murder chicken bbq? Any of your local dishes, with Lady Meg's magic touch, would be fine."

Sam took the bottle and slipped it into his inventory before downing the sample and returning the glass to Harmon. "You got it! Just let us know when, and we'll go all out!" He looked at all the empty glasses on the table, then scooped them into his ring as well. "I'll go run these through the dishwasher and get em back to you."

Harmon and Allistor followed Sam out of the room, the orcanin and the marine chatting about spider spit as they got on the elevator. Allistor waved good night before heading to his own quarters. After confirming his wakeup call with Nigel, he slipped into bed. His head barely hit the pillow before he was asleep.

Chapter 9

Allistor was pleased to find that he wasn't even slightly hung over when Nigel woke him two hours before the first sunrise. Amanda, who hadn't been in bed yet when Allistor retired early with a snootful of brandy, groaned and tried to cover her head with a pillow.

"Oh, no you don't. I need you and your lovely smile to help me win over Master Daigath this morning. After that, we've got a big day storming the castle.!" He spanked her lightly on the butt, then pushed her toward the edge of the bed. She had to plant her feet on the floor to avoid rolling out and faceplanting.

"You snored like Fuzzy last night." She complained, getting to her feet and stretching a bit before heading toward the shower.

"Must of have been the spider spit I drank last night." He offered as he followed her, dropping his shorts as he went. Once in the oversized shower, he grabbed some soap and began to rub her back.

"Let me guess… Harmon? How hung over are you?" she asked before ducking her head under the water and grabbing the shampoo.

"Not at all. We tasted a few brandy samples, strictly for science." He moved his hands up to help massage the shampoo into her hair.

"Riiiight. Science. So where does the spider spit come in?"

He told her the whole story as they quickly and efficiently soaped each other up and rinsed off. Ten minutes after Nigel's wakeup, the two of them were dressed in clothes Lilly had fashioned for them. They weren't exactly formal, but were well made and fitted to them perfectly. Allistor wore mostly black, with red and grey accents. In contrast, Amanda wore a cream colored dress that was modestly cut, but hugged her figure quite attractively.

Allistor quickly confirmed that he had the box with the Ancient Shellback heart, the bottle of Hennessy, and several other rare crafting materials in his inventory. Taking Amanda's hand, they walked onto the waiting elevator and headed downstairs. Harmon had suggested that they serve their visiting VIP one of Meg's delicious breakfasts, saying it might be a swaying factor in Master Daigath's decision.

One by one, the advisors that Allistor had requested to join them began to arrive. Some through the teleport, others just coming downstairs. All four analysts attended as well, anxious to meet the legendary elf. Gralen arrived at the same time as Harmon, and had barely stepped off the teleport pad before Nigel's voice rang out.

"Master Daigath has confirmed permission to teleport to this location. He will arrive momentarily."

The AI only just finished speaking when the pad lit up, and the ancient elven master appeared.

Harmon stepped forward, bowing deeply to his old mentor. "Welcome, Master Daigath. I thank you for granting my request. You honor us with your presence." He stood upright and smiled at the elf.

Daigath looked like any other elf Allistor had seen, though instead of appearing to be twenty two years old, he looked more like thirty. He was dressed in forest green leather from head to toe, the stitching simple but somehow elegant at the same time. When he stepped forward to embrace Harmon, his movements were fluid and economical, displaying both agility and grace.

"Harmon, my old friend. It has been too long." He smiled kindly at the orcanin, glancing down at the blade tucked into Harmon's boot. His voice was just as smooth as his gait. "I see you still carry that old thing."

"Until the day I die." Harmon replied solemnly. "It remains the most precious gift I've ever received..." he paused and nodded toward Allistor. "and Prince Allistor recently gave me several billions of klax!"

"Ha! Flatterer! It's but a simple blade. But come, let us not keep your friend waiting. Introduce us!"

Both of them turned toward the waiting crowd, Allistor with Amanda at his side in the center of the group. "Master Daigath, may I present Prince Allistor of Invictus, Planetary Prince of Earth, and Emperor of Orion, and his mate, Lady Amanda."

Allistor stepped forward with Amanda at his side, and Daigath bowed his head. Allistor had the urge to return the gesture, but a slight shake of Harmon's head kept him upright.

"Welcome to Invictus, and Earth, Master Daigath." Allistor smiled at the elder elf. "We are most grateful that you were willing to come and meet with us."

"Thank you, Prince Allistor, Lady Amanda. I am most pleased to meet you. I admit to having followed some of your recent adventures, and being most impressed. It is rare to find a prince who cares so much for his people. Even rarer to find one who rose to such heights from, please forgive me, such a low station."

Allistor maintained his smile. "There is nothing to forgive, Master Daigath. I did begin with nothing but my clothes, and my friends, most of whom you see here before you, and a little bit of luck." He looked at all the friends, old and new, standing behind him. "If you'd like to accompany us to our dining area, our chefs have prepared a morning meal I believe you will enjoy." He motioned for the elf and Harmon to walk alongside Amanda and himself. They were silent for a few moments as they crossed the lobby while Daigath took in their surroundings. He paid special attention to the sunken garden visible through the glass lobby doors as they passed. "Harmon tells me your first encounter with my race nearly resulted in war?"

Allistor did his best not to gasp even as Harmon winked at him. "Y-yes, that's true. I'm afraid I am woefully unprepared for the situation I find myself in. We accidentally offended a commander of the Or'Dralon during our very first foray into space. Fortunately, I was

183

able to apologize and establish more friendly relations before he disintegrated us."

Daigath shook his head as they approached a long table, taking the seat indicated by Allistor after waiting for Amanda to take hers. "The Or'Dralon. Among the worst of the bunch. My people have become entirely too prideful, too full of themselves. So focused on honor and etiquette, politics and power, that they've forgotten how to live." His tone was sad and his voice quiet as he finished.

Not knowing how to respond, Allistor sat in his own seat and nodded along. Amanda saved him by answering. "I'm afraid we've had very limited interaction with your people so far, though L'olwyn here is helping us to understand them. I think you'll find we humans are much less rigid. We've spent the last year so concerned with simple survival that we've not had much time to focus on niceties." She paused to indicate the simple dining area and the uncovered table at which they sat. "I'm afraid we're much more... humble than what you might be used to."

Daigath's gaze snapped up to L'olwyn as Amanda mentioned his name. Then returned to Amanda with a smile. "You are most gracious, Lady Amanda. My home is in a tree, deep within an ancient forest. My neighbors are creatures of land and bough, and visitors are few. My days of pomp and noble etiquette are millennia behind me."

Turning to the only other elf at the table, he said, "L'olwyn. I have heard that name. You are *unhoused*, are you not?" His tone was friendly, a simple question.

L'olwyn lowered his head, blushing slightly. "I am, Master Daigath."

The ancient elf chuckled. "Fear not, child. I have heard your story. Your predicament is no fault of your own. As far as I know, you have only ever acted with honor and loyalty. I, too, am *unhoused.* Though it happened so long ago that no one living remembers. And back then it did not carry the stain it does now." He turned back to Allistor. "That you have taken in an unhoused also speaks highly of you, and resolves one of the issues I believed might stand between us. This pleases me."

Allistor's pulse slowed as he began to feel comfortable with the elven master. "Please, allow me to introduce the rest of my advisors." He went around the table, introducing each human and alien and stating their title or function. Just as he was finishing up, the food arrived.

"And this is Lady Meg, with her husband, Sam. Our two most talented chefs." Meg set a plate in front of Daigath first, followed by Amanda, while Sam put his in front of Allistor and Harmon. Behind them, a long string of kitchen staff brought plates for everyone at the table. When everyone was served, Meg and Sam joined them, sitting across and several seats down from Daigath.

"Please, enjoy." Amanda smiled at their guest. Daigath took a moment, folding his hands in his lap and closing his eyes. Everyone else waited in silence, allowing the elf to observe his pre-meal ritual.

Opening his eyes to find everyone else waiting, he smiled. "Apologies. A habit so old I do not even notice it anymore. Just a simple gesture of thanks to the creators." He lifted the fork next to his plate and examined its contents. There were scrambled eggs with diced onions, spices, and peppers sprinkled in, a cup of fresh fruit, several strips of crisp bacon, and freshly baked bread. Meg had hastily confirmed with Harmon the day before that Daigath wasn't a vegetarian. On the table in front of him were pitchers of water, orange juice, and coffee.

As Daigath scooped some eggs onto his fork and took his first bite, the others at the table dug in. All of them trying not to stare as they awaited his reaction.

Except Meg. Meg stared unabashedly. Which caused both Sam and Allistor to have to resist smiling. Sam nudged her gently with an elbow, and she turned to glare at him for a moment before resuming her observation of the elf.

Daigath set down his fork as he chewed and swallowed, then took a sip of water. "Harmon has told me that you are an artist when it comes to food, Lady Meg, and I must agree. This is delicious!" He smiled at Meg, who was beaming back at him.

"Thank you, Master Daigath. Cooking for my family and friends is one of the joys of my life."

With that, the rest of the group dug in, all of them making sure to compliment Meg and Sam in one way or another, usually around half-full mouths. Which earned them a hostile glare from both Meg and Amanda.

By the time everyone was finished eating, it was nearly time for the first of the suns to rise. "Master Daigath, would you like to accompany me to the roof? The suns will rise soon, but it should remain cool and comfortable up there for a while."

"Certainly, Prince Allistor. Sam, Lady Meg, thank you for a wondrous meal. It has been decades since I've eaten so well." He bowed his head slightly to Meg, who just blushed.

Allistor led Daigath, Harmon, and Amanda to the elevators and up to the roof, where they took seats in the lounge area. Daigath eyed Allistor's smithy before sitting. "I had heard rumors that a planetary prince was crafting his own weapons, but I doubted the gossip-mongers. It seems I should give them a bit more credit."

Allistor chuckled. "I'm no master craftsman. I've just recently began to train in *Weaponsmithing* and *Enchanting*. The former I sort of picked up by accident, along with *Improvisation*, in the early days of the apocalypse. I was simply trying to figure out a way to stay alive."

Daigath nodded. "Self-preservation is often the best motivator. And I'm glad to see you pursuing a crafting skill or two. Far too many nobles think themselves above such pursuits."

"I've been a noble for less than a year, and frankly, I know even less about ruling and the politics involved than I know about *Weaponsmithing*. I've surrounded myself with the best friends, advisors, and analysts that I can, to help with the ruling. I'm hoping you'll consent to help me with some of the other knowledge I seek."

"Ah, yes. You wish to advance as a battlemage. I can indeed assist with that particular need." The old elf favored them with a half smile, pausing to gaze eastward, where the brighter sun had crested the horizon. "Assuming I choose to remain here for a time."

Amanda leaned forward in her chair. "Allistor has set aside his morning to speak with you, to show you around, in hopes of convincing you to stay. Is there anything in particular you'd like to see?"

Daigath took in the view, frowning slightly. "I dislike cities. Even ones so sparsely populated as this one. I prefer the deep forests and solitude of nature. Do you have such a place where I could reside while I'm here?"

Allistor nodded. "I believe we do. I became a prince when Lady Helen awarded me all of our former nation's national parklands. We have a Stronghold called Wilderness that I believe you'd enjoy. Or, if that is not remote enough for you, we can create one in a suitable location."

"I would like to see this Wilderness of yours."

"We can travel there right now." Allistor and company got to their feet, and five minutes later they were stepping off the teleport pad at the Wilderness Stronghold. Though he couldn't see anything beyond the high walls, Daigath smiled. Taking a deep breath, he said, "Yes, I can smell the forest."

Allistor led them to the main tower, and up the elevator to the top floor lookout post. From there they took the short staircase to a landing pad he had created before he realized the sheer size and weight of the yacht he'd been promised by the system.

Daigath looked around, his gaze passing over the mountains in the near distance, the old-growth forest, and the lake below. He frowned slightly when he noticed the clearing just beyond the lake. Harmon coughed, embarrassed. "Yes, uhm, I'm afraid that was me. I needed space to land my ship when I delivered Prince Allistor's yacht on the first day."

Daigath nodded, though his frown didn't fade quickly. Allistor shot the orcanin a grateful look for his taking the blame. He'd been in favor of having Master Daigath there to train him before today, but now he found he genuinely wanted to impress the old elf and convince him to stay.

"If this place is to your liking, we can set you up with a home and a workshop here. Whatever you need." Allistor offered. He notice Harmon staring at him, and when he raised an eyebrow at his friend, Harmon tapped his heart, then nodded toward Daigath.

It took a moment for Allistor to realize what the orcanin meant, but when it clicked in his head, he jumped to it. "Oh! And... as a gesture of our appreciation for you taking the time to visit with us..." He removed the decorative wooden box from his ring. "I believe this is the rarest crafting component we have obtained so far. None of us is worthy of it, nor will we be for many years, I'm told. I hope a master such as yourself can find a use for it."

Daigath accepted the box from Allistor's outstretched hands, running his fingers across the smooth surface for a moment before turning to Harmon. Without needing instruction, the orcanin extended his massive hands and held the box with the latches toward his old mentor so that Daigath could undo the latches and open it. The master's eyes lit up as the purple glow of the Ancient Shellback Heart reached them.

"This is indeed a rare gift, Prince Allistor. Thank you." He lifted the heart from the box and closed his eyes for a moment. "There are many possibilities that come to mind. I shall have to consider them all for a time, before choosing." He set the item back in its box, closed the lid, and nodded to Harmon, who stored the box away somewhere.

Daigath studied the horizon, staring off toward the mountains. After more than a minute, he said, "I think that I shall stay here a while. Though young compared to my home forest, this place calls to my soul. You seem a worthy student, Prince Allistor. From what I have been told, and have observed myself, you are a noble who truly cares for his people. And though I believe your ultimate goal of vengeance against the ancient ones who brought you here is doomed to failure, I would help you to become stronger for the sake of your people." His gaze dropped to the clearing Harmon had cut into the forest. "I shall establish my home there, and begin healing the damage wrought by axe and saw." He shot Harmon a look, and the orcanin looked sheepish.

"Thank you, Master Daigath. I'm thrilled that you're willing to stay, and to teach me. Do you need anything to help you build your home? Materials of any kind? Hands to help with the construction?"

Daigath turned away from the view to face Allistor. "No, thank you. I will not be constructing my home so much as shaping it. And I have all that I require. It will take me several months to convince the young trees to form properly, so with your permission I shall reside here in one of the towers in the meantime?"

"Of course, Master Daigath! Anywhere you like. And we can set aside space for you to work, or for training, whatever you need."

"Then let us formalize our agreement." The elf stepped forward and placed a hand on Allistor's shoulder. "I, Daigath of the Elves, Grandmaster Battlemage, hereby agree to accept Planetary Prince Allistor as student and ally. I shall serve him and his people to the best of my abilities, keep his secrets, and agree not to intentionally harm him or his interests, until we mutually consent to part ways, or he violates the terms of this agreement. In return, Prince Allistor of Earth shall provide me with shelter, space to work, and more of that delicious food!"

Allistor couldn't help but smile as he replied, "I, Prince Allistor of Earth, whole-heartedly accept the terms of this agreement."

A silver glow wrapped the two of them as Daigath lowered his arm. Allistor looked at his hands, watching the light being absorbed into them even as he felt the physical thrill that indicated he had leveled up. He blinked a few times as his interface filled with notifications. Ignoring them, he asked, "Silver? I've never seen that before."

Daigath chuckled. "Yes, well. When you enter into a formal agreement with a being as old as myself, even one as simple as ours, the System takes special notice. I am afraid you'll find that many nobles will be jealous of you now. While others will seek to gain your favor in hopes of obtaining permission to commission works from me. Permission which you cannot grant, by the way. That is not part of our agreement."

Allistor nodded. "Harmon has told me how rarely you create and gift weapons like his blade. I would never presume to make such a commitment on your behalf, even if I were able."

"I think we will get along just fine. Now, before I get to work on my new home, there are a few items we should address immediately. First, Harmon go remove all the cut lumber from my clearing." He glared at the orcanin, who was already moving toward the stairs and talking into his wrist communicator. When he was sure Harmon couldn't see him, he winked at Allistor. "He's a good boy, but I have to keep him on his toes."

Allistor suppressed a laugh, and Daigath continued. "As for you, there is much for you to learn. You have done well, learning several useful spells that have served to keep you alive through Stabilization and beyond. In no small part because you found clever and imaginative ways to use them. But no Battlemage that I have ever heard of has reached level fifty without learning more than the base skills awarded upon choosing the class."

Once again he raised a hand, this time placing it on Allistor's chest. "The motes have been hard at work within you. Much of your body has been reconstructed and repaired."

Amanda snorted. "He's let a *LOT* of things bite him over the last year." A second later, when the ancient elf's words sunk in, she gasped. "Motes? The little nanobots I see inside him?"

Daigath removed his hand and looked thoughtfully at her. "Nanobots. Hmmm. If I gather your meaning correctly, that is an apt description." He looked around the empty platform, then down at the courtyard below. "Come, let us find a place to sit, and I will explain."

Allistor led them down the stairs, then down another level in the elevator to the suite he had claimed for Amanda and himself. They took seats in the lounge area, and Daigath began his first lesson.

"We all exist within the *Neutrocosm*. It permeates everything in this universe at its most basic level. Matter, antimatter, dark matter, whatever you call the basic elements of existence, all are built upon the framework of neutrocosmic particles. Those particles provide the energy, the will, of our universe. And make no mistake, our universe is a living thing. One so vast and intricately complex as to be incomprehensible to most minds. The few ancient beings who delved so deeply into its secrets that they achieved a significant measure of understanding, were the ones responsible for creating the System. A sort of governing entity that enforces the will of its creators upon the rest of us. A few others, such as the ancient ones you have sworn vengeance against, attained enough understanding to further develop and modify the System's operational instructions." He paused as Allistor's face twisted into a scowl.

"What we call the *motes* are the physical embodiment of the system's will. As I said, they exist within all matter. Neutrocosmic particles that serve as the source of energy for all things. They exist unformed, neither positive nor negative, good nor evil, until given instruction. When you cast a spell, you are in effect requesting an action, which the System directs the motes to carry out. And they act on their own, to an extent, as they follow the base functions given them by the System. For example, within your own body, Allistor. When your physical form is damaged, the System dictates that it heal at a specific rate, based on a complicated formula that factors in uncounted variables, including your personal attributes. The motes take form, gather in and around the damaged tissue, and repair it at the subscribed rate. This rate of repair is increased by a healing spell, for example. Or decreased by factors such as depleted stamina, poison, debuffs of various kinds, and so on."

Amanda asked, "And that's why the areas where his bones have been repaired are stronger? Because they have a higher concentration of... motes?"

"Indeed. Or, more accurately, where healing magic was applied. If a simple broken bone were allowed to heal at a normal pace for humans, the strengthening would be less evident. But since your world was relocated, the entire planet has a higher than normal density of motes."

"Why is that?" Allistor was fascinated.

"There are a few reasons. First, the method of relocation. The ancient ones destroyed your original sun, harnessing energy that should have powered the star for billions of years, and using a considerable part of that energy to transport your world a great distance. Not all of that energy was contained, however. Some of it was absorbed by your planet and everything on it, including the flora and fauna. Which is you." Daigath pointed to the two of them.

In addition, once the System declared humanity to be a contaminant, and undertook to eliminate most of you, it transferred millions, if not billions, of new creatures from the menagerie to Earth. Each of those creatures with their own supply of motes. They proceeded to kill humans and other local life forms, absorbing some of their motes, and releasing the rest into the environment. And they were in turn killed by humans or other creatures, with the same absorption and release of energy. The result being a massive amount of energy from billions of deceased life forms floating freely across your world."

Daigath took a few breaths, watching the faces of the humans in front of him to make sure they were following him. "Another big contributor has to do with the reason humanity was declared a contaminant. The pollution you soiled the planet with, and most especially the power generation methods you used. The System destroyed your... I believe you call them nuclear power plants?" He waited for them to nod. "And in doing so, unleashed tremendous amounts of primitive and harmful radiation, which it then proceeded to begin converting into safe, usable energy in the form of motes."

Allistor ventured. "So, not only did we humans level faster than normal because of the large number of creatures sent here to kill us, but we've become more powerful from the higher concentration of motes?"

"It is not quite that simple, but yes. The higher density of energy here makes your spells more effective at a faster than normal rate. For example, your *Barrier* spell has leveled up several times in the last year through regular use. Each time you've cast it, and it fulfilled its purpose by absorbing energy, your proficiency has increased. On my homeworld, where the energy density is lower, you would have had to cast that spell roughly twice as many times to reach your current proficiency."

"Cool!" Amanda held up a fist for Allistor to bump. He did so, but with less enthusiasm. His mind was on the cost of the increased energy more than the benefits. Billions of human lives.

"Thank you, Master Daigath, for explaining all of this. I have many questions, but one seems more urgent than the others." He looked up at the sky briefly, and Daigath caught it.

"The answer is yes. The energy levels on Earth make it more attractive to the many factions out there. To start with, they can send their lower level nobles here to hunt and train, leveling more rapidly than normal, just as you have. Though, few could match your pace." He grinned at Allistor. "You have reached level fifty more quickly than even most nobles would dream. And the average citizenry of stabilized worlds, those without the money or power of nobles to assist them, are unlikely to ever reach level fifty."

Allistor nodded, setting his anger aside as best he could. "Harmon and Gralen explained a bit about that. And about how they were higher levels because they were soldiers in several wars."

Daigath didn't reply, as Allistor hadn't really asked a question. Instead, he changed the subject. "As a Prince of Earth, you will need to be able to defend your holdings. And the best way to do that is to be as strong, well-informed, and prepared as possible. Toward that end, let us see about your neglected class training. To begin with, I need you to share your attributes and skills with me, so that I can help you choose the best path going forward." He held out his hand, and Allistor took it. "Just focus on sharing them with me."

Allistor did as instructed, first pulling up his character sheet, then concentrating on sharing it with Daigath. The elf tightened his grip slightly to let Allistor know he'd been successful, then spent some time reading what he saw.

"You have done well, for someone new to the System." The old elf observed. "You have sufficient *Strength* to inflict respectable melee damage, but are lacking in *Agility*. That is understandable since your focus during stabilization was on ranged fighting. Your focus on *Intelligence* and *Will Power* reflect that as well, and they are the primary attributes for a Battlemage. Tell me, where would you assign the six free attribute points currently available to you?"

Allistor had been thinking about this, so it didn't take him long to answer. "My situation has changed recently. Since I am expected to do more melee fighting now, I would add a single point each to *Strength* and *Constitution*, two to *Agility*. As a noble who's about to be thrust into politics, I would put a point into *Charisma*, and a point into *Luck*?"

Daigath chuckled at the last one. "Sometimes *Luck's* influence *can* make up for lack of planning, or *Intelligence*. Were I you, I would forego the point in *Strength* and move it to *Constitution*. As you said, you will be expected to fight in close quarters more often, and survival is key. You possess sufficient physical strength to effectively wield sword and spear, and as a Battlemage your focus will be on spell damage more than melee attacks."

Allistor was grateful for the feedback, and quickly assigned his points as suggested.

Daigath nodded his approval, then released Allistor's hand. "And now, the reason I suggested we find a place to sit. I have a significant quantity of spells and skills for you. Since you have achieved level fifty without training every five levels as one normally would, this could take quite a while. I recommend we go slowly, a few spells at a time, as learning too many in a short period can cause side effects ranging from confusion and dizziness to excruciating pain, even coma."

Allistor had experienced some of the pain of learning higher level spells, and wasn't anxious to repeat the sensations. "I agree, Master Daigath. Slow is better. Especially as I have a battle planned for this afternoon. I don't want to be incapacitated."

"A battle?"

"A goblin horde attacked a stronghold in Invictus City the other day. We killed all that we could see, but have since found a nest not far away. This afternoon we plan to clear it once and for all."

"I see. Well, then you will likely be fighting underground, in tunnels and enclosed spaces. Let us start with a few spells that would be useful in that setting."

Daigath put a hand on Allistor's forehead and closed his eyes. A moment later Allistor felt a rush of warm energy, his brain tingling as information poured in.

He was glad he was seated, closing his own eyes against the dizziness he was experiencing.

When Daigath removed his hands, Allistor had two new spells and a new skill at his disposal.

Shatter
This spell will cause its target to explode, any hard components shattering into a spray of shrapnel that extends ten feet in every direction.
Cast time: Two seconds. Spell cost: 200 mana. Cooldown: One minute.

Allistor assumed this was a level fifteen or twenty spell, as the mana cost was low. But he nearly drooled as he pictured shattering weapons in an opponent's hands, doing AoE damage. Daigath was right, this would have come in handy in many of the fights he'd endured over the last year.

Silence
Casting this spell will render the target unable to speak or make sounds for ten seconds.
Cast time: One second. Spell cost: 100 mana. Cooldown: Two minutes.

Another spell that would have been extremely useful. Allistor made a mental note to get the trainers for the rest of his people going as quickly as possible. How much stronger could Invictus as a nation be if they'd had access to training over the past year?

The last bit of information Daigath had passed on was a skill, rather than a spell.

Quicken

Battlemages possess the ability to temporarily speed their perception, movement, and reflexes, while simultaneously boosting Strength and Agility by ten percent. Effect lasts thirty seconds. Cooldown: Six hours. Minimum level: 25

"These are amazing, Master Daigath. Thank you!" Allistor bowed his head to the elf. "They will indeed come in handy during the upcoming battle, I'm sure."

"I wish you the best of luck, Allistor, I'll leave you to your preparations. If you'll authorize my use of your teleport network, I will return to my home briefly to retrieve some personal items. Then begin work on shaping my new home near the clearing."

Allistor grimaced. "I'm sorry about the clearcutting. I authorized Harmon to clear a space for his ship to land, not giving much thought to the trees. At the time I planned to make use of the lumber for construction."

Daigath held up a hand. "No need to apologize, Allistor. None of the trees Harmon's droids felled had reached sentience. I simply found a handy excuse to poke at him. There is, however, an elder tree close by that has just begun to awaken. Along with a few others not far away. I shall commune with the nearest when I return, and began to shape my home within his boughs. When you have won your battle, come back and visit me. I shall introduce you to him."

"Th-thank you, Master. I had no idea there were sentient trees. I mean, some of our legends and folklore speak of Ents and the like. But to actually speak to a tree..."

Daigath just chuckled as he got to his feet. Allistor and Amanda accompanied him back to Invictus, where they parted ways. Daigath disappeared back to wherever he'd come from, and Allistor took a seat in the lobby to go through his notifications and review his attributes.

The vast majority of notifications were of fame and infamy points awarded for recruiting Daigath. There was also the standard level up notification for level fifty, and the award of two accompanying attribute points.

Designation: Emperor Allistor, Giant Killer	Level: 50	Experience: 1,100,000/35,000,000
Planet of Origin: UCP 382, Orion	Health: 65,000/65,000	Class: Battlemage
Attribute Pts Available: 0	Mana: 15,000/15,000	
Intelligence: 24 (28)	Strength: 10 (18)	Charisma: 11 (15)
Adaptability: 8 (10)	Stamina: 12 (19)	Luck: 7 (13)
Constitution: 21 (26)	Agility: 13 (19)	Health Regen: 2,000/m
Will Power: 24 (32)	Dexterity: 7 (11)	Mana Regen: 1,100/m

Chapter 10

After a quick trip up to the conference room to meet with Selby and share his latest round of fame and infamy awards, Allistor moved to the rooftop lounge area for some privacy. He checked in with Bjurstrom and the other raid group leaders to confirm they'd be ready to go after lunch.

"Nigel, please ask Master Longbeard if he's available to meet with me? If he is, ask him to join me here."

"*Of course, sire.*" There was a brief silence before Nigel added, "*He will join you momentarily. Also, Master Daigath has returned and has claimed a small suite in the main tower at the Wilderness Stronghold.*"

"Great! Thank you Nigel. I have another task for you. I need you to privately notify the parents of any children under level fifteen, that I am inviting their kids to join this afternoon's raid. The kids will stay on board the *Phoenix*, completely safe. They should receive enough experience points to level up several times, as well as receive a quest and the loot that comes with it. Have them bring the kids to Invictus Tower for lunch."

"It shall be done, sire."

Master Longbeard got off the elevator and joined Allistor in the lounge area, hopping into a chair without ceremony. "Ye did good convincin' Master Daigath ta join ya."

"Yes, I think his presence here has already been very helpful. I've learned quite a bit this morning, including a few new spells and a skill. Speaking of which, I would like you to take the lead on recruiting our little army of class trainers."

"Aye, that be easy enough. Just a few questions that need addressin'. First, d'ye want to contract with a trainer's guild? Or hire 'em individually?"

Allistor considered for a moment. "I think individually if that's possible. Ideally, I'd like to recruit them as citizens of Invictus, have them take the oath, and stay here. Bring their families if they'll swear, too. I intend to keep them busy, having a whole planet's worth of humans to train, as well as our non-human citizens. I'll pay them a salary, and we'll work out some *affordable* fee they can charge each client for training above that. If they wish to sell their services to non-human non-citizens, like members of some of the alien factions, they can charge more. Since, as I understand it, those factions would have charged us a great deal for access to their trainers."

Longbeard snorted. "That might earn ya some enemies, but I like it!"

Allistor wasn't really listening. His mind was reeling with visions of ferrying a small army of class trainers around the globe, finding human communities and helping them level up their class abilities. Once his own people had been thoroughly updated, of course.

"What would you consider an appropriate salary for a trainer?"

The dwarf stroked his beard for a moment, considering. "Some be more expensive than others. Rare classes, and trainers with higher levels, cost more. But on average, ye might pay a million klax per year. A bit less if ye allow 'em to charge fer services as ye mentioned."

"Nigel, how many different classes do we need trainers for at the moment? Include all citizens, human or otherwise."

"There are currently one hundred seventeen different classes among your citizens, sire. I can provide the list to Master Longbeard for his convenience."

Allistor's eyes bulged for a moment. The number seemed high to him, until he thought it over. While the system that now governed their lives was much like the VR games he'd played, it was also much larger and more intricate than any game. It stood to reason that instead of the few dozen class options most games offered, there might be hundreds or thousands of them in the real world.

"Okay, let's say just for rough budgeting we'll have a hundred and fifty trainers, at one million klax each." Allistor paused. "We'll need to build some kind of housing and training facility for them."

Longbeard nodded, "That be a common practice. Some nobles keep barracks fer trainers, with arenas and practice facilities. If it be yer plan ta provide housing and food, ye'll likely get a discount on the salaries."

"We can build that. Somewhere here close to the tower. But let's sweeten the offers this way. If they are willing to become permanent citizens, I'll award them the same ten acres that our other citizens are entitled to. Either here on Earth, or on Orion. They can choose some of the parkland I own, or if they hurry, I can claim some other land and gift it to them. That should have some value."

"Aye! If they be lookin ta purchase permission to claim a plot here on Earth through the normal system channels, it'd cost em ten years' salary at least."

"Good. Then make them that offer. Get as many as you can, as fast as you can. Needless to say, no goblins. Or other races you might consider hostile or unfit. Like… races that might find us tasty?"

Longbeard chuckled. "I'll get on it right now. And while we're on the topic of citizenry… there be a significant number o' dwarves what have asked about pledging to ye. The crew that performed yer planetary survey on Orion spent some time on the planet, and on the trade station, and spoke to yer beastkin citizens. Word got back that ye be a good Emperor, and that be a rare thing."

Allistor nearly smacked himself. "The survey! I completely forgot about that. When did they finish it? Do you have the results?" He paused, a sly grin appearing on his face. "Did they manage to find someone to 'leak' the reports to?"

Longbeard's face went flat, thinking Allistor had ignored his question about dwarven immigration. "Aye, the survey be finished. I expect results later today or tomorrow. And they'll have no trouble findin' buyers, don't ye doubt."

"Great!" Allistor hadn't noticed the look on his analyst's face. "As for the dwarves, of course they're welcome. As long as they're willing to swear the oath and become citizens like everyone else." Allistor paused. "Uhm… how many are we talking about? And which planet do they want to live on? We're going to need more housing."

The smile returned to Longbeard's face. "A few hundred o' me own clan. And maybe five thousand others, so far. As for which planet they'd prefer… I'd like ta bring my family here, to Earth. The others, I be thinkin' most will feel the same."

"Well then, let's do it! We'll get together tomorrow afternoon, and go over the survey results. You can update me on more specific details on the dwarves, and the class trainer hunt. Feel free to bring in the other analysts to help with the trainers. And speaking of the other analysts, do they also have families they wish to bring?"

Longbeard nodded. "I know Selby be considerin' it. Though I think she be waitin' to see if ye survive the next lil while." The dwarf grinned at him. "The others have no' spoken about it either way."

"Ha! Well please let them know their families are welcome as well. In the meantime, lunch should be about ready, and then we've got a goblin horde to deal with." Man and dwarf rose and boarded the elevator, riding together down to the lobby level. As soon as he reached the lobby area, Allistor was flooded with greetings from scores of children and their parents. Many of them from among Remy's people. Fuzzy was in the middle of the large space, being petted and scratched by more than a dozen kids, randomly victimizing a kid here and there with a lick to the face. From the looks on those faces, his breath was as foul as ever.

"Welcome, everyone! I'm glad to see you all here. We'll be having a quick lunch to get everyone well fed and buffed, then heading out to the *Phoenix* and *Opportunity* to…" his voice trailed off as a question occurred to him. "Hey, I see a bunch of you from Remy's Stronghold. How did you get here? He doesn't have a teleport pad as far as I know?"

A woman with a small child, a girl maybe six years old, stepped forward. "We drove over in a couple of school buses. It's not far, only a couple of miles straight down the FDR and then across on Liberty, and only took about twenty minutes."

Allistor cringed. "Well… I appreciate your enthusiasm! But we haven't cleared all the area inside the walls yet. Next time, please just let Nigel know you want to come, and we'll arrange to stop and pick you up. We'll be flying right past your Stronghold on the way there anyway." The woman, and several others in her group, nodded their heads.

Allistor's pulse slowed a bit as he calmed himself. "Alright, here's the plan. You kiddos will be part of the raid group, but we're going to keep you on the ships during the fighting. In fact, you're going to get a little training as ship's crew. How does that sound?"

There was jumping and clapping and cheering from the mob of kids. Several of the parents, who'd been looking less than enthused, relaxed a bit.

"We know from past battles that the kids will receive a share of the experience even though they're not directly participating in the battle. They'll be safe behind the shields, and the pilots know to bail if anything goes wrong. Any questions?"

Another woman, this one with a boy maybe ten and a smaller girl, asked, "Can we go with them? Not that I doubt you, Prince Allistor. It's just that, I haven't let them out of my sight hardly at all for the last year…"

Allistor smiled at her. He understood completely. "I'm sure that between the two ships we can find room for parents too, if you'd like to accompany your children." Most of the heads nodded, several smiled in relief and appreciation. The fact that they'd been so worried didn't go unnoticed.

"Uhm… guys, you all know that this is strictly voluntary, right? I had Nigel extend the invitations so that we could level up the smallest and weakest among us. But it's only an invitation, an offer, not a demand. Any of you who felt otherwise, I apologize. You're free to bail without any repercussions."

A man holding his daughter in his arms stepped to the front of the crowd. Allistor thought he recognized him from Cheyenne. "We understand, Allistor. I think I can speak for everyone here when I say we want our young'uns to get stronger. And this seems like a good, safe way to do that. Not like when you killed that void titan at the Citadel, and little Pip here leveled up. I was on that wall, watching that thing come for us, and for a while there I was sure we were all gonna die. So yeah, I'm here to sign her up for this, and I have faith you'll keep her safe. But that don't mean I won't worry a good bit till it's over."

Allistor smiled at the man. "Thank you for that. And I know how you feel, to some extent. I don't have kids of my own, but I've made myself responsible for all of you. Also, have you met Bjurstrom and Goodrich? They're like two twelve-year-old kids in full grown bodies. I'm worried about them every time we go out. Luckily, I have Fuzzy there to look after them."

Fuzzy grinned at him, tongue hanging out one side of his mouth as people in the crowd chuckled and patted his back.

"Any other questions?" He waited for a moment, and when nobody spoke up, he said, "Okay let's get everyone fed, and we'll get going."

Ramon, Nancy, and Chloe joined him at his table while he was eating, followed by his raid leaders and core group. Gene, Kira, and their girls showed up with Gralen, who'd brought Gene's bombs along on the *Opportunity*, which was now waiting at Battery Park. More than a hundred raiders who were high enough level to participate in the fight joined them for lunch, along with Gralen's beastkin crew and Kira's human crew trainees.

Meg had recruited Addy and Sydney to buff the food during prep, so when everyone finished eating they

210

had buffs of ten percent to both health and *Stamina* regeneration, as well as +3 *Strength*, +3 *Constitution*, +2 *Stamina*, and +2 *Intelligence* for six hours.

The crowd adjourned to the lobby, where Bjurstrom and the raid leaders organized everyone into groups and sent out raid invitations. Meg and Sam passed out jerky and water bottles to everyone as Nancy and Chloe handed out health, mana, and cure potions.

While they were doing that, Allistor opened his interface and created a couple of quests. The first was just for the kids.

> **Quest: The Prince's Pirates**
> *Board one of Prince Allistor's ships and assist the crew during the raid on the goblin horde. Keep to your assigned station, and follow orders. No leaving the ship!*
> *Reward: 50,000 Experience, 5,000 Klax, plus a share of the loot!*

When he finished that one, he included the parents and allowed them to accept on behalf of their offspring, not being sure whether all the kids could read. There was a general wave of laughter among the parents, and squeals of joy from the kids. The next one was for everyone.

> **Quest: Finish Them!**
> *Seek out and destroy the remaining occupants of the goblin horde's nest.*
> *Reward: 500,000 Experience, 100,000 klax.*

Allistor knew each raider would also get their share of the kill xp plus a share in the monetary value of the loot. This was just a little icing on the cake, mostly for the kids, ship crews, and parents who would be remaining on board.

With everyone organized, stocked, and properly motivated, they headed for the ships. Gralen assigned a few of his crew to supervise and 'train' the half of the kids that would be on the Phoenix, then took the rest through the teleport to Battery Park to board the *Opportunity*. Allistor had Remy's people drive the busses into the *Phoenix* cargo bay, since they'd be stopping at Remy's Stronghold to pick up his raiders anyway.

*****

They made a short stop at Remy's Stronghold, dropping off the busses and people, picking up raiders. Remy informed Allistor that all but ten of the holdouts had decided to join. The two of them quickly made arrangements for supplies, and a droid platoon to escort those ten safely outside the walls of Invictus. Allistor ordered Prime to keep the droids with them until they had established a Stronghold of their own.

By one o'clock they were ready to begin the attack on the nest. One hundred thirty human raiders, forty orcanin, and one grizzly cub, stood in the cargo bays of the spaceships as they hovered high over the Con Ed plant. Prime's droids formed a wide perimeter, keeping watch on the exits they'd found from a distance that would keep them safe from the detonations to come.

212

Aboard the *Opportunity*, Gene and his techs had rigged two of the pressure wave bombs that they were now calling *gutbusters,* as well as a half dozen conventional bunker-buster type bombs they'd claimed from the air force supply in Cheyenne.

The kids had all been assigned various sections of their ships, a few on the bridge, others in the galley, engineering, and such. Parents stood nearby, observing as patient beastkin crew members gave the children basic instructions and simple tasks to complete.

When Bjurstrom reported to Allistor that everything was set, he said, "Let's do this!"

Kira landed the Phoenix directly onto the FDR freeway, outside the brick wall that separated it from the Con Ed plant. The ship's guns blasted a small hole in the wall, maybe ten feet wide, reducing the brick to dust that quickly drifted away on the breeze. Allistor and about half the raiders stepped down off the cargo ramp and moved fifty yards closer to the wall, waiting for the goblins to emerge. When they didn't show up right away, Fuzzy let out a roar of challenge.

That did the trick.

First a few goblin heads poked out from either side of the gap in the wall. There was shouting, the clamor of weapons, then a fireball shot up over the wall from inside, arcing through the air toward the raiders.

"Back inside the shield!" Allistor ordered, casting his *Barrier* spell directly in front of the fireball while it was still high above them. As soon as he cast the spell, he turned and ran to catch up with his people. The invisible barrier from his spell lasted just long enough to disrupt the momentum of the fireball, causing it to drop harmlessly onto the road between the opposing forces. The raiders held up about ten yards in front of the cargo ramp, inside the shield that Kira had pushed outward from the ship.

Fuzzy let out another roar, and the rest of the raiders joined in. "Rawr!"

Several of the tanks started shouting insults at the goblins, taunting them as best they could. "Your mother was a horny toad!" made everyone laugh even as more fireballs emerged from inside the walls to splash against the shields.

Amanda, standing next to Allistor, observed, "It really does seem like this horde has a lot more shamans than the others we've fought. Even the developed clan on Orion."

Allistor nodded, answering as he tested out one of his new spells, using Shatter to cause one of the loose bricks near the gap to send shrapnel into the enemy gathering there. "You're right. And we need to identify them as quickly as possible. Burn them down before they can cast that enraged-explodey spell they use." Bjurstrom heard him and began to broadcast instructions through raid chat.

The goblins continued to gather inside the walls, but none had ventured out so far. The shamans continued to lob fireballs, and seemed content to try and wear down the ship's shields. Deciding they needed some motivation Allistor counted the spells. He saw five fireballs shoot up over the wall within about three seconds, indicating at least five of the shamans hiding back there. Doing his best to follow the arc of the last one back to a spot behind the wall, he took his best guess and called down a column of fire using *Flame Shot*. When nothing happened, he did the same for the next fireball he saw.

That one worked.

There was screaming, then increased shouting for a moment, and small green bodies waving clubs and spears began to pour the gap in the wall. The raiders opened fire with spells, arrows, and guns as the creatures emerged. Allistor cast *Identify* on a few of them.

Goblin Scout
Level 45
Health: 19,240/23,000

Goblin Warrior
Level 43
Health: 22,900/30,000

These goblins were higher level than the ones that had perished outside Remy's Stronghold. Allistor began to be concerned about taking his people, most of whom were lower level than these enemies, into the nest.

More of the little monsters scrambled out onto the highway, stumbling over the brick debris before getting sure footing and charging toward the ship. The first several dozen that had led the charge all lay dead or dying on the pavement, having been mowed down by the raiders. A few smart ones had made it to the K-rails in the center of the road and taken cover, waiting as more and more of their comrades filled in behind them. They clearly planned to zerg the ship once they had built up their numbers. The raiders all backed up the ramp into the cargo hold.

When Allistor estimated that there were maybe three hundred of the little goblins exposed, and the flow through the gap began to slow, he spoke in raid chat. "Okay Kira, lift off. Raiders, keep them interested. Gene drop your first bomb right outside the wall in ten... nine..." he counted down as the Phoenix gained altitude. Kira kept her within range of the raiders' spells and guns until the countdown reached three. Then she quickly increased their altitude even as the bomb was falling past them. The first gutbuster impacted the road just outside the wall, knocking some of the emerging goblins back through the gap. Those outside were blasted into bits if they were at the point of impact, or crushed against the K-rail. A few were flung into the air, flying dozens of feet before landing limply.

Most of the raiders leveled up, some more than once. The kids and parents in other areas of the ship got multiple levels, and Allistor could hear the celebrations. But he had more work to do. Seeing that the *Opportunity* had descended considerably, he ordered. "Drop the second one, Gene. Inside the wall this time."

Five seconds later the second gutbuster detonated, causing some of the brick on either side of the gap in the wall to bulge outward, then slowly fall into the street. Again, most of the raiders leveled up. Kira landed the Phoenix back in its same spot as Opportunity moved slightly westward and hovered.

Without waiting to be told, the orcanin scrambled down the cargo ramp and dashed inside the wall, quickly looting the goblins and gathering whatever bits they considered tasty. Allistor ordered everyone to assign their newly earned attribute points while the orcanin did their thing. He watched as eyes all around him unfocused, and a few of his people moved their hands as they navigated their interfaces.

The orcanin finished their work inside the wall, and moved through the bodies on the outside. As soon as they were clear, the leader waved at Allistor, indicating he should resume his bombardment. "Gene, the orcanin are clear. Let's knock the place down. Start as far west as you can, just to make sure we don't bury our friends in rubble."

The Opportunity adjusted further westward and increased its altitude several thousand feet, then dropped the first of the bunker busters. The impact nearly caused Allistor to piss himself! The ground beneath them heaved upward, and a deafening thunder caused nearly everyone to cover their ears. Most of the orcanin and raiders stumbled, or outright fell over. A plume of ash and smoke rose into the air near the opposite end of the facility.

Just as Allistor was recovering, the second one hit. Two of the towers that rose high above the power plant swayed, then tumbled down, adding to the growing cloud of debris, and shaking the ground yet again. The orcanin decided they'd done enough gathering and returned to the *Phoenix* on unsteady legs, looting bodies as they passed.

After the third bomb struck, much closer to Allistor and friends this time, the last of the towers collapsed, as did the skybridge between the two largest buildings, and a good bit of the remaining brick wall.

"Gene, hold your fire." Allistor called out. He couldn't see much through the still-growing cloud of smoke and ash, but he doubted there was much left of anything in there. "Prime, we're done dropping bombs for a bit. Tighten up your perimeter, and report any contact with the enemy."

Allistor watched as the ring of battle droids, who had been waiting out near his city wall that ran along the river, began to pace inward. He waited for the breeze to clear away most of the airborne debris, leaving just the rising smoke from several fires inside. "Gralen, how does it look from up there?"

"I see nothing moving, Prince Allistor." The beastkin observed. "No signs of life on the surface, or the visible lower areas. The last three bombs penetrated through at least three underground levels that I can see. Fires are reducing visibility."

"Alright, let's get in there. Hopefully there are just a few left to mop up, and we can go celebrate. Bjurstrom, no groups smaller than ten. Keep it at twenty unless we absolutely need to split up further." Allistor stepped down off the cargo ramp along with his people.

They picked their way through the goblin bits as they crossed the highway, then stepped through the much wider opening in the brick wall. The orcanin returned to finished looting and harvesting the goblins outside the wall. They had agreed to serve as a supplement lookout force, in case any goblins attempted to escape.

Allistor surveyed the destruction before him. What had once been a complex of large four and five-story buildings with several towers was now a sea of rubble and craters, twisted metal and broken pipes. Not a single living thing moved, only the flickering of fires and billowing smoke catching his attention. The acrid smell of scorched stone, metal, and plastic burned his nostrils and irritated his eyes, making them water. While he waited for his raiders to pick their way through the rubble behind him, he looked for an obvious route underground. Not finding one, he moved forward toward the nearest crater. Standing back a couple feet from the edge, he could see down into the lower levels. The bomb that struck there had penetrated down to the third subterranean level, blasting open concrete tunnels, pipes, and power conduits.

The slope down along the side of the crater was steep, and filled with debris. There was no way the raiders could descend there without ropes, and only one or two would be able to go down at a time. "Prime, can you mark where your scouts have found entrances on my map?" He looked to the android general standing just behind him. A moment later seven red dots appeared on his interface. All but one of them were now covered in rubble. The last was on the far side of the complex. Allistor compared his position, the dot on the map, and what he could see with his own eyes in front of him, and decided the entry point was a small ten by ten foot concrete building.

Pointing at the structure, he said, "Looks like that's our best way in, now. We just have to get there." Not wanting to risk crossing the center of the rubble field and having the ground collapsing underneath them, he set off to his left along the facility's perimeter wall. The damage was less severe further from the center, and the path wasn't quiet as littered with debris. The others followed behind, all of them keeping watch for any sign of movement.

It took ten minutes to pick their way around to the structure. Allistor found it mostly intact, with the concrete walls only cracked, not broken. The metal entry door stood open, and the room inside was partially visible in the daylight. There wasn't much to it. A rack along one wall for hard hats, all of which now lay on the floor. A pallet of six-inch copper pipes on the floor near the opposite wall. And in the center of the room, a concrete stairway leading downward.

Behind him, McCoy commented. "Well, this isn't exactly like every scary movie ever. No sir." He paused while a few people chuckled. "If I was in the movie theater watching this, I'd be shouting at the hero not to go down into the dark, smelly hole."

Somewhere near the back, Goodrich accommodated him, calling out, "Don't go down there, dumbass! Something's gonna eat your face!" This time the chuckles sounded more nervous than amused. McCoy raised a finger high in the air so his pal could see it.

"Yep. This is a horrible idea." Allistor agreed, quietly enough that only those closest to him could hear. He really was concerned about the level of mobs they'd find down in this hole.

"Nothing to it but to do it, right?" He took a deep breath, cast *Barrier* in front of himself, and cast a light globe down about ten feet in front of him. "Here we go."

The stairway extended straight down for about fifteen feet to a concrete landing, then proceeded further at a ninety degree angle to the right. Fifteen more feet below the surface, the stairwell opened into a large room filled with machinery and thick pipes. The ceiling stretched out 20 feet above their heads, and the room was at least a hundred feet wide, and many times that distance long. The far wall was visible because one of the bombs had crashed through the room near the other end and left the ceiling open. Allistor pushed his light globe further out ahead of him as half a dozen others cast theirs and sent them out in different directions. It was soon apparent that there were three long aisles running between the pipes and machines that stretched forward across the room.

Bjurstrom took over, assigning teams of twenty to break off left and right to proceed forward, moving parallel with the main group. Allistor maintained the lead in the center aisle, his *Barrier* still active in front of him. Fuzzy walked next to him, the bear's nose going crazy as he sniffed at everything they passed.

221

About halfway across the room, Fuzzy paused, raised his nose as high as he could, then growled. Everyone froze, and Bjurstrom whispered into raid chat. The raiders had all learned to trust the bear's nose. From across the open crater ahead of them, they heard the screech of metal on metal, and one half of a double metal door opened. The sunlight revealed a figure standing there, its head pushed forward as it seemed to be scenting the air just like Fuzzy. The figure was tall and thin, at least three times the height of a goblin. Two arms, two legs, with humanoid proportions except for unusually long arms. Allistor quickly cast *Identify*.

Fomorian Guard
Level 47
Health: 60,000/60,000

Fuzzy growled quietly from deep in his chest. The hairs on his back bristled and he lowered his head, ears flat. Logan whispered, "Well shit, that ain't no goblin."

The creature's head whipped toward them, and it let out a high-pitched wail before stepping back and slamming the screeching door shut again.

McCoy's voice was barely more than a whisper when he added, "And now they know where we are, and which way we're coming."

The groups all advanced as far as the crater, not finding anything alive to challenge them. The crater was too wide for most of them to jump across at that point, but it was possible to drop down the fifteen feet or so to the level below. For Allistor, that drop was nothing. His improved Strength would allow him to absorb the impact from that landing with ease. But that was not the case for all of his people.

Prime solved the problem for him. The droid stepped off the edge, his hydraulic legs barely bending when he landed. Looking up, he said, "I will catch each of you."

Logan volunteered to go first. As the largest man in the group, he weighed more than anyone but Fuzzy. He hopped off the edge, holding his breath until Prime's four arms easily caught him, placing him back on his feet. After that the others jumped down one by one until it was just Allistor and Fuzzy. The bear had kept stepping back further from the edge, clearly not willing to jump. It reminded Allistor of the day they'd met, when the cub had been stuck on a ledge in the middle of a waterfall. Then he recalled that he'd caused the cub to fall off, bounce off some rocks, and plunge unconscious into the water below.

"Yeah, I'm sorry buddy. I guess you don't have fond memories of stuff like this. Hold still, and I'll *Levitate* you, then you can just drift down." Fuzzy growled and backed up, shaking his head. "What, you don't trust me?" Allistor was slightly offended, but he put his mind to trying to find an argument that might convince his several-hundred pound cub to just jump. Instead, an idea struck him. Removing a rope from his ring, he showed it to the bear. "You don't have to jump, buddy. Well, not far. You grab hold of this, and just step off, and I'll lower you down."

Fuzzy looked at him like he was insane.

"C'mon Fuzzster! I'm strong enough to do this, even with you as chunky as you've become! We really need to cut down on your snacks." Now Fuzzy was afraid *and* offended, shaking his head no and glaring at his human.

"Look, remember tug of war?" Allistor and the cub had played it quite often when Fuzzy was much smaller. He tied a knot in one end of the rope and held it out. "Here, Fuzzy. You take hold and pull. C'mon, you remember this game."

Fuzzy took a few hesitant steps forward, then took hold of the rope just above the knot.

"Okay, now tug! C'mon... pull!" Allistor dropped most of the length of rope on the floor and took hold about four feet from the bear's snout. He leaned back and put his weight into it, just as if he were the anchor in a tug of war contest. Feeling the pull, Fuzzy naturally growled and tugged back, digging his feet in and clenching tighter on the rope.

"That's right! Who's a badass rope-tuggin bear? You are!" Allistor moved his grip up on the rope until it was just half a foot from Fuzzy's jaws. Planting his feet, he lifted up on the rope with all the strength in his legs, back, and arms. Fuzzy's front feet lifted in the air as he growled a challenge. His massive neck muscles shook the rope back and forth. While he was distracted, Allistor cast *Levitate* on him, then tugged the rope gently even as his cub squealed in surprise and fear. The moment Fuzzy was

224

out past the edge of the hole, he pushed down gently, and his squirming, bawling cub, drifted down to the floor below. When he made contact with the floor, Allistor cancelled the spell. He quickly gathered up the rope, put it back in his ring, and called out "Geronimo!" before leaping over the edge himself.

A second later, Prime caught him and set him on his feet. A second after that, Fuzzy swatted those feet out from under him with one massive paw, causing him to fall and clunk his head on the concrete. The bear turned his butt toward his human and stomped away toward the back of the group, throwing Allistor a dirty look over one shoulder. Nobody said a word, and Allistor rubbed his head, getting to his feet again with Prime's assistance.

When she was sure he was okay, Amanda burst out giggling. A moment later, several of the others quit holding back, and joined her. She managed to say, "Guess we know who's really boss around here." before another laugh got her coughing.

None of them had remembered to send their light globes down, and now they were all out of sight. So they cancelled the spell and recast it, the lights moving down the tunnel ahead of them. They were now walking back in the direction that they had come in the room above, hoping to find an intact stair leading further down.

"Anybody ever heard of a Fomorian?" Allistor asked. He didn't recall the term from any of his games, but something tickled at the back of his memory.

Goodrich spoke up. "My gran used to tell this fairy tale about them when I was little. Some kind of fae monsters that lived underground. She used to say they'd come and steal the eldest child of a family if they misbehaved. I was the eldest." He paused to shake his head. "That's about all I remember."

Prime spoke up next. "Fomorians are an elder race. Long-lived, though not with the lifespan of elves. They do prefer to live underground, as their eyes do not work well in daylight or brightly lit areas. They possess formidable physical strength, and can move nearly silently. Most are able to cast spells, mainly earth magic and dark magic."

"Thank you, Prime. I think." Allistor said. Turning to look behind at the others following along, he asked, "Everybody get that?" He saw heads nodding all along the column of raiders.

A minute later the light globes drifting ahead of them illuminated a stairwell door. Stationing a group of twenty to watch that door, they continued down to the end of the tunnel. There were a few offices on either side, which were quickly cleared without incident. At the end, there was a control room of some kind, with several workstations, large monitors mounted on the far wall, and a bank of servers behind glass to one side. With no power, it was all just dead metal and plastic. They checked the room for any hidden goblins or other mobs, then returned to the stairwell, and prepared to head further down.

Chapter 11

Logan opened the stairwell door for Allistor, who stood in front of it with his *Barrier* shield cast in front of him. This was becoming standard procedure for breaching doors during raids. Allistor immediately pushed his light globe into the stairwell, but once it crossed the threshold, it simply disappeared.

"What the..." Allistor stared into the unnatural darkness in front of him. Suddenly panicked, he cast *Flame Shot* in the form of a fireball through the doorway. It too disappeared, though he could hear its impact a second later.

"Dark Magic." Prime observed. "Please, allow me. My sensors operate on several light frequencies." Allistor stepped aside, allowing Prime to move past him and through the doorway, one of his four arms holding his shield, the other his staff. To the watching humans, and grizzly cub, he just disappeared into a void. "This level and the stairs within sight are clear." He reported aloud.

Allistor reached one hand into the darkness. It felt cold, but not painfully so. He quickly checked his interface for any sign of a debuff, and found none.

"Fuzzy, you smell anything?" he looked down at the bear standing next to him. Fuzzy just shook his head.

"Alright... we move through the dark. Prime, you lead, reach out one of your hands so I can take it. Logan, hand on my shoulder. Michael, you and a couple tanks

227

next in line with shields ready, then a couple healers. The rest of you hold here until we figure this out. It has to be some kind of trap, or ambush, and I won't bring our whole group into it. I want two more tanks and some dps watching our backs, in case something drops down through the crater from above like we just did."

He took a deep breath and took hold of Prime's hand when it emerged from the darkness. He felt a hand on his shoulder, and a moment later Amanda's voice from behind him said, "Ready."

Allistor stepped forward, Prime leading him, and the others following. It was clumsy and slow, but eventually they made it down the first flight of stairs, across the landing, and down a switchback flight to the level below. The darkness continued to permeate the space, and the chill on Allistor's skin was increasing.

Prime spoke in raid chat. "There is a door at this level, and more stairs leading downward."

Logan replied, "We gotta go down, clear the stairwell first. We'll hear the door open if something tries to come through here." Allistor agreed.

"Let's make sure of that. Hold on." He reached out until he could feel the door, moving his hand up and down until he located the handle. He quickly removed one of his crafted swords from his inventory, and used the lanyard to hook it onto the handle. As an afterthought, he removed one of his early attempts at a shield and simply leaned it against the door. If anything opened that door, the shield

228

would fall, and the sword would bang against it, ensuring they would hear.

"Alright, I set a sort of alarm on the door. If you hear metal crashing, speak up. Now let's keep going."

Prime took hold of his outstretched hand, and the conga line of blind raiders continued down the next flight of stairs. As they were reaching the landing, Allistor heard a thud, and felt a vibration through Prime's hand. "Contact, sire. Fomorian at the bottom of the stairs."

Allistor directed a *Flame Shot* directly ahead and downward, hoping to strike the creature. He was rewarded with a high-pitched wail. A moment later something impacted his barrier, but he couldn't see whether it was a spell, or a physical attack.

Behind him, Logan said "Prime, Allistor, move left." The man waited two seconds, then opened up with his machine gun, firing short bursts downward. The first two bursts could be heard hitting the wall, the third caused a screech of pain, and words hissed in some unknown language. Logan managed two more bursts before something struck him, knocking him backward, groaning in pain.

Allistor shouted "Heals on Logan!" as he fired another *Flame Shot* at the sound below. Followed by a *Mind Spike*, which didn't take. Apparently one had to see the target for the spell to work. Another impact struck Prime's shield, the vibration audible. Prime let go of Allistor's hand and Allistor sensed forward movement. There was the sound of another impact, and a gurgling,

229

then an experience notification passed across everyone's interface. Immediately the darkness dissolved, revealing another fomorian at the bottom of the stairs. Or rather, its corpse laying at Prime's feet, the droid's staff driven directly through its face and out the back of its head.

> **Fomorian Mage**
> **Level 50**
> **Health: 0/0**

"Well done, Prime!" Allistor thanked his general. A quick look back showed Logan was back on his feet and at full health, but his leather chest armor had a large hole burned into it. "You okay, Logan?"

"That sucked. A couple inches to the left and I'd be dead. Dumb idea, having the two guys with shields step aside." He looked down at his chest. "Let's hope there aren't a lot of those mages down here. Fighting in the dark is bad news."

"That thing was level 50." Bjurstrom added. This might suck even if we're fighting in the light." He looked to Allistor, a question obvious in his expression.

Sam patted Bjurstrom on the back. "If it were easy, it wouldn't be any fun! I say we whup some fomorian ass!" The old Marine bent down to loot the corpse.

Allistor spoke in raid chat. "The rest of you, come on down. We need to talk." He waited for the raiders to bunch into the stairwell, filling up all the flights. Climbing to the middle landing, he spoke loud enough for all to hear.

"We're up against high level mobs we haven't faced before, and that we don't know much about. Logan nearly got one-shotted just now, and he's a higher level than most of you, with a bigger health pool."

He paused, thinking as he spoke. "We can bail right now, leave this place and drop more bombs, hoping to take these things out. Or we can keep going. But only with volunteers. I'm not ordering anyone into what might be a meat grinder. So take a minute and think it over."

While they murmured amongst themselves, he opened his interface's raid tab and looked for something he'd used often in his VR games. They'd almost all had a voting system where party members could vote yes or no on occasions like this. It was faster than a voice vote in large parties.

Not finding anything similar, he simply waited a minute or so, then called out. "Okay looks like we'll have to do this by show of hands. And let me be clear, any who vote to turn back will not be looked down upon in any way." He took a deep breath, clenching his fists to keep his hands from shaking. "All those in favor of continuing, show me your hands."

Sam's hand was the first to go up, followed almost immediately by everyone else's, except Meg's. Looking up at her husband, she shrugged, then raised her hand. "At least it ain't bugs."

Allistor found himself wishing they'd voted to turn around. His gut was telling him that more than a few of them would die down in this hole if they continued on. But he'd given them the choice, and they'd opted to keep going. Trying to calm his roiling stomach, he nodded. "Then we go. Let's take this slow and careful. Nobody take any stupid risks. Retreat is okay. We live to come back later, when we're stronger."

They had another difficult choice to make. There was a door leading out of the stairwell where he was standing, and a second door down at the bottom. The enemy could come from either direction, or from the door they'd entered a level above, through the tunnel they'd just cleared. He wasn't going to put this one to a vote.

"Bjurstrom, I need one group of twenty back upstairs watching that tunnel. Another group at the bottom guarding the door there. Find a way to block it, jam it closed, whatever. The rest can come with me through this door, and we'll clear this level before heading down."

The airman nodded and began calling out instructions. Twenty raiders started climbing back up, while another twenty formed up at the lower level and began discussing how best to keep the door from opening.

Allistor and Logan moved the remainder of the group up and down slightly, so that nobody stood directly in front of the door, then Allistor recast his *Barrier*, and Logan pulled the door open.

Four light globes immediately flew threw the door over Allistor's head, moving down the corridor in front of him. He led with a *Flame Shot* straight down the center before he could even see what he faced. The fireball flew unimpeded down the hallway to splash against the end wall. The light from the globes revealed a concrete corridor with more pipes and conduits running along the upper corners on each side. There were half a dozen doors on the left, and four on the right, before the hallway ended in a T intersection about a hundred feet ahead.

There was no sign of any monsters.

"Alright, by the numbers, let's clear these rooms." Bjurstrom spoke through the raid chat. Give me three tanks facing down the hall, just past the first two doors. One on each door, heals and dps behind. You know the drill."

The raiders quickly formed up, the three tanks facing down the hall in case enemies emerged from other doors while they cleared the first two. A tank stood in front of each door, and when another raider yanked it open, they went through with shields up. Healers and dps were poised to do their thing should the tank be attacked.

They weren't.

The first two rooms were clear, so they systematically moved down the hall, clearing each door as they got to it. As soon as the tanks established there were no targets, the breaching groups would move on, and the trailing raiders would search each room for usable items.

It took a little less than ten minutes to clear the corridor and side rooms, and Allistor advanced to the intersection. Poking his head out around the corner, he saw two short hallways, each with a single door at the end.

"Alright, we split into two groups. Logan, you take half our people and go right. I'll take the door on the left."

Allistor moved around the corner and closer to his chosen door as he spoke. It was a metal door with a small and narrow vertical window in it. The glass was clear enough to see through, but there was nothing but darkness on the other side. Allistor couldn't tell without opening the door whether it was simply lack of light, or another magical darkness.

He waited while the group divided, and then watched as Logan's team breached their door. Michael, shield raised, dashed into the darkness beyond even as a light globe followed. There was a brief pause, then the tank screamed.

Allistor's heartrate doubled, and he was about to push through his group to run and help, when Logan began to groan and shake his head. Then laughter echoed out of the room, and Michael emerged. "It's just a maintenance closet. Nothing in there. You should see your faces!" the man grinned, until he saw the look on Allistor's face at the other end of the hall.

"Uh, sorry boss." He looked sheepish, lowering his eyes. Nancy stepped up next to him and slapped the back of his head.

As Allistor turned back toward his door, which Sam was ready to pull open for him, Meg called out, "Hit him again, for me." Nancy did.

Clearing his throat to make sure his group was focused on him, Allistor nodded to Sam, who silently counted down from three, then pulled open the door. Light globes shot through, and disappeared the moment they crossed the threshold. A second later Allistor and three others cast Flame Shot, sending four balls of fire through the darkness ahead. Right behind those, Prime stepped through the door, all three of his eyes glowing, shield and staff raised.

"This is a large room, with three primitive generators, each about the size of a bus." the android reported. I see three fomorian guards, one mage. One guard and the mage have been struck by your spells. Recommend sending more, immediately. I am clear of the door."

Not waiting for orders, forty or so raiders cast fireballs through the doorway, high and low, from angles slightly to the left and right, which effectively filled a wide cone within the room with fire. There were wails of pain, and a second later a dark flash erupted into the light of the corridor. It sped from the doorway into the crowd, striking one of the tanks and knocking him back into the people behind him. The spell had flown over top of his shield, striking him in the face and removing most of it. He was dead before his corpse impacted the dps raiders behind him.

"Incoming!" Prime shouted as he launched his staff toward the mage, and another bolt burst from the darkness. This time the tanks were better prepared, and shields were raised higher. The tank whose shield took the impact was knocked back, but the spell was deflected upward into the ceiling. The folks behind him quickly helped him back to his feet to retake his place in the line.

Another volley of fireballs blasted through the doors and into the darkness. A moment later the dark spell dissipated and Allistor could see Prime fighting the three fomorian guards. The mage lay on the ground, one of Prime's feet on its head, which was badly deformed.

Even as Allistor charged through the door, one of the fomorians brought a club around and slammed it into the general's back, causing him to stagger.

Allistor cast *Mind Spike* on that guard, causing it to drop its weapon and wail, holding its head with both hands.

Behind Allistor, the full remaining group was charging through the doorway, casting *Erupt*, *Mind Spike*, and *Flame Shot* in columns that dropped from the ceiling onto the enemies. Allistor focused on the nearest, which was equipped with a shield and hand-axe. The ranged dps from scores of raiders was already taking its toll, despite many of the attacks being absorbed by its shield.

Fomorian Guard
Level 52
Health: 37,100/67,000

A quick look told him that the other two guards stood between his target and Prime, so Allistor tested out one of his new spells. He cast Shatter on the guard's shield. For about half a second, nothing happened. Allistor was starting to wonder if the spell failed when the metal shield exploded. There was no fire, or smoke, and not really much of a sound. One second there was an intact shield, and the next there were thousands of metal shards accompanied by a sort of metallic ting. The guard holding the shield was simply shredded, what little was left of his arms falling to the floor as the shrapnel passed through and around him and into his companions. Both of them took some damage, and were bleeding from dozens of wounds.

"Holy crap." Sam whispered from somewhere behind Allistor.

The barrage of magic had paused for a moment as everyone reacted to Allistor's spell. But the raiders quickly resumed their attacks on the other two. Prime backed away, pulling his staff from the mage's chest as he got clear of the kill zone. Allistor noticed he was limping as he moved.

> *Fomorian Guard*
> *Level 55*
> *Health 31,450/75,000*

One of the remaining guards turned and screamed at the raiders, the sound rippling toward them and stunning about half of the group. Others dropped weapons and shields to cover their ears. Taking advantage of the moment, both guards hurled short spears at the raiders. Their extremely long arms worked as well as any atlatl, a last second flick of their wrists giving the projectiles tremendous added momentum. The first whistled past Allistor, striking Sam in the shoulder and blasting all the way through to puncture the gut of one of the healers behind Sam. The second spear actually struck Allistor's magic barrier, shattering the spell, but got deflected enough that it bypassed Allistor and took one of the tanks in the knee. The spear disregarded the man's armor as if it wasn't there, penetrated through the leg, all but severing it at the knee.

Allistor tried to ignore the screams around him as he shook off the effects of the fomorian's sonic attack. He left the wounded in the hands of the healers, focused on bringing down the enemy. Each of them had equipped another spear, and were preparing to throw. Allistor cast *Mind Spike* on the nearest, then cast *Barrier* just half a foot in front of the second. The first guard screamed again, causing several of the raiders to drop to their knees. The second cocked its arm back for a throw, but when he began to push the spear forward, it struck Allistor's barrier and lost nearly all momentum.

Wasting no time, Allistor cast *Shatter* again, this time on the spear the second guard still held. When the metal weapon shattered, its right arm and a large portion of its right side disappeared in a bloody mist. Allistor could see its exposed ribs and the punctured organs behind them. The guard fell, not quite dead, but definitely out of the fight.

The remaining guard recovered from *Mind Spike*, and opened its mouth to send out another sonic blast. Allistor cast another of his new spells, *Silence*. The guard took a deep breath, then visibly pushed with its gut, but no sound emerged. Its confusion only lasted a few seconds before it bent to retrieve the spear it had dropped.

Allistor quickly cast *Levitate*, raising the guard several feet off the floor in its bent position. It tried to turn itself mid-air to reach the spear, but fell short. Allistor used his last new acquisition from Daigath, activating his *Quicken* ability and charging forward. As he moved, he waved one hand leftward, causing the guard to slam against one of the giant metal generators. A second later his improved speed brought him within a step of the monster.

Allistor drew his sword, not slowing at all as he passed the now upside-down guard, severing its head from its body. Just to be sure, he stopped and stabbed the mage and the other two guards through the head.

Level up! You are now Level 51 ! You have received two Attribute Points.

After looting the bodies by kicking each of them, Allistor moved back to his people, Prime limping along next to him. Without slowing, Allistor said "Prime, take whatever time you need to effect repairs." The android saluted and sat right where he was, lifting the pack off his back.

Sam was back on his feet, but looked pale. The healer who'd taken the spear to the gut after it passed through Sam wasn't so lucky. She lay dead on the floor, her skin also quite pale. The tank with the destroyed leg was being hooked up to one of the regeneration machines. Amanda had decided that healing wouldn't be able to repair the mostly severed knee joint, so she'd had someone finish the job with an axe. Even with multiple heals and the regeneration machine working on him, the tank looked pale as well.

"The spears were tipped with some kind of poison. We got to him, and to Sam in time, but Lucy took the spear very near her heart. She was gone before we even knew there *was* a poison." Nancy reported to Allistor.

Allistor recognized Lucy as one of Remy's people. He knew she had a little girl, slightly older than Chloe, that was right now on one of the ships above. He wasn't sure of the identity of the tank that had been killed, as there wasn't a face to recognize.

Bjurstrom walked over to stand next to Allistor, both men watching the regeneration process. It was both disgusting and fascinating at the same time. Bjurstrom cleared his throat. "We've killed five of those things now, and it cost us two of ours. Nearly cost us two more. That's not a good ratio."

Allistor nodded. "We don't know enough about these fomorians. They keep surprising us. And their levels keep getting higher. There's a whole other floor below us to clear."

Sam, still breathing unsteadily, added "And fightin in the dark sucks. They can see us, but we can't see them."

Allistor had a solution for that. "I can get Prime to bring more droids down. They can see through the darkness to some extent, and can be our front line. But yeah... I came here expecting to fight goblins. Not these things."

"I say we get the hell out of here, drop some more bombs, come back when this whole place is just a glassy crater."

Walking over to where Prime was still replacing a bent component of his right leg, Allistor asked, "any reports from your scouts outside?"

"A small party of goblins attempted to escape. My troops killed two, captured eight. They have been handed over to the orcanin."

"Okay, have your troops wait ten minutes, then move back. We're getting out of here, and dropping some more bombs. I don't want your battle droids so close that they take damage, but have them keep a sharp eye out for any more escape attempts."

Prime didn't stand, but saluted with one arm that held a tool of some kind. "I shall be fully repaired in approximately three minutes."

Allistor left him to it, going back to the group. The regeneration of the tank's leg was nearly complete. "Bjurstrom, sweep the room, check for the usual, then we're outta here." A few seconds later most of the raiders were fanning out in groups of ten to loot and check the room.

In raid chat, Allistor said, "Gene, Gralen, I need you guys to head back to Battery Park. Andrea, I want a couple of your guys back at Cheyenne to load up half a dozen more bombs in a storage ring and teleport to meet *Opportunity*. Gralen, get back here with those bombs as fast as you can. We're heading back up and out of this place. The new plan is we blast these things into charcoal."

He could hear Andrea telling Gene who to call back at the Silo to get the ordinance. Allistor knew they still had a few bombs on the *Opportunity* now, but he wanted more. He was dealing with the losses reasonably well, getting better at not blaming himself. But these things were going to pay for killing his people. And they weren't going to get to kill any more.

With Prime and the tank both back on their feet, the raiders retraced their steps. Prime carried the dead tank's body, Logan carried the healer. The group guarding the lowest level joined up, leaving the door blocked behind them. They picked up the group guarding the upper door, and made their way back down the tunnel to where it opened into the crater. From there, several of the raiders with high strength and agility stats were able to simply leap up to the higher level. Prime reversed his previous job of catching jumpers, this time gently tossing people up into the higher tunnel. And the rest, including Fuzzy, Allistor used *Levitate* to lift up. The last one to go, he had them clear a spot before he used *Dimensional Step* to join them.

The entire raid party jogged down that last tunnel, back to the original stairway, and up through the concrete building at the surface. Their pace was a bit faster on their return trip around the perimeter, since they were just retracing their own steps, and were reasonably sure the ground was safe.

Back aboard the Phoenix, Allistor examined the loot he'd taken. They had a few more minutes before Gralen would be back with the bombs. He'd gotten one of their spears, a pair of thin metal bracers, two gems, and ten thousand klax.

Fomorian Spear
Item Quality: Rare
Attributes: Strength +2, Constitution +2
This weapon, constructed of shadow steel, is imbued with a slow-acting poison concocted from the deathcap mushroom.

Allistor took a moment to inform Nancy and Amanda of the source of the poison, in hopes that it would help them to better counteract it in the future. Nancy thanked him, her eyes unfocusing to check her interface for any relevant information. Amanda put a hand on Allistor's arm. "Lucy, the healer who was killed, her daughter is here on the Phoenix. She's part of the raid party, and saw her mom's name go grey. I'm going to go talk to her."

Allistor nodded, not trusting his voice. He did his best to express his thanks with his eyes as Amanda kissed his cheek and departed. Promising himself he'd spend some time with the little girl when the battle was over, he went back to the loot. The next item of note was a staff about eight feet long, made of some type of very hard wood, a shade of grey so dark it was nearly black, with streaks of deep crimson swirling within the grain. Embedded along the top third of its length were several dark stones.

Fomorian Mage's Staff
Item Quality: Epic
Enchantment: Darkness, Void Bolt
Attributes: Intelligence +2, Will Power +3
This staff acts as a spell storage device, spell enhancer, and melee weapon. The enchanted stones hold (3/5) charges of the AoE spell Darkness, and (9/12) charges of Void Bolt. Stones can be recharged with current or alternate dark magic enchantments. Spells cast using the staff as a focus will have increased range (10%) and potency (variable).

The last item was a small dimensional storage bag. When Allistor accessed it, he found several dozen gems of various sizes and shades. Closing the fifty-slot bag, he made a mental note to share them with Michael when the two of them had time to identify each stone and any enchantments they already held.

Gene's voice came across raid chat. "We're about one minute out. Got six more bombs, plus the three we already had."

"Great. We're all clear. Prime's troops have retreated to a safe distance. Try and drop the first three into the craters you've already made. After that, we'll see how things look."

Kira lifted off without needing to be asked, having heard that more bombs were imminent. Allistor stood at the open cargo door and studied the compound, more of it coming into view as the ship ascended. The three craters sat in a nearly straight line down the middle of the complex. Crossing his fingers, Allistor took a deep breath. "Please let these bombs finish the job. I don't know if I can take my people back down there. Or if they'd follow me when I ask."

He watched, along with most of the other raiders who'd gathered around, as Opportunity dropped the third wave of bombs, one at a time. After each impact, Gralen waited a bit for the dust and smoke to clear. When the third bomb slipped into the final crater and exploded, Allistor heard more than one of his people whispering prayers of their own.

Just as the impact sounds died down and the clouds began to disperse, there was a tremendous secondary explosion. Allistor could see a ripple pass through the ground below, rubble being tossed up and remaining structures crumbling as the wave rolled underneath. A moment later the ripple could be seen advancing outward, damaging other nearby buildings and causing a wave to extend out across the river. The small perimeter structure that housed their previous entry point disappeared in a cloud of concrete dust.

Level up! You are now Level 52! You have received two Attribute Points.

Every single person on board both ships leveled up along with Allistor. But a quick check of his interface showed that the quests he'd given out were not complete. Which meant there were still living enemies below.

Prime appeared next to Allistor. "Sire, my scouts have engaged a small party of Fomorians to the north."

Allistor's interface map now showed half a dozen or so red dots tightly clustered about a hundred yards north of the western end of the complex. "Kira, take us there!" Allistor shouted into raid chat. If the enemy was within combat range of Prime's droids, he couldn't just drop a bomb on them. It would take out any of their nearby droids. Allistor considered doing it anyway, but feared that would hurt not only his reputation with Prime, but with any observing factions. He cursed the System and his new responsibilities under his breath.

The *Phoenix* shifted smoothly westward and began to descend rapidly. Allistor felt the urge to hold onto something even though the floor underneath them was completely stable. He could see the flashes of plasma rifle fire from the battle droids, and the much larger bodies of the fomorians pushing toward them, using broken walls, trees, and large chunks of concrete as cover.

Kira landed in the closest open area she could find, about fifty yards west of the battle. The moment the Phoenix set down, Allistor shouted, "Let's go!" and leapt off the cargo ramp, jogging toward the fight. As soon as he was close enough, he used *Identify* on the enemy monsters.

Fomorian Guard
Level 55
Health 73,000/77,000

Fomorian Guard
Level 60
Health 81,450/85,000

There were four guards, all roughly the same levels as the raiders had faced below, between fifty and sixty. But the ones that caught Allistor's attention were bigger, and smaller, than the others.

Fomorian Patron
Level 75
Health 165,000/165,000

Fomorian Scion
Level 20
Health: 28,450/30,000

The Patron stood at least a dozen feet tall, with alabaster skin and eyes that glowed blue. In his arms he held the much smaller Scion, maybe four feet tall and very thin. The Scion's eyes also glowed, but with a bright green shade rather than blue. And it held a bundle against its chest, wrapped in fabric or leather, that leaked a similar green glow in several places.

The guards were acting as shields, using their bodies to protect the other two. The smaller one's lower left leg was dangling at an odd angle, clearly broken. All of them were covered in a thick layer of debris dust, and a few had what looked like scorch marks on their skin.

"Spread out! Form into your groups!" Bjurstrom called out in raid chat. "Focus on the guards first. The others don't seem to be holding weapons. Start with the guard closest to the big guy. Hit them with everything you've got, and stay behind your tanks!"

Allistor decided to leave the guards to his people. They outnumbered the fomorians roughly twenty to one, and since none of the enemy were identified as mages, he had faith that the raiders could take them quickly. His concern was the glowing eyes of the Patron and Scion. They seemed likely to be magic users.

Steeling himself, Allistor cast *Mind Spike* on the little one first. It began to scream, dropping the bundle it held and thrashing so violently that the larger one had difficulty holding on to it. Allistor hit the Patron with *Restraint*, and the spell failed. He tried *Mind Spike* again, and that failed as well. The Patron was simply too many levels above him.

Thinking furiously, Allistor decided to try a more physical approach. He channeled a Flame Shot for three seconds before calling it down atop the enemy's head. It did some minor damage, and caused the Patron to lose his grip on the little one.

Wailing in anger, the Patron turned his back to the child and stepped between it and Allistor. The ground between them shivered from the sonic attack, and Allistor found himself on his knees, holding his hands over his ears and gritting his teeth. His eyes unfocused slightly, and he thought they might be bleeding. He could feel warm drops of liquid running down his cheeks.

The giant fomorian lumbered toward Allistor, a familiar-looking spear appearing in its right hand as it strode through the debris. Its mouth now closed, the sonic attack ceased, and Allistor struggled to focus. He managed to cast *Barrier* in front of himself, but had no faith that it would stop that spear. Focusing on the ground just in front of the Patron, he cast *Erupt*, hoping to slow it down.

And it did. The stone spike shot upward at an angle, penetrating the right leg of the giant and causing it to scream in pain. This time it wasn't a sonic attack, and Allistor's mind was recovering quickly enough that he could cast *Shatter* on the spear.

A second later the weapon erupted, sending shrapnel deep into the body of the Patron, his arm and leg peppered with more shards, and his hand simply disappearing into a bloody mist. The force knocked him back, freeing him from the stone spike in his leg, and blood began to spurt from the wound.

Allistor became aware of screams behind him on either side, and in front of him. A quick look around showed half a dozen of his people down, but still moving. Michael had a spear poking through his shield and shield arm, the sharp point just inches from his heart. But he was still on his feet and advancing with the other tanks.

The Scion, visible now that the Patron had been knocked to one side, was crying and attempting to get to its feet. Allistor mercilessly cast another *Mind Spike* on the creature, and it began to roll around on the ground, screaming.

The Patron used his good arm to push himself up onto his knees and shouted a short series of words. A black flash appeared in the air directly in front of him, bursting outward to strike Allistor's barrier. The spell's momentum was cut by maybe a third as the barrier burst with a small popping sound, and the spell struck his shoulder. Allistor was knocked off his feet, his armor melted and his shoulder burning. He nearly passed out from the pain, but managed to hang in there as several heals washed over him.

Staying on his back, partly to make himself a smaller target, and partly because he didn't think he could get up, Allistor cast *Levitate* on a large chunk of concrete with jagged edges. With a flick of his hand, he moved it away from the Patron about fifty feet, then reversed its direction. The momentum of the projectile as it crashed into the enemy caused him to stop the next spell it was chanting, and Allistor heard some bones break.

He quickly cast *Mind Spike* on the Patron, and this time it worked. The thing grabbed its head and shook it violently.

Fomorian Patron
Level 75
Health 119,105/165,000

Not waiting for it to recover, Allistor cast *Shatter* on that same chunk of concrete, now sitting just a foot or so from the giant. The explosion did another several thousand points of damage, and left bleeding wounds across most of its body. Allistor's own health was up to about ninety percent, and he still had plenty of mana.

Just as the *Mind Spike* was wearing off, Allistor cast *Levitate* on the Patron. He flicked one hand upward, sending the monster shooting high into the sky. Allistor kept it moving upward until it was out of his spell range, at which point the Patron slowed, then fell. Allistor estimated the fall would be more than a hundred feet, and was already anticipating the creature's death when it began to slow, using magic of its own. Rather than smashing into the rubble and bursting apart, it settled slowly on its own two feet and began chanting again.

"Dammit. This thing just won't die!" Allistor rushed toward a nearby bit of wall, about four feet of it still standing. He reached it just as the Patron completed its cast, crouched as low as he could get, and held his breath. A second later he was knocked over and buried under shattered pieces of brick as the wall fell on him. His health bar down to sixty percent, he was blinded by the brick and mortar dust in his eyes. Wiping frantically, he cast a heal on himself and began to blink rapidly, trying to clear his vision.

He could see the giant fomorian's blurry outline ahead of him. It was advancing again, limping badly and stumbling over rubble in its path. When he started chanting again, Allistor tried his new *Silence* spell. And as with the other magic attacks, it failed.

Just as Allistor was resigning himself to being blasted into oblivion, Prime darted in from his left and stabbed the Patron with his staff. The weapon didn't penetrate the skin, even with the android's considerable strength behind it. But it did interrupt the cast and give Allistor a moment to breathe. The fomorian swung its handless arm at Prime, blood spraying from the stump as it knocked the droid away like a rag doll.

Desperate for a way to stop this monster, Allistor tried something stupid. Focusing on the ground right behind the Scion, he cast *Dimensional Step*. He staggered when he appeared behind the little creature, still not steady on his feet from the hits he'd taken and the instant change of location. Drawing his sword, he cast Restraint on the Scion, then wrapped his left arm around its throat and lifted it up against his chest. He pointed the sword at its neck, and shouted.

"Hey! Over here! Surrender, or I kill this one!"

The Patron, who had been searching the ground where Allistor had just been, spun around and glared at him. It spoke in a language he didn't understand, but sounded vaguely Gaelic. Its remaining hand raised, pointing a finger at him. Allistor began to feel sleepy, and more dizzy than he'd been a moment before. Growling through the effects of the spell, he pressed his sword harder against the Scion's skin, the tip sliding into flesh.

Immediately, the spell effects faded, and the Patron dropped its hand.

"Prime, can we negotiate with this thing? Do you understand it?"

"I do not, sire. Fomorians are a scattered and reclusive race, rarely encountered. But they have a reputation of having no honor or sense of mercy." Prime moved to stand next to Allistor, all three of his eyes focused on the Patron, his shield and staff at the ready.

As if to confirm Prime's words, the Patron screamed at them, unleashing its sonic weapon again. Allistor didn't hesitate, pushing his sword through the Scion's throat, levering it forward and nearly decapitating the little creature just as the wave hit him.

The Patron's scream ceased immediately, and it flew into a rage, charging toward Allistor and Prime. Spells began to hit it from all sides. Allistor saw that his raiders had finished off the guards and had all turned their attacks on the last remaining fomorian. It mostly shrugged off the attacks, until three stone spikes shot up in front of it, one penetrating its knee, another its left foot.

Three tanks rushed forward with shields raised, slamming into the thing from slightly different directions, then hacking at it with swords while it was recovering. They quickly backed off, placing themselves between it and Allistor as the dps raiders slammed the thing with more spells. Allistor, on his knees after the sonic attack, let go of the corpse he held and tightened his grip on the sword. Casting *Dimensional Step* again, he appeared behind the Patron and swung as hard as he could manage at its spine.

The blade cut deeply, but didn't sever the tough creature's spine. Allistor quickly stepped back and stabbed upward through its back, hoping to hit something vital. He felt the blade scrape against bone, either the creature's ribs or its vertebrae, and it shuddered. He twisted the blade as he pushed further, then twisted the other direction as he ripped it out.

Finally, an experience notification flashed in front of his eyes as the Patron dropped to its knees, then forward onto its face.

Level up! You are now Level 53! You have received two Attribute Points.

Allistor sank to his own knees, his hands shaking from the fading adrenaline rush. His raid interface was showing a few more greyed out names, and he didn't want to look to see who it was. About a quarter of his raiders were at or below 50% health, and he could hear cries of pain as they were being healed.

"Get up and help." He growled to himself, pushing aside the inner conflict that threatened to disable him again. Getting to his feet, he took a few seconds to survey the battlefield, then started casting heals on those who needed them.

Michael screamed like a little girl, then passed out when Logan yanked the fomorian spear free of his arm and shield while McCoy held the arm still. One of the healers poured a potion directly onto the wound even as she cast *Mend* on it. The spear's blade had split the radius and ulna – the twin bones of his forearm – shattering both. Allistor was glad his friend was unconscious and not feeling the pain of the mending bones.

Three more raiders were beyond healing. All of them damage dealers. The fomorian guards had managed to throw several spears each before being taken down. A man with a bow still gripped in his left hand was on the ground with a spear through his forehead. A woman holding no weapons who must have been a caster took one to the chest. And a second man must have been killed after the guards ran out of weapons, as his face had been smashed in by a large chunk of concrete.

Nearly all the tanks had been injured, doing their best to block incoming projectiles while their fellow raiders burned the monsters down. One man had three separate holes punched through his shield, and through his armor. He still looked pale from the effects of the poison from three different spears. Nancy was working hard to keep his health up and get a cure potion into him.

When everyone that could be healed was back on their feet, Allistor moved to loot the two fomorians he'd killed. He received thirty thousand klax, and several items that he didn't take the time to inspect closely. He saw three pieces of armor, a knife, a head piece, and a scroll, none of which glowed with any tempting colors. When he was done, he turned toward the ship and nearly tripped over the glowing bundle the Scion had dropped. Since it was no longer in the smaller fomorian's possession, it hadn't showed up as loot.

He took a few seconds to unwrap the leather around it, then used *Examine*.

Ancestral Orb

Item Quality: Artifact

There was no further description, so Allistor wrapped it back up and stuck it in his inventory. He'd ask Master Daigath about it later.

Several of the raiders wanted to explore what was left of the lower levels, to see if there was any viable loot. Prime had one of his scouts point out the tunnel the fomorians had exited from, and McCoy led a group of twenty into the darkness.

Chapter 12

It turned out that nearly all of the underground nest was destroyed, either blown apart or caved in. McCoy's group followed the escape tunnel back to a large room that contained several beds and chests, and a rack of weapons made of the same shadow steel as the spears. All other exits from the room were caved in, and some of the debris filling the tunnels was melted. They decided against trying to dig through any of it, returning to the *Phoenix* with what loot they'd found. In addition to the weapons on the rack, which were too large for most of the humans to wield, there was a considerable bit of armor, some more of the various colored gems, and some books that appeared to be bound in goblin skin.

Kira stopped at Remy's Stronghold to drop off his people, including Lucy's body, and her daughter. He apologized to Remy, tears in both men's eyes. A few minutes later they were landing back at the tower.

Allistor gathered everyone together for a memorial service, and the names of the lost appeared on the lobby wall with the others. Dinner was a mostly quiet affair, with just a few small groups raising glasses to toast lost friends. Allistor and Amanda joined them for a short time, wanting to share a few happy memories, then retired to their quarters early.

They sat down on a sofa, Amanda with her legs across Allistor's lap, holding his hand and just letting him think. Nigel's voice, its volume low as if he were aware of their mood, broke the silence.

"Sire, Master Longbeard wishes to inform you that he is ready to meet with you at your convenience."

Allistor sighed. "That's right, I told him we'd talk about Orion and the dwarves this afternoon. Please ask him to join us here." He looked at Amanda. She was feeling their losses just as much as he was. "Or I could go downstairs if you prefer."

"No, I'm curious. I'd like to hear what he has to say." She shuffled her feet onto the floor and leaned her shoulder against his, still holding his hand as they waited for the dwarf to join them.

When he exited the elevator, he walked into the sitting area and plopped down across from them without ceremony. "I heard ye had a rough day. Never see'd a fomorian meself, but I heard plenty. I don't envy ya the experience."

Allistor removed one of the spears from inventory and passed it across to the dwarf. "They were using these. Strong bastards, able to throw these like ballista bolts. And they're poisoned."

Longbeard whistled. "Shadow steel. There be few alive that know the secrets o' forging this metal. It's said the fomorians use dark magic in the forging process. Mebbe even sacrifices."

"Well, let's hope that's not true. The metal is strong, yet light. I was hoping maybe between yourself and Master Daigath, we could figure out how to duplicate it."

The dwarf eyed the spear a while longer before setting it down. "Aye, maybe. How many o' these d'ya have to experiment with?"

Allistor grinned. "We looted a small armory after the battle, and our people looted several from the dead. We also pulled maybe a dozen out of our own wounded and dead." He paused, and Amanda squeezed his hand. He cleared his throat. "So in all maybe fifty pieces? Plus some armor.

Longbeard just nodded, then changed the subject. "Ye wanted ta know about the survey of Orion?"

"Yes. Please." Amanda answered first. Allistor just nodded his head.

"There be significant iron ore deposits scattered around the planet. Not enough for a large scale mining operation like me people had before the cataclysm. But plenty for small mining companies or individual miners who want ta hammer away at somethin', maybe train up their skills. It be the same for more precious veins like gold, platinum, and the like. And less valuable ores like copper, magnesium, cobalt." The dwarf looked up from the pad he was reading to make sure Allistor and Amanda were following along. When Allistor nodded, he continued.

"There be three saltwater oceans, and two freshwater lakes that nearly be big enough to call themselves seas, and thousands o' smaller lakes and rivers. The lumber in the old growth forests that cover most o' the land has significant value, but only if yer willin' ta let it be harvested. Which I do no' recommend. Ye might allow some land ta be cleared for farming, which I'm afraid is likely ta be yer main industry on Orion."

"That's fine, nothing wrong with farming. If there aren't too many natural predators, maybe we'll start shuttling herds of cattle, buffalo, and other stock to graze there. With the larger cargo capacity we have in the captured goblin ships, we could even go get reindeer, water buffalo, maybe elephants, if any still live."

Longbeard nodded. "Aye, and there be plenty o' factions that need land fer agriculture. Ye captured yerself a good lil gem there."

"What about the rest? Are the orbital stations up and running? The defense satellites?"

"The orbital defense be installed and operational. The trade station ye traded to Harmon be at about fifty percent operational status. One o' the housing stations be fully repaired and occupied, the other likely the same by the end o' next week."

"That's great news, Master Longbeard. And… do you have better numbers for me on the great dwarven immigration?"

The dwarf snorted. "I be wantin' ta bring three hunnert of me own family here to Earth. Some be miners, others farmers, crafters, engineers. Me own da be a distiller of fine spirits." He winked at Allistor before continuing. "As for the rest, I've received just over seven thousand requests for citizenship. They all be willing to swear the oath, live, work, and fight next to ye."

"Fantastic!" Amanda clapped her hands together, a sincere smile on her face. "Your family and your people are most welcome here, Master Longbeard."

The dwarf returned the smile, gazing fondly at Amanda as if she were his own daughter. "Even better, there are more than thirty among them that qualify as trainers for classes from Nigel's list."

"Excellent!" Allistor thumped the table with one hand, the other having been recaptured by Amanda. "And any progress on the rest of the trainers?"

"Aye, with the help o' me colleagues, we've identified and contacted nearly a hundred candidates we think would make a good fit, counting me own people. By the end o' the week we should have a complete list. I recommend ye get ta work on buildin' yer trainin' facility and housing."

"I'll start on it first thing in the morning. Thank you, Master Longbeard, for brightening a rough day for us. I'm excited to meet your family."

"Ach, no. That'd not be proper. They be simple folk, not of a level ta be rubbin elbows with a Prince such as yerself."

"Nonsense!" Amanda leaned forward. "Allistor may be forced to accept his titles and responsibilities for the good of our people, but Invictus will *not* have anything resembling a caste system, where any citizen should feel unworthy of sitting and chatting with us during a meal."

Longbeard took in the fire in Amanda's eyes, then Allistor's smile as he nodded agreement with his future princess. "That'll take some getting used to fer many o' my folk. The beastkin, too. Maybe more so for them, as they generally be treated as little better than slaves or battle fodder across most o' the Collective."

"Well, we will just have to work with all of you to help you get past that." Amanda got to her feet, causing Longbeard to do the same. "But not tonight. We'll start first thing in the morning. Thank you, Master Longbeard. We wish you a pleasant evening."

The dwarf actually bowed, then favored her with a wide smile. "Thank ye, m'lady, and the same to ye both." He turned and exited via the elevator.

"Tomorrow's going to be busier than normal. We've got a lot of projects to set in motion. I don't know about you, but I think it might be past my bedtime." Allistor stood and led Amanda toward their bedroom.

*****

Morning started at sunrise with a loud knock on their bedroom door. Allistor groaned, then asked, "Who is it?"

Without bothering to answer, their two teenage suitemates burst through the door, both speaking at once. Amanda opened one eye, and was about to scold them, when she noticed the smell of bacon and caught site of the trays they each carried.

"Next time, do not enter someone's bedroom until you are invited. And 'who is it?' does not count as an invitation. Allistor could have been walkin around with his cute lil butt hanging out." The two girls giggled. "Now, give me bacon. And speak one at a time."

Allistor and Amanda sat up in bed, propping pillows behind them as the girls placed a tray in each of their laps. There was bacon, eggs, toast, a small cup of apple and orange slices, and coffee.

"We figured out how to add even better buffs to the food!" Addy practically erupted with the news.

Sydney nodded her head. "We got a bunch of levels from the raid yesterday. Chloe was with us on the Phoenix, and we were all in the galley together, being trained. She mentioned how she was helping to raise chickens and rabbits, and maybe the big murder chickens, and her mom had been using a version of the *Grow* spell on them."

When she stopped to take a breath, Addy took over again. "So you know how we've been singing with Meg while she cooks, to increase the food buffs. Well, we thought, what if we sing to the animals? So we talked to Meg about it, and after dinner we went to see Nancy and Chloe. They had some baby chickens at their place, so we

263

sang to them while Nancy cast the growth spell. This morning, Chloe brought Meg a basket of eggs, and…"

"Taste them!" Sydney pointed at their trays, practically vibrating with excitement.

Allistor and Amanda both took a bite of eggs. They were scrambled with milk, lightly sprinkled with pepper, and mixed with diced onions. Allistor was savoring the flavor when the buff kicked in. He saw Amanda's eyes widen at the same time.

"Holy crap! Plus twenty percent health and stamina regen for twenty four hours!" Amanda beat Allistor to the punch.

The girls squealed, hopping up onto the bed and nearly upsetting the breakfast trays. Addy's smile stretched from ear to ear. "Yep! And Meg thinks if we do the same with pigs, it'll be even better. Imagine magic bacon!"

Allistor grinned at them. "All bacon is magic. But if you two can make it *super magic*, you'll be the most popular young ladies in the whole world!"

"Yessss!" Addy fist-bumped Sydney. "Okay hurry up and eat so we can take those trays back to Meg." The two girls got up and left the room, very conspicuously hovering around the sitting room and occasionally eyeing the two diners' progress.

Allistor and Amanda obligingly scarfed down their food, the bacon and coffee both adding additional minor buffs. Five minutes later they handed the trays back to the girls, who zoomed off back to the kitchen.

After getting showered and dressed, the two made their way down to the kitchen as well. They found Meg slicing and dicing ingredients like a master chef. Allistor pretended to tip-toe up close to her, making a smoochy face as he went.

"Don't even think about it, young man. My husband is due back here any second, and he's bigger than you!" She gave him a mock glare, and he took a step back. Amanda advanced in his place and gave Meg a quick peck on the cheek.

"Breakfast was delicious. And the buffs are amazing!"

"Yep." Meg nodded. "That's actually where Sam is right now. With the girls, that woman Dawn that went on the road with you, and one of the strippers from Laramie. Seems they both can sing really well, and are gonna work together with Scottie with the blue hair to see about teaching a group of kids how to sing those buffs. Then we can have kids at each property that's raising livestock or food crops singing to them as they grow. Chloe's already demanding to be part of the group after last night's results."

Allistor actually did give the woman a kiss this time, and she waggled her knife at him in a vaguely threatening manner as he said. "That's friggin *awesome* Meg! The buffs we'd get from every meal… and it'll give the kids something to do. We can have their local leaders give them some kind of daily quests for it, so they earn experience and money too!"

Amanda added, "Not to mention when they get older and stronger, we could have bards buffing every raid group with songs."

Allistor looked left and right, hunching his shoulders slightly as he whispered in a conspiratorial manner. "And just imagine what it'll do to the moonshine they're making in Cheyenne."

Meg just snorted. "Unless you're planning to help cook lunch for a few thousand people, out with you. You're holding up progress!"

After fleeing the kitchen, they walked hand in hand to Allistor's customary spot in the lobby. They sat there making small talk or answering questions for citizens who stopped by. It was sort of an informal royal court. A few folks came to them with problems like a shortage of crafting material, or a disagreement over a trade with another citizen. Amanda mostly handled the problems, leaving Allistor to jot down an updated list of things that needed his attention. The list read:

Housing for trainers, and training facility construction. Nigel blueprints?
Housing for more immigrants – (where, in what numbers?)
Talk to analysts about auctioning parts of Orion
Visit Master Daigath – more training, ask about fomorian artifact and books
Talk to Harmon about defense satellites for Earth.

As he was writing, Fuzzy wandered up and sat next to him, nudging Allistor's arm to demand ear scratches. Allistor absentmindedly obliged as he considered the list. When Fuzzy belched in his general direction, he added, *Figure out breath mints for Fuzzy* to the list with a smile. Then he mumbled to himself. "In fact..."

Pulling up his interface and going directly to the Quests tab, he generated a quest for Nancy to figure out some herb or alchemical concoction to freshen his bear's breath. He giggled when he pressed the button to send the quest, causing Amanda to look over at him with suspicion.

"What'd you just do?" She raised one eyebrow and folded her arms in front of her chest.

"I, uhmm... just sent Nancy a quest. Like, a research quest. For the good of the nation." He concentrated on not looking at Fuzzy while he spoke.

Amanda seemed about to question him further when she was approached by Lilly, who had several samples of different lace patterns in hand. "Oh! I have a fitting with Lilly for the wedding dress." Amanda was on her feet and hugging the woman.

"Hey Lilly!" Allistor smiled at her. "I meant to go see you today." He had totally forgotten, hadn't even put it on his list, but there was no need to share that information. "My armor got pretty beat up yesterday. I'm not sure it can even be fixed." He produced the burned and damaged gear from his ring and set it on the coffee table in front of him. Lilly took one look at it and shook her head. "Be easier just to make you something new. I've got some hide from the drake they killed on the roof of the tower here, and I've been practicing my enchanting. Give me a few days and I'll have something for you."

"You're the best!" Allistor favored her with his brightest smile. Lilly and her small army of crafters had worked hard to outfit all the raiders with at least one full set of armor, either leather or cloth, depending on the individual's needs. And it seemed every week the gear was getting better and better attributes.

When Lilly and Amanda departed to discuss the dress, Allistor decided to visit Harmon. Exiting his tower and walking across the courtyard, he found L'olwyn puttering around in the sunken garden, a pair of clippers in one hand.

"Good morning, L'olwyn. Have you taken up gardening?"

The analyst looked at him for a long moment, as if to say "Duh, elf here." Then nodded his head slightly. "Indeed, Allistor. Elves, or at least light elves, have an affinity for growing and managing flora. I've taken note of this garden several times since my arrival, and this morning decided to undertake its recovery. I suspect it was quite lovely before the city fell."

While he'd been talking, Allistor pulled up his Quest tab again and offered the elf a quest to do what he was planning to do anyway. Smiling, he sent it over. A moment later, L'olwyn actually chuckled. "Very good, sire. I shall endeavor to accomplish the task in a timely manner."

"Take your time, my friend. My mother loved to garden. I think the attraction for her was more about the peaceful hours she spent tending the plants, and less about what actually grew. Enjoy yourself. I'm off to talk to Harmon about buying defense satellites for Earth."

The elf froze, his eyes widening. "That would be… premature." He made his clippers disappear into his inventory and turned toward his employer. "You were able to install the system on Orion as its Emperor and sole planetary authority. Here, you are simply a Planetary Prince. And though you are the only one on Earth at the moment, putting such a system in place would be overstepping the boundaries of your authority."

Allistor hadn't considered that. He was so used to the other leaders he'd encountered following his lead, or being killed… "I suppose the system would consider that as me somehow trying to limit settlement of Earth?"

"Very likely, yes. Also, it is not only common for the Council of a planet's Princes to discuss and approve such an undertaking, but to share in the cost." The elf's smile barely missed being condescending. "Such a network is designed to encompass an entire planet, after all."

"Thank you, L'olwyn. I clearly have much to learn. I'll put this issue on the back burner for now, and move on. Also, thank you for your assistance in locating class trainers for us. Master Longbeard told me all of you pitched in."

"It is my pleasure to serve, sire. Allistor." The elf blushed slightly. He was starting to relax around Allistor and the others, but his reserved and formal nature were deeply ingrained.

A question occurred to Allistor, but he was immediately hesitant to ask the elf, remembering his status as *unhoused*. After a few seconds, he decided to just go for it.

"One other thing, L'olwyn. As I'm sure you're aware, Master Longbeard has recruited a significant number of dwarves to join us here in Invictus. And we have tens of thousands of beastkin already. I'm told that Selby is considering inviting some of her family, assuming I live through the next few months. I hope I don't offend you by asking if there's anyone you'd like to invite as well?"

The elf's eyes lowered immediately, as did his hands. His normally perfect posture sagged slightly. "As you know, other than my ship's crew, none of my House survive."

"Yes, and I'm sorry if it pains you to discuss it. I just thought there might be..." Allistor paused, then rephrased. "I wanted you to know that you're welcome to invite friends or... whomever you think might be a good fit, and willing to join us. I didn't want you to feel left out."

L'olywn continued to keep his gaze lowered. His voice was thicker and slightly raspy when he responded. "I appreciate the thought, and the gesture, Allistor. Truly. I shall... consider it." He produced the clippers from his inventory again. "If you have no further immediate needs, I should like to make a little more progress here before I rejoin Master Longbeard and the others in the trainer recruiting efforts."

"Certainly. I'm sorry to have interrupted. I hope tending this garden brings you the same peace it brought my mom. Have a good day, L'olwyn." Allistor turned around and headed back to his own lobby, his reason for visiting Harmon now moot. He felt bad for... how did that guy in one of his favorite old vids put it? Harshing the elf's mellow. Which is why he didn't ask about auctioning bits of Orion. It could wait.

Back inside, he returned to his usual spot and called out to his ever-present AI. "Nigel, you heard my discussion with Master Longbeard about housing and other facilities for the class trainers?"

"Of course, sire. Would you like me to repeat some of it back to you?"

Allistor shook his head. "No, I remember it well enough, thank you. I was wondering if you had a blueprint for the type of facility he described. Some combination of housing and training facilities? I'm assuming they would include some fighting arenas, open spaces for shooting and spell casting, reinforced rooms in case of explosive enchanting experiments, that kind of thing?

"I have three options that fit my understanding of your needs. If you'd like to return to the conference room with the pedestal, I can display holograms for you."

"Great! I'll uhh… meet you in the conference room." Allistor felt silly even as he said it. Nigel was everywhere, all the time. "Would you ask Longbeard if he has time to meet with me as well?"

Allistor headed for the elevators, and by the time he rode up to the conference room floor, Longbeard was already waiting for him. The offices and quarters the analysts had claimed were only two floors down.

The two of them sat at the table, and Nigel displayed a blueprint above its surface.

"This first option is actually a military compound, but quite closely fits your needs. It features one or more barracks buildings, within which the size and function of the residential rooms can be adjusted. There is a wall around the entire complex, which also includes a large kitchen and mess hall, armory, medical facilities, and several combat arenas."

Allistor studied the hologram that rotated slowly in front of him. It looked like some of the gladiator ludus he'd seen in movies, rather than any modern military complex. He thought it was kind of cool. Looking through the hologram, he saw Longbeard nodding his head in approval.

"This is cool, but it may be that some or all of these trainers will have families, or just won't want to live in a barracks. What else have you got, Nigel?"

The hologram went dark for a moment, and the ludus design was replaced with a much larger display.

"This one is actually a design for a guild or crafter's village. There is a central square surrounded by shops that could be converted to small training facilities for more... sedate class activities or skill training. Surrounding the central square are concentric rings or blocks of individual housing units. This could also be modified to more dense residential structures like apartment buildings if space is limited. Large outdoor combat arenas, shooting ranges, and similar components can be added in at will. And, of course, the entire village can be surrounded by a wall."

Allistor liked this one much better. The small town aesthetic appealed to him. "Very nice, Nigel. I suspect this is what we'll go with, but you have another one to show us, right?"

Once again the display changed. This time Allistor was seeing a large dome. After a few seconds, their perspective zoomed in through the surface of the dome to reveal its contents.

"This one is generally used in contested territories where attacks by enemy factions are likely. Class trainers are a resource that must be protected. Failure to do so can negatively impact a faction's reputation considerably. Toward that end, this structure features a reinforced dome with more extensive defensive measures on the exterior. The interior generally only accommodates one or two large, open spaces or arenas for combat training. The housing is built up against the lower surfaces of the dome itself, much like your design of the Stadium Stronghold. Space is at a premium, and your hundred plus trainers

would likely need to share training facilities with those of similar or complimentary classes."

Longbeard nodded his head. "Aye, buildin' underground, or in this case under a dome, makes fer tighter quarters. Ye make the dome too big, it be less sound. Ye could easily expand the available space by creatin' a second level under the first."

Allistor shook his head. "I don't think we need to go to all this trouble, do you? After all, these trainers will be our citizens, not guild contractors. And I'll protect them in good faith, just as well as the rest of my people. With shield domes and anti-aircraft batteries and such."

Longbeard chuckled. "Aye, ye do tend to go all out when it comes to defense. I agree the dome be overkill. At least fer the current situation. If ye were to, for example, annoy the Or'Dralon... well then I'm doubtin' a dome would help ya anyway!"

"So I think we'll go with option two." Allistor tried to ignore the idea of an attack by the powerful elven faction he'd already angered once. "And let's say we include housing for... five hundred. There will be a hundred and fifty or so trainers to start, but we will surely need more in the future. And there should be room for support people. Shop keepers, cooks, healers, crafters, I don't know what else." He looked at the dwarf. "Master Longbeard I'll need a list from you of which trainers are coming alone, or with families, and how many in those families. So that we can be sure to construct proper houses to fit their needs."

"Ye need to think larger, Allistor. Ye be runnin' a whole planet, plus a large chunk o' this one already. I expect that'll grow, based on what ye've done so far. The size ye propose be fine fer now. But leave yerself room to expand. Or create more than one compound."

"Speaking of room to expand, where should I put this thing? I don't think here in the city would be wise. I mean, all the hunter and ranger type classes would need a forest nearby to train in, right?"

"And the alchemists will need to find and harvest herbs and other ingredients. Ye could grow em inside the walls, but that'd take more space." Longbeard stroked his beard. "If there be a place near mountains or a mine, that'd help as well. Both fer trainin' and for resource gatherin'. Yer crafters will need materials ta train with."

"Well, the first place that comes to mind is the Wilderness Stronghold. Deep in the forest, near the mountains. But I doubt Master Daigath would appreciate all the explosions and people running around his home gathering herbs and shooting animals for crafting bits." Allistor thought it over for a while. "I'll talk to Helen. She's my minister of parks n stuff, she should know a good spot. And I like your idea of having more than one compound. We could have training rooms and residences reserved for visiting trainers, and let them move around some. I still plan to take them traveling with me to visit other human survivors. Maybe some of the larger human settlements, or friendly off-world factions, will get the same idea and hire trainers that might travel to visit us."

Allistor was getting excited about the prospect of training up all his people. Making the human race in general stronger, and better prepared, would speed up his plans to take the fight to the aliens who'd nearly wiped humans from the face of the earth. Just the few spells Daigath had taught him already had made a huge difference in the last battle.

"Master Longbeard, you mentioned before that you thought most of the dwarves would want to settle on Earth. Is that still true? And if so, will they want their own separate community? Or would they be willing to mingle with us humans and beastkin, join some of the existing communities?"

"I'll make sure me own family spreads out a bit. You humans are a bit strange, but friendly enough." He winked at Allistor. "But I be thinkin' most o' the others would prefer a community o' their own, at least to start. We can work on integrating them over time."

"Alright, then if you can stay for a short while, we'll get Helen up here and discuss locations."

Longbeard just nodded, getting up and heading for the door. "Be back in a jiffy. I'll just be poppin' down to visit lady Meg n beg some o' them tasty pastries. Can I bring ye some back?"

"Always." Allistor grinned. Fuzzy snorted his agreement, getting up to follow the dwarf. The bear never missed an opportunity to visit the kitchen. "Nigel, could you ask Helen to join us if she's not busy?"

"Of course, sire." Nigel answered as the village concept hologram reappeared above the table. A moment later, it shrank to half size and another hologram appeared next to it. This one showed a map of the former United States, with green highlights indicating each of Allistor's parks and properties. Seeing it visualized in this way, he was surprised by the sheer quantity of land he was responsible for. Something regarding the parks niggled at the back of his mind, but he couldn't quite put a finger on it.

Helen and Longbeard got off the elevator together and joined him. She already had a half-eaten scone in hand. Using her elbow to point toward the dwarf, she said "I like this guy. Every time I see him, there's treats!"

They took a seat, and she got right to the point. "Beardy here told me what you're looking for on the ride up." Longbeard gave her a sideways glance for calling him Beardy, as she looked up at the holo-map and her eyebrows bunched together for a moment. "There are lots of parks in the mountains. The biggest and most obvious being Yellowstone. But that one is, you know, basically a giant volcano. That's actually how I *thought* our world was going to end. Massive eruption, ash cloud covers the earth, blocks out the sun…"

"Uh, okay. That's terrifying." Allistor interrupted her.

Longbeard chuckled. "Do no' worry, Allistor. Me people can work with ye to relieve the pressure in a volcano. We can even make use o' the stored power ta run mining or manufacturing operations. We'll not let our new home perish so easily."

"Okay, good. Does that mean your people would like Yellowstone? It has mountains, forests, fields, natural springs... though I'm told it does get very cold in the winter."

"That would seem to be a likely option." The dwarf mused. "Be it large enough for several thousand of me people?"

Helen snorted. "Nigel, please zoom in on Yellowstone." The hologram obligingly adjusted the display so that the park filled most of the image. The nearly square park in the upper left corner of Wyoming began to show its mountain ridges, rivers and lakes. Longbeard's eyes widened as Helen added, "It's roughly two million acres, so you tell me."

"Haha! Aye, that be just enough." He winked at her. "If ye'll let me do some explorin' with a few o' me cousins, we can select a proper location in a day or two."

Allistor said, "Take one of the goblin colony ships we captured. That way you can load it up with supplies, droids for security, one of the juggernauts, whatever you need. When you establish a location, we'll create a Citadel, install a teleport pad, and so on. If you need a pilot..."

Helen interrupted. "Actually, I'd like to go. I've been studying under Kira, and I can pilot one of those ships now. Assuming Gene and his guys have labeled the controls in English, and put in proper sized seats. Unless you need me for something the next couple days?"

Allistor was slightly jealous. He hadn't learned how to pilot anything other than airplanes so far. And he kind of wanted to tag along himself. He loved the idea of exploring the majestic park, of getting away for a couple days and creating a new home for the dwarves. "Nope. Well, except before you leave, we need to select a location for the class trainer village."

The three of them returned their gazes to the map, and Helen pulled a few of the park service books from her inventory. They began to discuss locations and their features as described in her books. The map was surprisingly detailed, and a question arose in Allistor's mind.

"Nigel, these maps. Where did you get them?"

"Alpha from Phoenix, and the other ships' AI's, shared their data with me, sire. I have complete scans of the planet's surface. Minister Helen provided the information on the parks. Thanks to the orbital defense satellites, and the survey that Master Longbeard shared with me, I have even more detailed information on Orion."

Allistor leaned forward. "Nigel... can you use the images you have of Earth to locate likely human settlements?" There was a pause, and the holo-image shifted to a representation of the globe.

"I do not have detailed scans of Earth, but the goblin ship that you captured in Cheyenne did complete a

few passes above the planet under cover of night before landing. I have located several places where significant light sources were detected, implying human habitation at that time. Without a more complete scan by one or more of our ships, that is the best I can do." The globe lit up with hundreds of points of light, mostly north of the equator. Allistor's Stronghold locations, minus those in New York, showed up among the others.

"Master Longbeard, I spoke with L'olwyn this morning about my intent to place defense satellites around Earth. He informed me that I would be exceeding my authority if I did so. But what if I were to place a sensor satellite of some kind? One that could scan the planet?"

"Aye, that would be within yer rights as a Prince. As long as it has no offensive capabilities, the System will no' object."

Allistor's excitement was building! Now he could put in place a means to locate other human settlements. Or friendly alien settlements, for that matter. He was about to take one more step toward uniting the human race!

Chapter 13

Allistor left Helen and Longbeard to plan their trip after they'd agreed upon a location for the trainer's community. He was tentatively calling it Skill School, a name which nobody else liked so far. After authorizing Helen to create a Citadel on Yellowstone, and making sure she and Longbeard would take along sufficient resources that the system would allow it, he was going to take his own little adventuring party and go establish the Skill School.

But first, he was headed back across the courtyard to see Harmon.

Stepping into the shop, he was greeted by Scrit, the same imp that had escorted him on his last visit. The little creature bowed deeply, one arm behind its back and the other sweeping outward in front of him, just as before. "Welcome, great Prince, to our humble establishment. How may we serve?"

"I'd like to talk to Harmon so I can give him a whole bunch of money?" Allistor ventured, watching for the little imp's reaction.

"Ah, no wonder you are the boss's favorite Earthling. Please follow me." Scrit led Allistor across the store, which seemed a good bit busier than the last time he'd visited. Once again the imp sat him in a waiting area before going to alert Harmon of his presence.

"Allistor! Good morning." Harmon emerged from his office, a big smile exposing all of his sharp lower tusks. "What brings you to my humble establishment?" Behind him, Scrit stuck out his tongue and crossed his eyes, then turned and headed back to his post.

"I thought I'd come and taste some goblin stew, or whatever your chefs use the meat for." Allistor kept his best poker face as he stood to shake the orcanin's hand.

"Ha! Were you actually willing to partake, your reputation with my troops would increase greatly! But I suspect you are... what is that human term? Pulling my finger?"

Allistor couldn't help but laugh. "Pulling your leg. And yes, I am. I actually wanted to talk to you about satellites. For Earth, I mean. Thank you for installing the defense net over Orion, by the way."

"You are most welcome. I think I got the better end of that deal, of course. The orbital trade station is now up and running, and already making me money. There is a great deal of interest in Orion, and at least a hundred factions have sent representatives in hopes of buying land at auction. Apparently there was a leak of the planetary survey results." The merchant grinned. "Those representatives are filling my available visitor's suites, and spending money while they await the auction."

"Awesome! And speaking of spending money, I need to know two things. First is what it would cost to install a similar network around earth." He held up a hand as Harmon opened his mouth. "I know, I'm not allowed to do that. Yet. But I have plans." He winked as Harmon closed his mouth and rolled his eyes. "More immediately, I would like to put a satellite in orbit that can scan the planet for me. One I can use to find settlements across Earth. I plan to start visiting them, taking trainers and supplies with me, and do what I can to unite the remaining humans."

Harmon looked concerned. "Allistor, I can provide the tech you want, even have it in place later today. It's not expensive, really. But I... can I offer advice without you taking offense?"

"Of course, my friend." Allistor braced himself.

"Your thirst for vengeance has motivated you to achieve what you have so far. And that is probably a good thing. But your constant references to humans versus aliens and the need to make humans stronger while excluding the other settlers on Earth... it is beginning to cost you. And it will likely cost you more if you continue as you have been."

"What do you mean?" Allistor had a suspicion, but wanted Harmon to spell it out.

"Well, I'm sure you're aware that your anti-alien statements have created some friction between your human and beastkin citizens. This will likely carry over to the dwarves as well. Beyond that, the non-humans who have settled here already, or plan to settle here, are concerned that the only Planetary Prince of Earth may target them for being non-human. While I know you well enough to know that your vengeance is focused specifically on the ancient ones who acquired earth on behalf of the Collective, others are not aware of the distinction. It sounds to them as if you despise all non-humans." Harmon took a deep breath. "And, as I've warned you before, you are many, many years from being powerful enough to enact your revenge. If you ever will be."

Allistor had indeed been thinking about Gralen's previous comments regarding fear among the beastkin immigrants. But he hadn't realized his own attitude was having such far-reaching and misguided consequences.

"I'm... I'm sorry, Harmon. I'll try to do better. I'm... damn." He shook his head. "Doesn't the fact that I've recruited so many non-humans already alleviate that concern?"

Harmon shook his head. "There are many thousands of species in the Collective, my friend. Elves, Dwarves, Humans, my own people, we're all variations on the same original species. What you would call *humanoids*. The much wider variety of species that look less like you and I, who have come to Earth and not been included in your faction so far, are growing concerned."

"I understand." Allistor was getting tired of every word or deed having some larger impact on himself and his people because of the whole reputation system. "Thanks for saying something. I'll try to do better." He sat back down, biting his bottom lip as he thought.

Harmon extended an olive branch. "I might be able to assist you with a few introductions. To some of the more... alien races, for lack of a better term. You might establish friendly relations, or even trade agreements. And of course, some of them are looking to gain your favor in order to procure prime locations on Orion."

Allistor nodded. "Let's do that. Maybe in the next couple days? And uh... try to warn me about anything I shouldn't say, or do? Like, don't introduce me to somebody who will declare a blood feud if I offer to shake a hand. If they even have hands. Shit."

Chuckling, Harmon replied, "We'll start you off with the very friendliest of species. Let you get your feet wet, so to speak."

"In the meantime, you can get that satellite up?"

Harmon nodded, using his wrist device to pull up some information, then a hologram. "We have a few options, all of which you can easily afford..."

*****

When he was through speaking with Harmon, Allistor headed back to the Tower. There were arrangements to be made for the Skill School. As he walked, Allistor looked up at the sky. He still spotted the occasional ship entering the atmosphere as more colonists arrived, and wondered how many were going to be friendly, and how many would need to be eliminated. Despite Harmon's comments, which Allistor really did appreciate, he wasn't going to apologize for putting humans first.

The satellite Harmon sold him had capabilities he hadn't dreamed of. It could transmit everything from simple images of the planet's surface, to heat-sensing, motion detection down to a target the size of a housecat, and three dimensional holograms complete with topography. It could even scan below the oceans' surface and give him an accurate picture of the landscape down there. It was solar powered, and had its own collector for hydrogen molecules to use as thruster fuel when necessary, to hold its orbit or shift to a new position. And, of course, Nigel was able to assume its operation and communications functions. It had the added benefit of being able to bounce signals to areas around the globe that Redd's short wave radios weren't reaching.

Back at the tower, he requested that three raid groups of five low level citizens meet him at the Citadel in Cheyenne. He was also bringing along Amanda, Prime, and William. As they passed through the teleport and began to walk toward the waiting group, the squire practically stomped along behind him, disappointed because he couldn't join Chloe and the others in learning to be bards. He apparently couldn't carry a tune in a bucket. Allistor brought him along to distract him.

Before heading out the gate, Allistor called for a half dozen battle droids to join them, two to escort each of the small raid groups. They were going to be clearing several buildings, where the mobs, if they found any, would likely be low level. But he wanted the droids available to step in as tanks in case his people got in trouble. He,

Amanda, William, and Fuzzy would clear buildings as a fourth group.

His discussion with Helen and Longbeard hadn't offered him up the perfect location for his first Skill School compound. He'd wanted one with everything his people could need nearby, including forest, water for fishing, a mine for training, and space for farming outside the compound itself. Not finding exactly what he wanted, he was tempted to wait until the new satellite's scans could be reviewed in depth, and use that information. But time was not on his side, and he needed to get the accommodations ready for at least the first hundred and fifty right away.

So they'd chosen a safe location that offered most of what he wanted.

Right between the Citadel in Cheyenne and the Silo on the Air Force base sat the Cheyenne Frontier Days complex. It was huge, with several buildings including a rodeo/auction arena, an old west museum, an exhibition hall, and several large parking lots that accommodated hundreds of trucks with horse trailers. He intended to use the existing buildings as part of the school, and place the new compound on the parking areas.

In addition, to the east of the complex, between it and the Citadel, right next to the airport, was Lions Park. It featured several useful structures as well, like a botanical garden for the folks looking to practice herbology and alchemy, and an aquatic center, which Helen said was a building with a bunch of indoor pools and water recreation stuff. And the park surrounded Sloan Lake, which could be used for fishing as well as boating.

Also, to the north and west the complex bordered on Abscarra Lake and recreation area, as well as Kiwanis lake, next to the Cheyenne Country Club and two different golf courses. There were small wooded areas and overgrown fields where hunters and rangers could train, or farmers could use to skill up. And Helen said there was an old silver mine in Cheyenne, though she didn't know where. Allistor would have to rely on the miners, or maybe the dwarves, to locate it.

Since it was so close to the Citadel, the groups simply strolled out the front gate and down the switchbacks. He handed out bits of dragon jerky to everyone so that they'd have the buffs. There was regular vehicle traffic between the Silo and Citadel at this point, with foraging crews traversing the area regularly. Allistor didn't expect to be attacked as they walked, and suspected all the buildings in the Frontier Days complex would have been cleared already, but one never really knew.

When they reached the airport, they turned straight southwest and took a short cut across the airport's runways and open grassland. Crossing a four-lane road, they stopped just inside Lion's Park. Gathering his raiders around him, Allistor said, "Okay, let's make a loop around the lake to the south. Each group take a building as we reach them." Amanda sent raid invites to everyone as he spoke. "Keep an eye out for ambush predators in the trees and bushes. And don't get too close to the lake." He pictured the massive lake sturgeon he'd found in another lake early on.

"Call out in raid chat if you need help. The battle droids will simply observe, or move heavy obstacles, unless you get in trouble. In which case they'll step in and tank while you recover, or retreat. I want nobody getting hurt here today, understood? There's just no reason for it. If things get dicey, retreat and call for help."

His people all nodded. Most of them were between level fifteen and twenty. He took a moment to create a quest for them, in case they didn't run across any mobs that would grant experience.

> **Quest: Conquer the Frontier!**
> *Clear and secure the Frontier Days complex and Lions Park so that Prince Allistor can claim them and construct the Skill School.*
> **Reward:** *100,000 klax; 200,000xp; First in Line*
> *status when the Skill School opens.*

He hit the button and watched as everyone unfocused to read and accept the quest. Amanda snorted. "Skill school. Worst stuff-naming-skills ever." Fuzzy nodded his head in agreement. So did William.

The groups split up, walking in a wide line through the park, one group after another taking the buildings as they came. The parties ran across nothing more dangerous than a level fifteen canid that had been wandering about in the botanical garden. There were some lower level vermin that must have spawned near the end of Stabilization. In a little over two hours, the park was clear.

Crossing the next road, they moved into the complex grounds. This went much slower, as there were dozens of abandoned horse trailers to check in addition to the scores of buildings. There were more fights here, but nothing the individual parties couldn't handle. There *was* one incident where a matted and hungry-looking golden retriever was startled by one of the groups. It shot out from behind some rotting hay bales and surprised them, the groups tank screaming like a little girl. Allistor and his group came running, but by the time they arrived, his people and the dog had calmed down. The tank was on his butt, legs out in front of him, trying to tempt the dog with some jerky.

Amanda had to grab William as the boy tried to run forward to play with the dog, potentially scaring it away. Max had been a beloved member of the Warren family since almost the first day, and everyone in the group was hoping this dog would be friendly as well.

Eventually the dog's hunger won out, and it took some food from the man's hand. After that came some ear scratching, more treats, then some face licking and cheers. The dog consented to some mass petting as the group members closed in two or three at a time. Allistor kept Fuzzy at a distance.

The dog followed his new buddy the tank, getting the occasional treat as they continued to clear buildings.

By the time the day was through and the complex was clear, the pair were bonded just like Allistor and Fuzzy.

Opening his interface, Allistor claimed the complex, and spent nearly half an hour placing, then moving, all the various structures he wanted. When he finally had it right, he pushed the button, and the place was transformed. Another wall went up, surrounding both the complex and the park. He'd decided to leave the golf courses and the other two lakes open. The rodeo arena and other buildings remained, and most of the rest of the space was taken up by individual homes, sized from a single bedroom to four bedrooms. He'd added a fountain near the center, next to the kitchen and dining area, just for ambience. Around it, in a rough circle, were a row of shops that could serve as either trainer offices or crafter stations where goods could be traded or sold.

Allistor held off placing a teleport pad within the walls. There were already pads at the Citadel and Silo, and he didn't really want to put a third one so close by. It was a short walk from either facility, and he could have droids escort anyone who needed it back and forth. His next Skill School compound would have a teleport, as he planned to put it somewhere in Europe or one of the other continents. Once he had more time to research locations and find other survivors.

About half of the raiders leveled up from the quest experience, and were congratulated by the others. And everyone appreciated the extra spending money. One hundred thousand klax was nothing to Allistor, but for the average citizen, especially ones who were not normally raiders, it would buy some sweet gear, or allow them to build themselves an outpost or something.

*****

Back at the tower, Allistor checked his list again. He was making decent progress on getting things done. The next item he saw was to discuss with the analysts the details of auctioning parts of Orion. He knew that Longbeard was off with Helen at Yellowstone, and the others were probably occupied with recruiting trainers. Not wanting to interrupt that effort, he opted to go and visit Daigath. With William and Fuzzy in tow, he teleported to the Wilderness Stronghold.

There were only a few people moving around. Less than a hundred citizens had opted to live at Wilderness full time. Most of them were hunters and crafters. Others dropped by for a few days of fresh air and fishing, or to visit the place where Helen and Allistor had fought the murder chickens. It was becoming sort of a tourist attraction.

"Nigel, is Daigath inside the walls?"

"No, sire. He left before the first sunrise and has not returned."

Allistor equipped a shotgun, sliding it into its sheath on his back, then did the same with his sword. Looking down at William, he said, "We might run into hostile creatures out there, so have your staff ready." The boy was small, but he was already higher level than most creatures

Allistor had encountered in the wild. His squire nodded his head, producing his staff and gripping it tightly in both hands.

The trio exited the gate, Fuzzy taking the lead and using his sensitive nose to track Daigath. Not that they really needed it, as Allistor knew the old elf was planning to set up his home in or near the clearing on the other side of the lake. They followed Fuzzy down the slope and into the forest, the bear often meandering, sniffing at trees and munching on tasty mushrooms or berries. William snagged more than a few berries for himself, and soon had sticky juice smeared around his mouth. When Fuzzy tried to clean it off for him, the kid was quick enough to evade the tongue and the bear breath behind it.

Allistor let them take their time, as he was in no particular hurry. And it was nice to spend some quiet time with his bear and his squire. The birds sang at them from the ancient trees above, and every once in a while Fuzzy startled a squirrel or rabbit, sending them dashing away into the brush. When they reached the creek that fed the lake, Allistor was able to find a spot where several large boulders offered a way to cross. William made a big deal of hopping from stone to stone, waving his arms about as if he were off balance. Fuzzy simply plowed through the shallow water, splashing both humans with cold mountain water as he passed. Allistor stopped at the other side, producing a cantine and filling it in the creek, which was fed from snowmelt high in the mountains. Taking a sip, he broke into a smile. "Ahhhh. Nothing like fresh clean water."

William bent and scooped a handful for himself. Taking a sip, he copied his prince. "Ahhh."

Fuzzy, observing his two humans with his head tilted to one side, bent down and lapped up some of the water as well. Not tasting anything particularly interesting, he looked at the both of them for a moment, then tried again. William giggled, and said, "I think it's a people thing, Fuzzy." The bear gave something close to a shrug, and continued on toward the clearing.

It took them another half hour to reach the clearing. The first thing Allistor noticed was a series of indentations in the ground. It looked almost as if bombs had been dropped around the clearing, and it took Allistor a moment to recognize that these were spots where trees had been cut and stumps removed. Probably by Harmon's demolition droids. There was also a large patch of dead grass over to one side where the cut logs had lain, until recently. Allistor scanned the area, looking for a sign of the ancient elf as Fuzzy sniffed at the nearest of the holes. Reaching out with one sizeable paw, he scratched at the dirt, revealing a mass of wriggling insect larvae. As he quickly licked up the squirming treat, William made gagging noises.

"Ew. Fuzzy how can you eat those?"

Laughter from behind him caused Allistor to turn. Daigath emerged seemingly from nowhere, simply appearing between two trees at the edge of the clearing. "For a bear, young William, those are like candy. And they're good for him, too. They'll help keep his coat shiny and warm."

Clearly not convinced, William held his tongue. When Allistor bowed to the old elf, William copied him. "Sorry to disturb you without notice, Master Daigath. A few things have come up that I wanted to ask you about."

"A visit from my host is no bother, Allistor. Come, let us leave this scarred place. I have only just begun work on my new home, but there is a place we can sit comfortably and speak." He led them out of the clearing, back the way he had come. Slightly uphill from the clearing, and across a small brook that trickled down a rocky path, he brought them to a giant old oak tree whose thick, gnarled roots rose up from the ground and formed several comfortable spots to sit. The elf motioned for Allistor to sit first, then he and William followed.

Looking up at the branches above, the lower ones being thicker than Allistor's shoulders were wide, he asked, "Is this your sentient tree?"

Daigath chuckled, "No, though he may not be far from awakening. Another century or three, I would think. He is a great, great grandson of the awakened one, who himself is only just becoming aware. But this one will make a good home. He has already shown an affinity for being shaped." The old elf patted the roots on which they sat. "Soon I will begin to shape my home in the branches above. Now, what did you wish to ask me about?"

Allistor cleared his throat. "Well, first, I wanted to thank you. The new spells and skill you gave me made a big difference in the last battle. We went into the goblin horde's nest expecting high level goblins. Instead we found something called fomorians. They were much tougher, and they surprised us. Some of my people died as a result, but many more would have died without the magic you gave me."

"I'm sorry to hear that." Daigath looked thoughtful. "I have not heard of fomorians making an appearance in at least a thousand years. And you say they were within a goblin nest? And the goblins were high level?"

"The highest we've seen so far here on Earth. And they had a larger than normal number of shamans among them."

Daigath nodded. "It would seem the horde was in service to the fomorians. Which would imply that a noble was present, and they were establishing a clan here on Earth."

Allistor nodded. "We killed a giant one called a Patron, and a small one that was a Scion. Which is part of what I wanted to talk to you about. The young one was carrying this." He produced the wrapped artifact and handed it to Daigath.

The ancient elf carefully unwrapped the glowing stone. It was about the size of a bowling ball, though much lighter, and its surface wasn't smooth. There were thousands of tiny facets, each one refracting the emerald glow from within. As the elf studied the artifact, Fuzzy sniffed at it, then backed away and sat down. William just stared with his mouth open.

"You have indeed encountered something rare, young prince. In my lifetime I have seen only one other Ancestral Orb. That one had been captured, much like this. It was traded to an Emperor in return for his planet. Within a few days, that Emperor was assassinated, and the Orb stolen. The assassins killed more than five hundred imperial guards that day, and left no witnesses to identify them. It has often been speculated that it was fomorians reclaiming their property."

"What exactly is it? And why is it so valuable?"

Daigath rewrapped the artifact and handed it back to Allistor, indicating he should put it away. "Fomorians are an elder race, one half of a pair of races born on the same planet, who fought a war that spanned millennia. Their enemies, the Tuath De, were surface dwellers and masters of what is now commonly referred to as *light* magic. While the Patrons and Matrons of the fomorian clans most commonly favored the *dark*."

"Like good and evil." William observed.

Daigath shook his head. "No, young one. The manipulation of the motes, what you know as magic, is neither good nor bad." He paused for a moment, then reached out and took hold of William's staff. The boy let it go without resistance. "Much like your staff here, magic simply exists. It has the potential to do harm," he spun it with one hand and smacked the boy lightly on his arm. "or it can be used for more benign purposes." He extended the staff so that it touched the same spot on William's arm. A pulse of green light flowed from the elf's hand, down the staff, and into the squire's arm, healing what might have become a bruise. "The staff doesn't have an opinion either way, it simply exists as a tool."

William, who'd been scowling at the old elf and rubbing his arm, asked. "So it's the person? The one holding the staff? Or, the one using the magic, that is good or bad?"

Smiling patiently at the boy, Daigath corrected him. "Good or bad is a matter of perspective. Both sides in that war considered themselves good, and their enemies bad. Which of them were correct? If Lady Meg kills a pig to roast for your dinner, from your perspective she is doing good. But would the pig agree?" He left William to consider that, turning his gaze back to Allistor. "Dark magic is no more *evil* than light, and no more *good*. They simply are. Light magic can be used to injure, and dark magic can heal, under certain conditions. But I have digressed from your original question."

The ancient elf began to pace back and forth in front of the two humans. "The Ancestor Orb is a sort of… storage vault. Every few hundred years, a Patron and Matron produce a Scion. One with the potential to grow into a leader that could unite the clans of their race. They are trained almost from birth toward that end, and bonded to their clan's Ancestor Orb. The Orb contains the life energy and memories of past Scions. Each Scion that falls as he or she pursues their destiny is given to the stone. As they breathe their last, their essence is absorbed by the Orb, which grows larger, brighter, and more powerful. As far as I am aware, no Scion has ever succeeded in uniting the clans. Which is why, though the fomorians have always greatly outnumbered their ancient foes, they were never able to defeat them. Always there was infighting among the clans, keeping them from presenting a united front."

Allistor was fascinated. He'd always loved the lore of the games he played, and this sounded like the introduction to an epic quest. The kind that led to a world event! Looking around, he saw that even Fuzzy was leaning forward slightly as the elf spoke.

"My guess is that the fomorians traveled here to Earth before it was claimed by the Collective. Several of the elder races have visited this world in the past. They have been the basis of many of your myths and legends, yes?" He waited while Allistor nodded. "This is the case for most new acquisitions. Fomorians have been known to enslave lesser races to use as laborers and soldiers. They must have found a horde that had spawned here sometime in the last year, and used their abilities to alter and strengthen the horde. Probably killing humans within the city. That would explain the increased number of shamans among the goblins, as well as their higher levels."

Allistor was suddenly angry. "But I thought we were supposed to be safe from the other races during Stabilization."

"That is correct. There are harsh penalties imposed by the System upon anyone who is caught violating that rule. And I suspect that, in this case, you were the instrument that enforced the penalty. You say you killed the Patron and the Scion. Which died first?"

"The Scion. I took it hostage and attempted to negotiate, but the Patron attacked, so I killed the Scion, then the Patron."

"And was the Scion holding the artifact when it died?"

Allistor thought back for a moment, then shook his head. "It dropped the orb earlier, when I hit it with *Mind Spike.*"

Daigath shook his head, a look of sorrow on his face. "Then I suspect that the penalty for the clan taking action during Stabilization was the most severe. The clan destroyed, their final Scion unable to transfer its essence into their Ancestor Orb upon its death. And the orb in your hands. You did not see the Matron... so either she was killed inside the nest, or she remains alive elsewhere. Even should she live, without the artifact, her clan will wither and die."

Allistor felt his gut clench. "Unless she could reclaim the artifact, like you suspect they did with the Emperor? Which means I might have a great big green glowing target on my back?"

Daigath chuckled. "You became a target as soon as you earned your first noble title. More so now that you're a Prince and Emperor. But yes, if any of that clan lives, you now have an additional target on your back, as you say. They will stop at nothing to reclaim the artifact."

"Then how do I get rid of it? Can I destroy it? Or will it explode and flatten everything within a mile, or something."

Daigath looked horrified. "No! The power and knowledge contained within that Orb is… unquantifiable. Priceless. If you do not wish to risk retaining it for your own use, it could be used to your advantage. You could literally purchase a planet from one of the greater factions. Or commission a fleet of warships."

"What's so valuable about it? I mean, I understand its value to the clan, but what use is it to others?"

"Were you a higher level, and better trained, you could tap the stored essence within the artifact. Use it to power other artifacts, create legendary weapons, or cast immensely powerful spells. And you would have access to the aggregate knowledge of an untold number of Scions. Based on the size of the artifact, I would guess that the clan was comparatively young. Still, their race is from a planet that formed near one of the galaxy's early stars. Nearly as old as that of the elven homeworld. So even a younger clan's artifact might contain a thousand souls."

Allistor's instinct was still to get rid of the artifact. The last thing he wanted was to have everyone around him killed by pissed off fomorians trying to reclaim it. But his gamer instincts wouldn't let him not ask… "You said I need to be a higher level to use it. How much higher?"

The old elf laughed loudly. "You have done well to reach your current level as quickly as you have. But even should you maintain that pace, which you will not, it would take you fifty years or more. And even then, I am unsure a human mind would be compatible."

"Could *you* use it?" Allistor was already calculating an agreement between them.

Daigath nodded. "Indeed. I have the experience, and the knowledge, to make use of the artifact. But I will not." He saw the look on Allistor's face, and sat back down. "I am old, Allistor. Older than any other living elf, and most of the other beings in the Collective. Only the Ancient Ones, some of the elder dragons, and the Unnamed Ones who first created the System have lived longer. And no one knows if the Unnamed still live. If I desired power, I would have it. I would rule all of the elven factions, and a significant swathe of the galaxy. In fact, in my youth I dreamed of such conquest. Foolish dreams that cost me more than I will say." He paused, remembering something.

"I have chosen a different path, and prefer a simple life of observation and reflection. I have no use for the power that the artifact would grant me." He chuckled softly. "Though the idea of using the energy within the artifact to create a uniquely powerful weapon does tempt me slightly."

"Then can you advise me on the best way to dispose of this thing?"

"I will put some thought into it. Make some discreet inquiries. For now, my advice is to keep it hidden, and do not speak about it."

Allistor sighed, making a mental note to bury the thing in the lowest level of Fort Knox or something. Almost dreading any additional knowledge, he pulled the books bound in goblin hide from his ring and handed them over. "We also got these."

Daigath gazed at the books Allistor held out toward him, an expression of distaste on his face. He made no move to take the books. "Bound in goblin leather, written in blood. Those are foul things."

"Can you read them?" Allistor pushed them closer, encouraging the elf to get a better look.

"I can not. Fomorian is not one of the many languages I speak. And I know of no others who could read it, either. Though I could ask around, maybe find someone who could help you, I would prefer not to. I suspect nothing good can come of whatever is in those pages."

Disappointed, Allistor put them away, Daigath sighing in relief as if their presence had been a burden. Next he brought out one of the metal spears they'd looted from the guards. "I showed this to Master Longbeard, and he told me it was made of shadow steel. We were hoping you might know enough about the metal to help us make use of it?"

Again, Daigath looked with distaste at the item, but he did take hold of it. "Yes, I know shadow steel, unfortunately. And I will agree to help you learn to manipulate it, on one condition. You will swear upon your life never to attempt to create more of it."

Allistor looked up from the spear to the old elf's face. His eyes were hard, his lips pressed together. "So Longbeard was right, the making of this steel requires sacrificing lives?"

"It does. And that is all I will say on the matter. Do I have your word?"

"Of course. I swear I will not attempt to create new shadow steel." Allistor waited as the glowing silver light that seemed to be unique to the ancient elf surrounded them both, sealing the oath.

Daigath leaned back against his tree. "I am sure you wish further training, young battlemage. But I think we have spoken enough for today. I have much to consider, and some traveling to do. Let us return to the Stronghold together."

Without waiting for a reply, Daigath began to walk back toward the clearing and the Stronghold beyond the lake. Allistor and William jumped to their feet to follow, Fuzzy padding along in front of them.

Chapter 14

Back at the Wilderness Stronghold, they parted
ways with Daigath. Allistor decided to give William a
special treat, and a new responsibility as part of his squire
training. "I've got something to show you, but it's top
secret. Can you keep a secret? Even from Chloe and the
other kids? Even when they're talking about bard training,
and you want to show off?"

William gazed up at him, looking slightly hurt. "I
can keep a secret, I promise." He made a cross-my-heart
motion with his finger.

Allistor pretended to consider the promise for a bit,
just to impress upon the boy that he was trusting him with
something important. Though actually dozens of people
knew the so-called secret, if not hundreds.

"Alright, come with me." He led his squire to the
teleport and through to the Silo. From the pad, they took
the elevator down all the way to the lowest level. Stepping
off the elevator, they proceeded down the corridor and
through a large vault door. Right inside, they found a desk
and a military cot. Daniel, Allistor's official dragonling
wrangler, sat at the desk. He immediately jumped to his
feet and saluted when he saw Allistor.

"Sir! Uh... Prince? Sire? Welcome back."

"None of that, Daniel. Just Allistor, unless we're in
some formal court setting. This is William, my squire.
He's going to assist you in your duties from now on."

Daniel reached out a hand, and William shook it. The man's eyes widened at the strength he felt in the ten year-old's grasp. "Pretty strong grip there, William."

The boy beamed at him. "I'm almost level twenty! Been working on my Strength and Stamina."

Daniel looked up at Allistor, who explained. "Some of the kids have been coming on raids. Easy and safe way to level them up." He paused, looking past Daniel to where the dragon eggs were clustered. "How are things down here?"

"Pretty much the same, though I think they're going to hatch a bit sooner than Amanda expects. In the last week or so the eggs have begun to tremble, off and on. The little guys, or gals, inside are getting more active."

William's gaze had followed Allistor's, and when he saw the large eggs on the floor of the cavern beyond, he gasped. "Are... are those the dragon eggs?"

"So much for them being top secret." Allistor chuckled.

"Chloe told me about them. She says she's going to have a dragon of her own to raise."

"Well, we won't be just passing out dragons to everyone who wants one." Allistor frowned down at him, trying to look serious. "But *you* get to help Daniel here take care of them, and maybe even help raise them when they hatch. But like I said, you have to keep all of this *top secret*. You don't talk about the dragons with anybody but Daniel, Amanda, and me. Can you do that?"

William nodded so hard it made both men rub their necks. "I promise! What can I do? Can I hold one? Do we need to keep them warm?" his excitement had Daniel smiling.

"Well, come with me and I'll teach you everything I know about dragon eggs. Which admittedly isn't much..." He winked at Allistor, who was turning to leave.

"I'll send Amanda to check them again ASAP. Shout if you need anything at all. And make sure my squire gets home at a reasonable time every evening. Like, before dinner." Allistor didn't think he needed to say that last bit, William was a growing boy, and with his increased stats, he was an eating machine. He watched for a few seconds as the boy practically hopped all the way over to the nearest cluster of eggs, clinging to every word Daniel spoke.

*****

Baldur sat in the orcanin merchant's office. They were old friends, and the merchant made it a point to ensure that Baldur was comfortable when they met, even going so far as to install mist generators that filled his office with the soothing moisture meant to replicate his ancient race's homeworld environment.

"Your human friend is doing well for himself." Baldur transmitted through the mist, causing it to swirl slightly.

"He deserves his success, Ancient One. Allistor is a true noble, a rarity these days. He thinks little of himself, always looking to improve the lives of those he protects. Risks his own life to save others, even strangers, on occasion. I truly consider him worthy of being called friend."

"And he has great focus. At least when it comes to vengeance." The ripples in the mist held both amusement and sorrow.

Harmon nodded, a half smile tugging at his lips. "He is *quite* determined to kill you and your kin. Though I am trying to lessen his thirst for revenge, make him see that it is neither practical, nor wise."

"We have time enough to prepare for that eventuality, my friend. In the meantime, more urgent matters bring me here. What can you tell me of the fomorian encounter?"

"Nothing that you don't already know, I'm sure. Your information gathering resources are far superior to my own. Allistor went into what he thought was a goblin horde nest. Instead, he found fomorians, including a Patron and a Scion. When things calm a bit, I will have my people excavate what remains of the ground to see if they can locate the Matron. With the ordinance Allistor dropped, it may be that she was simply vaporized."

Baldur nodded his bulbous head, two of his tentacles rubbing together much as a human might wring their hands. "Let us hope you find remains. I would not like to imagine a fomorian Matron stalking our young prince to retrieve her Orb. He is not prepared, and though he himself might survive, anyone between them would perish. I suspect that would destroy him."

Harmon simply nodded, not responding for a moment.

"There will soon be two more human princes of Earth. They are gathering followers, and claiming resources, though not as rapidly as Allistor. You might encourage him to expand his holdings to other continents, otherwise our hopes for him might become more difficult to achieve."

"He's already thinking along those lines, if on a small scale. He told me recently he wants to install a defense net around Earth, and has a plan to make that happen. I'm sure he's planning some kind of alliance with other leaders, and a vote of approval. Then he'll pay for it himself, knowing him."

"That would not be such a bad thing, if our plans fail. Having control of a planet's defense net is having control of the planet, if one is ruthless enough to use it so."

"Allistor can be hard when he needs to be. He's shown that often enough. But I don't think he has it in him to become a tyrant. At least, not unless it was absolutely necessary to preserve his race. And putting him in that position would be playing a dangerous game indeed."

Baldur shook his head, all of his tentacles waving slowly, pushing the mist toward the merchant. "Let us not consider that, yet. I also wish to preserve the human race, as they are a favorite of mine. We shall let things unfold as they will, and apply pressure, or provide a small bit of assistance, here and there. If a heavier hand is needed at some point, we will consider how to proceed at that time."

"Speaking of heavier hands, do you suspect Loki of installing the fomorians?" Harmon looked left and right as if worried about eavesdroppers, despite knowing that his security measures prevented that. Even speaking Loki's name where it might be overheard could mean a death sentence.

"Oddly enough, I do not. I know he has interfered in other ways, like with Xar'Dakra appearing during stabilization. I suspect he was behind the Occulant, the Leprechauns, and the goblin colonists attacking one of Allistor's people. And, of course, it was Loki and Hel that triggered the acquisition of earth ahead of schedule, at a time when the System would view the humans' industry and pollution of the planet as grounds for extermination." The mists vibrated off of Baldur in waves of anger. "They will pay for that."

"I'm told that Loki has claimed his own territory here on Earth. A large island in the ocean to the west of us."

"He will not stop at one." Baldur confirmed. "He will claim more islands until he has secured enough land to earn the title of Prince. As he does with each new planet."

Harmon shook his head. "What is the point of that? He is already more powerful than any planetary prince. Or emperor, for that matter."

"I suspect it is simply a matter of habit, at this point. In the beginning, he played the games of planetary politics to increase his own power, and for the enjoyment of destroying other powerful leaders, friend or enemy. Now I think he just doesn't want to break the streak." He paused, his head tilting to one side. "Though, he does seem to have taken a special interest in Allistor and Earth. That may be my fault."

Harmon made a mental connection. "Which is why you're going to such efforts to assist Allistor."

"In part, my friend."

"Well, your suggestion to bring Master Daigath to meet Allistor has already borne fruit. He likely would not have survived the encounter with the fomorians had Daigath not given him some training just before the battle."

Baldur chuckled, the sound more like a gurgle to Harmon's ears. "And as usual, our young prince took a suggestion that was meant to assist him personally, and expanded it to include class trainers for everyone on Earth. This is another of the reasons I choose to support him."

"Any other… suggestions you'd like me to pass on?" Harmon grinned at Baldur.

"Yes. The Orb. Until we know that the Matron is no threat, encourage him to secure it someplace far from himself. A place with as few guards as possible, to reduce losses should she move to reclaim it. I'd rather see it returned to her than see Allistor suffer over its defense."

"And if the Matron is dead?"

311

"Then you and Daigath can guide him in how best to make use of it. I suggest a trade of some sort, and quickly. Others will learn of its existence and location, and would stop at nothing to claim it for themselves. As long as that artifact is in his possession, it is a danger to him and his people."

"Agreed." Harmon nodded. "Daigath has already told Allistor the same. And warned him that it would be decades, at least, before he could make use of its power himself."

"Thank you, my old friend. Let me know what payment you desire for your service here, and it shall be yours."

Harmon shook his head. "No, old friend. No payment needed. I like Allistor, and would help him regardless. Plus, he has gifted me a ridiculous amount of wealth in just the short time I've known him, hoping only for friendship in return."

"He has good instincts. He could find few better friends in this life or any other than Harmon, Emperor of the Orcanin."

"I am but a simple merchant here." Harmon grinned. "But I thank you for the kind words, Ancient One. May you find peace and harmony." He bowed his head. There was a faint pop, and a rapid motion of the mists as they filled in the vacuum left by Baldur's instant exit. Harmon pressed a button on his wrist, and machines began to pump the mists from his office.

*****

Amanda was examining a woman who'd been injured while clearing a nearby apartment building, when Allistor stuck his head into her infirmary office. "Hey, pretty lady!"

When both women looked his direction and smiled, he blushed slightly. "Pretty… ladies. I uh, wanted to see if one of you would like to have a quiet, romantic dinner this evening."

When both women nodded their heads, then laughed in unison, he realized he was digging himself deeper. "Er… I mean, the one of you that's currently engaged to marry me." He looked at the woman, an apologetic smile on his face. "Not that a quiet dinner with you wouldn't be lovely, I'm sure."

Now the woman was blushing, and Amanda gave him a mock scowl. "Am I that easily replaced? You cad!"

"Oh! Before I forget, Daniel needs you ASAP." He gave her a significant look. "There's been some recent activity…"

The woman on the exam table exclaimed, "Oh! Are the dragons hatching?"

He shook his head. "Is there anyone who doesn't know about our *secret* stash of dragon eggs?"

She took the question seriously, thinking for a moment before shaking her head. "No… I think it's pretty common knowledge. Everybody is excited to see whether we can tame them. Like the murder chickens. Imagine if we had murder chicken cavalry on the ground, and dragonriders in the air!"

Amanda laughed, patting the woman's shoulder. "Okay, we're all done here. Thank you. It seems I need to head over to Cheyenne right away if I'm going to be done and get back here for a romantic dinner with a semi-handsome prince!"

The two women shared a smile, and Amanda moved to give Allistor a peck on the cheek. "I'll see you tonight. Tell Meg I want the special." She moved on through the door without further explanation.

Curious, Allistor went to the kitchen to find Meg. She was coordinating the ever-growing kitchen staff in their preparation of the evening meal. The Tower's kitchen was feeding several thousand mouths three times each day, and producing remarkably good food with significant buffs each time. He was very proud of them.

"Hiya, Meg!" He gave a little wave as she looked up. As usual, she had a knife in hand.

"Allistor. Is there a problem? Have you come to tell me you just recruited ten thousand more people I need to feed in the next few hours?" Her tone was harsh, but she used the tip of her knife to stab a cookie from a nearby plate, then flick it in Allistor's direction.

He caught the sugary projectile and grinned, before taking a bite, then speaking with his mouth full. "Nope! I mean, we did just recruit several thousand dwarves, but they'll be setting up a home in Yellowstone, and cooking for themselves." He paused to swallow. "Good cookie!"

Meg glared at him, but there was a small smile on her face. "The girls baked those."

"I'll be sure and compliment them when I see them. Also, I'm here to deliver a message from her royal highness. I asked her to have a quiet dinner with me tonight and she asked me to request *the special*." He waggled his fingers as he spoke the words, giving them extra emphasis.

Meg paused her meal prep for a moment, her smile widening just a bit. "Understood."

Allistor stared, waiting for more. When Meg just resumed chopping some vegetables, he asked, "That's it?"

"Your request has been received, Prince Allistor. The meal will be prepared per Lady Amanda's specifications, and delivered to your quarters at the appropriate time." Meg didn't look up from her work.

Feeling dismissed, Allistor turned in time to see Fuzzy gingerly lifting a cookie off the plate. Both man and bear retreated before Meg noticed.

Back at his usual spot in the lobby, Allistor took a little time to talk with his people, just sort of hanging out. Fuzzy went outside to romp around with some of the kids, his new favorite pastime. The children had taken to 'kidnapping' his Fibble doll, Fuzzy chasing them down to retrieve it. The whole process involved much roaring, screaming, giggling, and slobber.

After a while, he found himself alone in the lounge area, and pulled up his interface. Something had been poking at the back of his mind, as if he'd forgotten something important. The last time that happened, he'd neglected to investigate the other Strongholds within the new Invictus City walls, and some folks had died before he got to them.

"Investigate!" He shouted, causing some folks crossing the lobby to start, then stare questioningly. He gave an apologetic wave, then focused on his interface tabs. He was looking for old notifications regarding his parks. Ones that he'd tagged and set aside when Helen first awarded him the whole list of park service properties. It took a minute, but he found them.

"Let's see here…" He mumbled as he scrolled through the notifications. The System had alerted him when he took ownership of the parks that there were trespassers in several of them. Just like with the Lakota tribe he'd encountered at Thunder Basin, these people were probably getting hostile notifications every time they entered or hunted on the parkland. Which meant that they likely felt a little hostile toward Allistor in return.

Leaving the lobby, he took the elevator up to the conference room with the pedestal, and sat at the long table. "Nigel, please display a map delineating all of the parks I own." A thought occurred to him. "Do you have access to my notifications? Can you highlight the parks that have trespassers?"

As a map of the continent flashed up, including the Hawaiian islands, Nigel replied, "*I do not normally have access to your interface or notifications, sire. But as you've asked me to retrieve information from them, I have limited access that allows me to do so. Much as I am able to share enemy locations to your interface map when requested.*" As he spoke, the blue hologram map developed green shaded areas signifying each of the parks. A moment later, several of them were marked with a red dot. Nigel didn't bother to explain the marking.

"Thank you, Nigel. Good to know."

Allistor examined the map, using hand motions to zoom in and out, or move the perspective in various directions. There were more red dots than he expected, and another question arose. "Nigel, can you add the dates of the first trespass notification for each park?"

"*Certainly, sire.*"

Each of the red dots now had a date underneath it in gold lettering. The dates were all three-digit numbers. It took Allistor a moment to realize that they corresponded to the number of days since Earth was seized and transported. Earth's old calendar system had been tossed aside, and a new one put in place.

It was easy enough to identify the date that Helen had made him a prince by assigning him the rights to all the parks. The vast majority of the notifications were from that date. But about a third of them had more recent dates marked, including one that was very recent. "So, people are moving into the parks post-stabilization. Which means they either didn't have a safe place, or they decided to abandon it once the System stopped spawning new monsters."

Allistor decided to take that as a good sign, imagining people spreading out into the open areas of his parks to do some farming. Something that would have been difficult and dangerous during stabilization, especially if the people were low level.

The closest park showing a recent notification was Fire Island National Seashore, just east of old New York City, running parallel to the southern shoreline of Long Island. Allistor checked the time on his interface.

"Nigel, where is Kira?"

"*She is aboard the Phoenix, performing drills with bridge crew trainees, sire.*"

"Please connect me, Nigel."

It only took a few seconds for Kira's voice to fill the conference room. "What's up, boss?"

"Feel like taking a short hop out to the east? I have trespassers to investigate at a bunch of the parks, and Fire Island is the closest. We can hop over, talk to whoever it is, and be back for supper."

"Sounds good to me. See you in a few."

Allistor was already up and moving, stepping onto the elevator that Nigel had ready for him. When he got to the ground level, Fuzzy was still playing with the children, and Allistor decided to leave him to it. Five minutes later he was aboard the *Phoenix* and heading up to the bridge as Kira lifted off. When he arrived on the bridge, he was surprised to see several kids at the various stations.

Kira didn't wait for him to ask. "Turns out, as a Master Instructor with the Pilot class, I can give quests to learn the various skills required to operate the ship. And they get the same skill level bonus you got when I started teaching you to fly. Let me show you."

Quest Received: Fly Like An Eagle
Pilot Kira has offered you a quest. Learn to pilot the Phoenix.
Reward: 100,000xp; Aviator Skill Level Increase; Ability to pilot space vessels up to and including Galleon Class. Accept? Yes/No

Allistor selected yes, then hopped into the captain's seat when Kira vacated it. She took up position next to him, and walked him through the controls as the ship hovered a thousand feet above the parking garage.

"This is... a lot like some of the flight simulator games. Except in three dimensions with holographic controls." Allistor mumbled, tentatively touching the holo-controls where Kira indicated.

"This is all just to help you learn the skill." Kira nodded her head in approval of his actions. "You could technically just ask Alpha the AI to take you to the spot you indicate on the map, and the ship can fly itself." As she spoke, she made a motion in front of Allistor, and a map hologram appeared before them both. There was a flashing golden dot on top of the Fire Island park. "But for our purposes today, you use these thrusters to alter our heading, and then these to move forward and adjust our speed..."

In all it took about ten minutes for the *Phoenix* to make the trip to their destination with Allistor at the controls. Kira had him stop, turn, and go the wrong direction a few times, then correct his course, reminding him that navigation was a big part of piloting. Under her direction, he carefully landed the ship in a vacant lot not far from a lighthouse on the narrow strip of sand that made up the island. Allistor was disappointed when he didn't get a quest completion notification, or a skill level up. It seemed he needed to do more flying.

Kira remained on the ship with the kids, continuing their training as Allistor used the smaller ramp to exit the ship. Taking a moment to make sure the immediate area was clear of any dangerous critters, he took in the sight of the waves lapping along the beach, inhaling the clean salt air.

Kira's voice came through the radio earpiece. "Our sensor technician in training says there are three infrared signatures inside the lighthouse. Probably human."

Allistor grinned. The sensor technician in training was a little girl about seven years old.

"Thank you, Sensors. Great job!" he called back, knowing Nigel or Alpha would transmit his reply for all the crew to hear.

The lighthouse and its accompanying building were less than a hundred yards away to his east. Hoping to make friends of whomever was inside, he elected not to equip a weapon. But not being a total idiot, he did cast *Barrier* in front of himself as he walked.

Allistor was less than halfway there when a door opened and an elderly man stepped out. He stood nearly six feet tall, his back and shoulders still straight. Dressed in khaki pants and a plaid shirt, he had a full head of long white hair that fluttered slightly in the breeze. "That's good, hold it right there!" he spoke just loudly enough for Allistor to hear, his gaze flicking around nervously. "What do you want?" A shotgun appeared from behind his back, pointed at Allistor.

"I came to introduce myself. I'm Allistor. You may have heard of me?" Allistor kept his empty hands up where they could clearly be seen.

The shotgun went from being held at hip level, to tight against the old man's shoulder as he took better aim. "The asshole we keep seeing notices about." It was a statement, not a question.

"Uh, yeah. That would be me. I can explain about those. Any chance you might lower that weapon so we can talk? What's your name, by the way?"

"You can call me Jones. At least until I blow yer head off. This is *my* place, no matter what them damn messages keep sayin. Leave. Now."

Allistor kept his hands up. "I officially grant my permission for mister Jones to occupy this property." He watched as the old man's eyes unfocused for a second.

"Well la dee da... you got rid of the whole trespassing nuisance. So what? Give me one reason I shouldn't still blow your head off right here and now."

Allistor was starting to lose patience with the cranky old fart. "Okay, first, it probably won't kill me. Second, it'll piss me off, and make us enemies, and I'd probably have to kill you. Which might anger whoever else is in there with you, and make *them* want to kill me..." He took a deep breath. "Look, I really do just want to be friends."

"How do I know this ain't just a trick to get me off yer land?"

Allistor lowered his hands. "Look, Jones. I already own this land, along with every national park in what used to be the United States. Do you know how much land that is? Millions of acres. I'm not here about land. I'm here because the System sent me a message that there were trespassers on this particular land... and that's you. *You* are what I'm interested in. I mean, whatever humans I found here. I'm trying to keep as many of us survivors alive as possible. Help us all grow stronger. So I came here to see you. See what I can do to help you."

Noting the man's expression hadn't grown any friendlier, he nodded toward the ship behind him. "If I wanted you gone, I could have just hovered over this place, blasted it into tiny bits, and gone on with my day, instead of walking over here and dealing with your cranky old ass face to face."

Jones chuckled, lowering his weapon. "Good point, son." He stepped forward a single step, clearing the doorway, and motioned for Allistor to approach. When Allistor got close enough, Jones extended a hand. "Sorry about that. It's a rough world out here, and a body can't be too careful."

Allistor shook his hand, noting extensive callouses. "I hear you. And like I said, that's why I've come. I'm forming a nation of survivors, and bringing in as many as possible. We've got safe places to live and work across the country, from coast to coast. The nearest is in what's left of Manhattan."

Jones had continued to scan their surroundings as Allistor spoke, clearly uncomfortable.

"Is there something in particular you're worried about? Has something been attacking you?"

Jones nodded. "More than one thing. We're kind of exposed out here. Those canid things roam up and down the beach, eating anything that washes up. There's things out in the water, too. And last week I swear I saw a dragon fly overhead."

"Would you feel better if we talked aboard my ship? Nothing's going to attack it, except maybe that dragon. And it wouldn't last long."

Jones considered it for a moment. "Come inside. It's safe enough in here." He motioned for Allistor to step through ahead of him. Releasing his *Barrier* spell, Allistor did just that. When his eyes adjusted to the dimmer light inside the building, he saw two women, obviously a mother and daughter by how closely the younger resembled the elder. "My wife Carrie, and my daughter Kaitlyn."

Both women smiled nervously at Allistor as he waved hello. Carrie motioned for him to take a seat in a wooden rocking chair near the sofa where they sat. "Please, have a seat. Welcome to our home."

"Thank you." Allistor sat, folding his hands in his lap as he looked around. The place looked old, like historic old, pretty much the way you'd expect the inside of a lighthouse to look. Everything was crafted of dark wood, oiled until it shone. The windows were round, like portholes, and set high on the walls. Allistor assumed that was in case of floods from heavy storms.

Jones quickly filled in his wife and daughter, and Allistor gave them his standard recruitment speech. When he was through, he offered, "You are all welcome to join us as citizens of Invictus and live in whichever location you like. Or you can remain here, with my permission." He watched as the two ladies got the same notifications the old man had gotten a few minutes earlier, officially no longer trespassers.

Jones grunted. "This place has served us well enough since we got here. But I ain't all that attached to it." Both women nodded.

Curious, Allistor asked, "Yes, I noticed you are sort of recent arrivals here. Where were you before?"

Carrie answered, "Here and there. My husband is a sailor and fisherman. We've spent a good part of the last year on the water, moving from island to island, port to port. Only hitting dry land when we need supplies."

Allistor didn't remember seeing a boat when he was outside, but he figured it could have been docked somewhere on the leeward side of the island. "And... you always wanted to live in a lighthouse?" he nudged her, smiling as warmly as he could.

"Ha!" the old man thumped the arm of his chair. "You know the expression 'any old port in a storm'? Well, we got run aground in a storm a few weeks back."

Kaitlyn shook her head. "You know it wasn't a sandbar, or a rock. It was one of those monsters."

Jones looked at his daughter, shaking his head. Allistor, though, was nodding. "I've run across at least one of those things. Out on the west coast. It was called a Mosasaur, and it was bigger than the two hundred foot boat we used to catch it. I nearly shit myself when I saw it." He bobbed his head slightly, looking at Carrie. "Excuse my French."

The woman laughed, a light and pleasant sound. "I'm married to an old sailor, young man. Don't mind your language around me."

Jones was more serious. "You went out *fishing* for one of those things?"

Allistor grinned. "It was sort of self-defense. I created a Stronghold called Pelican Point out on an island just off the Santa Barbara coast. My guys... uh... liberated a small fleet of boats from the marina, and were taking them to the island to use for a fishing fleet. We planned to provide fresh fish for the rest of our people. Anyway, one of those sea monsters took out one of the smaller boats as they were making the trip to the island. We figured if we were going to operate any kind of fishing fleet, we needed to get rid of it."

Seeing all three of them leaning forward with interest, he continued. "We had this big research vessel that was a trawler in a former life. Had a couple big cranes on it. So we went fishing. Used bait with explosive compound strapped to it." Allistor didn't know these folks well enough to explain that the bait was a goblin. "Caught a massive shark by accident. Thirty feet long. I thought *that* was scary enough. But the most experienced fisherman on the boat said we should leave it in the water, as bait. And a short while later this massive monster bit the shark in half. We set off the explosive, and boom! Sushi for everyone for like a week."

Jones look at him, skepticism clear on his face. "I'm betting it wasn't that simple."

Allistor nodded. "Yeah, that was the short version. Let's just say I needed clean shorts afterward, and it nearly broke our boat in half."

"Well, our boat just got bumped by one of those things, and it did enough damage that we barely made it to shore before she sank." Kaitlyn said. "I'd be fine with never going out into deep water again."

The old man sat quietly for a moment, then asked, "And you say you've set up a fishing fleet out there?"

"Well... we have a bunch of boats. Lots of fishing poles, a few nets, and half a dozen guys who know how to drive a boat. I don't know if it qualifies as a fishing fleet. It's also doubling as our navy, by the way."

Jones looked at his wife, who nodded. "I think we'd like to join you, if you'll have us. As long as we can go to... what did you call it? Pelican Point?"

Allistor warned them. "You need to know, there have been some big earthquakes out there. The Stronghold is high on a cliff, on pretty solid bedrock. But tsunamis are a very real threat. It might be safer to live somewhere else and commute to work each day through the teleport pads."

Kaitlyn snorted. "Just casually throw it out there that you can 'beam me up, Scotty' all over the place. Do you have hearthstones, too? Like, just close your eyes and port to your home base?"

"Ah, a fellow gamer!" Allistor smiled at her. She was maybe a year or three older than him, and cute.

Blonde hair bleached nearly white by the sun, and a deep tan.

Jones beamed at his daughter. "She sure is. She's what kept us alive and safe in the early days."

"Well, sorry to disappoint. No hearthstones. But we do have teleportation between most of our facilities that are Stronghold sized or larger. And, you know, spaceships."

And just like that, Allistor had increased his population by three.

Chapter 15

Allistor and Amanda were both back in their private quarters in plenty of time for supper. They were nestled together on a sofa when Nigel announced that their meal was on its way up from the kitchen. Allistor looked at Amanda, one eyebrow raised. "The special?"

"You'll see." She gave him a small smile. "I knew Meg wouldn't spill the beans."

The elevator doors opened, and two of the kitchen staff wheeled out a cart, upon which sat several covered dishes and a pitcher, along with the usual cups, flatware, napkins, and plates. Without a word, they guided the cart over to the spot Amanda indicated, then retreated back into the elevator.

Amanda got to her feet, pulling Allistor with her, and walked over to the cart. "I asked Meg to make this particular meal for us once in a while, when we need to be reminded..." She looked expectantly at her prince.

Allistor, now more curious than ever, sniffed in the general direction of the cart. When his nose couldn't identify anything in particular, he reached out and lifted one of the dish covers. His brow furrowed in confusion for a moment, surprised by what he saw. Reaching out, he poked at it with one finger, then lifted part of it.

"Is this... a peanut butter sandwich?"

Amanda beamed. "Peanut butter and orange marmalade, to be exact. The peanut butter is from a jar that Meg and I grabbed from that first convenience store we found after the void titan smashed the town. I stashed it away when you built the Warren, and food started coming in pretty regular. The marmalade is actually new, made from the oranges that Nancy's been growing. But with all that we have now, this tower, the small army of hunters and farmers feeding everyone, even a luxury space yacht, I thought it might be good to have a little reminder of the days when we would have considered this sandwich a feast."

Allistor set down the dish cover and hugged her close. "You are amazing."

"Somebody has to keep you in line, prevent you from going full Fancypants." She poked him in the ribs gently, then reached for another cover. "But wait… there's more!" She lifted the cover, exposing a pair of Ho-Ho's on a plate.

Allistor snorted. "I would have killed for those back then. Like, actually shot a guy in the face to get my mouth around that sweet chocolate goodness."

"Right? I had such chocolate cravings in those early days. You don't know this, but when we went out foraging, I took ridiculous risks when I thought there was a chance I'd find chocolate."

Allistor reached for the last dish cover as he replied, "Me too. I think we all did. Except Dawn. She was fascinated with those pink snowball things." He lifted the cover, and there sat a small package of teriyaki beef jerky. "Yessss!" he grabbed the package and, one arm still around Amanda, used his teeth to rip it open. He just stood there for a moment, inhaling the scent of year-old jerky wafting out of the bag.

"No hogging! Your better half wants some jerky!" Amanda's hand brushed past his nose as she reached in and claimed the first piece.

"Fine, but I'm starting with a Ho-Ho! I'm the prince around here, I can eat dessert first if I want to!" he handed her the bag of jerky and snatched up the tubular snack cake, biting off half of it and moaning at the flavor.

The two of them carried the food and drink back to the sofa, and savored their simple meal, feeding each other messy bits of sandwich and pieces of jerky. Amanda caught Allistor eyeing her Ho-Ho several times, and moved the plate out of his reach.

They'd just finished eating and were settling back for some full-tummy sofa cuddling when Nigel's voice came down from above. *"Pardon me, sire, Lady Amanda. I have an urgent request to speak with you from Eric in Detroit."*

"Put him through." Allistor sat forward, looking at the ceiling as if Nigel were up there somewhere. Amanda's grip on his hand tightened.

"Allistor? We've got a… shit, I don't know what it is. But I'm guessing it's a problem. A big problem." Eric was speaking quickly, breathing hard, clearly uneasy.

"What kind of problem? Are you under attack?" Allistor was on his feet now.

"Maybe? There's this big ship... orb... ball. I don't know what it is, exactly. Just came down out of the clouds and is hovering over Lake Huron." He paused, and Allistor could hear him gulp.

Amanda looked confused. "Eric, you're in Detroit, right? Lake Huron is north of you by several miles."

"Roughly sixty miles." Eric confirmed. "This thing is... big. Like, it should have its own gravity, big. Right now it's just sitting in the sky, but it's damned scary."

"Nigel, please contact Harmon and patch him in to this conversation." Allistor asked. They waited for a few seconds, then Harmon's deep voice rang out in the room.

"Allistor? Is everything okay?"

"I don't think so, Harmon. Eric, please repeat what you've just told us."

When the man mentioned the size and shape of the vessel, Harmon growled what could only be orcanin curse words. When he was done, he added, "We need to get there now. You bring the *Phoenix*, I'll get my ship. Tell Gralen and Gene we're going to need *Opportunity* and the goblin ship *Bellerophon*, too. Quickly!"

Allistor and Amanda were moving toward the elevator. "Eric, hang tight. Keep an eye on that thing, and call back if there's any change. Nigel, get Gene and Gralen onto their ships and on their way to join us. Tell them I need them *right now.* You can pass along what Eric has told us."

Not sure what they were facing, Allistor added, "Nigel, give me loudspeaker, everywhere." A moment later, as the elevator sped toward the ground floor, he broadcast. "Listen up everybody. We've had a sighting of a massive spherical ship hovering over Lake Huron in Michigan. We don't know for sure that it's hostile, but it seems likely. I need any raiders who are geared up and ready right this minute to join me on the *Phoenix*, or hop aboard the *Opportunity* or *Bellerophon* in the next five minutes. Volunteers only, this is not an order. We're going to go look at this thing, and for all I know it'll blast us out of the air."

When the elevator doors opened, he already saw Bjurstrom, McCoy, Goodrich, Sam, Meg, the girls, and several others running toward the lobby doors. He and Amanda dashed to catch up with them, and others were filling in behind. More than fifty of the regular raiders sprinted the four blocks toward the *Phoenix*. They were quickly joined by a horde of orcanin warriors led by Harmon, the massive soldiers' footsteps making broken glass rattle in nearby windows.

"What's going on?" Allistor asked Harmon as they approached the garage.

"My guess is that it's an Araneae ship. A harvester. They could not have purchased permission to harvest resources on such a scale this quickly, so they are probably poachers."

Amanda asked "Araneae?"

Harmon looked over at her. "You would call them… giant spiders? Round bodies, eight legs, armored exoskeleton. Similar to the Octians whose brandy you tasted, but more civilized."

"Oh, hell no!" Meg stopped running and was about to turn around when Sam scooped her into his arms and kept going. They were nearing the garage now. The elevator doors opened, but Harmon's troops just kept charging up the ramp. The humans packed themselves into the elevators, Meg smacking Sam about the head and shoulders and cussing at him.

Harmon, following his troops up the ramp, shouted, "Talk more from the ships!"

Allistor and the raiders boarded *Phoenix* a minute later, most of them remaining in the cargo bay where Bjurstrom and the other airmen organized raid groups, as Allistor, Amanda, Ramon, Nancy, Meg, and Sam dashed up to the bridge.

"Taking off!" Kira's voice echoed through the ship's corridors as the *Phoenix* lifted off the ground. Stepping onto the bridge, Allistor could see on the viewscreen that Harmon's ship was already airborne and heading off toward the northwest. Kira quickly followed his lead.

"Alpha, can you connect us to Harmon, please? And patch in Gralen and Gene, as well."

"Of course, Prince Allistor. One moment."

First Harmon's face, then the others' appeared on the center viewscreen. The remaining screens still showed the view outside as they followed Harmon toward Detroit. The moment Gralen's face appeared and he saw the others, he said, "Sounds like the big bugs. You agree, Harmon?"

The orcanin nodded his head. "My scout ship will be there in a moment, and we'll know for sure."

"Big bugs?" Gene asked, his eyes wide. Meg cursed quietly behind Allistor.

Harmon looked at his wrist, then grimaced. "Confirmed. It is an araneae harvester, one of the large ones. Hovering over a vast lake. Presumably, they intend to harvest the water and fauna within." He paused, registering Gene's question. "The araneae are the largest of the insectoid races. Both in individual physical stature, and in population across the Collective. Hence the term 'big bugs'. A relatively peaceful race, they breed quickly, each female hatching a brood of several hundred every few years. When there is an unusually rapid population increase, they colonize a new world and harvest its resources. Generally, they purchase these worlds legally. But when they become desperate, their base survival instincts override their fear of reprisal, and they become poachers."

"Nope. Giant spiders laying hundreds of eggs? I'm out." Meg turned to leave the bridge, Sam grabbing the back of her shirt and holding her in place. "Allistor, you just use the fancy guns on this ship and blast that thing out of the sky, and we can all go home." She looked suspiciously at Sam. "And no, we are *not* gonna be cooking spider meat!"

Harmon's head shook on the screen, even as he chuckled. "Their meat is quite tasty, Lady Meg. A chef with your skills could make some wondrous dishes..." His voice faded as she glared at him. Clearing his throat, he changed topics. "I doubt we have the capability to shoot down a large harvester. You will see for yourselves, momentarily. And even could we accomplish the task, it would devastate a large swath of land around the lake."

Ever the curious engineer, Gene asked, "Just how large is this thing?"

Harmon pushed a few buttons, and a hologram appeared on the screen where his face had been. It showed a nearly spherical structure with seams along its sides. "In your earth measurements, this harvester would be approximately one and one half miles in diameter." A red line stretched across the image at its widest point.

"Holy death star, Chewy." Sam mumbled, wrapping a protective arm around Meg, who had turned back to view the image. She elbowed him in the ribs.

"Did you just call me a wookie?"

Ignoring them both, Allistor asked "How would we fight a thing like that?"

Gralen actually responded before Harmon could. "Harvesters usually have minimal armaments, and those are mainly lasers meant for cutting stone or ice into easily loaded chunks. Still, one or more of them hitting our ships would be bad. As for taking it down, they are compartmentalized, with several outer layers of the sphere being storage bays. So doing any meaningful damage to the ship would require penetrating deep into its structure. If those bays are filled with water, for example, penetrating becomes exponentially more difficult."

The bridge of the Phoenix went silent as they reached their destination, and the size of the vessel in front of them hit home. The sun was setting, and the shadow cast by the harvester stretched further than Allistor could see. He couldn't put its size into words, couldn't find anything to compare it to.

Meg helped him out. "It's a damn floating egg-shaped mountain. Full of spiders. That's it. Time we all moved to Orion. I'm not staying here with those things." Even as she spoke, the vessel began to shift. The seams along its sides widened, and within seconds there were eight appendages unfurling from the main body and beginning to extend downward toward the lake.

"*What the actual hell is that!?*" Meg was nearly screaming now, moving behind Sam and sticking her head out under his arm. The harvester now resembled a gigantic spider god floating above the water, the sunlight highlighting its matte black surface.

Bjurstrom, who had just joined them on the bridge after organizing the raiders, added. "Yeah… no. That ain't right. How is a giant planet-eating spider even a real thing?"

"Planet drinking." Gene corrected him absently, their ship having just arrived as well. "It's here for the water."

"Yeah, that makes a big friggin' difference!" Meg grumped from behind Sam.

Grinning at Meg, Harmon said, "Allistor, if you would allow me to make contact? I have hope that we can resolve this without violence."

"Please." Allistor nodded, leaning against the captain's chair where Kira was huddled, feeling much the same as Meg about the ship in front of them.

Harmon's voice took on a formal tone, and he spoke loudly, the authority behind his voice unmistakable.

"Araneaen harvester, this is Harmon of the orcanin. I am here with Allistor, sole Planetary Prince of UCP 382, also known as Earth. Please respond."

There was a brief delay, then another face appeared on the viewscreen. Sam turned and clamped his hand over Meg's mouth even as she was taking in a deep breath to scream. The face was clearly insect in nature, most resembling a spider. It had multiple eyes in clusters across the upper half of its head, above a set of mandibles that bracketed a small mouth full of sharp...somethings. Allistor didn't know what to call them. They twitched as the creature spoke.

"Harmon, your name is known to us. Why do you seek our attention?" The voice sounded as if a dozen creatures spoke in unison. Allistor wondered if that was actually the case. Did they operate with some sort of hive mind?

"As I'm sure you are aware, this planet is newly stabilized, and is undergoing its first wave of colonization. It seems unlikely that the araneae have secured legal rights to harvest resources so quickly."

"We grow." The chorus of voices answered as the mandibles twitched. "We must harvest. We must have water and food, or the new generation of hatchlings goes feral. Many will die." A limb moved into view and pressed something off-screen, and a moment later the spider ship began to shift again. Four of the limbs that had been extended downward now lifted to point at each of the ships hovering around it.

"Do not interfere. We *must* harvest."

Harmon shook his head. "Please, wait. Allow us to discuss your situation. We do not wish violence between our races."

The araneae's face disappeared. Harmon let out a long sigh. The harvester's arms remained where they were, and did not fire.

Amanda was the first to ask. "Feral hatchlings?"

"Araneae are an intelligent race, and as I mentioned before, generally peaceful. When their offspring hatch, they have a fierce instinctive hunger. They must consume food and water sufficient to fuel a growth spurt that occurs within hours of their hatching." Harmon paused. "If sufficient resources are available to fuel this growth, they quickly mature into normal, sane adults. However, if there is a shortage of either food or water, they will be driven to find it anywhere they can. Most commonly, the hatchlings swarm their brood mother and any other adults nearby, consuming them for their flesh and fluids. If that still doesn't suffice, the strongest among them will begin killing and consuming their broodmates."

Gralen added, "And in that situation, if there is a shortage, the adults have to choose between allowing the hatchlings to run amok, or destroying them before they hatch."

"Sounds to me like there are too damn many of them already." Meg tossed in her opinion. "I say let them kill the nasty little eating machines with fire before they hatch." Most of the heads around the room nodded in agreement.

"As I said before, even were we able to destroy this harvester without suffering losses ourselves, imagine what will happen when it drops from the sky. The lake water would inundate the land for miles around. The earth would crack and shake, and a dust cloud would blot out the sun for days, if not weeks. All of that is assuming the harvester just falls, without its engine core exploding."

Allistor looked from the ship to the lake below. He thought he remembered from school that Michigan's lakes held something like a quarter of the world's supply of fresh water. And he didn't know the math, but it looked to him like the harvester could carry away a large portion of this lake.

"Harmon, is it safe to assume that they don't really need fresh water? They have a way to purify seawater, for example?"

"Of course. The harvester likely has such tech built into its structure. As well as ore refining capabilities."

"And... what is the penalty for them, being caught poaching like this?"

"Severe." Harmon shook his head. "The Collective will confiscate this harvester, should it survive any conflict that may occur here. Its crew of approximately a thousand araneae will be put to death, and their planet of origin cut off, a full trade embargo and military cordon put in place until penalties and fines are resolved."

"Why would they risk..." Gene started to ask, but Harmon cut him off. "They are aware of the risks. And the odds against their success. But they are not thinking rationally at the moment. Their own biological imperatives are flooding their systems with chemicals that drive them to provide the needed fuel, no matter what."

Allistor had a couple more questions. "Let's say we give them water. Is this enough? Or will they be back in a month for more? And how much are they planning to take?"

Harmon looked down at his wrist device. "A harvester this size has a capacity of... approximately two hundred million cubic feet of storage, or one and one half trillion gallons. As for the sufficiency of that amount, I don't think it matters. Even should you allow them to take

341

the water they need and go, you don't have the authority to approve the harvest. The Collective will punish them for the theft, and they will not be returning."

Gene coughed, raising his hand, then blushing. "Uh, I just did a little quick math. One and a half trillion gallons from the Earth's oceans isn't a big loss. Something like one millionth of one percent of the existing volume. Sixty percent of the planet is covered by quintillions of gallons of ocean water.

Allistor looked at Harmon. "I know I don't have the authority to authorize a harvest. But what kind of System-imposed penalties would I face if I just don't prevent it, and convince them to take water from the ocean, instead?"

Harmon thought it over, as did Gralen. "None that I'm aware of from the System. There will be factions who won't agree with your actions. Mainly those who don't like or approve of the araneae." Harmon concluded.

Gralen added, "Taking on a harvester with the ships we have would almost certainly result in losses. A wise leader would avoid that if possible. And since you are a mere prince…" The wolverinekin grinned, exposing sharp teeth. "It is not your responsibility to police the poachers. The Collective has been notified, so your obligations are fulfilled."

Allistor took a seat at a nearby station. He was feeling each second that ticked by as he considered options. Finally, he made a decision.

"Let's offer them this. We will agree not to attack, if they allow us to escort their ship out into the middle of the Pacific and harvest there. They will sink the ship gently into the water, so as not to cause any tsunamis, and raise it just as gently when they're done. In return, I ask that we agree to discuss a trade agreement, or possibly even an alliance, at some future date."

Harmon chuckled. "Very good, Prince Allistor. I will attempt to make such arrangements." A moment later the spider face reappeared on the screen. It seemed even more agitated than before. Harmon began. "The honorable Planetary Prince Allistor has extended the hand of friendship to the araneae, and granted you a boon. If you will agree…"

Harmon spent the next few minutes outlining a much more complicated set of conditions than Allistor had proposed, using extremely formal and flowery language. Allistor was impressed, both by the presentation and the terms Harmon had thought to include that Allistor hadn't. One of which being that none of their race attempt to harvest from Earth again, legal or otherwise.

"It is agreed." The multi-tonal voice answered within seconds of Harmon finishing his spiel. "We must go now. Our lives are forfeit, but we must return with the harvest before Collective forces intervene."

"Then we have a deal. Kira, please take us out somewhere in the south Pacific." Allistor's interface flooded with notifications, and without reading them individually, he glanced long enough to see that most of them were fame points, rather than infamy.

"Roger that, boss." Kira spun the ship southwestward, and they were off. All four of his ships surrounded the massive harvester as they made haste across the western half of the continent and out over the water. Kira picked a spot as far from any islands as she could find, and hovered.

The harvester loomed nearby, its mass blocking out the stars across a wide area of sky. They all watched as it lowered itself surprisingly gently until it hovered a few dozen feet above the water's surface. Once again the spider arms extended downward, poking maybe a hundred feet down into the water, and began pumping. Each leg created a ripple that, for their immense size, was relatively minor. Ten foot waves pushed outward, losing momentum and size as they encountered other waves.

While they waited for the harvester to fill its storage compartments, the spider creature reappeared on the main screen. "We are grateful, honorable Prince." The creature seemed calmer now that it was achieving its goal. "Your kindness will not be forgotten. Our High Queen Xeria extends her appreciation, and an invitation to visit our world of origin."

On a side screen, Harmon was discretely nodding his head. Allistor smiled at the spider, his lips remaining closed, just in case showing teeth was an offense of some kind. "I am honored to accept the invitation."

The araneae nodded its head. "Two days hence. We are sending coordinates. We regret we shall be unable to greet you in person. The Collective's price must be paid. It has been an honor for us to have met you, noble one. May you rule long and wisely." The screen went dark before Allistor could reply.

Amanda moved to sit in Allistor's lap. Looking up at Harmon's face on the screen, she asked, "Will the penalty really demand the deaths of a thousand crew members?"

Harmon nodded. "The Collective enforces strict laws when it comes to planetary resources, new acquisitions, and colonization. It demands stiff penalties, out of necessity. If it did not, there would be chaos throughout the galaxies. Weaker races like your own, no offense, would be wiped out without mercy, and the strongest factions would fight endless wars that escalated beyond reason. Planets destroyed, countless lives and resources wasted." He looked from Amanda to Allistor, then back again. "Though Lady Meg will not be happy to hear it, this harvest of water and the biomatter that it contains, will save the lives of likely tens of millions of hatchlings."

Meg stayed silent, but gave Harmon the stink-eye.

A few minutes later, the massive legs, each of which was thicker and taller than the Invictus tower, retracted gently from the water and back into position within the sphere. The crew wasted no time making their getaway, the ship rising quickly out of the atmosphere and jumping away.

Amanda got to her feet. "Guess we should head home. Two days to prepare to meet the queen of an entire race of beings. What does one wear to meet a spider queen?"

Chapter 16

After a short night's sleep, Allistor shared breakfast on the roof with William, Amanda, Fuzzy, Addy, and Sydney. Their little adoptive family ate slowly, sharing their activities from the previous day. All three kids wanted to go with Allistor and Amanda to meet the spider people, but Allistor felt uneasy about it.

They'd had some further discussion with Harmon on the way back from their Pacific adventure, and it seemed the visit would be safe enough. Especially since the queen felt friendly toward them. The humans would be taking the *Phoenix* to the araneaen homeworld, which was nearer to the twin suns of their system than Earth. He surmised that Earth's recent relocation within their solar system was the reason it was targeted. Normally they would have had to travel farther, raiding other systems within the galaxy.

Promising the kids he'd think about them tagging along, he left the table and went to fire up the forge. Since taking up crafting, Allistor found he liked to pound on metal while he was thinking. Today, rather than standing behind Allistor trying to brain him with a stick, William headed to the Silo to help Daniel with the dragons. Amanda had confirmed that they seemed to have hit a growth spurt, and might hatch within the week. William was determined to be there when it happened.

Allistor really wanted to be there, too.

He decided to experiment with one of the shadow steel spears. Taking it from his inventory, he slid the pointy end into the furnace and waited for it to heat up, observing the unusual metal as it changed colors. When it was a bright, glowing, reddish gold hue that suggested it was ready to be shaped, he used his tongs to pull it from the forge and set the heated point on the anvil. Taking his hammer in hand, he gave a few experimental swings. The impacts sounded dull compared to normal steel, and he saw no difference in the shape. Swinging harder than he would for normal steel, he struck near the sharpened point, intending to bend it.

Still there was no change.

"This is some hard stuff." He mumbled to himself. With his *Blacksmithing* skill still pretty low, he wasn't aware of any methods or tricks that might help him shape this metal. So he let it cool on the anvil, putting away his tools and deciding to wait until he had a chance to consult more with Longbeard and Daigath.

Thinking about Daigath, he headed toward the elevator. He wanted to see about additional class training. On the way down, he pulled up his interface and the Citadel tab. There were two listed, the one in Cheyenne and Ramon's on Governor's Island. So Helen and Longbeard were still looking for a good spot in YellowStone.

Stopping in the kitchen, and as usual, finding Fuzzy there trying to mooch treats, he asked Meg for some pastries to take to the ancient elf. She happily handed him a dozen almond pastries in a paper bag, saying, "I like him. He doesn't take me to places filled with giant spiders."

Allistor took the bag, grinning. "There's still time to change your mind and come with us. We're not leaving till morning."

"I'm going to spit in your food next time you eat here." She grumped at him.

"Does that give it extra buffs?" He gave her his most innocent face.

"Out of my kitchen before I skin your walking bear rug there and feed you the meat."

Fuzzy looked hurt, taking two steps back and eyeing Meg, a small whine escaping from his throat. She looked down at the bear, and instantly felt bad. "I'm just kidding, Fuzzy bear. I would never hurt you." She tossed him one of the pastries, which he caught and swallowed whole. His tiny nub of tail wagged slightly.

Allistor and his bear left the kitchen, Allistor slightly jealous that the cub had gotten a pastry, and he hadn't. He was tempted to eat one from the paper bag, but thought Daigath might be suspicious if he showed up with eleven treats, rather than a dozen.

They teleported to Wilderness Stronghold, and after confirming with Nigel that Daigath was not inside the walls, they headed out. Their walk around the lake went more quickly this time, as a path was beginning to form from the traffic back and forth. They crossed the stream and were a few hundred yards from the large clearing when

Fuzzy froze. His nose went into the air, moving back and forth as he scented something on the wind. Spinning around, he huffed quietly and peered off into the brush. Allistor moved closer to his bear and whispered, "What is it, buddy?"

Fuzzy huffed again, sitting on his haunches and looking up at Allistor, then back into the brush, his nose going a mile a minute. There was a low growl deep in his throat, but Allistor thought it was more curious than hostile.

Setting a hand on his bear's head, he followed Fuzzy's gaze and squinted slightly, trying to locate a forest creature or monster. Failing to find anything, he closed his eyes for a moment and just listened. To his surprise, two things happened at nearly the exact same time.

First, he heard a rustling in the underbrush ahead of them. A half a second later, an image came to him. More than an image, actually. It was live, and moving, like a feed from a camera. He could see the trees and shrubs he'd been looking at before he closed his eyes, but from a lower angle. His vision darted to where the rustling sound originated from, and suddenly his sense of smell told him what was coming.

A bear. A female bear.

Allistor gasped as he realized what was happening. He was somehow seeing and smelling what Fuzzy was seeing and smelling! Removing his hand and opening his eyes, he looked toward the same spot Fuzzy had shown him, and sure enough there was a brown muzzle with a black nose poking through some shrubs about forty yards away. He could no longer smell her without the connection to Fuzzy's nose, but he was sure she was female.

Fuzzy let out a small, confused roar that sounded like he couldn't decide whether he was claiming territory or calling out an invitation. The nose quickly disappeared amidst some additional rustling. The cub looked up at Allistor, a question clear in his beary expression.

"Go ahead, bud. Say hi if you want to." Allistor motioned toward the shrubs.

Fuzzy sat there for a another several seconds, clearly unsure what to do. Allistor had found him when he was a young cub, and Fuzzy had had no experience with other bears since. Allistor didn't push him, just stood next to him and waited to see what he'd do.

The oversized teddy bear snorted a couple times, shaking his head as if trying to rid himself of the female's scent. He got to his feet and took a few steps forward, then sat down again and sniffed at the forest floor. Another reserved roar, and this time he got an answer. A much louder roar erupted from the bushes, and the female stepped out into the open.

She wasn't as large as Fuzzy, but Allistor got the impression she was older. The lines of her head and jaw were harder, more defined. Allistor wondered whether that was because she was more developed than Fuzzy, or just because his bear was overfed.

Fuzzy got back to his feet and hopped forward, bobbing up and down in a playful manner Allistor had seen him use with the kids. He grunted a few times, and gave the female his best bearish smile.

For her part, the other bear seemed confused. She halted, standing on all four feet, and tilted her head to one side as she watched Fuzzy's antics. She briefly switched her gaze to Allistor, who took a few steps back and sat down, making sure she knew he wasn't a threat. As soon as she turned her attention back to Fuzzy, Allistor *Examined* her.

> *Grizzly Bear, Female*
> *Level 27*
> *Health: 31,000/31,000*

Allistor relaxed. She was roughly half Fuzzy's level, and only slightly more than half his size. Even if she decided to get hostile, Allistor doubted she was any threat to his bear.

The two bears approached each other, Fuzzy practically prancing, wanting to play, while the female was more cautious. Eventually they got close enough to touch noses, and spent a little while sniffing each other. Eventually, the female relaxed. Fuzzy raised a paw and swatted at her, much like a kitten taking on a ball of yarn. She gave a growl of protest, rearing up on her hind legs before smacking Fuzzy on the head with both forepaws.

"Stay here and play, Fuzzster. You know where to find me." Allistor turned to continue his journey to Daigath's home, wanting to give Fuzzy his privacy. Just in case the phrase "bears do it in the woods" took on a whole new meaning for Fuzzy. That wasn't something Allistor wanted to see. Fuzzy barely acknowledged him, pouncing on the female and chewing on one of her ears.

It didn't take long for Allistor to complete the trek through the woods, across the large clearing, and up the hill to Daigath's new tree home. He spotted the ancient elf sitting on a branch about thirty feet up, both hands on the tree trunk, eyes closed. Not wanting to interrupt whatever the elf was doing, Allistor took a seat on the same root as before. While he waited, he pulled up his list and reviewed it. Everything was already either checked off, or underway. He resolved to make a new, updated list when they returned from visiting the giant spiders' planet.

"I hear you had quite the evening." Daigath's voice drifted down, followed a moment later by the elf himself. He dropped to the ground in front of Allistor as gently as a falling feather.

Allistor handed him the bag of pastries. "If you mean the araneae, yes. We averted what could have been an ecological disaster near one of our Strongholds, and still sent them away with the resources they need. Though, as Harmon explains it, the cost to them will be high. Will the Collective really kill the crew?"

Daigath nodded. "And many more of their brood will starve when the planet they departed from is sanctioned. Thankfully, they were wise enough to send the harvester from a colony world, rather than their homeworld."

Allistor shook his head. "I wish there was some way I could help them. If I were Earth's emperor, I could have given them permission to harvest, or so I'm told."

The ancient master caught Allistor's eyes with his own. "You can not help everyone. And not every race conforms to the norms of your world. For example, the sacrifice of a thousand, or even a hundred thousand araneae means little to their queen. And that crew willingly made the sacrifice, knowing their lives were forfeit, in order to save millions. The harvester is of more importance to her than the lives lost, or even those that will suffer deprivation on the colony. The loss of the harvester makes it more difficult for her to gather the resources needed to feed the next wave of hatchlings. Araneae are a thinking, civilized race, except for their overriding imperative to reproduce and expand."

Daigath paused, then added, "The fact that you, as a noble whose interests lay in preserving your planet's resources, assisted her harvester crew... That is of more significance to the queen than the loss of lives or her ship. Few nobles in the Collective now would act in such a manner. She will be very curious to meet you, to find out for herself if you are sincere, or insane." The elf grinned at him.

Allistor thought he understood. He was going to have to learn not to make assumptions about other species, factions, or civilizations.

"I told them I was hoping for a trade agreement, but I spoke before I knew anything about them. Do they have anything we'd want, that I can't just purchase through Harmon?"

Daigath chuckled. "There are few things you cannot purchase through Harmon. But yes, they are a worthy trade partner and ally. Araneae are builders. They are experts at large projects, be it planetary structures, space stations, or large ships like their harvesters. The queen has a nearly unlimited labor force to draw upon, with each laborer able to carry heavy loads, perform multiple tasks at once with their separate appendages, and the ability to pass on their basic knowledge from brood mother to hatchlings. This means that within a few months of their birth, they are functioning adults able to contribute to their society."

"So if I wanted to purchase a space station to orbit Earth above my territory? Or more colony ships?"

"They could certainly provide you with both." Daigath stared at Allistor for a moment. "I assume you didn't come here just to ask about the upcoming visit. You wish more knowledge of the Battlemage class."

Allistor nodded, changing his focus. "I do, Master Daigath. The spells you've already given me were extremely helpful."

"Those were lower level skills and abilities that you could have learned when you achieved level twenty. I have in mind another for today. One of my favorites. You just barely meet the level requirement, having reached level fifty. But you have already learned the *Dimensional Step* spell, which shares a good bit of the required knowledge

355

for this one." He placed a hand on Allistor's head, and closed his eyes.

Allistor's mind began to swirl. It felt as if a low flame had been ignited inside his brain, steadily growing warmer as seconds ticked by. There were flashes of visual input that came and went too fast for Allistor to consciously comprehend. At the same time, he could feel connections being made, almost like a flow chart forming in his head, tying the new information to knowledge he'd already picked up from *Dimensional Step*, and a few other spells.

When it was all through, his brain hurt. The pain was about as severe as your average migraine, and he'd dealt with much worse. Blinking a few times, and grabbing hold of the root for balance, he read two new notifications.

You have learned: Dimensional Manipulation Level I

> *Dimensional Manipulation I allows the caster to circumvent the barriers between dimensions, manipulating the void to create pocket dimensions with stable openings. Mana cost: Variable depending on size and quantity of pockets created. Cooldown: N/A. Advancing this spell to higher levels will allow caster to create larger and more complex structures.*

> *Quest Received: Master Manipulator Part I*
> *Advance the Dimensional Manipulation spell to Level II by creating stable dimensional rifts and pocket dimensions. Don't die in the process.*

Allistor snorted when he read the last bit. "Don't die? I take it there's some special risk involved in casting this spell?"

Daigath nodded. "Every time any spell is cast, there is a small risk of failure, and an even smaller risk of backlash. This particular spell literally rips a hole in the fabric of our reality, so yes. There is some risk involved. At level one, you are able to pierce only one other dimension, that being the one known as the void. It is exactly as it sounds, a null-space where time holds no sway. You can create and stabilize a pocket within the void, useful for storing inanimate objects, among other things. Should you fail to stabilize the spell before you cease channeling, you will be drawn through the rift you created, and perish."

Allistor thumped his hand on the root next to him. "I can make storage rings!"

"Eventually, yes. It takes some practice to be able to create a compartmented pocket dimension. The higher your skill level, the more compartments you'll be able to create within the same space. But that is not the spell's only practical use. As you practice, you will see." Daigath looked around briefly. "Now… go someplace far from me before you attempt your first cast. And away from others, as well." He pulled one of Meg's pastries from the bag and took a small bite. Allistor wasn't offered one.

Not sure if the elf was kidding, Allistor thanked him and headed back to where he'd left Fuzzy. He could hear the two bears long before he could see them. There was much thrashing about in the bushes, and growling. When he was as close as he could get without intruding, he called out. "Hey, Fuzzy bear! Time to head home."

There were two surprised growls, and Allistor chuckled. Normally he'd never be able to sneak up on a bear. But the two had been so distracted, neither had heard or smelled him coming. Fuzzy emerged from behind a large tree a moment later, with the female right behind him. Both bears' muzzles were stained a deep purple shade that indicated they'd found some blueberry bushes. "Ooh! I love blueberries. Did you bring me some?"

Fuzzy shook his head, looking momentarily ashamed. Allistor just chuckled. "We'll have to figure out some kind of harness for you, with pockets. So you can carry stuff." Even as he joked with his bear, he kept a wary eye on the female, who was still approaching. She was, after all, a wild bear. And at least twice his size. Fuzzy approached and sat at Allistor's feet, headbutting him to demand ear scratches. The female halted a few feet behind and sat down as well. She watched Fuzzy close his eyes and growl softly as he enjoyed the scratchings, and Allistor could swear the female's face adopted a look of longing.

Looking down at Fuzzy, he asked, "What do you think? Is it safe to pet your new friend?" He closed his eyes, and immediately got a vision from Fuzzy of himself scratching the other bear's ears. "I'm gonna take that as a yes." Trusting his bear cub's instincts, he motioned toward the female. "It's alright, come here. I'll scratch your ears, too." He held out a hand and wiggled the fingers at her.

She just sat and stared for a while, clearly unwilling to approach any closer. After a minute or so, Fuzzy walked back and retrieved her, pushing at her with his snout until she got to her feet and moved next to Allistor. He held out his hand for her to sniff, which she did, before carefully lowering her head slightly. Grinning, Allistor proceeded to gently scratch behind her nearest ear. She almost immediately leaned into his hand, her way of telling him to scratch harder.

Fuzzy resumed his previous spot, and Allistor found himself standing in the woods, bracketed by softly growling grizzly bears. "I wonder... can I bond with more than one bear? What do you think, Fuzzy? Should we bring her into the family?"

He closed his eyes again as Fuzzy shook his head and growled a bit more loudly. A mental picture of the female bear getting headscratches from Amanda came to him.

"Oh, so you don't want to share me, but you want to keep her around? I'm not sure Amanda would *want* a bear companion. But let's head back to the Stronghold, and we can find out. Maybe if Amanda isn't interested, Helen would be."

Fuzzy looked thoughtful for a moment, then grunted his agreement before getting back to his feet and walking toward the gates. Half an hour later they stopped outside, the female unwilling to walk through. They were close enough to the structure that Nigel could hear them, so

Allistor called out. "Nigel, please ask Amanda to meet us here. And tell her to bring some meat."

"*Of course, sire.*"

Allistor sat down with his back against the wall, watching as Fuzzy and the female resumed their play in the clear space between the wall and the forest. She had just tripped up Fuzzy and knocked him off balance, causing him to roll a good distance down the slope, when Amanda walked through the gate. She took a moment to watch the bears at play, then laughed.

"I thought you'd found more murder chickens you wanted to try and tame."

"Nope. Not murder chickens. Though, that's a good idea. We should try to find more. And it isn't *me* that's going to be doing the taming. Fuzzy found himself a girlfriend, and he told me he wants *you* to try and bond with her." He watched her face as her eyes widened.

"What?? He *told* you? Me?" She spluttered a bit, then crossed her arms. "Explain."

"Well, it seems that my bond with the Fuzzmeister has grown strong enough that we can talk through images he shares with me. He sent me an image of you scratching her ears. She likes ear scratches quite a bit, by the way. Anyway, that's his way of telling me you should bond with her. Or if you don't want to, Helen is apparently an acceptable substitute."

"That's why you had me bring meat." Amanda surmised. "Was that part of your bonding process with him?"

"Yep. I fed him. I mean, first I made him fall off a cliff, knocking him unconscious and drowning him. But I saved him, then fed him, and we sort of took a little nap on some warm rocks… So I'm not sure exactly which parts matter. But in most of the games, bonding with a pet involved feeding them. I'm hoping that's all it takes, because she's a little too big to dump in a pond."

Amanda absent-mindedly smacked his arm as she watched the bears growl and tumble, swatting at each other. "I'm… not opposed to bonding with her. She's beautiful." She took a step toward the bears and paused. "We should talk to Helen. I don't think Fuzzy's old enough to be mating yet, and he's not behaving that way right now. He's still acting like a playful cub. But if we're not careful, we might have a litter of cubs romping around before long."

Allistor snorted. "Yeah, William and Chloe would just *hate* that."

Amanda had more concerns. "You tamed Fuzzy as a cub. He learned to live around people, to go outside when he needed to… go." She looked around. "What if she can't learn those things?"

Allistor shook his head. "I don't know. She was pretty quick to accept me, once Fuzzy told her I was okay. And to be honest, I didn't really housetrain Fuzzy or anything. From day one he let me know when he wanted out. I think the bond made him smarter pretty much from the beginning." He watched her face carefully, trying to see what she was thinking. "Listen, you don't have to do it. Like I said, Helen, or someone who lives here at Wilderness, could bond with her. Or we could just let her roam free out here in the forest, warn the hunters not to kill her. Fuzzy can visit her here easily enough. I don't think there's anything in these woods that could harm him at this point."

Amanda didn't speak, but took a few more hesitant steps toward the wrestling bears. The female's ears perked up, and she froze, staring at Amanda. Fuzzy, now on his back and waving his paws at her, took a moment to realize playtime had ceased. He looked up, spotted Amanda, and rolled to his feet. Trotting over, he licked her extended hand, then demanded scratches. Amanda stared back at the female as she obliged, speaking softly.

"You're a very pretty girl, aren't you? Your fur looks soft, and you have big brown eyes."

The female bear sat there, head tilting first to one side, then the other, as she listened to Amanda speak. Allistor was sure she didn't understand the words, but the tone was friendly enough.

"Toss her a chunk of meat."

Amanda took his suggestion and pulled a canid steak from her ring. To Fuzzy's dismay, she tossed it so that it landed about halfway between herself and the other bear. Fuzzy got up and was about to go claim the prize when Allistor said, "No, buddy. That one's for her. Come over here with me, and I'll give you one."

Fuzzy instantly abandoned Amanda, leaving her in a staring match with the sorely tempted female grizzly. The steak had been cooked with whatever herbs and spices Meg had been using at the time, and even Allistor was salivating a little at the smell.

The grizzly got to her feet and strode forward, her nose in overdrive, never taking her eyes off Amanda. When she reached the steak, she quickly snatched it up, then retreated several steps before sitting down to gnaw on it.

"That's a good girl!" Amanda sounded pleased. She'd adopted the baby-talk tone that most people seemed to automatically use when speaking to animals. When the steak was gone, she added, "I have more. You want another one, pretty bear?" Amanda produced another steak from her inventory and held it out, dropping into a crouch to seem less intimidating. Allistor held back a laugh, as the bear out-massed Amanda by about two hundred pounds, and was equipped with sharp teeth and claws."

The girl grizzly approached, her nose and belly leading her closer. Allistor held his breath as she got within biting range of Amanda, who was still speaking softly to her. Allistor couldn't tell what she was saying, but it seemed to soothe the bear. He let out the breath when she gently took the meat from Amanda. This time she sat down where she was, and trapped the steak between her paws as she ripped it apart. It was unsettling, seeing this wild grizzly, a mere two feet from Amanda, gnawing on the steak. When he saw Amanda's hand twitch, he spoke quickly, but quietly.

"Stop! I wouldn't touch her while she's eating. Just let her finish, then you can try it."

Amanda pulled her hand back a bit, nodding at him. "Thank you. That could have been bad." She stayed in her crouch, close enough to the bear to feel her breath, waiting for her to consume the steak. Which didn't take long at all. Still laying on her belly, the bear licked both paws clean, then looked up at Amanda expectantly.

"Can I pet you? Scratch your ears?" Amanda asked, reaching forward slowly. The bear looked from her over to Fuzzy and Allistor for a moment, and seemed to make the connection. She stretched her neck, pushing her head forward slightly, and allowed Amanda to scratch. After a couple minutes, she scooted closer and pushed harder against Amanda, nearly knocking her off balance. When Amanda began scratching under her massive chin, she growled happily and opened her eyes to meet Amanda's gaze.

"There you are." Amanda smiled, increasing the scratchings by adding a second hand. "Such a beauty. I think your name should be... Fiona."

As Amanda was completing her bond, Allistor's interface displayed a notification that a new Citadel had been created.

Chapter 17

As he and Amanda escorted Fiona into the
Wilderness Stronghold to meet everyone, Allistor got a
call, Nigel's voice echoing out from the walls.

"Sire, Minister Helen wishes to speak with you."

"Go ahead, Nigel." Allistor had been waiting to
hear from Helen and Longbeard, and was excited to know
how things were going.

"Hey, Allistor. Just checking in. We picked a spot
in the mountains at Yellowstone, and the dwarves are
already at work. Thought I should warn you that a few
thousand of them will be coming through the Cheyenne
hub shortly."

Before Allistor could respond, Amanda interrupted.
"Helen! I bonded with a bear! Just like Allistor did with
Fuzzy. Now it's Fuzzy and Fiona!"

There was a moment of silence, then, "Noooo way!
How did you do it? What's she like?"

Allistor waited, rubbing Fuzzy's head as the two
women gushed over the new development. When things
slowed down, and Helen was complaining about how
jealous she was, Allistor interjected. "How about we meet
you in Cheyenne. You can meet Fiona, we can greet the
dwarves as they arrive. Bring Master Longbeard if you
can. I wanted to ask him a few questions."

"You got it, boss. See you there in a few."

They took some time to let the gathered citizens and Fiona get to know each other. Several of them offered treats to both bears, and a couple of the children who lived at Wilderness tackled Fuzzy, demanding loot after they 'killed' him. Fiona was initially distressed at this, but when she saw Fuzzy playing along with the tiny humans, she relaxed.

When everyone had met everyone, and the bears had been given more treats than was probably good for them, the four teleported to Cheyenne. Helen was there to meet them as they stepped off the pad, along with Longbeard and a few other dwarves.

"Oh, she's beautiful!" Helen approached Fiona slowly, holding out a hand for her to sniff. After being mobbed by humans at Wilderness, the new bear pet was calm and friendly, licking the hand before allowing Helen to pet her. "And she must be pretty tough. Level twenty seven means she must have been killing and eating more than her share of forest critters or monsters…"

Allistor stepped aside to allow more introductions, motioning for Longbeard to join him after the dwarf took his turn greeting Fiona. The two of them sat at a table in the outdoor dining area near the old food court.

"Helen tells me you found an good spot?"

"Aye, more than acceptable. There be a mountain with much potential fer both mining and buildin' a proper underground settlement. There be a lake fer fishin', and plenty o' open space fer crops and stock. Two o' me experts on geology already be tracing the lava tubes to see about mappin' the volcano. Ye were right, she be a big 'un!" He made an expansive gesture with his hands. "We placed the Citadel at the base of a tall cliff, so we can dig right into it from there. There be quartz deposits in the stone, and the mornin' sun shines on the cliff, makin it sparkle like a million diamonds. Lady Helen let us name her, so she be called Lightholm."

"That's very good to hear, Master Longbeard. I hope your brethren are very happy there. If there's anything you need in the way of supplies or equipment, you just let me know." He took a moment to withdraw a shadow steel spear from his inventory, the same one he'd tried to bend earlier. Holding it up, he said, "I tried to work the tip of this in my forge this morning. Heated it until it looked workable, then pounded on it. But I didn't even scratch it, let alone bend it."

Longbeard took the spear in hand, examining the sharp end closely. "Aye, makes sense. This metal be forged with magic, and it'll take magic to unforge or alter it. Its creation required the sacrifice of a soul, usin' dark magic and blood magic. We'll not be doin the same." He looked sideways at his prince.

"No, of course not." Allistor shook his head. "I wanted to learn about this metal mainly to increase my crafting skill. If we can't alter the weapons, so be it. We'll find a way to use them as they are, or trade them to someone who can."

"We'll work on it together, when we have some time." Longbeard assured him, even as he gestured toward the teleport pad. "Me people have begun to arrive. Lady Helen will administer the oath once they're all here, and they'll share a meal with the local folks here before movin' on to Lightholm."

"That's an excellent idea." Allistor got to his feet. "Let's go welcome them, and get the introductions started."

*****

After the settlers had taken their oaths and shared a big lunch with their new fellow citizens, they departed for the Lightholm Citadel in Yellowstone. Allistor snagged Helen, who was already making noise about wandering off into the woods to claim a pet of her own, and asked her to meet with him and the analysts later that afternoon back at Invictus tower. Longbeard accompanied them over to view the new class trainer village, giving it his approval and praise before returning to the Invictus Tower, and heading directly upstairs to catch up on the trainer recruitment progress.

Amanda and Helen spent some time escorting Fiona around, then watching as the still tentative bear was eventually drafted into a battle with the children in the courtyard. They swarmed over her just as they did with Fuzzy, not pausing to consider whether or not she was a volunteer. There were a few moments of suspense, as the adults worried about her reaction. But she took it in stride, recognizing that human cubs like to play just as much as bear cubs.

Allistor had a mandatory date with Lilly, who had some final fit adjustments to do on the formal attire he'd be wearing to meet the spider queen. She grumbled at the fact that he seemed to have grown, and Allistor realized that he'd added a couple points to *Strength* since the last time she'd measured him, and was slightly taller and bulkier now. He actually had more points available to assign after killing the fomorians, but he'd decided to wait.

Lilly assured him that the necessary alterations would be complete by the end of the day, and practically chased him out of her workshop.

Making his way up to the floor his analysts used, he stuck his head into their meeting room. "How goes the recruiting?" When they all began to stand, he motioned for them to sit.

Selby spoke first. "We've filled nearly all the positions on the list. Several of them will arrive today, the rest over the next week. I even convinced my cousin to accept one of the positions, and bring his wife."

Allistor chuckled. "So you've decided I'll live long enough that it's safe to bring your family?"

Selby blushed slightly, as Longbeard roared with laughter. When he calmed a bit, Longbeard gasped, "Tell him!"

Looking uncomfortable, Selby mumbled something Allistor couldn't hear. When he held a hand up to his ear and raised his eyebrows, she repeated herself at a higher volume.

"Well, you see… I hired him to be the trainer for the *Survivalist* class skills." She kept her eyes on her hands avoiding Allistor's gaze.

Allistor didn't immediately make a connection. He stared at the little gnome for a moment, then looked to Longbeard, who was staring right back, a huge smile on his face.

Then it hit him.

"And once he's here, even if I'm killed and Invictus falls apart, as a survivalist he's more than capable of just fading into the wilderness and fending for himself."

"Ha! Ye got it in one guess!" Longbeard slapped the table. Now Allistor was smiling as well.

"I'm sorry, Allistor, I-" Selby stopped as she saw the grin on his face.

"Don't sweat it, Selby. I don't blame you one bit. You know so much more about the universe we live in than I do. I'm like a toddler wandering around in a jungle with just a sharp stick and a little luck to keep me alive. It only makes sense for you to be cautious about my chances for survival."

He spent a little more time with them, making sure they had all they needed as far as funds and supplies to get the trainers' village up and running. When Helen appeared, he was reminded that he wanted to cover something else. He sat her down, and had Nigel pull up an image of the globe that incorporated their new satellite scan data.

"I want to expand our holdings on other continents." He began

"I thought you put an end to the raid groups going out to claim more land." Helen raised one eyebrow as she spoke.

"I did. At the time, I was concerned about looking greedy, or seeming like some kind of imperial overlord. But over the last several days, some things have happened that changed my mind. I'm told that as a planetary prince, my authority is pretty limited. I can't put a defense net around Earth, which puts the whole of humanity at an increased risk. I couldn't authorize the harvester to take the resources they needed, which would have saved the entire crew from being executed. So maybe it's time I expand Invictus to include enough territory to become Emperor of Earth."

There was silence in the room as his surprised audience absorbed his words.

L'olwyn was the first to speak. "That may be… complicated, Allistor. There are already colonies from large and powerful factions established here on earth. They might be resistant to your plans, as it would negate their ability to raise a prince of their own, and have input on the future of this world."

"Like the Or'Dralon" Allistor nodded. "I've considered that. I must try to create alliances with them in any case, and I think I'd rather do it from a more powerful position than I have now. I can't spend the rest of my life afraid of the big bad wolves."

Droban the minotaur offered his own advice. "Courage is commendable. And your bold actions to date have elevated you to a position of power quite rapidly. But courage must be tempered with wisdom, lest you overstep. It is not just your own life that you risk."

Helen snorted. "That's a polite way of saying don't let your ego write a check that your ass can't cash."

Allistor shot her a dirty look before turning to Droban. "Wise advice, Droban, thank you. And I don't plan to seize the entire planet today. I want to start with another skill school someplace overseas, where there are large numbers of survivors. Maybe take some useful properties like mines, fertile farmlands, that kind of thing. I plan to gather as many human survivors together under my banner as I can. Along with the lands they have claimed for themselves. I'd like you folks to research just how much of the Earth's land and resources I have to control before I can become emperor."

Longbeard nodded. "Aye, we can do that easy enough."

"In the meantime, please work with Nigel and Helen to review the satellite scans and find me some likely targets for settlements, and for the next trainer's village."

"I have some cool ideas already." Helen volunteered. "Places I've seen or read about. Like, historic castles and landmarks, that kind of thing."

"Such as?" Allistor was immediately curious. He liked the idea of claiming his own real life castle.

"Well… off the top of my head, how about Dover Castle? It's a huge structure on the coast of England, with its own port. And it has a very cool network of tunnels on multiple levels underneath. It was used as a sort of command bunker during world war two."

"Sold! Let's go claim it as soon as possible. Assuming nobody else has, yet. Get Nigel to focus on the area and check for signs of survivors." Allistor was excited.

Nigel obligingly altered the display, first zooming in on the region Helen indicated, then zooming in further when she located the castle complex. There didn't appear to be any surface activity in the daylight, so Helen had him switch to previously recorded data from a night passover. There were no indications of lights in the darkness, or infrared signatures.

"Let's do it!" Allistor thumped the table. Nigel, please ask Kira or Gene if one of them is available to fly us to England. And alert Bjurstrom that we could use a raid team. Also let Sam, Meg, Ramon, Nancy, Michael, Chris, Lars, Logan, George, Dawn, Remy, Leila, and the girls know as well, in case any of them want to tag along."

"*Of course, sire.*" Nigel's calm reply didn't dull Allistor's excitement at all. A moment later the AI added, "*Lady Kira and her crew can be ready in fifteen minutes.*"

"Alright, let everyone know we're heading out in half an hour." Allistor headed for the elevator, but halted when Longbeard asked, "Ye mind if I tag along? The underground bits sound interestin'."

Allistor hadn't even considered that his analysts might want to join. For that matter, he didn't know what levels they were, or whether they had any interest in leveling up.

"Damn. Of course you're welcome to join us. Any of you. You have a standing invitation to join any raid that you'd like. It may not be polite to ask this, so please let me know if it's improper. I don't know what level you guys are. Could you benefit from joining the raid groups, clearing buildings, that kind of thing?"

L'olwyn replied for the group. "You are currently a higher level than all of us except Master Longbeard. Most analysts live sheltered lives, and earn experience from performing our duties, or crafting, and such. As a result, we are generally slow to level up." He looked at the others, who nodded. "You could simply have *Examined* each of us to determine our levels."

Allistor grimaced. "I was told it was rude to do so outside of combat. Especially to friends."

Shelby giggled. "That is true. I'm lowest at level thirty. The big fella here is thirty two, and L'olwyn is level forty eight. Master Longbeard is-"

"I be high enough level that none o' ye can use *Examine* on me n get more'n me name." Longbeard grinned at them. Helen laughed.

"Okay then. Good to know. Any of you who wish to join us this afternoon, meet us in the lobby in twenty five minutes. I don't know if we'll find survivors at this castle, or monsters. So be prepared to fight. Or, heal. Shit. I don't know what your combat roles would be. But we'll figure it out once we've got the group together." He thought for a second, then added, "Any of you who'd like to accompany us to visit the spider people are welcome as well."

"Araneae." L'olwyn corrected him. "The queen would not take kindly to being called a spider person. It would be similar to calling you a hairless ape."

"And that's why you should come with me." Allistor smiled at the elf. "To help me avoid needless mistakes that might, I don't know, start a bloodfeud?"

*****

Half an hour later the group was aboard the Phoenix and heading out to cross the Atlantic Ocean. Allistor left the flying to Kira and her crew of trainees, instead gathering the group in the larger mess hall. Everyone he'd invited had opted to join him, along with Amanda, both bears, and a few of Remy's and Leila's people, and the room was buzzing with speculation. Allistor stood up and got their attention.

"Okay so we're going to Dover Castle, to see if we can claim it. From our satellite info, it doesn't look like anyone is living there, so this might be a five-minute job. I'm actually kind of hoping there's a bunch of creatures in the underground levels, so we can clear it like we did the Silo."

"Dungeon run!" Selby pumped a fist into the air.

Allistor sighed, "I wish. I wish there really were dungeons like we had in the VR games. We've cleared several underground areas full of monsters, but once they were clear that was it. No respawns or big loot chests." He paused, grinning. "Except for the gold depositories, of course. There was plenty of loot, and the leprechauns left us actual pots of gold."

Shelby said, "Oh, there will be dungeons. They take a little while to form, but I'm sure several would have been created during Earth's Stabilization. They will grow larger with time. And as you mentioned, once you have cleared them, they will repopulate over a period of several days."

Droban added, "And the loot is better inside actual dungeons. The system provides bonuses based on individual circumstances. For instance, if you conquer a dungeon full of creatures that are on average ten levels higher than you, the loot awarded will be substantially better than if the situation were reversed."

"As a Planetary Emperor, you can also create your own dungeons on Orion, using a specifically enchanted core, and significant sundry resources."

The mouths of every human in the room dropped open. Goodrich actually drooled a bit. Nobody spoke for several seconds. Allistor finally asked, "A real dungeon? Like, the kind with quests and bosses and big chests full of loot at the end?"

"Aye, real dungeons." Longbeard confirmed. "They be most often used to train an emperor's troops. Weed out the weak, and strengthen the survivors. It be a benefit to the emperor either way. The weak die, makin' the dungeon monsters stronger. Then the stronger troops who kill 'em get more benefit."

Amanda shuddered, her face turning red. "Who would force weak troops into a place that is sure to kill them?"

Longbeard shook his head. "Few need to be forced. Clearin' a dungeon be among the fastest ways to level up. And most dungeon owners let 'em keep whatever loot they get from kills. So even the weak ones be willing to take a chance in a dungeon."

Droban added, "The weaker soldiers know that when battle comes, they must face enemies that were likely strengthened by their own dungeons. Their odds of survival are better in the dungeons as part of a group. And should they survive the dungeons, they improve their odds o' surviving battles."

Allistor nodded. How often had he sent his people into combat to level them up? Clearing buildings, claiming territory, or hunting. This didn't seem all that different to him. And he'd purposely sent his lowest level people into harm's way for the same reason. So that they'd survive unexpected attacks of unknown strength. He did his best to make sure they were safe, sending higher level experienced raiders with them. But it was basically the same.

"We need a dungeon!" Bjurstrom's smile was a little disturbing. He'd taken on the responsibility of coordinating raids for the lower level citizens.

"I agree." Allistor was already picturing giant loot chests, glowing with golden light, bursting with epic gear. He looked to L'olwyn. "Where do we get one of these cores?"

"They can be purchased on the open market, though they are priced too highly for any but the larger factions and emperors to afford. You can commission a master enchanter to create one to your specifications. And again, this is quite costly. Occasionally a core is given by the System as a quest reward or world-first achievement, like your yacht."

"Or they can be stolen when you conquer a wild dungeon, or one belonging to someone else." Selby happily offered.

Droban cautioned the obviously excited humans. "Stealing a dungeon from an emperor or faction is generally grounds for war. Most simply wait for a wild dungeon to make itself known, and rush to be the first to conquer it."

Allistor looked to Longbeard. "Would the planetary survey have picked up a dungeon if there was one on Orion?"

Longbeard shook his head. "Nay, lad. Dungeons be a place outside normal space."

"So we might have dungeons on Orion, and on Earth. We need to find them." Allistor mused.

Drobon nodded. "Almost certainly on Earth. Though several of the colonists will already be seeking them out. As for Orion, it may be that the dwarves already conquered and destroyed them. A dungeon is a valuable asset to control. Beyond using it for your own people's benefit, you can sell access to interested parties. If the core can be taken without being destroyed, and moved elsewhere, like a secure homeworld…"

Kira's voice echoed through the mess hall. "Okay guys, approaching the coast of England. We'll be at the castle in less than five."

The entire group got to their feet and filed out of the mess, heading down to the cargo bay. When Allistor felt the ship's forward motion cease, he opened the cargo bay doors. Kira was hovering about a thousand feet above the main castle structure.

"That's just awesome!" Allistor took in the massive stone walls, towers, and buildings. The grounds were overgrown, and the deep grass showed no signs of passage.

Kira descended, landing the ship in a large parking area south of the fortress proper, just west of a building that, based on its cross-shaped construction, must have been a church. The moment *Phoenix* touched down, Allistor and the others walked down the ramp and onto a paved street that led directly through the main castle gate. The walls and towers stretched maybe thirty feet above them, ancient stones projecting a sense of strength and power. The very definition of a bulwark.

"This is the coolest place ever!" Sydney shouted, then ducked her head between her shoulders as the rest of the raiders shushed her. They were in hostile territory, and shouting could bring monsters from every direction. "Sorry." She whispered, blushing furiously.

Bjurstrom broke the raiders into small groups, dividing up the analysts by their various roles. Unsurprisingly, Droban and Longbeard were both melee fighters who could wield a shield and double as a tank if needed. L'olwyn was a healer, and Selby could alternate between firing a tiny gnomish crossbow or casting lightning and fire spells.

The sisters began singing a song that buffed *Stamina* and *Constitution* by two points each, choosing an old tune that Allistor couldn't quite place that had a driving beat. One of the girls sang the equivalent of a bass line, while the other took the melody. The range of sounds the girls could now make with their voices was amazing.

As usual, Allistor led the way. There were dozens of structures here to clear, including the massive walls and towers that rose every hundred feet or so along its length. Several buildings lined the insides of the wall, all surrounding the massive main tower in the center. Outside the walls were other structures like the church, another gatehouse, and more. Those could be cleared later. Allistor was anxious to get inside the main building and down into the tunnels.

Passing through the high arch of the gateway, they found themselves in a courtyard paved with flagstones, facing the massive central tower. It rose four stories, thick stone walls and narrow windows, built for defense as well as light and air, looking down on them. Allistor couldn't help but imagine knights in full armor striding up the stairs to the tower's door, squires leading horses toward the stables over to one side. Silence reigned as the others took in the sight for themselves. There was a feeling of history here, as if one could almost hear the battles and celebrations of the past.

Bjurstrom broke the silence, issuing quiet orders. "Groups one and two, move left, clear the buildings. Groups three and four, go right. Only clear from the ground up, and report any access points to the underground. Maintain radio contact. Check-in's every ten minutes, and call for help if you even *think* you *might* need it."

The group spread out as directed, taking one building each as they began to leapfrog each other around the outer wall structures. Allistor stayed in the courtyard near the tower entrance with the sisters, Amanda, and the two bears, to keep an eye on the gate and serve as backup if anyone called for help. In less than an hour the others had checked and cleared every room in every building in the loop. None of them reported any contact with monsters, or any life forms at all. Which made them all a little nervous.

Amanda was the first to say it. "This is the first place I'd have come if I were a local. And there's no way that nothing spawned here or took shelter here for the last year. So either some*body* already cleared this place, or some*thing* has killed everything else around."

Meg shook her head. "We didn't get a trespass notice when we came in. If this place was cleared, they didn't claim it. Maybe they died in the process?"

Bjurstrom nodded. "Makes sense. They probably did just what we're doing, started by clearing up here, then worked their way through the tower and down to the underground levels."

Sam finished the thought. "And like that asshat Colonel Potts, couldn't get the job done. Or maybe they're down there right now, still tryin'."

"Only one way to find out." Allistor looked around. "Everybody take five to grab some food, get buffed up, and we'll head into the tower." All the raiders took a seat there in the courtyard, munching on sandwiches or jerky, while the girls renewed their musical buff on everyone. Fuzzy took the opportunity to teach Fiona the proper way to mooch treats, leading by example.

Chapter 18

Allistor got to his feet, the rest of the raid right behind him. Without a word, they broke into their previous groups, spreading the healers and tanks out. Allistor took the lead, climbing the few short steps to the tower door. Casting Barrier on himself, he stepped through.

It took a few seconds for his eyes to adjust, the interior of the tower not getting much sunlight through the narrow windows and doorway. When he could see clearly, he scanned the hall in front of him. Exposed stone walls with hanging tapestries, heavy wood plank floors, all with a thick layer of dust that looked undisturbed.

Moving quickly, he stepped forward to the next door, which led to a much larger room. A corridor led left and right, with several thick wooden doors along each side. Bjurstrom spoke quietly into his mic, sending groups left and right to start clearing rooms. These were experienced raiders, for the most part, and didn't need much instruction.

Allistor and his group, which included Amanda, the bears, Ramon, and the girls, moved into the large room and started checking the walls and corners for anything hidden. It was only five minutes before his radio transmitted the all-clear, and the groups began to move upstairs. Allistor and company waited in the throne room, checking out the blocky twin thrones and other historic items. The castle had been operating as a museum when the world ended, and didn't seem to have been disturbed much since.

The smaller groups found a few vermin on the upper floors. Normal earth rats, not the monsters from the menagerie. And some pigeons nesting on the top floor. The rats perished, the pigeons were chased away, at least temporarily. Allistor shook his head when he heard that report. In the early days, the opportunity for pigeon meat would have made their mouths water. When everyone had returned to the ground floor, Ramon pointed out the stairway leading downward on the map he'd been creating to level up his *Cartography* skill. He'd actually found some tourist pamphlets on a rack, one of which included a map of the castle and its underground levels.

Knowing that they were moving into confined spaces, the group configuration altered. Allistor still took the lead, with Logan next to him to open doors. Behind them were several tanks, followed by most of the dps and healers, with another small group of dps and tanks at the rear. The bears, and the teen sisters, stayed near the center of the group.

Allistor led them down the stone staircase, which ended at a thick wooden door with heavy iron bands reinforcing it. The ancient looking door had a modern round knob made of brass. Executing their usual drill, Logan opened the door, clearing the way for Allistor to step through.

Three light globes glided past Allistor's head as he passed the arched doorway. Straining to see down the hallway in front of him, his peripheral vision picked up dried bloodstains on the walls and floor ahead and to either side of him. Continuing forward with his *Barrier* spell active in front of him, he made room for the others to filter in behind.

"Something died in here." Sam observed.

"Captain obvious." Meg snickered, elbowing her husband.

"Several somethings." Helen added, winking at Meg. "Look at the splashes on the walls. Some are round splats like a gunshot spray. But most are long splashes, from deep blade cuts, or maybe claws." The group took a more careful look at the walls, nodding their heads in understanding. There was a jumble of broken furniture further ahead, also liberally covered in dried blood.

"No bones, though." Remy observed from near the back. "And whatever it was, it wasn't strong enough to break that door behind us, and didn't know how to work a doorknob."

Everyone knew what no bones meant. Whatever had been victorious in the fight down here had either moved, or consumed, the bodies. Sam, rubbing his side where Meg had attacked, looked down at her with a wide grin. "Maybe it was giant spiders." He stepped to the side before a second elbow could land.

Allistor couldn't help but smile. His people were seasoned and confident enough to joke with each other in what amounted to a bloodstained dungeon corridor. This is what he wanted for them. To be strong enough to thrive, despite living in a world that pretty regularly tried to kill them.

Moving forward, they cleared the furniture by pushing and stacking it to either side, leaving them a clear path, as well as potential cover to hide behind if necessary. For an hour they slowly made their way through the first level of tunnels, clearing as they went. McCoy pointed out some spent shell casings, both for shotguns and rifles. The absence of any handgun casings puzzled them for a little while, until Leila pointed out that handguns were illegal in the UK, except for military personnel.

There were also large burn marks on some of the furniture scraps, as well as deep gouges. So the battle had included both magical and melee attacks. Fiona sniffed at what appeared to be a set of three claw marks on a chair leg, and growled, her hackles rising. Amanda petted her head to reassure her. Fuzzy took a sniff too, and shook his head. Allistor got the impression it wasn't a scent he recognized.

"Might be a new monster, guys. Fuzzy hasn't smelled it before, and he's been almost everywhere I have."

"Let it not be bugs." Meg whispered, and several of the folks nodded their agreement.

After clearing the first level of tunnels without incident, the group moved to the next stone stairway that spiraled downward. Halfway down, both bears began to growl, their noses sweeping back and forth. Allistor held up a hand, and the entire group froze.

There was a rustling noise echoing up from below. The limited light from the globes hovering ahead of him didn't reveal any movement, or any creatures waiting in ambush. Refreshing his *Barrier*, Allistor continued forward, whispering to the bears to be quiet.

He needn't have bothered. Whatever was down below already knew they were there. The rustling increased, followed by rattling sounds, and several short, barking noises. Allistor drew his sword, and heard the tanks behind him equipping shields. The light globes pushed further down the stairs as the party advanced. Allistor had taken just three more steps when the first of the monsters appeared around the bend in the stairway. It paused, surprised by the large number and size of invaders above it.

Oviraptor Juvenile
Level 40
Health: 21,000/21,000

The little thing, less than three feet tall, looked much like a dinosaur. It ran mostly upright on two powerful hind legs with three-clawed feet, and had two short upper arms with three claws each. Its head was elongated, with two rows of sharp teeth in a wide jaw, and eyes on either side of its head. Down its back ran a line of what looked like multicolored feathers protruding from its grey scaled skin.

"It's a tiny murder chicken." Goodrich called out from further up the stairs. His voice squeaked slightly. The man had a definite aversion to the murder chickens after his last encounter. McCoy patted him on the shoulder.

Hearing the voice, the raptor barked back in challenge, the sound quickly joined by several more behind it. Two, then four, then nearly a dozen of the creatures crowded into the stairway within sight of Allistor. More could be heard barking down below.

"Shit." Logan muttered from right behind and above Allistor. "This is gonna leave a mark."

With one final bark, the lead raptor dashed forward, speeding up the dozen or so steps between its position and Allistor's. When it was maybe four steps away, its powerful legs bunched, then uncoiled with a burst of strength, launching the little monster right toward Allistor's face.

It collided with the magical barrier in front of him, and much to Allistor's surprise, the invisible shield held! The raptor was stopped cold, it's head knocked back as it fell straight down. Unfortunately, the three that leapt in right behind it smashed through the shield. The one coming straight at Allistor lost its head as he swung his sword, its corpse falling atop the stunned raptor at his feet. Logan used his massive axe to split the second one nearly in half while it was still in the air. The third missed Allistor's shoulder by inches when he ducked, flying past him to impact the shield of one of the tanks.

Allistor straightened back up to find the entire mass of tiny raptors coming at him. One leapt for his face, while others attacked his legs. Several more used him as a springboard, leaping at him, and digging in with their hind leg claws before continuing on to leap over top of the shield wall, landing among the fighters and healers. When one of the tanks tried to prevent a second wave getting past him by raising his shield high, two of the little monsters simply charged underneath, biting and clawing at his legs as they passed.

In seconds, the entire raid group was chaos. Allistor felt heals wash through him as he cast *Mind Spike* on a raptor that had its jaws inches from his face. The thing screamed and thrashed, its claws unconsciously slashing his face and neck. Ahead of him, stone spikes shot up from the floor, skewering several of the little monsters before they could leap into the crowd. Fireballs and lightning shot past Allistor even as he stabbed a raptor that was latched onto his right leg. Another sank its jaws into his sword-arm wrist, biting through the leather amor and deep into his flesh.

He used all the strength he could muster to slam the little beast into the stone wall of the tunnel once, twice, and again until he heard its skull crack, and it let go. His health was down below fifty percent, and it had been a little while since he'd felt a heal. Looking back, he saw several of the raptors rampaging through the center of his group, distracting the healers, keeping them from casting. One of them leapt up and latched on to Dawn's face, its claws digging into her neck and chest to secure a grip. Her scream was cut short as it flexed its powerful neck muscles, shaking its head and ravaging her face. Allistor cast *Restraint* on it, and Ramon reached in with his bare hands, prying the monster's jaws apart and ripping it free, tearing his own skin in the process. He threw it to the ground, and it was stomped into oblivion as Nancy caught Dawn's falling body. Allistor saw several heals land on her even as she fell.

Not far behind them, Droban pulled one of the little monsters off a healer's back, and simply pulled its head from its neck with a quick snap of his bulging forearms.

Allistor couldn't do anything to the raptors that were in tight among his people without potentially harming them too, so he turned toward the monsters still ahead. He began to channel *Storm*, the clouds quickly gathering over the enemy that were trapped on the stone spikes, and those still coming from behind. The first lightning strike burned one of the skewered lizards to a crisp. Within a few more seconds, lightning was filling the stairwell below him, striking target after target and wearing down their health pools even as they were repeatedly stunned.

He stopped channeling after about twenty seconds, when all of the little monsters below were no longer moving. Turning back, he saw that the raiders had control of the situation again. Several of the tanks had turned and pinned the lizards to the floor, or stunned them with shield bashes. The damage dealers were quickly burning through their enemies' health bars, while the healers were doing their best to bring everyone back up.

Except the three who were already dead.

When the last of the raptors had perished, Selby, Remy, and a few of the others leveled up. Addy and Sydney had stopped singing, both of them collapsing to sit against the wall, their eyes wide and unfocused. Addy had

Dawn's blood splattered across her shoulder and face, and was too dazed to wipe it clean. Looking down, Allistor saw what his interface's raid icon had already told him.

Leila, the leader of one of the Strongholds he'd just folded into Invictus, was gone. The raptor that killed her still had its jaws locked onto her neck, her hand gripping a knife that pierced its chest. The teeth still lodged in her flesh and severing her arteries kept the healing spells from being able to save her. One of her people was trying to pry the dead lizard off of her, and Michael bent down to help.

The next body Allistor saw, lying just two feet from Leila, was one of his own people. A member of Bjurstrom's regular property acquisition raid team, his name was Scott, and Allistor had only met him a couple of times. A leaping raptor had managed to drive one of its long rear claws through his eye and directly into his brain. Even with all the healing magic available to them, some injuries were fatal, no matter what.

The last body on the floor brought tears to Allistor's eyes. He walked over and dropped to his knees next to the ravaged body. Amanda, Nancy, Ramon, Sam, Meg, Michael, all the members of his core group from the Warren that were present joined him, hanging their heads in sorrow.

There lay George, the old man who'd been running Luther's Landing, who had joined them so early in the first year of the apocalypse, and helped Nancy to develop the greenhouses that fed so many survivors through that first hard winter. He lay on the cold stone floor, very nearly decapitated. It was clear from the clean wound that he hadn't been killed by a raptor, but by a stray blow from sword or axe when the monsters sowed chaos within the ranks. Someone had panicked, or simply missed their target, and killed George as a result.

Allistor didn't look around to find the guilty party. That could be dealt with later. He laid a hand on George's chest, and spoke softly. "I will miss you, old man. We all will. You were tough as nails, with a kind heart, and a sharp mind. I hope you're with Luther somewhere, now."

The others hugged and consoled each other, eventually moving aside so that McCoy and his team could put all three of the lost raiders into body bags. They set each bag gently into a side room to be retrieved for burial on their way out.

Sam pulled Allistor into an uncharacteristic hug, then pushed him out to arm's length. "He went quick, and he went down fightin'. That's the way he woulda wanted it."

Allistor nodded, knowing Sam was right. George was an old soldier to his core.

Surprisingly, L'olwyn approached, and offered. "May he awaken in Valhalla, and fight at Odin's side."

Sam grunted in agreement, and Allistor nodded. He had questions for the elf, but it was not the time or place. Sweeping the room with his eyes, he saw expectant gazes directed his way. The raid was looking for him to lead them on, or lead them out.

"We go on." He stated. "We've paid for this place in blood, and it's ours now. Anyone who doesn't feel up to this, and wants to return to the ship and wait, is welcome to do so. No repercussions." Allistor didn't wait to see if anyone left. He recast his *Barrier* spell, and started walking down the remainder of the stairs, kicking each corpse to loot it as he passed. He didn't even glance at the notifications, keeping his focus on each new step that moved into his line of sight as he descended.

When they reached the bottom, they found a chamber filled with nests. Scattered around the floor, the nests were made of bits of torn cloth, leathery skin, and bones. Some of the bones were quite obviously human. Dawn mumbled, "I guess we know what happened to the folks who came down here before."

Helen kicked one of the nests, dislodging several of the bones, and some egg shell fragments. "A lot of these bones look like they might belong to the raptors. My guess is they've been hatching and fighting amongst themselves down here. That's how they got to such high levels, and didn't starve."

Nobody had anything else to add, morale being low after their losses. Allistor and Logan led the way through the second level tunnels, the group getting back to business. They cleared rooms and side tunnels, finding a few individual raptors here and there, putting them down quickly and without mercy.

At the far end of the last section of tunnel, they reached a heavy metal door with a padlock on it.

Longbeard pulled a hammer from his belt and smashed the lock open with a single swing, the two pieces dropping to the floor with a metallic clang. The old dwarf bowed politely, sweeping one hand toward the door. "After you."

Allistor nodded at Logan, who waited for him to get into position, then yanked the door open. The moment the opening was wide enough, half a dozen light globes shot through ahead of Allistor. He cast Flame Shot in the form of a fireball ahead of him as well, then stepped through.

Another staircase, cut directly into the stone, led downward into the darkness. Everyone was silent as he listened for more raptor sounds, or any indication of what might be waiting below. Allistor could hear both Fuzzy and Fiona sniffing behind him, but neither made any growling noises. When Fiona sneezed, Allistor looked at the stairs more closely. The dust here was thicker than up on the ground level, and also undisturbed.

Feeling confident that nothing was waiting to ambush them on the stairs, he started down. The light globes lowered themselves slightly, then pushed ahead of him below the stairwell ceiling as it sloped down. This stairwell was cut in a straight line, and the raiders were able to see much further ahead of themselves than before. Eventually Allistor spied the bottom landing, and an archway with another door. The floor was wet, with puddles here and there, and what looked like a thin layer of mud atop the stone.

When he stepped off the last stair onto the landing, Allistor's foot squished and slid slightly. Looking down, he saw that the mud wasn't really mud, but thousands of squirming worms. He quickly lifted his foot back up, motioned for those behind to hold back, and Examined one of the worms.

Common Earthworm
Level 1
Health: 10/10

"Relax guys. They're just earthworms." He looked across the landing. "Tens of thousands of them, but they're harmless."

"Are we going to have to kill them all to claim this place?" Logan asked from one step up.

"Are we going to *have* to kill them?" Dawn asked. "Of course we're going to kill them. They're creepy and squiggly, and... and icky!" She shuddered. Somewhere behind her, Meg nodded. Not waiting for Allistor to disagree, she tossed one of her glass grenades out into the center of the landing, where it shattered. A moment later she tossed a *Flame Shot* spell into the same spot, lighting the napalm that had splattered across the floor. The worms curled and crisped by the thousands.

The raiders began to cough as the smoke naturally drifted upward at them, the smell of burnt mud and crisped worm carried with it. "Ugh! That's even worse." Dawn complained, holding her nose and trying to breathe shallowly through her mouth.

Allistor stayed where he was, waiting for the flames to burn themselves out, doing his best not to inhale the stench. His mind was pondering a different issue. After a moment, he asked the question aloud.

"Where'd the mud come from?"

Logan was the only one who heard him over the coughing and complaining. "What?"

"Where did the mud come from? Allistor asked louder. "These tunnels were dug more than a hundred years ago. Right into the stone of this hill. We're far above sea level, so it's not like the tide washed it in."

Logan shrugged, as did several others who'd heard. "Maybe there was a partial cave-in somewhere ahead? Or just seepage from rainwater above, bringing in some mud a little bit at a time?"

Allistor nodded slightly. "I guess that makes sense. Let's keep going. This is the last level. We clear this, claim the place, and take our dead home." He led the way across the landing, stepping carefully so as not to slip on the burnt worm carcasses. The landing ended at another metal door, which was not locked. Once again, Logan pulled the door open, and Allistor pushed through, light globes just ahead of him.

The floor beyond was also damp, with some kind of fungus or moss growing here and there on the floor and walls. Allistor looked down the corridor for a moment, then said, "Call back your globes."

He waited as the glowing balls of white light retreated back into the stairwell. As soon as they were gone, he pulled the door mostly closed, and confirmed what he'd thought he saw. The corridor was glowing a soft shade of blue. It was barely there, just bright enough to keep the place from being totally dark.

Opening the door again, he said, "Nancy, there's some kind of glowing blue moss or something in here. Gotta make a good alchemy ingredient, right?"

He stepped aside as the others filed through the door, moving down the corridor to make room for Nancy. A few of them reached out as if to touch the softly glowing substance, but Nancy stopped them. "Don't! Colorful things in nature are often poison." She said as she stepped through the door. Taking a knife from her inventory, she gently scraped some of the substance from the wall into a vial, and stared at it, her eyes unfocusing. A moment later, she said, "It's as I thought. This substance contains low levels of cyanide!"

Those who'd been tempted to touch quickly pulled their hands back from the walls. When she noticed the nervous shuffling, and people crowding toward the center of the hall away from the walls, Nancy chuckled. "Relax. It would only hurt you if ingested, or if some fool started burning it, and you inhaled the smoke. Or if it got into your bloodstream directly, somehow." Looking directly at Bjurstrom, she added, "Or if one were to lick the walls."

Bjurstrom put his hands behind his back, an innocent look on his face. "Yeah, Goodrich! No lickin' the walls."

Rolling her eyes, Nancy turned to Allistor. "This could indeed come in handy for several potions. Mostly poisons, but also a cure potion. Let me harvest some more."

As Nancy did her thing, Allistor continued farther down the hallway, now casting a light globe ahead of him. The blue light from the moss was enough to keep him from tripping over furniture, but he needed to be able to see anything hiding in the corners. Logan followed behind, and the others spread out, one by one, still sticking to the center of the floor, away from the walls. Several more light globes floated above the line of raiders.

Which, as it turned out, saved their lives.

Allistor was maybe a hundred feet beyond where Nancy was working, when someone screamed behind him. Even as he was turning, another scream rang out, then several shouts and grunts of pain. People were pointing up at the ceiling, while others were slapping themselves and gyrating crazily. He was about to run back to help, when something blue dropped right in front of his face. His eyes reflexively followed it to the ground, where it instantly curled into a ball, small jets of something shooting out of it. Allistor thought it was a bug of some kind, and he used *Examine.*

Motyxia Scavenger
Level 10

Health: 100/100

The screaming intensified, and Allistor could see health bars dropping on his raid screen. Another of the creatures fell onto his shoulder, and he felt a spray of something on his neck. A moment later it began to burn, and he felt slightly sick. He could see it was some kind of segmented millipede, its body pulsing with the same blue glow as the moss. It had wicked pincers on its front segment, which were now nearing his neck. He quickly brushed it off, then stomped it into oblivion.

"Out! Everybody back to the stairs!" He shouted, running toward the door and pushing Logan ahead of him. Another of the little creatures landed on his face as he looked up, seeing hundreds of them dropping out of tiny holes in the tunnel ceiling, landing on his people. The one that hit his face rolled off, but not before it squirted him with a noxious liquid. Some of it splashed into his left eye, instantly blinding it. He moved his *Barrier* spell so that it floated above his head, and elongated it as much as possible. Now about ten feet long, it sheltered him, Logan, and a few others as they rushed toward the door. Many more of the nasty little things were falling to his left and right, hitting the ground and rushing on tiny legs toward his feet. If his raiders had been walking anywhere other than the center line, they'd likely have been buried in the falling millipedes.

Ahead of him, his people were stumbling, many of them crying in pain as they moved through the door and up the stairs to make room for those behind. The healers were doing their best, but the substance the millipedes squirted them with were both acid and poison. Nancy was passing around poison cure potions to those that didn't have them, and Allistor pulled one from his own inventory. Before he was even through the door, he greedily chugged the entire vial, his gut feeling slightly better right away. Without the use of one eye, he missed the door on his first try, slamming his shoulder into the frame on the left side. Backing up, he turned slightly and dove through the opening.

The moment Allistor was through the doorway, Logan slammed the heavy metal door shut, then leaned against it. "Well, that sucked." He let out a long breath, one hand gingerly touching his face where he'd been hit by more than one of the millipedes.

Allistor agreed. But not as vehemently as Meg. The woman cursed long and loud, stopping twice to take a deep breath and continue before she finally ran out of colorful words to describe exactly where Allistor could stick things. A few people actually laughed through the pain as her tirade progressed. Sam beamed with pride. "That's my girl."

Dawn, who had recovered from her previous injuries only to have half her face disfigured by the Motyxia poison, grunted as she sat down on a step. "We just got our asses kicked by a bunch of level ten bugs."

Meg had a grenade in each hand, facing the door. "Logan, open that thing up! I'll teach the lil smurfy blue bastards who's boss."

Logan was turning to oblige, when Nancy shouted, "No!" All eyes went to her, and she held up a glass vial with some of the blue mold in it. "Cyanide, remember? You start a fire in there, you create a poison cloud. And who knows whether there's any kind of vents in there? Or where that cloud might come out?"

Meg didn't look like she much cared. She looked at Logan, then glared at him when he didn't open the door. When he shook his head and leaned back against it, she started cussing again. Sam gently removed the grenades from her hands, putting them in his inventory before pulling her into a hug. Everyone could hear her muffled voice still ranting into his shoulder as he squeezed her tight.

Everyone cast heals on themselves, and helped to heal others, as they waited for the cure potions to neutralize the poison. A few, who had taken hits on bare arms as well as faces, puked up their lunches. Two went into seizures before the focused heals of several comrades and a second dose of cure potion eased their symptoms. Both bears seemed to have been protected by their fur, though there were some bare spots here and there. Amanda fed them each a potion.

Bjurstrom turned his back on the vomiting and stared at the door. "We can't burn them with fire. Or lightning, I'm guessing. Andrea could dissolve some, but her cooldown is…" He paused and looked up at her.

"Thirty seconds." She supplied, looking pale herself.

"Bugnado." Dawn suggested.

Meg instantly brightened, turning away from Sam. "Yeah! Like you did with those friggin meat bees!"

Allistor nodded. "Logan, get ready." He turned to the door and cast *Barrier* yet again. "Okay, now."

Logan opened the door, and Allistor extended his magical shield to cover the entire opening. Then he and the others who knew the spell commenced casting *Vortex* into the hall. Winds began to pick up, forming multiple small twisters within the corridor. As the wind speed increased, bits of moss peeled off from the walls and ceilings, along with some of the millipedes that were still dropping from the ceiling.

Allistor noticed that the larger motyxia on the floor were killing and eating their smaller cousins. At least, until one of the vortexes passed over them.

In less than a minute, they could no longer see through Allistor's barrier, which was now coated with a thick layer of blue slime from millipedes and moss being hurled against it. When the spells all faded, Allistor released the shield, the slime dropping to the floor. Then he recast it, and said, "Again! This time, one at a time. I'll go first. Form your *Vortex* right in front of the door, then push it down the hallway. One every ten seconds, please." He started his own spell, allowing the tornado of bug bits to grow from floor to ceiling before pushing it down the tunnel. Behind him, he heard Bjurstrom coordinating everyone who had the spell, calling them by name when it was their turn. One by one they scoured the long hall as far as they could push their spells.

Ten minutes later, Allistor cast yet another new Barrier above his head, and led three of them with the *Vortex* spell down to within about fifteen feet of the limit of their castings. When they stopped, Allistor looked up. Not a single one of the millipedes had dropped on them as they walked. Taking a deep breath, he shifted the shield so that it was in front of them, filling the tunnel opening, and cast another *Vortex*. The others followed behind, a new spell forming every ten seconds, and they cleared the rest of the tunnel. Allistor held the blue-slimed shield for a moment as he pulled up his interface and tried to claim the castle.

"Yessss!" He shouted when he saw the green button, pressing it instantly. There were cheers behind him as the entire area went transparent, all of the raiders having experienced it before, knowing that it meant they'd accomplished their mission.

Allistor quickly chose the usual settings, making Dover Castle a new Citadel. When the golden lights faded, the group returned to retrieve the bodies and carried them upstairs. All except Nancy and a couple of her students, who took some time to scoop up large quantities of millipede goo and moss.

Back up in the main courtyard, Allistor set up one of the teleport pads, and they carried their dead home.

Chapter 19

Allistor and the original group of survivors sent Leila and Scott's bodies to Invictus City for a memorial service, and took George home for his funeral. It was a solemn affair, with thousands attending from nearly all of Allistor's properties to pay their respects. George had helped keep many of them alive, put food in their bellies, and given some of them sage advice over the year since the apocalypse. The funeral and wake lasted late into the evening, Allistor and Amanda eventually stumbling exhausted into bed. Amanda cried herself to sleep as Allistor held her, tears in his eyes as well.

Five hours later, they were awakened by Nigel.

"Pardon me for waking you, but you have approximately one hour before the Phoenix must leave for Araneaea. Lady Lilly is insisting on a last minute fitting before you leave."

Allistor groaned. "Shit, I was supposed to meet her yesterday. Please tell her I'll be right down, Nigel."

"She is waiting in your sitting room, sire."

Allistor and Amanda both crawled out of bed. Lilly greeted them with coffee and pastries on a cart when they emerged from their bedroom. "I know, I'm not feeling so hot, either." She commiserated. "But we need to suck it up and get you ready to meet the spider queen." She handed Allistor a suit, and Amanda a dress. "Try these on. I'll give them one last check, and if any adjustments are needed, we can get them done on the ship."

They did as they were told, and ten minutes later Lilly pronounced them properly clothed for a formal state meeting. "Try not to get dirty, or tear anything, before you meet the queen." She admonished them as she stepped onto the elevator.

"You look beautiful." Allistor gave Amanda his best smile, trying to cheer her up. They had both looked at George as a sort of father figure, and his loss hurt.

She gave him a half smile in return, making an effort. "Thank you, sir prince. You look half decent, yourself."

He poured her a cup of coffee, mixing in a couple spoons of sugar, because she liked it sweet. Motioning for her to sit on the sofa, he handed her the mug along with an apple turnover on a small plate. Fixing himself the same, they ate their breakfast in silence. When several more minutes had passed, Amanda asked, "Do you think we'll have to eat some weird spider food while we're there? Like, fried beetle larvae, or liquified fly guts?"

Allistor grinned. "If we do, I'm totally letting you taste it first. This time *you* get to be the guinea pig."

"Speaking of food, do you think Meg will come along?"

Allistor shook his head. "Nope. Especially not after the whole blue bug encounter yesterday."

"I learned some new words from her. That was impressive." Amanda tried not to smile. "She really chewed your ass."

"I'm thinking about bringing her back some pet spiderlings." Allistor got to his feet. "But before we can bring anything back, we need to actually get there. Ready to fly across the solar system to meet a giant eight-legged monarch?"

Amanda joined him, and they headed for the elevators. "This is so surreal. Giant talking arachnids, monsters, dragons… our world is so completely different now."

"It's not all bad." Allistor took her hand, leading her off the elevator into the ground floor lobby. "I found you. That wouldn't have happened if the world hadn't changed."

She stopped walking, using his hand to pull him back to her, giving him a soft kiss on the cheek. "Keep talking like that, and I might pick you over all those cute cowboys."

"Allistor!" Harmon called out as he walked into the lobby from the courtyard. "Ready for your first official affair of state?"

"Nope." Allistor shook his head. "I'm terrified I'll do or say something wrong."

"You'll do fine." Harmon assured him. "The araneae are not big on formality."

L'olwyn joined them, along with the other analysts. "Just remember, do not turn your back on the queen until you are at least ten steps away. To do so within that range is both an insult, and invitation to attack." The old elf warned.

Allistor's eyes widened. "What? Where… why hasn't someone mentioned this before now? What else haven't you told me?" His pulse began to race.

L'olwyn's stoic face cracked slightly, and the other non-humans lost their battles to keep straight faces. Looking around, Allistor took in the laughter and smiles. Turning back to the elf, he asked, "Did you just make a *joke?*"

"You did request that I try to… lighten up?" The elf bowed slightly.

"Ha!" Amanda snort-laughed. "He got you *good*!"

Shaking his head, Allistor grinned sheepishly at his analyst. "Well played. Of course, you realize this means I have to get you back, somehow."

L'olwyn's face went stoic again. "I shall wait with bated breath as you plot your revenge."

There was a moment of silent disbelief at the elf's second volley, before the entire group laughed. Allistor patted his shoulder. "Thank you, my friend."

Kira walked past them, giving a little wave as she headed for the door along with her bridge crew trainees. "Bus leaves in fifteen!"

The others turned to follow, chatting quietly as they walked the few blocks to the parking garage and the Phoenix. It was a large and varied retinue accompanying Allistor and Amanda. Harmon and the analysts, Gralen and three of his beastkin, who would be guiding the bridge crew on the trip there and back. Logan and the three remaining lead airmen to act as security, Lars, Remy, Andrea, Dean, Ramon, Nancy, Chris, Helen, and both bears.

They boarded the Phoenix and got settled in a guest passenger's lounge on the upper deck. As Kira lifted off, Harmon produced a shiny metal box about the size of a loaf of bread, and handed it to Allistor.

"You asked about a gift for the queen. I think this would serve."

Allistor opened the box. Inside was a crimson lining that shone slightly, like some kind of woven metallic fabric, but was soft to the touch like velvet. Cushioned atop the lining was a long string of black pearls. Peering over his shoulder, Amanda reached out and touched it at the same time he did. "Oooh. I like those." She mumbled.

Allistor looked at Harmon, one eyebrow raised. "Pearls?"

Amanda said, "What? She's a queen, right? I'm guessing girls are girls no matter the species, and we all like shiny baubles."

Harmon chuckled. "They are not Earth pearls. These are harvested from a creature similar to your oysters, called incallions. They live in dark, dangerous waters filled with predators. The local divers who harvest them… well, let's just say they do not often live to retirement age. A string this size likely cost the lives of two or three of divers. This adds greatly to the value." Harmon paused, holding up a hand when he saw Amanda start to speak.

"I do not encourage this waste of life. This particular strand was harvested before any of us were born. It was a wedding gift to the wife of an emperor who perished after offending my people more than a century ago." He grinned, his tusks showing to frightening effect.

"In addition, these will be of particular value to the queen of the araneae. They are among the shortest-lived sentient species in the Collective. The queen will live longer than her people, but even she can only expect a life span of about twenty years. These pearls took more than one hundred years to form inside the incallions."

He looked at Amanda. "Before the acquisition, you could have expected to live maybe a hundred years?" She nodded. "Imagine if I were to present you with a gift that Master Daigath spent five hundred years crafting. What value would it hold for you?"

Amanda whistled. "I see what you mean." She looked down at the necklace again, a new appreciation in her eyes.

Allistor nodded as well, touching one of the pearls, feeling its smooth surface. "I guess it's a little like how we value diamonds, since they're rare and take millions of years to form."

L'olwyn immediately took the box from him and used some kind of cloth to wipe off any skin cells and DNA he might have just left behind on the necklace, liner, and box. "Indeed. And just as a reminder, you should touch nothing and no one while you are visiting. And do not eat or drink anything offered to you. I do not suspect the araneae of having nefarious intentions, but one can never be too careful."

Amanda snorted. "No pureed fly milk shakes."

"Thank you, Harmon. This seems like a very thoughtful gift. Let me know what I owe you, and we'll settle up as soon as we get back home." Allistor pulled on a pair of gloves that Lilly had included at L'olwyn's insistence. Amanda did the same.

"I would have gone with chocolate covered crickets, or something." McCoy mumbled from his seat near the door.

The rest of the trip was split between discussing potential trade agreement terms, and protocol instruction, like not looking the queen directly in the eyes, not raising one's hands higher than one's head in her presence, and one particular bit that made Allistor a little more nervous.

"One or more of her guards, who are all female, may challenge you. This could include verbal insults, a waving about of forearms in a hostile manner, or even a short charge in your direction. You must ignore them all. To do otherwise is a sign of weakness." Harmon instructed. "Also any one of them may challenge the queen herself, in an attempt to embarrass her in public. Unlike you, she may decide to respond. If she does, well… get out of the way."

"So, I'm supposed to disregard an eight foot long giant spider guard charging at me with hostile intent?" Allistor leaned back in his chair. "It's a good thing Meg's not here."

Longbeard laughed. "Do no' worry, Allistor. Any challenge put to you will be just fer show. To actually attack a guest o' the queen would mean instant death. It simply be a test o' yer courage, as well as the queen's patience. Each o' them guards is also one o' her offspring, and a potential replacement as queen."

Amanda sounded worried when she suggested, "Maybe we should leave Fuzzy and Fiona on the ship? I'm not sure either of them would react well even to a fake attack."

Allistor agreed, and the bears didn't seem to object.

Kira's voice came across the intercom a short time later. "We're approaching the planet, folks."

Harmon reached over to a control panel, and a section of the lounge's wall slid open to reveal a twenty-foot wide viewscreen that Allistor initially took to be an actual window looking forward across the ship's hull. He realized it was a screen when Harmon zoomed in, the view of the small planet in the distance suddenly becoming much larger. It was a dark planet, most of it a very deep shade of green, with black mountain ranges here and there. Huge storm clouds large enough to be seen from space obscured great swathes of the surface, and lightning flashes within the storms were nearly constant.

"Doesn't look like a real friendly place." Selby observed. Longbeard grunted his agreement.

Harmon gave some details. "I've been here once before. The gravity is slightly lower than Earth's, and the atmosphere more humid. The storms move quickly, but you don't want to get caught out in the open when one of them passes. On most of the surface, the trees protect you from lightning strikes. You can't tell from here, but they're massive, ancient monsters. I've seen some with a trunk diameter of thirty feet, rising as tall as your tower at Invictus. They can withstand the lightning strikes with little damage, and actually convert some of the energy to promote growth. You can tell the trees that have been struck recently, as their trunks glow slightly in the darkness."

"Cool." Goodrich leaned closer to the screen and squinted, as if that would allow him to see more detail.

"It has been speculated that the araneae achieved their size and intelligence through some mutation caused by the synergy between storms and trees. That they lived in the trees, and were altered by the converted energy flowing through the trees over thousands of generations."

"You want mutant spiders? Electricity and tree sap. That's how you get mutant spiders." McCoy poked Goodrich's arm as they all watched the planet grow larger on the screen.

Now they were able to see large structures, or clusters of structures, with lights. Harmon zoomed in on one of them. "This is their queen's cluster." Allistor tilted his head slightly sideways, taking in the details as they continued to get closer. Eventually he could make out several individual spires rising up from the surface fog, curving inward toward each other. He blinked a few times. "That... those look like giant spider legs. Like, if a dead spider were laying on its back, the legs sticking up into the air."

"They're huge. Tell me these creatures don't live inside the corpse of a giant spider world boss." Bjurstrom's voice was barely above a whisper.

Harmon chuckled. "No, they are artificial constructs. Many have made a similar observation. I believe it may have been a joke on their part, the amusement of some araneae architect long ago. Or maybe it is just a shape they admire."

Andrea shook her head. "Or maybe it's a giant battle droid that could flip itself over, get up and lay waste to the planet." For which McCoy gave her a fist bump.

Ramon looked thoughtful. "It's not that much bigger than the harvester ship. And Harmon said they're skilled builders. Maybe it *is* some kind of massive vessel."

Everyone was silent, taking in that possibility, imagining a spider more than a mile long rising through the sky and into space. Except for Bjurstrom, who was imagining it flipped over, stomping its way through Tokyo.

"Landing in five minutes." This time it was Gralen's voice on the intercom. "We've been told to land outside." His voice sounded slightly concerned, and Harmon frowned at the words.

"Was a reason given?"

"None. You'll need to move inside quickly once we've set down. A storm is approaching."

Amanda looked worried now, as well. "Will the ship be alright in the storm?"

Harmon smiled. "The *Phoenix* has shields that will absorb and store energy from any lightning strike. Or simply repel the energy if its storage capacity is full. No harm will come to her. The System granted Allistor quite a boon when it selected this ship. It is both powerful and versatile, while also offering luxury and comfort." The admiration in his voice was clear. "We should prepare to disembark."

Everyone got to their feet and made their way back down from the topmost deck to the cargo hold. They had just a brief wait before the ship set down, and the ramp lowered. Allistor could see that they'd set down on a large bedrock outcropping situated between two of the leg-like towers. The air was indeed as humid as Harmon had described, and it took them all several steps to adjust to the slightly lighter gravity as they moved down the ramp.

Fog rolled past, a stiff wind pushing it quickly through the trees and brush that surrounded them. A deep purple cloud bursting with lightning was quickly filling the sky to their left. That was all Allistor had time to take in before a dozen massive spiders emerged from a door that opened in the bedrock's surface, and walked up a ramp.

The honor guard turned to take up position in two rows along either side of the stone ramp, and behind them emerged an even larger, armored araneae. With a body maybe ten feet long, its belly was suspended at least four feet off the ground by eight segmented and chitin-covered legs. The segmented body must have weighed at least a thousand pounds, the head segment looking down at them from about eight feet high. It halted in front of them, moving one of its forearms in what Allistor assumed was a salute.

"Welcome to Araneaea, your Majesties, honored guests. I am First Warrior Artax. Please, follow me inside. We must move quickly to ensure your safety, as a storm approaches." The creature turned and stepped to one side, motioning toward the door. When Allistor and the others stepped forward, it moved toward the doorway at a quick pace.

Passing through the door, Allistor found himself in a wide stone corridor, the walls at least twenty feet apart. He supposed for creatures the size of the araneae, it was necessary to have plenty of room to move about.

Once the last of the honor guard had followed them through and secured the door, Harmon asked a question. "First Warrior Artax, I am curious. Why have us land out here?"

The giant spider warrior turned to face him, bowing deeply. "Apologies, Emperor Harmon." There were gasps from all the humans in the corridor, but no one spoke as Artax continued. "There has been some... difficulty with the new hatchlings. The subterranean landing bays where we would normally greet such honored guests are not currently secure."

Behind him, several industrial sized hoverpads were making their way toward the group. Half of them had six chairs each fastened to their surface, making them look a little bit like cars with no roofs or doors. The others were simply bare platforms. "We have been forced to improvise some transportation for you. I hope this will not offend?"

Allistor stepped forward, shooting Harmon a look that made it clear he had some explaining to do. "We understand the need to improvise in times of trouble. These will work just fine." To ease their host's mind, he stepped up onto the closest pad with seats, and sat down. "Yes, this is quite comfortable."

Artax bowed his head again. "You are most gracious. We will arrive in the Queen's presence shortly." He waited for the rest of the guests to board hoverpads, then he and his soldiers boarded the others. A minute after Allistor sat down, they were hurtling down the corridor at considerable speed. The lights along the walls flashed by so quickly, it was hard to distinguish one from the next. Turning to look at Harmon, who was seated in the third front seat on their pad, on the other side of Amanda, he cleared his throat.

"*Emperor* Harmon?"

Harmon looked slightly embarrassed. "Did I not mention that?"

Amanda crossed her arms and looked up at him. "You most certainly did not."

With a long sigh, the orcanin met her gaze. "My official title is Emperor of Orcana, the orcanin homeworld."

Allistor followed up. "And that would make you... emperor of all orcanin?"

Harmon grinned sheepishly, which wasn't easy for an orcanin. "It would, yes."

"But... you said you fought as a mercenary." Allistor was confused.

"I did, for more than a century. When our people were freed from bondage, we had little in the way of resources. But we had been trained as warriors by the elves for hundreds of generations. It is ingrained in our culture, and our DNA, at this point. So we formed mercenary guilds, hired ourselves out, and used the contract proceeds and spoils to build our empire." He paused and looked down at his hands for a moment. "I have told you that our one unbreakable law is that we never take up arms against the elves. Or, specifically, the high elves. Our previous emperor was growing tired of that restriction, and spoke often of making war with them. Our empire has grown powerful, and we might well be a match for the elves should it come to that. But the cost would be unbearable.

And honor requires that we hold to the oaths that granted our freedom. He began taking actions that he hoped would incite the elves to violate our pact and attack us, freeing the orcanin from our oath. I was forced to… remove him from the throne."

"Wow." Amanda was looking at Harmon with a newfound respect. "So should we be calling you Majesty, or…"

"Harmon. I have little to do with running the empire these days. I leave that to my offspring. I much prefer the life of a merchant."

Allistor was trying to find words to respond to these revelations when the hoverpads slowed, then came to a halt. While Harmon had been sharing his surprising history, Allistor hadn't noticed the change in their surroundings. Instead of bare stone walls and floor, the corridor they were in now was constructed mostly of a softly glowing burnished metal. Stepping off the pad, he found himself in front of a large archway with ten-foot high double metal doors.

The honor guard, having practically leapt off their pad and rushed to open the doors, lined up inside and escorted the party into the room beyond. Allistor and Harmon led the procession, with Amanda between them.

The room was maybe a hundred paces long, and about half that wide. The ceiling stretched three stories above them in several graceful rounded vaults. Near the opposite end of the room stood a raised dais, one high step about four feet above the floor. Atop the dais were dozens of cushions, upon which rested the queen. She was at least twice the size of Artax, and her skin was nearly black, several shades darker than the mostly greyish araneae gathered on either side of the path Allistor was walking.

The massive doors clanged shut behind them, and the sounds of them being bolted created some concern. Allistor resisted turning back to look, keeping his focus on the queen, and a smile on his face as he approached. He could feel a trickle of sweat trailing down his back as his pulse quickened.

Luckily for him, the queen addressed Harmon first, obviously considering him of higher rank. Her multitoned voice was smooth and calm, despite whatever unrest was occurring within her domain.

"Greetings, Emperor Harmon. It is good to see you again after so many years. You are most welcome, as always."

Harmon bowed his head slightly, and Allistor wondered which of them outranked the other. Both seemed to be the leader of their species.

"Always a pleasure, High Queen Xeria. May I present my good friend Allistor, Prince of Earth, and Emperor of Orion, and his betrothed, Lady Amanda."

Both humans bowed to the queen, more deeply than Harmon had, per L'olwyn's careful instruction.

"Welcome! Thank you for accepting my invitation, Emperor Allistor. Your attempt to accommodate my peoples' need in a desperate situation was truly appreciated." She waved one of her forelegs at them.

"Thank you for extending the invitation, your Majesty. And I only did what I felt was right."

Harmon, concerned by what he'd heard in the queen's words, took a step forward. "Majesty, pardon my directness, but has something gone wrong? You mention Allistor's *attempt* to help, suggesting the harvest was unsuccessful. And the latest hatchlings have taken over your shuttle bays? Do you require assistance?"

The queen made a long, slow humming sound, then answered. "The timing of your visit is unfortunate. I meant it to be a celebration of our latest broods hatching. However, the Collective's enforcers acted more quickly than we anticipated, and seized the harvester before it could deliver the desperately needed resources Allistor so generously allowed them to gather. As a result, we had insufficient food for our hatchlings. A great number of them have gone feral."

The queen lowered her head slightly, and Allistor had the impression it was a gesture of embarrassment or shame.

Allistor was the first to respond. "Can we help in some way? Could you send a harvester to Orion? As emperor, I can authorize a harvest from one of the oceans there."

"Thank you, Emperor Allistor. Once again you show great kindness. But I am afraid it is far too late for that. We feared that even the harvest from Earth would not arrive in time. And the enforcers made sure of that. The hatching has begun, and will be finished long before a harvester could make the trip to your planet and back."

Harmon frowned. "The Collective's forces should not have been able to respond so quickly. And even if they were close by for some reason, they should have allowed the harvest to be delivered before confiscating the ship, rather than endangering so many lives. Was a reason given why they did not?"

The queen's voice took on a harsh tone, the multiple chords seeming to crash against each other as she spoke. "We have repeatedly attempted communication with them, but there has been no reply of any kind."

Harmon looked concerned, briefly turning back to L'olwyn, who shook his head. "I have never heard of such action being taken." Longbeard also shook his head. Harmon turned back to the queen.

"I will investigate this immediately, Majesty. Though I know it will not help today's situation, a break in protocol that results in the deaths of millions must be answered for." He looked back at the locked metal doors behind them. "If you wish it, I can have an army of orcanin warriors here within the hour to help… resolve your issue with the feral hatchlings. You need only grant access to your hub."

The queen rose from her cushion, stepping lightly down off the dais and approaching the visitors. She reached out one foreleg and gently touched Harmon's arm.

"Thank you, my old friend. But you know that is not our way. My warriors and workers are striving even now to deal with the feral ones. They shall either be strong enough to destroy them, or perish in the attempt. It is the way of our kind."

"Weakness!" one of the araneae standing near the dais shouted, the word echoing off the ceiling above. "Your weakness has led us to this ruin! Millions of lives forfeit! A harvester lost to us! You are no longer fit to rule, Xeria." The room was instantly filled with quiet chittering from the gathered araneae.

The queen turned to face the speaker, who stepped forward from the ranks. She was larger than most of the others standing nearby, but considerably smaller than the queen.

"You believe you could have done better, little one? I don't believe I know your name."

The volume of the chittering increased, and the other female twitched visibly. Allistor guessed that the queen not knowing, or pretending not to know her name was quite an insult.

"I could scarcely have done worse! You grow old, Xeria, and clearly senile if you don't recognize Ixam, your eldest granddaughter. Your time has passed. Surrender the throne, and I will allow you to live out your days overseeing the next brood in the egg chambers."

"And if I refuse?" The queen took another step, putting herself directly between her visitors and the challenger.

"Then I will take your head, and mount it above the dais as a reminder to all of our people that weakness is death."

The two giant females faced each other, all of their many eyes laser-focused on the other. L'olwyn leaned forward and whispered, "I hear the sounds of battle nearby." Allistor couldn't hear anything, even the chittering of the court having gone silent. But elven hearing was supposed to be far superior to human, and he trusted L'olwyn.

Allistor was about to speak to the queen when Harmon held up a hand and shook his head. He took a single, slow step backward, followed by another. Allistor and the others followed suit.

"Little one, you have neither the strength, nor the cunning, to supplant me." Xeria practically growled. "Withdraw your challenge, and I will allow you to live and grow stronger."

The smaller female nodded her head. "You are correct, in that I am not as strong as you. Were I to challenge you in single combat, you would surely defeat me. As for cunning... there you are mistaken. I have cultivated allies, and raised soldiers of my own. A wise queen knows when to delegate!" She nodded toward the locked doors, and several araneae who'd been hovering at the back of the crowd dashed toward it. Two of them undid the simple bolts, while two more flung the doors open wide.

Out in the corridor, battle was raging. Allistor couldn't tell one side from the other, but dozens of the giant spider people were slicing and bashing at each other with swords and maces, spears and hammers. The fight quickly spilled through the door as several of the combatants leapt upon the four who had opened the doors. Obviously not trained warriors themselves, all four were quickly dispatched, their heads crushed or simply removed.

There was a scream of rage from the queen, and Allistor turned back from the door just in time to see her leap at her granddaughter. A long scepter appeared in one of her foreclaws, and she swept it downward onto Ixam's head. Several of the smaller spider's eyes burst, and her chitin exoskeleton caved in with a loud crack, Ixam's legs going limp beneath her.

Even as her body hit the floor, Xeria backed away. Several of the other females around Ixam dashed in and began to tear her body to shreds. Their way of demonstrating loyalty to their queen.

Breathing hard, the queen turned and faced the door, walking back to stand next to Harmon. "That fool! The young have no respect for tradition! To involve our warriors in a challenge for the throne... even had she been victorious, our people would not have accepted her. And to pull warriors from their duties dealing with the hatchlings? Disgraceful!"

The sounds of battle out in the corridor caught her attention. Raising her head, she shouted toward the door. Her multi-toned voice was so loud, Allistor winced. L'olwyn and Selby covered their ears, the elf dropping to his knees. "ENOUGH!" her voice echoed through the room. "The challenge has failed! Ixam is no more! Return to your duties!"

The warriors who had entered the room and killed the traitors had stepped back out and formed a barrier across the doorway, striking out at any enemies who got too close. When the queen's orders ceased to echo through the room, one of them turned to face her.

"Majesty! We no longer battle the misguided fools who followed your granddaughter. The hatchlings have broken containment!" The warrior turned back to face the corridor, and Allistor could see that the other three fighters with him were already engaging the hatchlings, as were the opposing adult warriors they'd been fighting a few seconds before. Much smaller than the adult spiders, each of the hatchlings was maybe two feet long. They looked much like the adults, but with wild red eyes and slavering jaws that seemed to never stop gnashing. Each swing of sword or spear crushed one or more of the little monsters, but each one destroyed was replaced by five or six more. They flooded across the floor and walls, and a few dropped from the ceiling onto their prey.

The hatchlings bit at the warriors, but their sharp teeth didn't penetrate the chitin exoskeletons. Tiny legs with spearpoint sharp tips pounded at the armor, seeking out weak points and joints. Any two or three of the little feral creatures would be no match for an adult warrior, but each of them was being swarmed by dozens of the hatchlings.

"The bodies! Feed them!" The queen shouted, dashing back to Ixam's bloody corpse. She easily lifted her granddaughter and hurled her body across the room to land near the door. Several others ran to grab her body, and the four bodies that lay inside the door, and toss them out into the corridor. The moment they hit the ground, hundreds of the feral hatchlings swarmed them. The distraction gave the warriors a slight reprieve, and they worked together to clear each other's backs of gnawing hatchlings.

"All of you, fight!" The queen instructed, not waiting for her people to respond before she charged toward the door. Now in addition to her bloody scepter, she held a wicked looking curved blade in her other foreclaw. The warriors blocking the door parted to let her through, then followed her into the corridor where she was already mowing down hatchlings in a wide swathe.

Allistor stepped toward the door himself, but Harmon grabbed his shoulder and held him back. "They will not thank you for interfering. If the hatchlings break into this room, you may defend yourself. Though, at that point..." The orcanin didn't finish his thought. Allistor and the others all knew what he meant.

"Bjurstrom, raid group!" Allistor called out, sending invites to him, Amanda, and Harmon. "Include the queen and everyone else!" Bjurstrom nodded, and his eyes unfocused as he started sending out invites. Allistor turned to Harmon. "I don't want any friendly fire problems if I have to burn them down." The orcanin nodded his approval, drawing twin scimitars and gazing with longing toward the battle. The others in their group drew weapons as well.

Amanda snorted. "Sure wish Meg was here with her grenades right about now."

Chapter 20

The raiders stood with weapons at the ready, watching the queen and her people battle the ravenous hatchlings outside the door. First Warrior Artax had followed his queen into the corridor and was inflicting even more devastating damage than she was. His armor protected him from the dozen or more hatchlings that rode his back, legs, and belly, trying to bite or stab their way through.

Several of the female guards who'd torn apart Ixam's body took up station in the doorway, replacing the four warriors that had moved out into the corridor to protect the queen. Occasionally a few of the hatchlings would slip past the door guards, only to be massacred by several of the courtiers standing behind them. When one of the female guards was overwhelmed, one of the hatchlings having managed to bite into her throat, her body was tossed into the corridor to distract the mass of hatchlings, and another took her place.

"That's just brutal." Amanda muttered.

Harmon nodded. "It is their way. To their thinking, you are either predator, or food. They waste nothing here, including their own bodies. The dead are fed to the young, or used as fertilizer if there are no hatchlings. Adults who are too weak to feed or fend for themselves are left to die, becoming a resource rather than a drain."

"Just another reminder that the other species out here in the universe don't share our views or morals. That's going to take some getting used to. I keep catching myself looking at everything from a human point of view." Allistor kept his eyes on the doorway as he spoke. "I could drop a lightning storm out there and take the pressure off of them. Since they're in our raid group, it wouldn't hurt them."

"Do not." Harmon warned. "The queen needs to claim victory here, or perish, on her own. Her strength and judgement have been publicly called into question. Many of her people will feel the same as Ixam did – that this chaos is her failing. She would not welcome your assistance." He looked at Allistor and winked. "But be ready, should she ask for it."

The group of visitors stood their ground near the dais, watching as araneae died by the score. For every few hundred of the hatchlings killed, one of the adults would fall. Even worse, the hatchlings that fed on the corpses seemed to grow right in front of their eyes. They quickly became stronger, and more voracious. Some even turned on their fellow hatchlings, finding them much easier prey than the adults. Allistor noticed that the adults rarely attacked the cannibals, wisely leaving them to their grisly work.

About five minutes after the queen charged into the fray, the sounds of battle began to decrease. Another minute or two, and the corridor grew silent. The guards at the door parted, and the queen limped through, her body completely covered in blood, more than a little of it being her own. She climbed atop the dais and settled down amongst the cushions, staring down at the nearby females.

"Anyone else wish to challenge me today? I am weakened from battle, now is your chance." Her head shifted left and right, scanning the crowd. No one stepped forth.

"Emperor Harmon, Emperor Allistor, my most sincere apologies for these unfortunate events taking place during your visit here. You have witnessed my greatest shame." She lowered her head, blood still dripping from her chitin armor onto the cushions.

"There is no shame in doing what must be done. We have all found ourselves in impossible situations, forced to make decisions that we'll regret, whichever option we choose. You had the strength and courage to act swiftly in the best interests of your people." Harmon bowed his head slightly. "Your people should appreciate your actions, and honor you for them." He eyed the quiet crowd around them.

Allistor nodded his head. "As you know, I'm new to the responsibilities I hold now. I can't imagine how I'd handle a situation like this. I just hope that none of us will ever have to again."

The queen's head drooped. Allistor suspected she had lost a considerable amount of blood. "I am afraid I must cut our visit short. There are yet more feral hatchlings to be hunted down and dealt with. But before you go, I wish to make an offer of friendship and formal alliance with you, Prince Allistor of Earth, Emperor of Orion. And ask that our factors discuss mutually beneficial trade agreements."

Allistor's screen lit up with notifications, including a couple level up notices. He bowed at the waist toward the fading queen. "I am honored to accept, High Queen Xeria." He panicked briefly, not having more words, until one of the phrases in his notifications caught his eye. "May you rule long and wisely."

The queen nodded once, then rose unsteadily from her cushions. Three of her guards escorted her through a door near the back of the room. First Warrior Artax, himself covered in blood and bits of hatchling, motioned them toward the main door. "I will escort you back to your ship."

When they reached the corridor, Allistor and the others were shocked by the sheer number of bodies piled up. There were tens of thousands of the hatchlings, and hundreds of adult corpses, many of them wearing the armor of the queen's warriors. As they waited for the hoverpads to arrive, Harmon took a couple discreet steps to the side, and whispered something to Artax. The warrior nodded grimly, and turned to face Allistor.

"It is known that the blood of hatchlings has value as a component in various crafts. I am sure our queen would be honored if you were to harvest some to take back with you."

Surprised, Allistor stammered. "Th-thank you, First Warrior." He glanced at Nancy, who immediately got to work. She enlisted Andrea and her airmen to assist her.

When Artax turned toward the approaching hoverpads, Allistor discretely bent and grabbed a hatchling corpse, quickly sliding it into his inventory. When he caught Amanda's stern look, he whispered, "I'm bringing back some spider legs for Meg."

*****

The trip back was mostly quiet, everyone absorbing what had happened. After the encounter with the blue millipedes, and the losses that came with it, the battle with thousands of low level spiderlings had struck a chord with most of them.

Bjurstrom tried to lighten the mood. "So, Prince Allistor, what are the rules for challenging you for your throne? I'm asking for a friend." He grinned as a few of the others chuckled.

"Challenge me? Right now, I'd just give it to you. Just leave me Orion, and Lady Amanda here, as the start of my harem."

Bjurstrom recoiled in mock horror. "And take on all that responsibility? That's for officers and foolish kids who run around saving people!"

Allistor held up his inventory ring, then made like he was about to reach into it with his other hand. "You positive? I'm sure I have a crown in here somewhere for you…"

"I'll take it!" Helen held out her hand as if to accept the crown. "My first act as Princess Helen will be to have Lilly make cute lil leather outfits for all the cowboys."

Andrea snorted, then held up a hand for a high-five. "I vote for Princess Helen!" Selby nodded in agreement.

The group became a little more talkative for the remainder of the trip. Nancy spent a little time examining the hatchling components, mumbling to herself and Ramon occasionally. The airmen and Andrea got into a discussion about proper names for murder chickens. Amanda convinced Harmon to let her scan him with *Internal Analysis*. Ten seconds into the scan, she said, "Damn. I thought Allistor had a lot of injuries. There's hardly a part of you that hasn't been damaged at some point."

"I was a front line fighter for several decades." Harmon shrugged. "And orcanin children begin combat training at age four."

Reflecting back on the day, Allistor asked Harmon, "Will they be asking to send a harvester to Orion?"

Harmon shook his head. "Not for several years, I would imagine. This hatching was an anomaly, with a much larger than normal number of broods hatching at once. Hence the rush to obtain resources, even at the risk of forfeiting a harvester and crew." He looked down at his hands. "The loss of life was… significant, from what I could see. And we only observed the one segment of the battle. There would have been food for some percentage of the hatchlings, but those were likely consumed by the ferals soon after. And many breedable females likely lost their lives to the ferals as well. I am confident the queen, and her replacements, will ensure that this situation does not arise again."

"And the harvester's cargo? You sounded surprised that it was seized."

"Indeed." Harmon's bushy eyebrows furrowed. "The Collective's forces should not have been able to respond so quickly. Unless they already had a fleet in this system, for some reason. And there was no reason that I'm aware of, prior to the harvester incident." He took a deep breath, looking thoughtful as he rubbed his chin with one hand. "Even then, the enforcers should have allowed the resources to be delivered once the situation was known, rather than endanger the lives of millions. The seizure of the harvester, punishment of the crew and the colony world it originated from, are all that the System's rules demand. I suspect someone is behind this."

Allistor looked thoughtful himself. "You're saying someone maneuvered the enforcers to be here in time to take the resources, meaning that they alerted the enforcers before the harvester actually visited Earth?" When Harmon nodded, the room grew quiet.

"Which means that whoever alerted them... might have had something to do with either the lack of resources, or the anomalous timing of so many simultaneous hatchings?" Amanda ventured.

"And potentially the fact that the harvester was sent to Earth, which has already had more than its share of odd occurrences." Harmon confirmed. He looked around the

434

room, then sighed. "There is something you should know. Earth was acquired centuries ahead of schedule. During a time in your development when the pollution and ecological damage you humans were inflicting on your planet was sure to trigger a harsh response from the System."

"What do you mean, ahead of schedule?" Allistor's face was growing red, and his hands squeezed the arms of his chair so tightly it creaked.

"Like all of the worlds within the Collective, your planet has been visited and… guided by the elder races. Likely since the early stages of life on Earth. It is why they appear in so many of your myths and legends. It was the same with my world. The ancient ones foster growth and evolution, monitoring the worlds until they are deemed ready to join the collective. In the case of Earth, you should have had several more centuries to develop before the planet officially joined the Collective. Time to advance your science, art, and physical characteristics to a point that would have put you on a more even footing with the rest of us."

Allistor's rage was building, his heart racing as he let go of the furniture and clenched his fists. Getting to his feet, he began to pace.

"And why did these ancient ones claim our world early? The way you phrased it, you made it sound like the extinction of the human race was the goal."

Harmon shook his head. "Not the ancient ones as a group. Earth wasn't acquired via the normal process. We suspect one of them, or a small group of them, went rogue and triggered the early acquisition of Earth. And whether or not genocide was their goal, they would certainly have been aware of it being a certain consequence of their actions."

"We?" Allistor growled. "Were you somehow involved in this?"

Harmon leapt to his feet, towering over Allistor, his eyes blazing and his tusks bared as growled. "I should kill you for even suggesting such a thing!"

Everyone else in the room was instantly on their feet, weapons drawn, as the two Emperors glared at each other, breathing heavily. After a long moment, Harmon blinked, and stepped back, relaxing his posture. "But I will not. I understand your anger, and forgive you for the accusation."

Allistor took longer to come to his senses. He stood there glaring at the giant orcanin, his fists and jaw clenched. He could hear the blood rushing through his veins. Amanda moved to his side, putting an arm around him and pulling him close. "Allistor. Take a deep breath."

Slowly, Allistor calmed. His jaw loosened, and he unclenched his fists. He took a few deep breaths, lowering his gaze. "I'm sorry, Harmon. Truly. You have been a friend and mentor to me since the day we met, and did not deserve to be accused. I... it's hard for me to hear all of this after what we've gone through this year." He returned to his seat, pulling Amanda down with him and squeezing her tightly.

Amanda asked the question that she knew Allistor would ask next. "Harmon, you said 'we suspect'. Allistor's question is valid. Who is 'we'?"

Harmon took his seat as well. After a moment of careful thought, he answered. "I have lived a long time, and seen many things. I am emperor of an entire race, and as such I have had contact with ancient and powerful beings like Master Daigath. And yes, that includes some of the Ancient Ones." He paused to gauge Allistor's reaction to this news. When the human just nodded at him, he continued. "I have spoken with them on more than one occasion since Earth was taken. They have suspects, but no proof, as yet. I ask you to trust me when I say that the perpetrators will be found and punished. I will also tell you that some of them have worked on your behalf over the last year, though the laws of the System prevented them from acting directly."

Allistor was still breathing hard, but was trying to calm himself. He thought back over the major events of the year. "The yacht? The titan scroll?"

Harmon nodded. "Though I have no direct knowledge, I would say that both are correct. Though the scroll itself was likely generated by the System as a reward for killing the elite void titan, which had no business being on a planet still in stabilization. I expect his presence was arranged by the same renegades."

Allistor knew better, based on the letter that accompanied the scroll. The scroll was deliberately placed. But another thought came to him. "The message I got, the one reminding me to use the titan scroll, and to equip the Prince's Seal."

Harmon grinned. "Again, the System severely limits any direct action on a stabilizing world. But a simple anonymous reminder of an action that the System itself had taken, in this case a reward waiting to be used..."

Allistor's thoughts spun. He had been pretty sure that the scroll had been placed by the person or persons that had sent the titan to destroy him. Which meant that whoever sent the reminder message had figured out a way to help Allistor use his enemy's actions against them. Whether that was just by sending the reminder, or it was also them that provided the titan scroll, he needed to take some time to think things through. For all he knew, it could all be the same person or persons just messing with his mind.

The fact that beings with nearly unlimited power were messing with him, and had potentially killed hundreds of thousands of araneae in some scheme that included him, was terrifying. Not just because they might simply decide to kill him, though that was a major fear. But because in doing so, they might kill Amanda, or others close to him. Or the whole human race, for that matter. They didn't seem to care what consequences their actions had.

The rest of the trip home was mostly silent. Allistor eventually stood, offering his hand to Harmon. "I truly am sorry, Harmon. For calling your honor into question."

Harmon stood and engulfed Allistor's hand in his immense paw. "Let us forget it happened, my young friend."

"Ha!" Amanda poked Harmon in the ribs. "Not likely. I don't know about Allistor, but when you jumped up and growled at him, I nearly soiled myself. I won't be forgetting that anytime soon."

*****

Baldur entered Loki's chamber without warning, the mists practically fleeing ahead of him as anger radiated from his entire being.

"Loki! You go too far!"

Frightened by his brother's rage, but keeping a calm outward demeanor, Loki responded. "What is it this time, Baldur?"

"Are you so petty as to destroy an entire generation of araneae just to strike at the human I showed an interest in?"

"I don't know what you're-"

"Do *not* finish that statement, brother. You are no innocent. I have had *enough* of your games! The enforcer command ship *Retribution* and its fleet were ordered to that system a week ago. Yet no one seems to be able to verify where those orders originated, or the purpose of their mission. And the orders to refuse communication with

Xeria, while confiscating the resources that might have saved her hatchlings?"

Loki's upper tentacles waved in his species' version of a shrug. "Lay your accusations elsewhere, Baldur. It was not my doing. Though I admire the ingenuity of whoever was behind it. A masterful bit of manipulation, that."

"More lies!" Baldur's stumpy legs shuffled as he stomped toward Loki, leaning in close. "I give you notice, Loki. Should more mysterious mishaps happen to, or around, the human… I will end you myself! System be damned! I will sacrifice my own mortal existence to end yours! Do you hear me?" The righteous rage pouring from Baldur nearly boiled the mists between them. Loki quailed, flinching slightly despite himself.

"I do not lie, in this case, brother. It wasn't me." The mists that transmitted his reply seemed hesitant to even approach Baldur, who ignored the words in any case.

"Were I you, I would use my resources and cunning to ensure that nothing untoward befell the human. You have known me long enough to know that I *do not* make idle threats, brother. I tire of the limitations of the physical world. It would be no hardship for me to follow our elders into the next plane of existence, and to take you with me."

Loki had no response as Baldur turned and stomped back through the exit. When the door closed behind his brother, he cursed long and loudly to himself.

In another chamber not so far away, Hel watched the feed from a cleverly concealed monitoring device. Baldur, and likely Odin as well, had reacted exactly as she'd hoped.

*****

Back on Earth, Allistor was restless. He paced back and forth on the rooftop of the Invictus tower, his thoughts confused and angry. He'd already tried heating some steel and trying to forge a weapon, planning to test a new enchantment theory that had come to him recently. But he found he couldn't focus enough to even shape the metal properly, and abandoned the work.

He gazed up at the evening sky above, the density and brightness of the stars so much more than the sky he'd grown up under. The nearest and brightest of the stars were even visible under the light of the dual suns in daytime.

Moving over to the rooftop lounge area, he retrieved a bottle from under the bar without looking. When he'd taken a seat and went to open the bottle, he found it was one of the bottles of Brandy that George had given him.

With a sigh, he opened the bottle and, not bothering with a glass, took a sip. He imagined how offended George would be by the action, actually hearing the old man's voice in his head saying, "Respect the quality of the drink, boy!". He took another swig, staring up at the sky.

By the time he stumbled on unsteady legs into his bed, the bottle was nearly half empty.

*****

Morning brought bright sunshine and an instant headache for Allistor when Amanda threw the blinds open wide, allowing the sunlight a critical hit on his face.

"Gah! Nooo. Light bad. Go away." He grabbed a pillow to defend himself against the onslaught, his next words being muffled as he placed it over his face. "Close! Close blinds! Evil woman!"

Amanda just chuckled. "Can't have our fearless leader lazing about in bed all day! There are things to do! People to see! More castles to storm!" She pounced on him, beginning to tickle his sides without mercy. "Up! Up, prince lazybones!"

Squirming and trying unsuccessfully to defend himself without dislodging the protective pillow, he finally gave up and let it fall. Instead, he grabbed Amanda and pulled her in for a kiss. She initially complied, for about three seconds, before she realized he was using her head to block the sun instead of the pillow. "Nope! None of that." She quickly moved her head aside, allowing another critical hit before he even had time to raise his hands. "Hit the showers. You smell like a distillery. If you get up right now like a good boy, I won't tell Nigel to shut off the hot water."

"Nigel would never do that. I'm the prince in this castle. Tower. Whatever." Allistor grumped as he got to his feet. His head was pounding and the light was still way too bright.

"Nope, Nigel likes me better. Isn't that right, Nigel?" She looked up at the ceiling.

"*Lady Amanda is correct, sire.*" Nigel's voice drifted down.

Allistor froze. "Whaaat? How is that even… what?" He looked at Amanda who had crossed her arms and was giving him an 'I told you so' smirk. She only held for a moment before she burst out laughing.

"Thank you, Nigel. That was perfect!"

Allistor smelled a rat. "Nigel, did she put you up to this ahead of time?"

"*She did indeed, sire. My apologies. She said you would be amused, and that she would encourage you to upgrade my Interface Level again.*"

The effects of the hangover plus Nigel, his supposedly faithful AI, messing with him was too much. "I'm going to shower now. When I get out, we'll talk about your upgrade. Any chance you'd be willing to leave *Lady* Amanda stuck in one of the elevators for a while?"

"*Of course, sire. For what period of time?*"

"Ha! That's better." He stuck his tongue out at Amanda. "Nigel's a daddy's boy."

Amanda flipped him off before heading out of the bedroom and through their quarters toward the elevator. Allistor waited patiently until he heard, "Nigel you better *not* leave me stuck in an elevator."

Grinning, he got back to his feet and hit the shower. He took his time getting in, reaching in to test the water with one hand first, in case his treacherous fiancé had actually convinced Nigel to turn off the hot water.

Ten minutes later he was dressed and walking into the dining area seeking breakfast. He spent a leisurely half hour eating and chatting with residents. He laughed along with them as they observed Fuzzy and Fiona making the rounds from table to table, mooching treats.

Allistor was just contemplating a visit with Daniel and William to check on the dragon eggs, when Nigel informed him that Daigath wished to speak with him. Their relationship was still very one-sided, and Allistor didn't dare request that Daigath travel to him, so he took both bears, stopped by Amanda's office to let her know Fiona was going with him to the Wilderness, and headed out.

He enjoyed the walk through the woods to Daigath's home, the fresh air and exercise helping to ease his still slightly aching head and gut. The bears only stopped twice to nibble at some berries or mushrooms. Arriving at the ancient elf's small clearing, he was surprised to find both Nancy and Chloe there. They were sitting on a root, facing a female elf that, based on her white hair and coal black skin, had to be a dark elf. The three of them seemed to be in deep discussion. Both bears wandered over to greet Chloe. "Allistor! Welcome back." Daigath waved from a branch about twenty feet up, before jumping down to join him. Allistor noticed again that he slowed before he touched the ground.

"Thank you for coming. I wanted to speak with you about a few things, but first, come meet one of my dearest friends." He led Allistor over to join the others. "Prince Allistor of Earth, Emperor of Orion, meet Netsirk, former Matriarch of the Greywoods, and Master of the Druidic Order. She's your new druid class trainer, and one of three alchemy instructors as well."

Allistor extended a hand. "Pleasure to meet you... should I call you Matriarch?"

"Only if you want to be put over my knee, young human!" She grinned at him as she rose and shook his hand. "My friends call me Sirk, and I imagine we shall become great friends."

"She's been teaching us druid stuff!" Chloe shouted, then covered her mouth and blushed. "Sorry." She looked around at the now silent forest.

"So you're going to be a druid like your mom?" Allistor took a knee and held out his arms for a hug. The little girl launched herself off the root and into his arms, squeezing him tightly.

"Yep! And a bard, too. I've been singing with Addy and Sydney and Scottie. Watch this!" She began to hum a happy little tune, then pointed at a small shrub and

445

cast *Grow*. The shrub instantly began to grow taller, simultaneously breaking out in bright pink blooms of flowers. "Pretty cool, right?"

"Very cool!" Allistor clapped, and both bears chuffed as they moved to sniff at the new bush. Fiona sneezed, sitting down on her rump and shaking her head, making Chloe giggle.

Daigath put a hand on his shoulder, and Allistor stood upright. "Part of the reason I asked you here today is because of this charming young druid. She tells me that you have a bad habit of... how did you put it, Chloe?"

"Lettin' stuff bite him all the time!" Chloe helpfully supplied.

"Yes, that was it." Daigath patted her head. "Ladies, if you would excuse us?" All three nodded their heads, and the elf led Allistor into the center of a wide open grassy area. "Part of your training as a battlemage involves melee combat techniques. I had planned to address this later, but Chloe has insisted that you need immediate assistance." He grinned.

Allistor waved at the little girl, who had been watching him a little nervously. He knew she was worried she had just 'told on him' and gotten him into trouble. He flashed her a smile, then blew her a kiss, both of which she promptly returned. Turning back to Daigath, he nodded. "I hold no illusions about my melee skills. I've depended mostly on spells or guns during combat. The times I've used a melee weapon, it has been mainly just poke the pointy end at the bad monster."

Daigath chuckled. "I assumed as much. I'm told melee combat was a lost art among humans for more than a century. We shall strive to correct that, starting now. Draw your sword, and let us begin."

For the rest of the day, Nancy and Chloe trained with Sirk, or sat around nibbling on berries as they watched Daigath torture Allistor.

The elf was not just a master at creating weapons. He was just as skilled in the art of wielding them. He had Allistor begin with his sword, spending nearly an hour just on the proper way to hold the weapon. He had Allistor assume a defensive stance, and manipulate the weapon. Thrusting, swinging, blocking... with each move Daigath demonstrated a way to disarm Allistor. Ten minutes in, he had to cast *Restore* on himself, because his right arm was broken at the wrist.

The second hour was all about correcting his defensive stance, and how to move in various directions without losing his balance. Once again, Daigath highlighted his mistakes through action, and Allistor spent much of the time getting up off the ground, again and again.

From there they moved to offensive stance, then some basic sword forms. Daigath allowed him a short break for lunch, which they both shared with the ladies, and the bears. Then it was back to the stances and sword forms, with Daigath only occasionally using a thin switch to knock the weapon from Allistor's hand to remind him about his grip.

By the time Daigath called a halt for the day, Allistor was exhausted. Daigath had drained his *Stamina* more than once during the training, leaving Allistor panting and flat on his back in the grass while he recovered. Daigath assured him it was all part of his development, and that the more often he drained his *Stamina*, the more he pushed himself, the faster he would improve.

And the master was right. Allistor sat on a root, catching his breath and reviewing his notifications for the last several hours.

You have learned the skill: Swordsmanship! Level 1

You have learned the skill: Evade! Level 1

Attribute Increase! Your Stamina has increased by +1

Spell Level Increase! Your Restore spell level has increased by +1!

Skill Level Increase! Your Swordsmanship skill level has increased by +1...

The net result for the day was that he was now a level three *Swordsman*, had increased his *Evade* skill to level two, picked up a single point in both *Stamina* and *Constitution* from the abuse he'd taken, and leveled up his basic heal by a point.

After thanking Daigath for the training, and promising to return soon for more, he and the bears escorted Nancy and Chloe back to the Stronghold. Chloe rode Fuzzy's back for most of the trip, her eyes closed and head nodding as she drifted off to sleep. When they arrived at the teleport pad, Nancy expertly lifted the little girl into her arms, whispered her goodbyes, and teleported them both back to their Citadel.

Allistor and the bears headed back to the tower, arriving in time to join Amanda for a wonderful meal of steak and potatoes with fresh spinach and apple slices. After dinner they retired to the rooftop lounge, where a nearly exhausted Allistor shared the story of his training, and the results.

Soon enough, Amanda got up to make them a drink at the bar. Allistor opened his interface to look at his stats and assign some of his available points. While Daigath had been torturing him physically, he also coached him further on how he might want to focus his growth in attributes and abilities.

Because of the melee training, he added two of the ten points he had available to *Agility*. Because they were a battlemage's primary stats, he added a point each to *Intelligence* and *Will Power*. After a little consideration, he put a point into *Luck*, because why not? Finally, the last point he assigned went to *Charisma*, for the next time he had to do princely things like negotiate a trade agreement or avoid a war. He left four points free to be assigned later.

Designation: Emperor Allistor, Giant Killer	Level: 55	Experience: 7,200,000/57,000,000
Planet of Origin: UCP 382, Orion	Health: 72,000/72,000	Class: Battlemage
Attribute Pts Available: 0	Mana: 16,000/16,000	
Intelligence: 25 (29)	Strength: 10 (18)	Charisma: 12 (16)
Adaptability: 8 (10)	Stamina: 13 (20)	Luck: 8 (14)
Constitution: 22 (27)	Agility: 15 (21)	Health Regen: 2,200/m
Will Power: 25 (33)	Dexterity: 7 (11)	Mana Regen: 1,400/m

Chapter 21

The following morning Allistor had a meeting first thing with the analysts. He found them waiting for him in their conference room with a breakfast bar already set up to one side.

"Good morning, folks! Thanks for having food sent up. I'm starving!" He took a moment to heap some scrambled eggs, toast, sausage, and fruit onto a plate, then grabbed a pastry before taking a seat. He retrieved a glass from the center of the table and poured orange juice from a chilled pitcher. "Okay, hit me."

Selby started off. "First, all of the class trainer positions on Nigel's list have been filled, the trainers have arrived, and sworn the oath. They are settling in at the village, and so far things have gone smoothly."

"Including your gnomebarian cousin the survival trainer?"

"Yep!" the little gnome grinned at him. "We're giving them the rest of today to get organized and acclimated, and training will start tomorrow. Priority is being given to your senior advisors, raiders, and the group who helped you clear the property, as promised."

"Great! Thank you all for organizing that, and for your hard work." Allistor said before shoveling more eggs into his mouth. His activity with Daigath the day before had made him ravenous.

L'olwyn was next. "We have been contacted by High Queen Xeria's factor to discuss a trade agreement. Which of us would you like to act as your factor? Or do you have someone else in mind?"

"It should definitely be one of you. None of my fellow humans have any experience with... interplanetary trade? Don't even know the proper term for it. Is one of you more experienced than the others?" He looked around the table, watching them look at each other.

L'olwyn bowed his head slightly. "That would be me, Allistor. I was often sent on trade missions for my House. That is, in fact, where I was when my faction perished."

"Well, I'll do my best not to destroy us all while you're away. Or do you even need to travel there?"

"The terms of the agreement can be negotiated from here, via hologram."

"Hologram! Dammit. One second guys." Allistor looked up at the ceiling. "Nigel, I'm sorry. I forgot about your upgrade. What additional attributes does Interface Level Five get you?"

"I will receive upgraded intuitive algorithms that will allow me to better anticipate your needs. In addition, my sensor and control capabilities will be expanded. Sensor range will double, and I will be able to communicate with you from a range of up to 1,000 feet from any of my structures. My defensive capabilities would be increased, allowing me to better resist attempts at a

takeover of my systems by a hostile AI. My capacity to manage multiple facilities will be increased as well, though you are currently in no danger of reaching that limit."

Just out of curiosity, Allistor asked, "What is your current limit?"

"I am currently capable of managing up to one hundred separate facilities such as Strongholds, Citadels, Outposts, and the like. Serving a population of up to one half million entities. An upgrade to Interface Level Five would more than double that capacity."

"Thank you, Nigel. I officially authorize your upgrade to Interface Level Five." Allistor opened his own interface, selected the *Nigel* tab, and purchased the upgrade. Once again, he was disappointed in the lack of trumpets or fireworks. Especially since he'd just spent a half billion klax on the upgrade.

"Thank you, Allistor. Your generosity is appreciated, as always. It is a pleasure to serve you."

Looking back at his analysts, he apologized. "Sorry, folks. I promised to do that yesterday, and got sidetracked. Where were we? Holographic conferencing over trade agreements, right?"

"Yes, Allistor. And congratulations on your upgrade, Nigel." L'olwyn replied. "Before I contact the High Queen's factor, is there anything in particular you'd like to prioritize as a trade item?"

"I have no idea what they have to offer, other than really big ships. Which we could certainly use, at some point. Do they build military ships? We have the *Opportunity,* but I think we might need more firepower in coming days. And I guess larger colony ships? Or cargo haulers? I really don't even know what I don't know about this." Allistor shrugged, a little frustrated. He pictured the immense harvester that had visited earth.

"Hey… guys? What about the harvester that just got confiscated. What happens to that? And the resources inside it? Will it go up for auction or something? Do we have any claim on it, since the cargo is from earth?"

Longbeard chuckled. "Aye, ye might be able to prosecute a claim fer the cargo, as the sole planetary prince. The vessel itself will be held by the Collective until the punishment has been administered. At which point the colony world it belonged to will have the first option to purchase it back. Should they decline, or be unable, it'll go to open auction."

"Great! Let's start the process of filing a claim for the resources. No point in letting someone else have them if there's a chance we can get them returned. Especially if someone was scheming against us to seize those resources, or deny them to Queen Xeria."

L'olywn, shaking his head at how easily Allistor was distracted, continued. "As for trade goods, I believe Nancy will tell you that the blood she harvested is quite useful. And the araneae currently have an overabundance of it, so values will drop. They also have skilled builders that can be hired under contract, and I believe they sell the wood from those wonderful trees."

"Would they also sell us saplings? Or seeds, even? With Nancy and the other druids being able to grow things quickly, we could surround our properties with tall trees that absorb lightning, and keep dragons from swooping in." He was thinking of the area behind the Citadel in Cheyenne where his cowboys were grazing cattle.

"I can certainly inquire." L'olwyn nodded.

"Alright, rather than spend a lot of everyone's time on this, I'll leave it up to your best judgement. We can meet privately if you want to discuss details in the coming days. Unless… do any of you others have any recommendations."

"If they have any interestin' ores to trade, we can always use more o' that for crafting." Longbeard offered.

"Or blueprints for structures and ships, if you're interested in trying to build your own, Allistor." Selby added. Her little gnomey face was alight with the prospect of tinkering with giant structures.

"I think we're a long way from that right now," He shook his head. "I want to focus most of our resources on expanding our territory and improving the lives of our people here on Earth and Orion. But that is a good idea for later, when we're more stable, and powerful."

Two of the topics of their discussion clicked in his head. Looking up at the ceiling, he asked, "Nigel, what is the average level of the beastkin who have become citizens?"

"The average level of the entire beastkin population is currently eleven."

Allistor looked at Longbeard. "And the dwarves?"

"Me people be fighters, as well as whatever their main profession be. I dunno the exact number, but me guess is their average level be near thirty."

"Alright, good. Then back to the beastkin. We still have about ninety percent of the area inside the Invictus City walls to clear. That includes surface structures, underground subway tunnels, and so forth. The monsters we've been finding here are mostly too low level for my fellow humans to benefit from, experience-wise. I propose we bring a thousand low level beastkin here each day, send them out in groups with battle droid escorts, and begin to clear the city. That should level up all of the beastkin to the point where they can choose a class and get some training. It'll also bring in a ton of loot drops for crafting materials, hopefully. Anyone see any issues with that?"

All around the table the analysts shook their heads no. "Droban, would you organize that with Gralen and Nigel, please?" The minotaur bowed his massive, horned head in acknowledgement.

"Thank you. Next, I want our higher level people, whether they be human, dwarf, beastkin, whatever, to start locating and claiming more significant sites like Dover Castle. They can start as soon as they've all visited their class trainers. We're all going to be much stronger, and safer, with the proper spells and skills. And I'm going to take a small group with me to start contacting other communities of survivors, try to recruit them. Or at least form alliances with them." He looked at each of them for a few seconds as he said, "And of course you're all welcome to participate."

Longbeard bowed his head slightly. "I thank ye for thinkin' of us. Meself, I'll be headin back to Lightholm instead. There be a few things I want to check on."

Allistor nodded. "Please thank your people for me. I'm sure Helen will be glad to know that the supervolcano won't be killing us all anytime soon."

His first meeting done, Allistor snagged several pastries and slid them into his ring. Riding the elevator down, he took a seat in the lobby and began to compose another list of priorities. As he was writing, Fuzzy came and sat by his side, Fiona nowhere in sight.

Check on Luther's Landing

Meet with Leila's replacement?

Talk to Harmon about Ancient Ones some more

Meet with Helen, pick more sites to claim.

Decide what to do with orb relic – talk to Daigath? Buy a planet? Fleet?

Visit Lightholm.

Check in with Daniel and William.

Test new enchantment idea. Maybe discuss with Michael.

As he sat there thinking about what other items to add to the list, the pungent smell of unwashed grizzly became stronger and stronger. Smiling to himself, he added:

Give Fuzzy a bath.

"Nigel, where is Helen?"

"Minister Helen is currently located in the dining area of this facility."

"Thank you, Nigel. How does the upgrade feel?"

"I am... quite pleased with my increased functionality, sire."

Allistor headed to the dining room, where he found Helen having a late breakfast with half a dozen citizens. Fuzzy, never one to be shy around food, immediately passed by Allistor on his way to mooch from Helen. He chuffed happily, alerting her to his presence well before he arrived. Allistor thought the bear almost hopped a little in his excitement.

"Hey Fuzzmeister! Where's your girlfriend?" Helen searched behind the bear, spotting Allistor and waving. Fuzzy gave a small growl that sounded very much like "Don't know." before planting his head in her lap and demanding scratches.

Allistor took a seat, grabbing an orange from a bowl on the table and beginning to peel it. "So I thought we'd discuss more places to claim overseas."

Helen nodded. "I've been giving it some thought. Been leaning toward historic sites that we could preserve. Like the palace at Versailles, the Great Pyramids-"

McCoy interrupted her with "Oh, no. Uh uh. If there's any place in the world you just know a dungeon is going to form, it's the pyramids."

Allistor grinned at him. "All the more reason to make sure it's ours, and not taken by some alien faction. You want them to get all the best loot?"

McCoy groaned, but shook his head. "No. I'm just saying, there's gonna be dudes with jackal heads and scarab beetles the size of donkeys. You wait n see." The others laughed at him.

A man Allistor didn't know spoke up. "I was on the Detroit team when we claimed the Stronghold. There's a great big salt mine nearby that goes like, miles deep. Might be that a dungeon forms there, too."

"Salt!" Allistor smacked his forehead. "I should have put that on my list. Too many things to remember. He looked at the surprised man. "Can you take a team back there and investigate? Don't try to clear it if you find monsters down there. But apparently salt is going to have some significant value, so we need to claim that mine." He held up a hand as the man started to get to his feet. "Not now. Wait until your group has all visited the class trainers. Then get Gene or Gralen to fly you guys out there. Take a bunch of droids with you. Report back on what you find." The man nodded, retaking his seat.

They discussed several other places where folks thought dungeons might pop up. The catacombs under Paris, the lower levels of the Vatican, London underground. One person suggested his childhood girlfriend's basement, because it had creeped him out as a kid. Another mused that the Great Wall of China could be one long dungeon stretching for miles. Allistor thought about that for a second. "You know, if we could claim that, it would probably give us a ton of new territory. Might be worth investigating."

Helen nodded. "Even if it doesn't, the structure is worth preserving."

They spent a little time spitballing more locations with the group, then Helen and Allistor retired to the roof. Helen suggested the location because Fuzzy was "Getting a little ripe." At which point Fuzzy looked hurt and snorted at her.

When they sat down in the lounge area, she pulled an old school paper world atlas out of her ring and set it on the low table in front of them. The thing was practically falling apart, but the maps were clear enough. Allistor saw that she'd circled several places with a red marker.

"We have to assume that at least some of these places have already been claimed, either by humans, or colonists. But with our very own super speedy space ship, we can hit a lot of them in a relatively short time." She began to flip to random pages and point out locations like Victoria Falls in Africa, the Roman Acropolis,

Neuschwanstein Castle, Buckingham Palace, the ruined castle at Dorset, and Allistor's favorite, Stonehenge.

"Alright, let's set aside... a week?" He paused and waited for her to nod her head. "We'll get everyone trained up, and head out in a few days. And if we pass over or near any human settlements, we'll stop and visit. Let's make sure that the *Phoenix* cargo hold is stuffed with food and supplies that might help them out."

With that settled, Allistor decided to spend some time crafting. He heated the furnace and retrieved the half-formed sword he'd been working on before. The new enchantment that had occurred to him in his sleep had been lurking in the back of his mind ever since. He'd simply been too busy, or too distracted, to try it out.

As he worked the metal of the sword, he found himself missing the constant barrage of blows against his barrier from William. His squire had become a fixture of his life in a short amount of time. Allistor caught himself wondering about the process of adopting the boy, then snorted. "You're the boss now, genius. There are no forms to fill out. Just declare him adopted, and it's done."

Letting the nearly finished blade cool for a moment, he said, "Nigel, please connect me with Amanda."

Seconds later, her voice rang through the smithy. "What's up, your highness?" Her tone was playful.

"I uhh... I have something serious I want to talk over with you. Are you available now?"

Her tone suddenly matched his, with a slight hint of worry. "Where are you? I'm coming right now."

"On the roof. No rush. Nobody's in danger or anything."

She didn't reply, so Allistor put the blade back into the forge for one last heat. He wanted to fine tune the shape a bit before quenching and hardening the metal. He was gently tapping it with his hammer when Amanda arrived.

"What's up?" She asked, a concerned look on her face.

He gave the sword a few final taps, then dipped it into a barrel of oil. "I want to talk about William. And... maybe the girls, I guess?" He pulled the blade free and wiped it down with a rag before setting it on his workbench. Taking her by the hand, he led her to the nearest sofa.

"I've been considering... what do you think about us adopting William. Like, officially. And just now it occurred to me, maybe Sydney and Addy, too?"

Amanda thought it over for a few seconds. "Well, first... we're not married yet. So there might be..." She stopped when she caught him grinning at her. "What?"

"You were about to say there might be some complications with paperwork or something?"

Her eyes widened, and she laughed. "Ha! I guess not. Okay, well there's another consideration. If you adopt the kids, they become your legal heirs. That might put them in danger."

Allistor hadn't considered that. Danger was everpresent in their world now, and he'd almost automatically dismissed that as a factor.

Amanda took his hand in hers. "Another thing. And this sounds so corny, but... what if we have a child of our own? The other kids are older, and if we go by all the old traditions, our biological child would be fourth in the line of succession."

Allistor had flashbacks of old stories and movies where jealous siblings murdered each other to take a throne. Then a vision of William bonking his newborn son on the head with a stick. It was ridiculous, and he shook his head.

Amanda continued. "I think we need to think this over for a while. I'm all for us continuing to take care of our little family. Maybe even give each of them their own planet to rule one day." She winked at him. "But let's talk to your advisors first, and take a little time. We also need to ask them if they even *want* to be adopted, assuming that's the way we decide to go."

Before he could find words, she leaned in and kissed him deeply. "I love you for wanting to adopt them, and for loving them the way you do. You are a good man, Allistor."

"I thought you just loved me for my big... holdings. And cuz I can lift heavy stuff."

Refusing to take the bait, she gazed into his eyes. "No. I love you for your heart. You're young, and decently attractive, and smart. But what makes me want to be yours is what's inside you." She placed a hand over his heart.

He covered her hand with his own. "I feel the same. Except when you try to cut me so you can test something. Then, not so much." He leaned forward and kissed her even as she smiled.

"I'm going to go back to my office. I'm working on an experiment, trying to better understand the motes, and how they work." She pulled away from him and got to her feet. "We can talk more about this tonight."

Allistor nodded, getting to his feet and pulling her close for one more kiss. "I'm going to be experimenting with a new enchantment. So if you hear a boom, and the building shakes, well... maybe don't come up here. I might be splattered across several blocks." He grinned.

She slapped his chest and turned away, boarding the elevator.

Picking up his newly formed sword again, he closed his eyes. He wasn't sure how to accomplish the enchantment he wanted. The idea had awakened him early one morning, and he'd been imagining and discarding different methods in his head ever since. When he thought he had a clear and viable idea in his head, Allistor went to work.

He'd left a hole in the pommel of the sword for inserting a gem. Digging through his inventory, he pulled a diamond from a bag of gems he'd looted. It just instinctively seemed the most appropriate stone for the enchantment he wanted.

Mounting the stone in the pommel, he used some wire to temporarily hold it in place. Once it was secure, he took the weapon in hand and looked it over. The sword wasn't a masterpiece, by any means. But it was a serviceable weapon, with a thirty-inch leaf shaped blade. The hilt was still just metal, as he hadn't taken time to wrap it in leather yet, so it felt cool in his hand. He supported the blade with his other hand, the edge much too dull at this point to cut him.

Once again closing his eyes, he thought back to his experiences in learning spells. Focusing on the way information flowed into his brain, teaching him complicated formulas and concepts that, as he learned more and more, seemed to tie together. He specifically looked at the process involved in the *Mend* and *Restore* spells, the way the motes came together to stitch wounded flesh, or regenerate missing tissue.

Then he did his best to reverse it.

For the better part of an hour, he focused his mind on creating the effect he wanted, never breaking contact with the weapon. Eyes closed, he was able to sense it when his own mana finally began to drain, and his intent was absorbed by the weapon. He felt it flow through his hands, into the metal where it flowed down the blade, imbuing the steel as it went. Finally, he felt it inundate the diamond, filling it with power.

When he opened his eyes, he caught sight of the gem glowing brightly for a second before the light faded. His interface was immediately filled with notifications.

Skill Level Up! Your Enchanting skill has increased by +1

Skill Level up! Your Weaponsmithing skill has increased by +2

Skill Level up! Your Improvisation skill has increased by +1

> *Congratulations! You have discovered a new enchantment! By focusing your will, knowledge, and intent, you have imbued a weapon with the enchantment: **Lacerate**. This enchanted weapon will cut deeper into flesh than a normal blade, doing an extra twenty percent above the blade's normal physical damage. Each cut will have a fifteen percent increased chance to generate a bleed effect, draining the target's health for the same amount as the physical strike damage over thirty seconds. Bleed effect can stack up to five times. Each added effect resets the thirty second timer.*

Allistor set the weapon down on the bench and shot a fist into the air. "Yesss!" He did a little victory dance up there on the roof, all by himself, except for the odd swallow that was nestled quietly in one of the planters next to its coconut. Calming down, he *Examined* the blade.

> *Unfinished Sword*
> *Item Quality: Common*
> *Damage: ??*
> *Enchantment: Lacerate*

Shaking his head, he took the weapon over to a grinder and began to sharpen the dull edges. When he was through there, the next step was to polish the blade's surfaces. Lastly, he took some of the crimson drake hide from his ring and carefully wrapped the hilt. When he was finished, he tried *Examine* again.

> *Cutter*
> *Item Quality: Good*
> *Damage: Slashing 900-950; Piercing 600-750*
> *Enchantment: Lacerate (+20% Slashing damage; 15% chance to inflict Bleed effect)*

"Who's the man? You da man!" He congratulated himself. This was by far the coolest weapon he'd created so far! Allistor spent a little time admiring the blade, tilting it so that the sunlight reflected off of the Damascus pattern he'd layered into the steel. The leaf blade had a fuller cut down the center of both sides, taking some of the weight from the metal and making it easier to wield. Not that it mattered much in his case, his *Strength* made it feel no heavier than a willow switch in his hand.

He immediately stepped out to a clear area beyond the lounge seats and took the defensive stance that Daigath had taught him. After a few practice swings, he worked his way through the forms, both offensive and defensive, again and again. The sword felt good in his hand, and after a few minutes of twinges from sore muscles, his body began to respond. He moved a bit faster, his transition from one form to the next getting less hesitant and jerky. His mind focused, and he began to imagine an enemy before him, a sword of their own in hand. His every thrust was answered by the imaginary foe, and he blocked or parried their thrusts in turn.

When he finally came to a halt, more than an hour had passed. He was sweating, and breathing hard, and his *Stamina* was down to about ten percent. Returning to his work bench, he carefully cleaned the weapon before putting it into his inventory ring. A quick ride down the elevator to his quarters for a shower, and he was ready to head out to Cheyenne. He wanted to show off his new weapon to Michael and the other smiths.

Allistor was walking toward the elevator, having just taken one of the breakfast pastries from his inventory to snack on, when William's voice came to him through Nigel.

"Allistor! Come quick! It's the eggs... they're... Daniel says they're about to hatch!"

*****

Loki sat in his chamber, the mists around him swirling in reflection of his agitation. He was still annoyed with his reaction to Baldur's rage, the momentary slip in his normal reserve. Worse, he had been successfully set up to take the fall for actions he had not taken. And he was certain he knew who was actually behind them.

Activating a holographic viewscreen with the touch of one tentacle, he observed an image of Hel as she moved across her own private chamber. The feed was from one of more than a hundred hidden devices he'd had planted in that particular room, and one of only three she hadn't located and destroyed.

She was watching a feed of her own, the human prince on her holoscreen practicing his sword skills. Loki had been watching him as well, but quickly grown bored. The weapon he had just crafted was interesting, though. Not its form, which was still crude, or its stats. What interested Loki was that the human had managed to teach himself a fairly complicated enchantment.

Allistor and his people had advanced exceptionally quickly during Stabilization. And now that he'd arranged for an unprecedented army of class trainers to actually join him as citizens of his princedom, they would grow even faster.

If Loki had possessed teeth, he would have ground them in frustration. His tentacles waved in annoyance, causing the mists to swirl even more emphatically. Loki was no fool. He took Baldur's warning to heart. The fact that he had to not only stop scheming against the human weakling, but now had to work to protect him against Hel's machinations, as well as those of any factions who might wish him harm… it was nearly too much to bear.

He briefly considered his best course of action. Trying to root out and foil all of Hel's various schemes would be a challenge, and require way too much time and resources. She was a master of misinformation, deception, and covert action. Possibly even his equal, in some aspects.

No, if he were to protect the human prince, and thus preserve his own physical existence, he would need to convince her to do the same.

From her previous comments, and the actions he suspected she was behind, he thought it might not be all that difficult. Hel admired Allistor's ruthless tactics, especially when eliminating fellow humans who opposed him. Loki suspected it was Hel who had delivered the summoning scroll when Xar' Dakra was defeated. And he was *sure* that Hel was behind the resource shortage, coordinated araneae hatching, attempted harvest of Earth resources, and subsequent movement by the Collective enforcers. All of which combined to draw Allistor into a volatile situation. What Loki wasn't sure of, was whether all of that was meant as some sort of trap for the human boy, or as a way to boost his reputation.

"Regardless, it should not be difficult to convince my offspring to support the young prince." He mumbled to himself. "The easiest way being to continue to *appear* to oppose him. She will, out of habit, work to oppose my will. And in doing so, she may do more than just support him. She may reveal herself, and suffer the wrath of Odin and Baldur in my stead."

The Ancient One rose from his seat and glided toward the door, on his way to begin the battle of wit and will with his daughter.

End Book Four

Acknowledgements

Thanks once again to my family for their love, support, and occasional ass-kicking when I need it. They are my alphas, my sounding board, and the ones who aren't afraid to tell me when something sucks! And a less enthusiastic thank you to my beta readers, who are rude, crude, and definitely socially unacceptable, but still good guys. A big thanks to Anders Hemlin for the wonderful cover art.

For semi-regular updates on books, art, and just stuff going on, check out my Greystone Guild facebook page https://www.facebook.com/greystone.guild.7 or my website www.davewillmarth.com where you can subscribe for an eventual newsletter.

And don't forget to follow my author page on Amazon! **That way you'll get a nice friendly email when new books are released**. You can also find links to my Greystone Chronicles and Dark Elf books there! https://www.amazon.com/Dave-Willmarth/e/B076G12KCL

PLEASE TAKE A MOMENT TO LEAVE A REVIEW!

Reviews on Amazon and Goodreads are vitally important to indie authors like me. Amazon won't help market the books until they reach a certain level of reviews. So please, take a few seconds, click on that (fifth!) star and type a few words about how much you liked the book! I would appreciate it very much. I do read the reviews, and a few of my favorites have led to friendships and even character cameos!

You can find information on lots of LitRPG/GameLit books on Ramon Mejia's LitRPG Podcast here https://www.facebook.com/litrpgpodcast/. You can find his books here. https://www.amazon.com/R.A.-Mejia/e/B01MRTVW3O

There are a few more places where you can find me, and several other genre authors, hanging out. Here are my favorite LitRPG/GameLit community facebook groups. (If you have cookies, keep them away from Daniel Schinhofen).

https://www.facebook.com/groups/LitRPGsociety/

https://www.facebook.com/groups/LitRPG.books/

https://www.facebook.com/groups/GameLitSociety/

https://www.facebook.com/groups/litrpgforum/

https://www.facebook.com/groups/541733016223492/